THE DARKEST LIE

ANGELA DAY

A Creative life
B an amplified life

ISBN-10: 0615724957
ISBN-13: 978-0615724959

DEDICATION

To my Gaidin, as always, for always.

And
To Mr. Hansen, who taught me to write.
To Mr. McMurray, who believed I could write.
To Mrs. Staheli, who made me write.

ACKNOWLEDGMENTS

This book would not have been possible without the help of some truly magnificent people. Special thanks to The Woodlands Taekwondo Academy for training my sons, loving my family, and giving me time to write while my boys were kept busy learning honor, perseverance, and self-esteem. Special thanks also to Laura McClellan Shingleton and Wendy Anderson Newman for their editing prowess and ability to understand what I meant to say, to Laurie Poulsen for her eleventh hour copy editing, and to all of my alpha readers who put up with my endless questions. Thanks to the Writing Excuses Podcast, my go-to cure for writer's block. Thanks also to my family for their endless support, especially my mom who signed up for Twitter to support me and then emailed me to ask what Twitter was, and thanks first, best, and most of all to my husband who is always my most valiant supporter and champion.

And thanks to the SMG. This is, after all, our story.

PROLOGUE

Time had run out hours ago. "Where are my pain meds?" the young woman screeched, momentarily overwhelming all the other noise in the room. Lieutenant Gage winced, standing at attention near the head of the bed. She had been put in charge of guard detail for Amelie and her unborn child as a highly classified assignment, and the details of the mission were sketchy. "Please, it hurts so much," Amelie's voice shook.

A highly dangerous hostile was in pursuit of the pregnant woman and their lead had been 36 hours. They were to protect her through childbirth and get them to a safe house.

The Woman answered, her gentle tones filling and soothing every space in the room left raw by the screaming. "Medications don't make the pain go away, dear heart. They only hide it so your mind can't feel it."

It had been 40 hours.

"That would be better, yes, please," Amelie said, panting.

Amelie had been in labor for the last ten of those hours and it looked incredibly painful, although Lt. Gage wasn't sure all the shrieking was necessary. Subconsciously the lieutenant covered her abdomen with one hand, thinking of the secret she carried there herself, and then resumed her grip on her gun. Even through the reinforced concrete walls Gage was sure everyone else in the subterranean military medical facility could hear Amelie's cries.

The room was claustrophobically small, the single hospital bed going almost from one wall to the other. Lt. Gage could have reached out and touched the back of the guard watching the door without extending her arm fully, while the guard at the foot of the bed crammed himself into a corner to give the doctor and the nurse room to work.

Gage didn't want to die in a box like this.

"I can't do this, I can't do this," Amelie begged, her voice trailing off as she started to cry. "What if my baby never comes?" The Woman stiffened.

"Give her pain medications." Her mild voice penetrated every object to the edges of the room.

Gage saw Amelie's eyes widen as The Woman watched her. "You said I couldn't have any pain meds because I need to be clear for the journey ahead. You said it would be too dangerous for the drugs to make my mind foggy." The young woman's eyes started to droop as the large dose of medication the nurse injected into the IV flooded her system. "Why is it not too dangerous now? What's happen...ning?" her mouth slurred around the words, but her slackening face did not lose its fear.

"What now?" asked the doctor. "She's too far under to push, and a C-Section at this point would be mortally dangerous to both mother and child."

"I will assist them," The Woman began with her eyes closed, this time her quiet voice wrapping around her like a coat, or a shield, and Lt. Gage felt the powerful presence of The Woman dim. The green eyes snapped open and focused with alarming intensity on Lt. Gage. "This child is coming to us unprepared for this world. I can complete the preparation, but only after the child is safely on the outside. You who will be a mother, please go and assist the doctor. He will need extra hands."

"Yes, Lady," Lt. Gage responded, too used to following orders to give in to the fear in her stomach. She set down her M16 rifle and went to the struggling doctor. Then she stood there, helpless, with her hands half raised.

"The danger will be in removing the baby without damaging the mother," The Woman instructed. "The baby's head will crown in a moment-- rest your hand on his head to hold the ridges in place."

"Ridges? Shredding holes!" the doctor exclaimed, staring at the hard triangular spines on the baby's head and then at Amelie's slack face. "Is she a full dragon? I needed to know that hours ago." The doctor placed his gloved hands over the spikes and tried to guide the infant to freedom. The line of spikes in the middle of the head continued down to the bottom of the neck. The infant's head came fully out, blue-tinged skin and slightly reptilian features tiny and well formed.

After the shoulders passed the birth went smoothly until the tail. The ridges had faded along the back of the neck but re-emerged along the tail. The umbilical cord was tangled with the tail and showed cuts where the tail spikes had lacerated it. The nurse hissed, and the doctor swore under his breath.

"Okay, lieutenant, here we go. Take the baby," the doctor instructed. "He'll need to stay with his feet elevated above the head. Nurse, once your hands are free you hold the leg and tail apart and I will untangle the cord. Don't compress it!" he snapped at Lt Gage, who was awkwardly trying to hold the babe around the tummy.

The guard tried to keep her hands from shaking as she adjusted her hold on the slimy infant. Although the sky color and faint pattern on the skin suggested scales, the skin was baby soft and slick. She knelt and adjusted her hold so that the infant's head was resting near the crook of her elbow, keeping the feet high. She drew the tiny body close, protected from his spikes by the long woolen sleeves of her uniform. He was warm. Being blue and scaly looking, she was surprised at how warm he was.

"Good," noted the doctor, carefully trying to separate the tail and the cord, "You need to clean the fluid from the mouth and the nose. The baby can't breathe until you do." The nurse pulled a bulb syringe off of the instrument table with her one free hand and handed it to the lieutenant. The doctor continued. "Suction the mouth and nose and squirt it into the cloth. You're doing well." Lt. Gage gave a quick nod but stayed focused on the task.

Monitors began beeping wildly. "She's coding!" the doctor shouted. He jumped to his feet and rushed to Amelie's side. "She's hemorrhaging internally.

We have to stop the bleeding." The nurse and the doctor frantically worked over Amelie's prone body, and Lt. Gage and the dragon baby were momentarily forgotten.

Three times she filled the syringe and emptied the baby's mouth. Three times she held her breath, waiting for the baby to inhale. There was no sound. The pulsing of the umbilical cord slowed. Time seemed to wrap itself around the barely pregnant soldier and the newly born child, starkly contrasting the activity and speed of the others around them.

"Why isn't he breathing?" Lt. Gage demanded.

"The umbilical cord was damaged by the baby's tail spikes. He likely hasn't had enough oxygen during the entire delivery." The doctor worked furiously to stabilize Amelie. "They've both undergone significant trauma. I doubt he'll survive."

"But..." Lt. Gage thought about the picture of her husband she kept in her pocket. They'd decided to wait to have children until the world settled down and they were more established in it, but that wasn't going to happen. She hadn't even had the chance to tell him that she was pregnant. Their baby was still inside her, no larger than a grain of rice. This baby in her arms was dying without his mother. What if she were the one laying on the bed while a stranger held her child?

"No," she whispered. She bent her head low over the small blue reptilian baby. "Breathe," she said, "please." She covered the strange wedge-shaped mouth with her own and forced air into the baby's lungs and then allowed the air to exhale. No response. Again she breathed for the little life in her arms. Again the child lay limply in her arms. Three, four, five more breaths, and then a little cough. A louder cough. A perfect baby wail. The newborn screwed up his face and had a proper first cry, telling the world how cold, bright, and empty it was.

Military training and field experience kept Lt. Gage's expression calm, but tears leaked from her eyes. The nurse glanced up from her work over Amelie. "I wouldn't have been sure that CPR would work."

"It had to work," the lieutenant whispered, "didn't it, Lady?"

She looked up from the child to the empty space behind Amelie's head, but The Woman was gone. The guards at the foot of the bed and door were also gone. She heard small popping and banging noises outside, like a fireworks display in the distance. Her comm piece buzzed to life in her ear.

"Ruan de Argos is approaching from south southwest with a contingent of Shae. They have opened fire on our position. Lt. Gage, what is your status, over?"

"We've been found," she said. Ruan de Argos was the hostile? She mentally cursed. This would not end in a firefight, it would be a bloodbath. The doctor's face was grim as he stared intently down at Amelie and Lt. Gage continued to speak. "We have to hide them."

"How?" exclaimed the nurse, "She's still unconscious and bleeding, and if we move her now she'll die."

A small circle of light flared behind Amelie and grew brighter and larger. "Give me the child," The Woman's voice came out of the light, and as it faded she was standing back at the bedside. Lt. Gage rose slowly, cradling the infant she took to The Woman.

"Little one, be well," The Woman instructed the squalling newborn. The wailing quieted, although the squirming did not. The Woman cradled the child close into her chest, snuggling with the baby while the sounds and screams of battle raged just outside the concrete walls. "This world is not the only one that will demand much from you, and yet it is vital that you do not know who you are." She smoothed the tiny forehead with the same comforting motion her hands had used to caress the mother's. "For that, you will need to be prepared in another way and your gifts secreted, to be saved for a different time."

The Woman wrapped both arms around the tiny bundle, and bent her head down to kiss it. Her flowing golden hair surrounded them, hiding the child from view. When The Woman raised her head, a normal pink human baby lay in her arms. The Woman turned to Amelie and placed her hand on the sweat-soaked forehead.

"This is a trial and a time you would also be best to forget," The Woman's voice was compassionate, but firm. Her hand rested gently over the closed eyelids of the prone woman. "Once I have taken Amelie and the child, there will be no reason to continue the assault, but Ruan will know that the child has been born."

"What if he didn't know, my Lady?" asked the nurse. "We could create the certificate of still birth and the one for the mother's death. He'd have nothing left to fight over."

"That won't stop him," Gage warned.

The Woman nodded. "I know. But if we can slow him down, I can hide them well enough to give them time." She looked at each of them in turn, and Gage felt like The Woman's too-green eyes were looking into her and not just at her. "All this must be a secret. The knowledge of this child must not leave this room." The Woman, still holding the now peacefully sleeping infant, placed her free hand on the lieutenant's head. Her hand felt like sunshine.

"The child you carry inside will be well, born whole and healthy, and will live to be proud to call you mother." The lieutenant took a deep, shaky breath, and a tear slid down her cheek. "You will survive this battle. But a darker day is coming, and for that, we are not prepared."

There was an earsplitting crash, the floor bounced, and an orange-red light flashed brightly enough that no one could see for moments after. When their eyes had readjusted, The Woman, Amelie, and the baby were gone.

"Did Amelie die?" the nurse asked.

"I don't know," Lt. Gage and the doctor responded together. Lt. Gage continued, "But we know the baby survived."

The comm unit in her ear buzzed again. "Lt. Gage? Alpha team has arrived on site. Ruan is redoubling his efforts but has informed us that he is open to negotiation as he has the right of parentage. Is that true? Lt. Gage, respond. Over."

"Right of parentage is no longer in effect. Child was stillborn dragon, mother was killed in childbirth. Internal hemorrhage and blood loss. Inform Ruan that hostilities are useless and negotiate cease fire. Over."

"He isn't going to believe that, lieutenant. Over."

"I don't need you to convince him, I just need you to stall him for--" Gage glanced at the nurse, who held up ten fingers. "Ten minutes. Over."

"Acknowledged. Over and out."

CHAPTER 1

There was one constant truth in Thane's life; they couldn't hurt him if they never saw him. This principle was first thing scrawled on the belief window through which he viewed the world. It even predated walking. Don't draw attention to yourself, don't react, and don't be seen. Everything else followed after.

Fifteen years had passed since the genesis of that rule, and now as a sophomore in high school it proved more important than ever. Thane surveyed the hallway in front of him with the same intensity a general would use to study the map of a critical battle. He knew the name of every student registered at Payson High, but he doubted that more than a handful knew him. That was fine, it gave him an edge in pinpointing their locations without them noticing.

Thane's path was set in milliseconds from entering the building: left side down opposite the Pit, swerve to the middle to avoid L hallway, and then past the front office and weave through the remaining crowds to green hall where his locker waited. It was Monday, so the front office would be busy finishing preparations for the school week.

He slumped his shoulders instead of squaring them, chin down instead of up. Confidence got you noticed. Conversations drifted around his ears, and although he mentally commented on a few, he did not speak, wave, or make eye contact with anyone he passed. Too dangerous. He lowered his chin more but was careful to maintain a steady pace past the football crowd. Girls giggled and boys tried to sound tough, but no one acknowledged him. Pit cleared. Small swerve, steady pace. Coming up on L hall... and through. Only the office was left before he could disappear into the crowds beyond.

"Thane! Excellent!" Mr. Hoffman's heavy hand fell on Thane's shoulder, halting him so quickly it threw him off balance. So much for being invisible. The assistant principal's perpetual smile beamed down and Thane looked back at him, waiting. Sometimes if he was quiet and still, people would get distracted and forget he was there. Mr. Hoffman's other hand was guiding a girl towards Thane, her grimace just as strong as Mr. Hoffman's smile. "This is Remi Gage and she's new in our school. Remi, this is Thane Whitaker. He would be happy to show you where your locker and your homeroom are! I know Thane will do a great job making you feel welcome."

Thane thought it was unlikely he could make her feel more awkward. Mr. Hoffman stood there, beaming at them both. Remi looked at Thane. "My locker is number five nineteen," she finally said, reading off her paper. Thane nodded and pointed down the hallway in front of him and started to walk. Remi followed, Thane working to stay just in front of her.

"I know you two will be great friends!" Mr. Hoffman's voice boomed down the hall, causing the students around them to snicker or stare. Thane kept walking, face expressionless. This was a nightmare. Everyone was looking at the new girl-- she was pretty and confident, with short black hair that stuck out like a fashion model or a rock star. Thane felt their eyes and heard their comments and walked faster. Trying to go unnoticed now was like trying to be quiet with a police escort. Only one more turn into green hall and he could rid himself of this attention beacon and get back into the safety of being nothing special and no one important.

The girl walked behind him until they were out of sight of the office, then bounced in front and cut him off.

"I wasn't going to give him the satisfaction of seeing me talk to you, random guy he picked out, but now I'm curious if you can talk at all." She smiled at him with one eyebrow raised.

"I talk," Thane answered, startled. She took a step closer to him, lifting her chin to look him in the eye and waited. Thane kept his mouth shut. He knew conversation was a bad idea. She obviously didn't.

"Not much, you don't. What do you think of this place?"

"The school?"

"The school, the town, your life, all of it." Her words got faster, her green eyes staring into his hazel ones until he looked away. "I'm new, I'm always new, and I want to know what it's like here. What do you do when you're bored? Is there a mall? What gang colors shouldn't I wear? How," she said, emphasizing each word, "do I survive here?"

"We don't have any gangs here," Thane responded, and couldn't stop from adding, "Why are you always new?"

"My dad's in the Air Force. We move a lot. I've gotten used to it and gotten used to making friends fast and leaving them faster. I am an excellent temporary friend." She smiled at him, but it was a painful smile that did nothing to lessen the tension around her eyes. Thane felt a flash of empathy for how lonely she was, and how nervous. No matter where she went she could never hide. He tried to smile back at her in what he hoped was a reassuring manner.

"You don't look so boring when you smile," she said, then flushed and grimaced. "Sorry, that wasn't what I meant. I tend to say things without thinking much about them first. I meant your smile has a lot of personality. So where's my locker?" Remi spun around and resumed walking. Thane hurried to catch up.

Her locker was two before his. She was still wrestling with the combination after he'd opened his, put away his extra books, and put on his backpack. "Here," he said, holding out his hand for the small paper with the combination. She relinquished it, and he spun the lock with deft fingers left, right, then left again and pushed hard with one hand while lifting the handle with the other. The thin metal door swung open. The scent of stale sweat and mold wafted out, encircling them like slow death. Remi gagged, covering her mouth with one hand and pointing to a small, dingy pile of gym clothes.

"How long have those been in there? Did something die in them?" she whispered, trying to use as little air as possible. Thane shut the locker and leaned against it. They both took a breath of non-toxic air and Remi looked dejected.

"What do I do now?" she said, a little of her bravado crumbling. Thane didn't think about it, didn't pause to consider. Her face was so sad and he had to fix it. He took the little paper she'd given him, flipped it over, and pulled out a pen.

"This is my combination; my locker is five twenty-three. You can use mine and tell Mr. Hoffman about the death smell in yours." He handed her the scribble and pointed to his locker. She smiled at him, beaming just like the assistant principal.

"Thank you for making me feel welcome," she said, doing her best Mr. Hoffman impersonation. It was awful. Thane found himself smiling back, the expression strange and a little uncomfortable, like stretching a muscle that didn't get much use.

All through his next two classes he thought about Remi. He wondered if he would see her again, surrounded by new friends impressed by her outgoing personality and the feel of the world outside all around her. She may have even asked about him, and her classmates would've said, "Who?" even though they'd gone to school together for ten years. Thane sighed. Invisibility wasn't great, but it was better than the alternative.

At lunch he sat with his tray of food at the end of an empty table on the far side of the cafeteria, close to the kitchen garbage. For him the smell was worth the protection. He'd only taken a few bites when a tray thunked down next to his and Remi slid onto the seat next to him.

"So I think I hate AP History," she began, biting into her sandwich and continuing with food in her mouth. "The teacher doesn't teach anything and assigns a ton of homework. I wonder if I could transfer to AP English or something, but then they'd just make me get up and introduce myself again, and I'm so done with that. I hate getting up in every class to tell everyone what my name is and where I'm from and what my favorite hobby is and what?"

Thane was staring at her. "You're sitting with me."

"Your powers of observation are superior. You should be a super hero."

"Invisibility is the only worthwhile super power," Thane responded.

"Who would want to be invisible all the time? My dad says that reading people is my super power. You are something of a mystery," she mused, staring at him so steadily it made him uncomfortable. "For most people, their personality and interests are plastered all over. They read a lot or spend a lot of time on the computer, so they squint a little and talk a lot. They're big into sports, so they have calloused hands and they just love flexing their muscles in your face. They're skinny and self conscious so they wear big clothes or tall and they slouch or short and wear big shoes or too much makeup because they don't like their skin or spike their hair to look taller or tough or something, but not you. You are so completely normal it's almost creepy."

Thane's lip twitched. "You think I'm creepy?"

"Not in a bad way," Remi amended, "it's just... there's no such thing as normal, you know? There are things that most people have in common but no one person is supposed to have all the most common traits, and yet, here you are."

She was still staring at his face, and Thane fought to keep the heat from rising in his cheeks. "If I'm creepy, you can sit somewhere else."

"Nope, sorry, can't." Remi grinned. "You fascinate me, so you're stuck with me for however long the Air Force allows. I am a temporary friend, and now, I am your temporary friend." She took a bite trying to be nonchalant, but Thane could see the tightness in her jaw waiting for his reaction. She really was lonely, and afraid, and probably tired of feeling like that.

Thane could see the loneliness and fear in her because he was an expert in both. He'd become reconciled to being by himself a long time ago. Never having a friend had meant never needing a friend. That's what he tried to believe. But here in front of him was a girl, a pretty girl, who wanted to know what he thought and listened when he spoke and asked questions. Part of him was reeling from all the emotional interchange and wanted to flee, find a safe place to hide, and wait until she'd gone away. But it was also that part of him that knew he couldn't leave someone when they felt scared and alone. "I haven't had a permanent friend before, so I guess a temporary friend would be a good start."

Remi's responding smile was so big and so genuine that it scared Thane. Wait, what had he just agreed to? The bell rang and he jumped to his feet. "I have to get to Chemistry." Her face fell a little, so he added, "Where are you going?"

She pulled a crumpled paper out of her pocket and scanned it. "Also Chemistry. With Rasmussen?"

"With me, then."

"All right, friend. Lead on."

Remi chatted all the way into the classroom and sat on the stool next to him, which was usually empty. Other voices echoed off the cinderblock walls and square-tiled ceiling. Their chemistry teacher, Ms. Rasmussen, leaned against the front of her desk and gossiped with some of her favorite students while posing so everyone could admire her. She favored the brainy and the beautiful, and if you were both, you were golden in her book. She allowed and even encouraged her favored few to call her by her first name. Thane was regretting his decision to befriend Remi-- everyone kept looking back at them, interested in the new girl. He tried to surreptitiously move further away and so be out of their line of sight when she sighed and put her chin down in her cupped hands.

"What?" he asked. Had she noticed?

"I wish I had hair like that." Remi said, watching Ms. Rasmussen. Thane looked at the teacher's longer-than-shoulder-length red hair, and back at Remi, waiting. She snorted. "Her hair is long, wavy, and a gorgeous deep red that most women can't pull off. Mine is short and dark and curls out everywhere."

"Your hair is nice. It fits you," Thane asserted, and Remi looked pleased. She seemed about to comment when the second bell rang, and Ms. Rasmussen clapped her hands.

"Everyone in their seats!" Her voice was deeper than most other women's voices Thane had heard. Everyone sat down, shuffling papers and pencils clicking loudly in the suddenly voiceless room. Ms. Rasmussen was known for being fun-loving and jovial, but she was also infamous for her hot temper and short fuse. "Bi-polar" was one of the nicest things said about her by the students, and even her favorites were afraid of her. She smiled, showing two rows of even white teeth as her eyes raked across the students and rested on Remi.

"What's this? A new student?" Remi nodded. "Stand up and introduce yourself! Do you have an add sheet?" Remi pulled one from her bag and took it to Ms. Rasmussen who made a show of reading it, and then smiled at Remi again. "Why don't you tell us your name, where you are from, and your favorite thing to do in your free time?"

Remi smiled winningly at Ms. Rasmussen, then rolled her eyes at the class. "My name is Remi Gage, I moved here from New Jersey but my dad's in the Air Force and we move all the time so my favorite thing to do is anything that isn't packing or unpacking." She got a few smiles and giggles with that, and Ms. Rasmussen handed her a well used Chemistry textbook. Remi returned to her seat. Ms. Rasmussen grimaced.

"Are you sure you want to sit there? There are some available seats up front," Ms Rasmussen suggested. "Maybe here by Jeran?" Thane wondered if the football jock remembered that they used to be friends. But that was a long time ago, second or third grade, before popularity meant winner take all and losers lose forever.

Remi was shaking her head. "I'm good here. Mr. Hoffman assigned me to Thane to help me find all my classes. I don't want to get lost," and she blinked at Ms. Rasmussen with wide, innocent eyes.

The red-haired woman shrugged and began the lecture. Remi waited until she turned her back to write on the board, and then leaned over to Thane. "What was that? I can go sit by Jeran, as if that was so great? What has she got against you?"

Thane had only known Remi for a few hours, but he was already sure that she wouldn't give up without an answer. "I'm not good looking and not smart, so she doesn't think I'm worth her time. It isn't a big deal," he said, seeing the look of indignation his new friend's face. "She's not my favorite person either, so we mostly just ignore each other. She must think your hair suits you too, or she wouldn't have offered you a seat up front." He meant it as an observation, but Remi gave him that genuinely pleased smile again before turning back to watch the lecture.

"Her facial expressions are creepy. She's happy, she's sad, she's annoyed, she's like a cartoon character. Is she always like this?"

"Mostly, yeah. My mom doesn't like her either, says she's fake."

Remi looked interested. "When did your mom meet her?"

"Parent night, back around when school started."

"Is your mom pretty?"

Thane was stumped. "She's my mom. She looks like my mom."

Remi gestured towards the teacher. "Ms. Rasmussen is tall and leggy with dramatic curves and gorgeous long hair. Women love to hate women like that, especially if they're used to being the prettiest one. That could be why your mom disliked her so much."

"No wonder you picked me for a friend," Thane whispered, Ms. Rasmussen directing a glare at him, which was probably the first time she'd ever looked at him in the three months since school began. "Girls must not like you much either." Thane paused, realizing that could be taken as a bad thing. "Wait, that wasn't..." but he trailed off seeing Remi smirk at his discomfort.

He fought off a blush again, and Remi patted his arm and turned back to face the front. Thane, relieved he hadn't offended her, did the same although he could still feel the warm pressure on his arm where she'd touched him.

After Chemistry Thane walked Remi to her last class, and was glad to go to AP Music. He loved music; it was the one thing he felt he was good at. The right song or phrase of music could make him feel almost free, and sometimes he daydreamed about becoming a bass guitarist. He loved the way the low bass notes vibrated in his chest and how the rhythm of the bass drove the song. Besides, no one had to see you to enjoy the music you made. The music spoke for you so you never had to be there at all, you could just fade away into the sound.

But that was a dream he would never admit, not out loud, not written down. This class was focused mainly on music theory, the whys and the hows of chords and scales and sound. It combined music and math and science. He loved it. Thane was relieved to sit at his desk at open his book so he could focus on something he understood. This was rapidly turning into the strangest day he'd had in a long time, and he needed space away from all the conflicting feelings this new girl brought.

After class Thane packed his things slowly and talked briefly with Ms. Sorenson, the music teacher. He was hoping that if he took long enough Remi would've gone home before he had to go to his locker. He did like her and there was a warm spot inside him that was new, but he was not used to all her questions or the way that people looked when she walked down the hall and he was starting to feel a little interrogated and overwhelmed. It was her first day, and she was probably in a hurry to get home and relax. It would be better for both of them if she'd already gone, Thane thought.

Remi was waiting at his locker. She didn't look impatient or in a hurry at all. "I like this math class much better than my old one. Mr. Greenwalt actually seems to get what he's talking about. I stopped by the office after class but Mr. Hoffman is in a meeting so I'll tell him about my locker tomorrow so they can send in a SWAT team to kill whatever is gaining sentience in there."

"Doing what?" Thane said in spite of himself. Remi grinned.

"Gaining sentience. Becoming self aware. Waking up to take over the world. All will flee before its death smell." She started putting her books in her backpack. Thane felt a surge of responsibility for her.

"Do you know which bus you ride?"

"Senior Airman Calder is coming to pick me up in the car. Do you ride a bus?" Thane nodded. "Do you live far from the school?" she asked.

"I don't think anything is far from the school. The army base doubles the size of the town." He set off for car rider pickup, Remi following.

"Air Force," Remi corrected. "It's an Air Force base, not army."

"What's the difference?"

Remi gave him a flat look, unimpressed. "The army is for foot soldiers. No one joins the army unless you want to be a ranger. The Air Force," Thane could hear the capital letters in the way she pronounced it, "is for people who can see beyond the horizon to everything else in the sky." She stuck out her tongue and pulled it back. "At least, that's what my dad says. I've heard more lectures about why the Air Force is different than any other branch of the military than any of his other favorite lectures. What's your family like?"

Thane paused. "They're... fine, I guess," he finally said.

That was not what she was looking for. "But what are they like? Do you have brothers and sisters?" Thane began to walk away, and she followed, still talking. "What do your parents do? Have you always lived here?"

The best way to get her off this seemed to be by answering her questions. "My parents moved here when I was a baby. My dad is an accountant. I have two sisters. Is that your ride?" Thane pointed to a man in a uniform standing next to a black car.

"Yep. You want a ride home?"

"I'm supposed to take the bus and meet my sister."

"I think you missed the bus," Remi said, pointing to the last big yellow vehicle pulling out of the school.

Thane jerked around, his face pale. "I need a ride to the middle school," he pleaded. Remi looked surprised at his vehemence and nodded. They ran together to the dark sedan and the man in uniform.

"Senior Airman Calder, we need to give my friend a ride to the middle school so he can pick up his little sister," Remi ordered.

Calder, in his pressed uniform and fresh haircut, was unmoved. "My orders are to take you and only you immediately home after school, Miss Gage. Those orders are not open for interpretation."

"Look, Airman," Remi put a scornful emphasis on the rank, "Thane has been helping me all day and both my father and I are grateful. Would you like me to tell my father about your ingratitude?"

"I would like you to tell your father that I followed his orders exactly," Calder was unintimidated by her ire. Remi opened her mouth to argue, but Thane growled and thrust his backpack into her hands. He turned, breaking into a run after the rapidly disappearing bus. He could hear Remi calling after him, but didn't turn back. Instead he ran faster, knowing he couldn't catch the bus, but hoping that he wouldn't be too far behind.

He panted as he ran, ignoring the way his too small shoes rubbed against his toes. The bus was out of sight ahead of him, but he knew the route it took. And he knew some short cuts.

He broke out past the side of the school and squeezed through the broken chain link fence into the Polar Queen parking lot. Thane's shirt snagged on a wire and he pulled against it hard and fast. If he could hit the traffic light at the top of the hill, the second oldest of the four traffic lights in town, he might be able to catch the bus at a red. He rounded the corner of the Polar Queen and saw the bus pass him, go through the intersection, and start down the hill. Thane bowed his head a moment, taking a few deep breaths, then started running again.

Racing down the hill was more difficult as the sidewalks were unfinished here. Thane stumbled twice and rolled his ankle, trying to keep his footing as the bus pulled further away. If Harper got on the bus at the middle school and he wasn't on it, she would tell their parents that she'd gotten picked on by the popular girls and that he hadn't been there to stop it. She'd make a big scene, crying and pouting, and his mom would throw up her arms in disgust and they would both tell dad all about it when he got home from work. Thane's dad Robert Whitaker, called Bert by those who knew him, was a tired middle aged accountant who would loudly complain that his life was going nowhere, and did not lecture his son. It was much worse than that. Thane shuddered, and tried to run harder.

He crossed the last street and saw the middle school. Thane entered the parking lot just in time to see the yellow monstrosity pull out, with Harper's face leering at him out the window. Some parents in the car rider line were pointing at him and talking, and the teacher on duty started coming towards him. Thane left the parking lot, beginning the rest of his two mile trudge home and favoring his ankle. He pulled his cell phone out of his pocket and texted his mom. "Missed the bus, couldn't catch it. Walking home. Harper's fine." His mother did not bother to reply.

As Thane rounded the final corner onto his street, the tall oak trees gave a shadowed feel made stronger by the clouds blowing in overhead. The houses were old but well cared for, and Thane doubted that his block had seen any changes in the last 5 decades. His house was more than halfway down, with brown brick on the bottom third topped by greenish aluminum siding. The large window in the front showed two faces, both female with blond, bouncy curls. As he approached Harper's face retreated into the house, undoubtedly to get mom, and the other disappeared and the front door opened with a bang.

"Thanie!" his six-year old sister Lanie shouted, as she barreled down the steps and threw herself into his arms. He caught her, barely, wincing and setting her down quickly. She pouted. "Carry me into the house, Thanie! I was good in school today and I got two stars. Miss Grady says I'm the best in the class at spelling!"

"You're always the best, monkey," Thane said, trying to calm his breathing. "You're the smartest first-grader ever. But I can't carry you right now."

"You have an owie? Let me see!" she demanded, and ran to his side. He'd meant his ankle, but she'd gone to the side with the tear in his shirt. "Oh!" she cried, and Thane was surprised to see sympathetic tears in her big blue eyes. "You're hurt and it's got blood!"

"Wait, what?" Thane twisted his head around to look. He'd thought the fence had only caught his shirt, but there was a jagged cut two or three inches long on his side and the shirt was torn through and stained with blood. Thane groaned. He didn't have that many shirts and the loss of one hurt.

Lanie started to cry. Thane's mom, Gwen Whitaker, came to the door. "What did you do now? Why is Lanie crying?"

"Thane's hurt! There's blood!" Lanie wailed.

"Thane hurt you?" Gwen demanded, turning on Thane. "Get away from her and get in this house now!"

"No, mommy, Thane has an owie, not me, and it's bleeding! We need to fix him!" Gwen seemed mollified and continued.

"Well he wouldn't have gotten hurt if he hadn't missed the bus. Look at you! Your shirt is ruined, your shoes are probably ruined, what were you thinking? But no, you weren't thinking at all, just doing whatever you wanted. Those awful girls picked on Harper again because you weren't there. Wait until dad hears what happened to your sister because you were too lazy to make the bus on time. Pick up your sister and get in the house."

Thane flinched, and his mom went back inside. Lanie wrapped both her little hands in one of his, and said, "You don't have to carry me, Thanie. I can walk in with you, and I'll fix the owie and you'll be all better." Thane felt a tightness in his throat that had nothing to do with running, and squeezed her hands in thanks. As they started into the house Thane saw Harper back at the window.

"Mom, he's making her walk instead of carrying her like you said to."

"Thane!" Gwen shouted. Lanie started to protest, but Thane picked her up and tickled her making her giggle instead. He carried her inside and put her down in her room, then walked downstairs into the unfinished basement. He took off his torn nondescript hoodie and revealed his bright yellow t-shirt underneath, and fingered the tear. The image of the bass guitar printed on the shirt was large and wrapped around his side so that the damage went through all four thick strings.

With a sigh, Thane pulled the t-shirt over his head and let it fall to the floor in a heap. He looked towards the rope nailed between two ceiling beams where he hung his clothes. It was a strange contrast-- he had several brightly colored t-shirts with logos or pictures on them that represented things he liked and was interested in like music and old movies, and then four solid colored hoodies in black, dark blue, grey, and a dark green. Every morning he'd get dressed in one of the t-shirts, then throw a hoodie on over it. He knew what he liked, but it was better to blend in. This had been one of his favorite shirts, one he'd bought himself with the money earned by doing yard work for his elderly neighbors. That was how he paid for his cell phone too.

He went into the unfinished bathroom and cleaned his cut as best he could and wondered if he could find a needle and thread to fix the shirt. He rinsed his socks and shoes in the sink of the bathroom and left them there to dry. He squeezed between the wall studs into the next room where a thick paisley rug and an old mattress lay on the concrete in the corner. The walls of the basement were all framed, but no drywall had been put up. That was another thing that Grandpa was supposed to do with Thane to help, since Thane's dad was always working. Thane pulled on an old shirt and lay with his hands behind his head, staring at the ceiling, and heard the first rumble of thunder.

Rain had been pattering heavily and the window well was just beginning to pool with water when he heard his dad's car pull into the driveway. The beat-up Buick had been a gift from Grandpa Whitaker to their family when Thane was ten, with the understanding that it would be Thane's car when he turned sixteen. Thane had been excited about it and about Grandpa's promise that they would fix it up together.

Then Grandpa had a stroke. It hadn't been fatal, but the old man seemed like a completely different person. Thane's family went and saw him once after he'd been moved to a care facility but he hadn't recognized them. Grandpa Whitaker had been Thane's best friend-- he'd call Thane up to tell him a new knock knock joke he'd heard, take Thane out to lunch on his birthday, just the two of them, and he would defend Thane when Thane's dad was harsh. Thane had been devastated after Grandpa's stroke, but when his dad found Thane crying he'd snapped, "Man up. Just be glad he isn't dead," and cuffed Thane roughly on the ear.

Thane heard his father open the door and stomp inside. He could hear Lanie's enthusiastic welcome and Harper's whine. Thane could hear the clicking of his mother's heels as she sauntered into the kitchen. There was a pause, and then the rustling of bags obscured the voices enough that Thane couldn't make out the words. But he knew when the storm hit.

"Thane!" Bert Whitaker's voice boomed loudly through the small house. Thunder crashed outside in the distance, pitiful and small next to his father's bellow. Thane knew making his dad wait would make things worse, and so he immediately responded.

"Coming, sir." He rose to his feet and began to climb the stairs, the cut in his side throbbing and his ankle stiff. He opened the door from the basement into the kitchen and saw his family; his mom, sitting at the table and inspecting her finger nails, Lanie getting silverware for the table and looking frightened, Harper setting out plates and seeming smug, and all of them a frame around his dad, red faced and furious. Thane noted that his dad was still holding a briefcase. Harper hadn't even waited long enough for it to be put down and away before tattling.

"Am I correct in hearing that you were too lazy to make the bus, ruined your shoes, your shirt, and abandoned your poor sister to bullies?" Bert Whitaker's voice was deceptively quiet, but Thane saw all the danger signs. The briefcase was wobbling in shaking hands, his jaw was clenched and tight, and his eyes were narrow. Thane knew his dad's job was stressful and that he was constantly under-appreciated at work because Thane's mom told him about it at least once a week. Today must have been a particularly bad day. Instead of responding, which Thane knew was the wrong choice, he lowered his head and tried to look guilty instead of numb.

"Do you know," his father continued, still quiet, "how hard it is on poor Harper to have those girls constantly pick on her?" Harper had told Thane those girls had stopped bothering her years ago, but she enjoyed the attention from her father every time she brought it up so she never stopped talking about it.

Thane had threatened to tell, but she'd laughed at him and said, "Who would they believe?" He knew then he'd lost, and tried to take it as best he could and never miss the bus.

"It isn't like you weren't aware of the problem. But clearly you don't care. You don't care about any of us!" His dad's voice was rising with each sentence, and his hands were shaking harder. Harper looked less smug, and Lanie was terrified. She was hiding behind mom's chair trying not to cry.

Today Thane had completely failed in his one and only personal law. Don't be seen. Remi had seen him as a friend. The entire school had watched him show the pretty new girl around. Ms. Rasmussen had glared at him in Chemistry, Harper had watched him miss the bus again, and now his father glowered at him and saw the source of all that was wrong with their lives. Lanie's eyes were wide with tears and suddenly, Thane could not take any more.

"You are the only bully here," Thane said. His dad went momentarily speechless, his face turning purple with rage. "Harper's lying. Those girls don't pick on her, they're afraid of her. She terrorizes them using everything she learned from you."

Bert dropped the briefcase and thrust his face an inch from Thane's. "If you're going to start throwing around accusations, you had better be ready to pay." Thane was done being yelled at, done being threatened, and tried to walk around his father towards the door. "Where do you think you're going?" Bert grabbed Thane by the collar and tried to hold him in place. Thane jerked to the side as his dad pushed, leaving his dad stumbling forward. The middle-aged man lost his balance and fell to one knee, so angry he was nearly incoherent.

Thane strode through where his father had stood and paused at the door. "Don't cry, monkey," he said, looking down at Lanie's tears. "If I'm not here, daddy won't yell anymore." Thane opened the door and walked barefoot into the rain, shutting the door gently behind him.

For a moment, the only sound was the rattle of rain on the oak leaves. Thane went to the side walk. He hadn't gotten past the edge of their small yard before the door to his house banged open and his father came hurtling out after him. "You get back in that house now," Bert screamed, and grabbed Thane by the arm and forcibly twisted. Thane flinched and jerked his arm away and tried to keep walking. He had all but killed himself trying to catch that bus, after a lifetime of trying to get his father to say something in approval of his only son. "Don't you dare ignore me!" his father shouted and faces appeared in lighted windows in other houses. So many of their neighbors watching him. Thane was embarrassed and in pain, and rage broke through the wall of distress and isolation.

"Ignore you?" Thane screamed back, turning and throwing himself into Bert Whitaker's face. "All you've done my whole life is try to forget that I exist, and now you don't want me to ignore you?" Behind his father, Thane saw Lanie leave the porch and come running. She would throw herself between them and beg them to stop, he knew from experience. Sometimes it worked. It wouldn't now. The anger and desperation Thane saw in his father's eyes were past reason. He saw his father pull back to take another swing. "He doesn't know she's coming," Thane realized, time seeming to slow, "he's going to hit her because he doesn't see her coming."

Thane yelled "Get back, Lanie," and knocked the larger man out of Lanie's path. Bert swung with the other arm too fast and too low for Thane to block and he felt the impact against his stomach. As he doubled over, a phrase of music burst through his mind.

Suddenly he and his father were engulfed in a flash of blue white light, and then there was nothing more to see. Thane thought he heard his mother scream and Lanie sobbing in the distance. He tried to comfort her. "Don't cry, Lanie..." but his voice wouldn't come out.

Slowly his mind sank into the blackness that already claimed his eyes.

CHAPTER 2

The first thing to penetrate the darkness was a sound. It worked its way into Thane's awareness, with an even tempo and low tone. The regularity of the beeping was comforting at first. Then it began to irritate him and he considered trying to figure out what it was. He slowly opened his left eye and his right followed, his vision blurry and indistinct.

Thane's eyes rolled around the room disjointedly for a few moments and he breathed in through his nose, deep and slow. His eyes snapped into focus as the smell of the room hit his brain. Disinfectant. Iodine. Ammonia. Thane was in a hospital.

His body jerked upright, ready to flee. Thane told himself to knock it off, but his eyes still searched for an escape. He almost screamed when something suddenly tightened around his arm. "Quit being a baby and start thinking!" he said to himself. He wasn't being attacked; it was only a blood pressure cuff. The sharp pricking in his arm was the IV. The beeping came from the heart-rate monitor. Nothing here was a threat. The squeeze of the cuff made him claustrophobic, and he took deep, slow breaths through his mouth to stay calm.

"Awake then?" a voice asked with forced cheer. Thane sprang back, ramming his back into the bed's side railing. The nurse flinched. "I'm sorry, I didn't mean to upset you. Your blood pressure and heart rate spiked, so I thought you were awake."

Thane stared at the pudgy women who tried to smile reassuringly at him. Her smile was off, like it was an expression she was mimicking. "What happened?" Thane's voice sounded scratchy and hoarse, and the words burned a little coming out.

The nurse blinked at him. "You were struck by lightning, dearie. Don't remember? Well, amnesia after a lightning strike is normal. You're a lucky young man. The strike hit you directly and passed through. Your father wasn't so lucky-- oh, but I'm not supposed to bring that up," and she bustled about the room. Thane froze, and wrenched his thoughts away from what she could have meant by that. He needed something else to focus on. "Dr. Bicknell ordered a blood sample. There's going to be a quick prick and then I'll need to fill these three vials. Is that all right?" she asked.

Swallowing, Thane nodded. He would never admit that he didn't like needles. He watched her wipe a section of his arm with ammonia, then pat just below the elbow. "Here's a good one," she said and picked up the needle. To Thane the needle seemed to move in slow motion, descending on him and barely touching his skin with its cool metal tip. Then it slid into his arm and Thane heard a few notes of music and saw a small burst of white-blue light in front of his eyes.

"Ouch," the nurse yelled, dropping the syringe and shaking her hand. The needle flopped to the side, still in Thane's arm while blood welled up through the opening it made.

"Sorry," Thane said reflexively.

The nurse looked sheepish. "No, no, I'm sorry. I should never let go like that!" She pulled the needle out of Thane's arm and put a wad of gauze on the tiny wound and a band-aid to keep it in place. "That's never-- I'm not even sure what that was. Let's try the other arm."

She reset on Thane's right side, and Thane focused on breathing and not looking at the needle. This time when the needle pierced his skin Thane flinched, but nothing else happened, no music, no spark. Nurse Pudgy filled the vials and labeled them.

"I've paged Dr. Bicknell, he's the specialist. He's been checking up on you but your father has needed more attention. You should be grateful that Dr.

Bicknell is here! Well, he's been here two months already, and you're the first two lightning cases we've had which is what Dr. Bicknell is interested in, so maybe he's lucky. Night and day that good doctor has been with your father, dear man. The doctor, not your father. Not that you father isn't a good man, I mean, I really don't know, he hasn't really been conscious yet, you just woke up and you were so much less hurt than he is..." the nurse floundered off into silence, fluttering her hands about as if trying to catch the right words to say.

"So he's not..." Thane trailed off, trying to decide what to say, trying to ask the question when his brain refused to form the final word. "When you said he wasn't as lucky, you meant..."

"Oh dear, no, he's resting, he's been hurt pretty bad and lightning strikes can have lots of secondary effects, but Dr Bicknell is very encouraged. The EMTs were already on their way and they were on the scene almost immediately and started CPR so his heart had only stopped for a minute at most." She seemed so bewildered by his discomfort that Thane briefly wondered why she decided to be a nurse, since she was awful at dealing with people. He decided he didn't like her. Then her words sank through his fuzzy thoughts.

"Why were the EMTs already on their way?"

Nurse Pudgy fidgeted. "Well, the neighbors were concerned, and you were shouting outside and one of them saw your father grab you so they called the police. The ambulance was coming along in case there were injuries. It was a good thing they did! Lightning strikes mostly do internal damage. They saved your father's life..." she trailed off, unsure how Thane was taking the news as he was careful to keep his face expressionless.

"What about Lanie?" he asked. She looked confused. "My little sister, is she all right?"

"You and your father were both standing with your feet in the same puddle. That acted as a conductor for the electricity and contained it to just the two of you."

"Where is my sister?" Thane asked.

"Your mother is in your father's room," the nurse replied helplessly. "I saw the girls last night but I haven't seen them today."

"Which room?"

"Not telling." The nurse grasped this statement and held on. "I'm not telling you anything else until you lie down and wait for Dr. Bicknell."

Thane nodded, and started pulling off wires and electrodes. Nurse Pudgy squeaked in disapproval and began flapping around like a trapped canary, trying to grab each electrode as he removed it. "What are you doing? Don't touch those. You have to stay in bed. The doctor hasn't cleared you for movement yet, you could have internal bleeding, and lightning strikes can rupture internal organs!"

"I'm fine." Thane asserted, and then paused. "Haven't you already checked for that stuff?" The nurse made a noncommittal waving motion with her hands, which Thane took to mean they had. "I need to see my sister."

Thane pulled out his IV, wincing as it tugged. "I can ask at the nurses' station." His mother was not good at dealing with emergencies, and if his sisters weren't here there was no telling where they were. Thane needed to make sure they were all right. He swung his legs off the side of the bed and started for the door while the nurse squawked in protest. He opened the door and the colder air from the hallway whooshed inside. Thane gulped and shut the door fast. The pudgy little nurse was still standing in the same place he'd left her, looking at him apprehensively. "Where are my pants?" Thane asked, while trying to hold his hospital gown closed.

Nurse Pudgy flashed a wicked grin. "The doctor will be here in a moment. I suggest you sit and wait for him, like a good little boy."

Dr. Bicknell was younger than Thane expected, and he had a beard unlike any Thane had ever seen. A line of facial hair less than an inch wide ran around the doctor's jaw from one ear to the other. That was it; no mustache or goatee.

It distracted Thane as he obediently sat in bed as the doctor poked and prodded, asking questions and shining lights.

"What were you doing before the electrical discharge? Take three deep breaths." "Why were you out in the rain? Does this feel sore?" "Do you and your father often fight? When and how did this cut happen?" "Has anything like this happened before? Blink and then follow my finger." Dr. Bicknell would fire the questions while listening to Thane's lungs and heart, checking his eyes, and applying pressure to various points and Thane did his best to keep up.

"I wanted to be outside. Rain doesn't bother me. No. Everybody fights with their parents. Cut on a chain link fence. Today. Never been hit by lightning before. Ouch!" Thane flinched as Dr. Bicknell's fingers probed the cut. The doctor immediately pulled back and looked apologetic.

"You seem to be fine, especially considering that your body conducted over one hundred million volts of electricity. The witness reports say that the lightning came up from below you and went through the water connecting you and discharged into your father. They all thought that was vitally important." Dr. Bicknell shook his head. "Public education is sadly misinformed about most science, such as the visible part of lightning always comes from the ground up. The interesting thing is most of it discharged into your father. I've never heard of the secondary contact generating more damage than the primary."

Thane found himself liking Dr. Bicknell, because even though he talked a lot he wasn't talking down to Thane. "I thought that it was weird it didn't hit any of the trees. Lightning is supposed to hit the tallest thing around, but that must be wrong too."

"Wait, there were trees?" Dr. Bicknell was enthralled. "What trees? How many? Where they big?"

"Yeah," Thane said, counting in his mind. "Maybe ten old oak trees. A couple of them have been hit by lightning before; one of them even got cut down because lightning killed it."

Dr. Bicknell sat, lost in thought. The stout brunette nurse came bustling in again, holding a clipboard with some papers. "The EKG results, Dr. Bicknell," she said as she handed them to him. Dr. Bicknell came out of his reverie and looked the papers over, and then checked them again.

"You are a fortunate guy, Thane. These results are normal, your eye exam is normal, and your organs all seem to be intact. Some conditions don't show up until later, sometimes weeks later, after a lightning strike. So if any time in the next three weeks you feel any pains in your chest, have blurry vision, or experience any unusual feelings or pains at all, come to the emergency room right away and have me paged. Here," Dr Bicknell searched in the pockets of his coat before pulling a card from his shirt pocket, "this is my contact card. If you give this to the doctor on call, he'll know to get in touch with me. Keep this with you at all times so that if something happens, if you have a seizure or you blackout, whoever finds you will know to contact me."

Thane felt a pain in his chest now that grew sharper with every scenario Dr. Bicknell laid out. The doctor must have noticed something was wrong, because he started backpedaling, "Not that any of that is going to happen to you! Usually these secondary or delayed occurrences have some indication in the tests, but yours are completely clean. I'm just trying to be overcautious. I didn't mean to frighten you."

"I'm fine," Thane stated, uncomfortable with the word "frighten." "What about my dad?"

The doctor hesitated, giving Nurse Stout a significant look. She looked blandly back at him. "I'm sure Mr. Whitaker is hungry. Go get a dinner menu for him, please." Nurse Stout left, disappointed. "That one is quite the gossip," Dr. Bicknell confided after she'd shut the door. "Your father is in pretty bad shape. Common secondary effects of a lightning strike are amnesia, confusion, loss of consciousness, heart problems and vision problems. Your father is showing all these symptoms. Your mother seems unwilling or unable to tell us much about what happened. Without the witness reports it is unlikely we would know anything about what was really going on."

Thane's stomach clenched. He could hear that Dr. Bicknell thought this was a big deal, and Thane wondered if he was in trouble. Dr. Bicknell was looking at him like he was expecting something and was willing to wait. Thane took a deep, shaky breath.

"I didn't mean to miss the bus and make him so mad," his voice tried to break and Thane paused, hoping that if he looked down hard enough Dr. Bicknell wouldn't notice the tears in his eyes. "If I hadn't missed the bus, he wouldn't have gotten mad and I wouldn't have left. He wouldn't have followed me, and neither of us would be in the hospital. She's right, everything is my fault."

"Who's right?"

"My mom. She says that dad's work is stressful and he works so hard and he wouldn't yell at me so much if I didn't cause so many problems." Dr. Bicknell rested a hand on Thane's shoulder and leaned forward until their eyes were level.

"None of this is your fault, Thane." Dr. Bicknell's voice was earnest. "I meant that without the witness reports we would have no idea that it looked like your dad was about to go ballistic on you. Your neighbor, a Valerie Knotts, said that she's often heard yelling from your house before. Promise me, Thane," Dr. Bicknell gripped Thane by both shoulders now, staring at him, "that if you are in a situation where a grown up is mistreating you that you get help. If you can't find an adult to trust, you can call me. You have my card. Promise me."

"I promise," Thane said, hoping that would end this conversation. "Can I go now?"

Dr. Bicknell blinked, then laughed and dropped his arm. "Yes. I apologize, Mr. Whitaker. Your vitals are strong and all your readings are within normal ranges. I do want to run some other tests, but for now, you look good."

"What other tests? Why?"

"You know lightning strike victims are my specialty area of research?" Thane nodded. "I'm going to do a full workup of your blood to see if being struck by lightning had any effect that we haven't seen yet. The results will take a week, maybe a week and a half. I'll call you if there's anything you should know. You seem fine now, so I don't see any reason why you can't go home today if you want." Thane nodded faster. "I'll get the paperwork started and we'll discharge you into your mother's care. Your dad's staying here for a few more days. I'll have Delilah bring you your clothes and take you to your dad's room." Thane nodded his thanks, and Dr. Bicknell entered a few more notes into Thane's file.

"Thane," he said, not taking his eyes off the screen, "anyone who tells you that this is your fault is lying. You're a smart kid. Don't believe the lie." With that, he left the room.

Thane sat on the table trying to absorb the conversation of the last few minutes. Dr. Bicknell had offered to help him with his dad. His dad had almost died. Thane could go home. His dad would be staying in the hospital. Dr. Bicknell said none of this was Thane's fault. No one had ever said that to Thane before and it gave him a warm feeling in his chest, even if he knew it wasn't true. The door opened again and Nurse Stout-- Delilah-- entered with some forms and his clothes.

"You can't sign anything, of course dear," she began, "but your pretty momma seems kind of flighty, so I'll go over all this with you first." She droned on about discharge instructions and follow ups, but Thane was still thinking about Dr. Bicknell.

"What if it isn't my fault?" he mused silently. "What would that mean?" His eyes were unfocused, thinking, and Delilah crossed into his line of sight, two short red horns poking up out of her dull brown hair. He blinked and said, "Horns?"

"What?" she asked, clearly confused. Thane could see them when she was looking down at her paper, but the moment she looked up at him, they were gone. He thought he heard a faint echo of a song.

"Do you have... horns?"

She paused, being completely still for the first time since Thane had seen her. Thane felt his cheeks start burning. "Never mind."

After he got dressed, Delilah took him out of his room and two steps more. "Here we are!" she announced cheerfully. Thane looked back over his shoulder at his room, then again at the room in front of him.

"Right across the hall?" he said. Delilah smiled at him and knocked on the door, then opened it. The room inside was dimly lit, with the beeps and hums of multiple machines. Thane froze in the doorway, remembering rushing into his grandpa's hospital room and the nurse shouting at him and his father cuffing him hard on the ear. His grandpa changed after the stroke, and Thane had believed deep down that his grandpa had died in that hospital bed but the hospital was too embarrassed to admit it, so they sent home someone else's grandpa instead and everybody went along with it.

"Go in honey," Delilah urged, and gave him a little push. Thane stumbled into the room as she shut the door behind him. A curtain hid most of the room but Thane could see his mom, one leg hooked over the arm of the chair she was lounging in, focused on the game she was playing on her phone. She brushed blond hairs out of her eyes. Thane stood there feeling both exposed and ignored in the cold little room.

"Hey mom."

Gwen Whitaker glanced up, then back to her screen. Thane put his hands in his pockets.

"How's dad?"

"I don't know. Read the chart," she responded, waving her manicured fingers vaguely towards the bed.

Thane glanced at the chart, then down at his bare feet. "Where are Lanie and Harper?" he asked.

"Mrs. Knotts took them home with her last night. She came to get the gossip first so she and all her old lady friends can laugh at us." His mom's voice bent with the sneer on her lips. Thane was relieved. He didn't particularly like their elderly neighbor, but she would keep the girls safe.

The silence stretched out, highlighted by the cheery background music and sounds of the game his mom was trying to play. Thane felt compelled to speak again. "Did the doctor come in?"

"Sure, they keep coming in and out. Could you go find me a bottled water? I asked that chubby nurse and she brought me a plastic cup, like I'm supposed to drink from the tap!" Gwen made a disgusted face, the contours highlighted by the bright digital light of her phone.

"Sure mom. I don't... it'll probably cost... do you have cash for the machine or something?" Thane shuffled his feet.

His mom's annoyed expression became almost martyred. "You seriously don't have any cash? Where is your lunch money?"

"Spent it on lunch yesterday. I think yesterday."

"And you don't have any extra in your backpack or something?"

"Don't have it."

"Why not?"

"Left it behind so I could catch the bus."

"How did that work out?" her voice was bitter under her bored tone. It stung more than usual.

"Dr. Bicknell says I can go home." She continued playing on her phone. "So, tell me what the doctor says when he comes back?"

His mother looked up at him then, and seemed to be struggling against something. Her mouth opened and closed, and then she squeezed her eyes shut and said nothing. In that moment before she hid them, Thane thought he saw tears in her eyes.

He did the only thing that might help. Thane turned around and left. He shut the door, taking care it made no sound, and leaned against it. His knees were weak and he put his hands back in his pockets so no one else could see how much they shook. He needed a place to hide. He crossed back to his room and found it being cleaned by hospital staff who shooed him out.

There were some chairs down the hall near the nurses' station and Thane sat heavily down on the bright blue fabric, drained. He put his head in his hands with his elbows resting on his knees and tried to process, tried to breathe. He focused on shutting out the thump of feet in the corridor, the quiet hum of the nurses' voices behind the desk, and the breathing of the man sitting next to him. Wait. There hadn't been a man sitting next to him. Thane peeked through his fingers and saw two hands holding a book open on the man's lap.

"You look like you could use a drink." Thane's head snapped up. The man shut the paperback and looked at him with one raised eyebrow. He was lanky with reddish orange hair and a face that was neither old nor young. Thane put his head back in his hands instead of responding.

"You've got that world-about-to-end look. Something go wrong?" The man half-smiled.

"I'm in a hospital. What do you think?" Thane shot back, irritated by the man and his pestering. None of this was his business anyway. The man grimaced.

"Right, sorry, someone doing poorly. Doesn't seem to be you, though." The man was staring at Thane despite his nonchalant tone. He seemed to be looking for something, and looking hard. It made Thane uncomfortable, and that made him angry.

"Did you want something? Because I'm not interested in entertaining you while you wait. Read your stupid book or don't, but leave me alone." Thane snarled, and was surprised at how angry he was and tried to shut it down. He must be more hurt about the exchange with his mom than he was letting himself acknowledge. Rather than being put off, the man seemed sympathetic.

"Bad day, eh kid? Don't worry, it'll get better." He rested his hand on Thane's shoulder, which was one step too far.

Thane jumped out of his chair, knocking the man's hand away. He stalked down the hall for a few steps, then whirled around and took one step towards the stranger who wouldn't stop talking. "It doesn't get better. You don't know anything about me," Thane said, slamming his fist into the wall next to him. The painted cinderblock did not yield, and there was a crunching sound. Several of the onlookers gasped, and the security guard at the nurses' station hefted himself to his feet and came over. "I am so sick of self-righteous self-centered adults talking down to..." he trailed off as the pain in his hand pierced the fog of his anger. Thane grunted, keeping his teeth together.

The red-headed man stood, intercepting the guard. "We've had a long day. I'll take care of it." The security guard looked the man up and down, and then nodded, pointing a finger toward the elevators. "Come on, little brother. Let's go get some ice." The man started walking. Thane gave the security guard a sideways look and the man in uniform glared at him, waiting. Thane turned around and went down the corridor to the elevators, head hanging down.

The man pushed the button for the Lobby and leaned against the wall. Thane's knuckles were throbbing, and tears swam in his eyes but he refused to let them fall. He shouldn't have yelled at his mom. This was the universe's way of punishing him for talking back to his parents. Thane knew better, and losing his temper had only gotten him in even more trouble. He was still angry at the stranger and realized what an idiot he was being.

"I'm not going anywhere with you," Thane stated. "I don't know you."

"Name's Brennan. I'm going to the cafeteria to get a drink. If you'd like to also end up at the cafeteria, there will be ice you can put on those knuckles.

There might even be a nurse there who didn't see you assault the hospital who could look at it for you." Brennan leveled his gaze at Thane. "If you're lucky, I might even buy you that drink."

"Fine. But I'm not telling you my name," Thane said, and Brennan nodded.

"Fine by me, kid. I'm being the Good Samaritan here, taking care of some stranger who punched an innocent wall. This way," he finished, stepping off the elevator and walking down one of the corridors.

Thane could see the sun setting through the glass doors in the hospital lobby. He wondered what time it was, and then what day. He considered asking Brennan but decided against it, not wanting to give the man the satisfaction. Remi would've asked him what he thought Brennan would be satisfied about. Thane had no idea. Of course, Thane had no idea if she would even talk to him again or if she'd already moved on to another friend. He wasn't sure anything could hold her attention for long.

His hand pulsed with pain. Curious, Thane probed at his knuckles with one finger. He hissed, the pain so sharp that spots momentarily danced in front of his eyes and his knees gave way. Thane staggered, and leaned against the wall. Brennan turned.

"You okay, kid?"

"Yeah," Thane gasped.

"Let me take a look." Thane tensed, and Brennan stood there, unmoving. After a few moments, Thane relented and held out his hand. Brennan took a step closer, gently took Thane's wrist and raised it to eye level. The skin around the knuckles was just beginning to bruise and swell, and any movement of the fingers made Thane grunt and wince.

"It'll be fine," Brennan announced. "A little bruised from its rapid impact with a wall, but just needs ice." Brennan patted Thane's hand and a sharp stabbing feeling shot up Thane's arm. His knees gave out and he sat down hard on the floor. Brennan looked contrite, and offered him a hand up.

"Don't touch me," Thane said.

"No, kid, I'm helping. How do your knuckles feel?"

"Fine--," Thane answered automatically, and then paused. The throbbing pain had been replaced by a burning deep in the tissue. The muscles and tendons felt strange and twitchy, like they were moving. Thane stared at his knuckles and saw a tiny puncture mark close up and fade away. After a moment there was a twinge, then a sharp snap that made Thane grateful he hadn't stood up yet. Then nothing. Gingerly, Thane straightened his fingers. They were stiff and sore and the bruising was still visible, but they moved without pain.

"It still needs ice," Brennan observed, and began walking again. Thane hurried to his feet and followed. Striding through the double doors of Mountain View's cafeteria, Brennan walked to a barrel of soda cans and scooped up a handful of ice and two root beers. Then he grabbed a sandwich in a plastic bag. Thane came in behind him, still cradling his hand because he felt he ought to and not because it really needed to be cradled.

Brennan handed the cashier a few bills and chatted pleasantly with her while she made change. Thane sat at a table, moving his fingers and staring at them in disbelief. The chair opposite scraped along the floor as Brennan pulled it out with his foot. He plunked down a can of root beer, then opened the sandwich bag with his teeth and emptied the sandwich onto the table, the bread coming apart from the stale turkey and Swiss and leaving a mayo smear. Brennan filled the bag with the melting ice from the soda barrel and offered it to Thane. Thane looked at it warily. Brennan sighed, and placed the ice bag on the table next to Thane's injured hand. They sat in silence, the humming of the refrigeration machines providing background noise.

Thane took the cold root beer can and cautiously rested it against the back of his knuckles. He let out a small sigh and his shoulders relaxed, just a little. Brennan tried to hide a smile behind his soda can, which became a grimace because he'd tried to take a drink without opening the can. Thane snorted and let go of a little more tension.

"Having a broken hand would've sucked," Thane commented. Brennan grunted agreement. Thane put down the root beer and placed the ice on his knuckles. He tried to open his soda can with one hand and fumbled it, and it rolled across the table. Brennan stopped it and put it back in front of Thane. The teenager considered for a moment, then lifted his injured hand and let the ice fall to the tabletop. He held the can with his left hand and popped the tab with his right, then lifted it and took a drink. The cold soda burned down his raw throat and he enjoyed the sensation.

"I'm Thane."

"Nice to meet you, Thane. It was starting to get awkward calling you 'kid'." Brennan grinned at him. "Who are you here for?"

"My dad and I got hit by lightning, but he got it worse. I'm waiting to go home," Thane announced nonchalantly. "You?"

He was expecting a reaction, but Brennan just nodded. "Sorry about your dad. Was he hit first or you?"

"Me. The doctor said I conducted over a hundred million volts of electricity." This time Brennan did look impressed and took a long look at Thane.

"One hundred million volts?"

"Yeah."

"And you're totally fine?"

"Yep."

"Huh. Who knew cinderblock walls were tougher than lightning?"

Thane deflated a bit. "My hand is fine now," he said. Brennan grunted.

"Anyone can get lucky once. The trick, kid, is to know how to make luck work for you. What most people think of as luck is really instinct, knowing the game and the rules well enough that you know which ones will bend when you push the right way. In the end, luck has nothing to do with our futures. We do."

Brennan took a long drink and crushed his empty can with one hand, then tossed it over Thane's head. Thane turned to watch it as it ricocheted off the wall and onto an empty tray a teenage girl was carrying. She squealed and jerked the tray upwards, propelling the crumpled can back into the air. It flew in a high arc across the room and fell into the bright blue aluminum recycling bin without touching any of the edges.

Thane turned back to gawk at Brennan. "There was no way you could've done that on purpose. You were--"

"Lucky? Haven't you been listening? I'm the luckiest guy on the planet, mostly because I know luck has nothing to do with it." Brennan stood up while he was talking and took a business card out of his back pocket. He flicked it at Thane, who caught it reflexively. "My card," Brennan said. "You seem like a person who could use a little more directed luck."

With that, Brennan turned around and started to walk out of the cafeteria. "Wait," Thane called, "why are you at the hospital?"

"Felt like this was the place to be," Brennan said, and left.

Thane looked down at the small wrinkled paper he gripped in his hand. He smoothed it out. "Brennan Tayler, Luck Specialist, SMG" with a phone number. "Luck Specialist?" Thane said, staring at the small card. He noticed he'd caught the paper with his injured hand. It should've still been immobile, or at least sore, but he'd used it without thinking.

Thane's stomach rumbled and he eyed the remains of the sandwich on the table. He scooped it back together and devoured it. He drank the rest of his soda, lifting the can with the hand he'd been favoring. Feeling unusually strong he crushed the can once it was empty. Who was this Brennan Tayler, and what had he done to Thane's hand?

CHAPTER 3

"I bet he escaped from the psych ward," Remi mused, fascinated by Thane's story. "He sounds like one of those savants, people who can do one thing better than anyone else on the planet but lack in their connection to reality."

They were at his locker in the school hallway during lunch, two days after Thane's mad dash to catch the bus and lightning strike. Remi had been glad to see him and drawn out everything that had happened since he left school on Monday, and he'd just finished telling her about Brennan Tayler. "Here's your backpack, Flash," Remi said, smacking him in the chest with it. Thane gave her a quizzical look, and she colored. "He's a comic book guy. Wears all red, runs so fast he's hard to see." Thane kept looking at her until she punched his arm. "Cool people like comic books."

"Sure," Thane said, smiling a little. It felt good to be doing something normal after the last few days. He stretched the fingers of his right hand, thinking about the hospital and Brennan again.

Remi noticed. "Let me see it?" Thane held out his previously injured knuckles for her and she stared at them like a jeweler inspecting a diamond. "There's nothing here. No bruising, no swelling, nothing. Are you sure you even hurt it?"

"Yeah," Thane answered. "It was broken. He fixed it."

"I wonder why," Remi mused, reaching out and taking his hand in both of hers. Thane stiffened, unsure, but Remi was too deep in her thoughts to notice. She rubbed his knuckles with her thumb, trying to feel for any inconsistency. Thane felt his face going red and was about to pull away when something inside his hand moved.

Remi froze-- she'd felt it too. Their eyes met over his hand. "What is that?" she asked him. He shrugged, pulling his hand out of hers to look at it himself. He pushed his finger down in the space between his second and third knuckles, and felt that same something hard roll away. It was so small he never would have noticed it on his own. He pulled his hand up to his eyes, and Remi stood on tiptoe to get a closer look. They both leaned in, trying to see any evidence of what they were feeling under Thane's skin.

The bell rang, startling them both. Thane and Remi realized their faces were only inches apart, and sprang back. Snickers around them in the hallway let them know their display had not gone unnoticed.

"New girlfriend, Thane?" Ben called from a few lockers down.

"You could do better, new girl," Jeran said, flexing his muscles. "I could show you a lot more than that weak loser." Thane's face colored, but Jeran walked off laughing with his buddies. Jeran was an entitled prick, the star of the second worst football team in the state. He wasn't smart enough to be the quarterback but as a wide receiver, you only had to get the ball somewhere near him and he would catch it. Tall and muscular, girls flocked around him and grownups loved to talk to him. Thane wanted to punch him hard enough to make it impossible for him to smirk for at least a week.

"Don't worry about those idiots," Remi started, but Thane spun around and left her behind. From the moment Mr. Hoffman introduced them, Thane had failed at his one cardinal rule. When he was with Remi everybody saw him.

Thane was one of the first into the room. Ms. Rasmussen didn't look up as he entered, engrossed in some magazine. He managed to slide onto his stool in the back row without exciting note or comment from anyone. He took out his notebook and pretended to read it as the rest of the class arrived in twos and threes.

Remi's voice, laughing and chatting, stabbed his ear and he couldn't help glancing up. She was walking in with Jeran, smiling at him and shaking her head so that her dark hair bounced. As they came in, Ms. Rasmussen's attention was diverted by Remi's giggle and she smugly observed them. "Know your way around now, sweetie?" she asked Remi in a satisfied voice. Remi gave her a half smile, but did not respond. Jeran flashed Ms. Rasmussen a grin calculated to charm, then turned to Thane and transformed it into a self-satisfied smirk.

"Thanks, Jeran," Remi said, and walked back to sit with Thane. Jeran's face darkened as she walked away.

"I found your girlfriend lost in the hall," Jeran swaggered down the aisle towards him, voice dripping with false sympathy. "I told her you were unstable." Thane was clenching his teeth, jaw taunt, and Jeran bent down in his face. "It's okay, loser. If your dad doesn't wake up, I'll take care of your hot mom, too."

Music blossomed in Thane's mind as his fist connected with Jeran's jaw. There was a crunch and a sizzle and the smell of burnt flesh as Jeran fell backwards and the second bell rang. Jeran landed on the floor, as surprised by the sucker punch as Thane was. Jeran sprang back up, blood in his mouth and rage in his eyes and oddly, a bright burn on his jaw. He moved at Thane.

"That is enough, Jeran!" Ms. Rasmussen snapped. Jeran hesitated, and then lunged for Thane. Ms. Rasmussen grabbed Jeran's shoulder and spun him around, her eyes flashing and her breath quick. "Get out of my class."

"What?" Jeran was stunned. "But Cressa--"

"You will call me Ms. Rasmussen. Go to the nurse's office, then the principal's. Now." Her voice had gotten softer, colder, and somehow so dark that Thane repressed a chill.

Jeran crumbled. He fled from the room, the door banging as he ran through it. Ms. Rasmussen came to stand in front of Thane and rested the tips of her fingers on his arm. "Aren't you a hero for defending your mother's honor like that!" She was sweet, but her green eyes glowed with something Thane didn't recognize. Greed? Insanity? She tugged at his arm a little, and he stood up. "Why don't you come up here and take Jeran's seat? He won't be needing it."

Thane obediently gathered his things and went with her to the front. Remi followed him. Ms. Rasmussen seemed delighted. She even clapped her hands to get the attention of the class, which was completely unnecessary as every eye was already on her.

"Change of plans today, everyone! We're going to be doing hands-on experiments instead of a quiz." Her announcement brightened the feeling in the room considerably. "Put away your books and keep out your notepads. You'll need to take good notes. Every team will need a Bunsen burner, a holding tray, one five hundred milliliter beaker, one hundred milliliter beaker, safety glasses for each of you, a thermometer, and a pair of tongs. We're going to talk about thermodynamics!" She seemed gleeful, as manic as Thane had ever seen her.

Thane got up and gathered the implements since Remi wouldn't know where they were. He felt awful for ditching her in the hall. Carefully holding as many of the implements as he could in his arms, he set them down gently on the table in front of Remi and spread them out.

"I stole his playbook," Remi whispered. Thane attached the Bunsen burner to the short tube that rose out of the center of their rectangular table. "I thought we could do some creative play changing."

A rush of gratitude warmed Thane. Having a friend had perks. Ms. Rasmussen continued to give instructions. "...and be sure, girls, to keep your hair away from the flames. I'll be around to make sure that the gas lines are connected. Place the holding tray about six inches above the flame and fill the larger beaker with water from the sink..." Remi grabbed the larger beaker and followed the line of students back to the sink. Soon all the students had their beaker of water in place on the holding tray and were turning the burners on, seeing the waving yellow and orange flame tighten into a straight blue and purple one. "Open the air hole to only about half, we don't want it fully on. We're just heating water."

The lean, tall woman walked around the classroom checking each burner to ensure that the gas lines were attached correctly and the flames were high and hot enough. She came to Thane and Remi, bending to peer closely at their set up. "I think you need to lower your holding tray slightly," she instructed, and Thane made the adjustment. The corner of Ms. Rasmussen's mouth twitched, and then she moved on.

Her foot slipped, the thin heel shooting into the air, and she flailed her arms. With one hand she grabbed the side of a table, and the other grabbed Thane's left arm, pulling his wrist directly across the open flame.

"Argh!" Thane grunted, jerking his hand back. There was a shiny red mark along the underside of his wrist as wide as two fingers. He stared at it as his teacher regained her balance and turned to him.

"Oh, Thane, I'm so sorry," she gushed. "Someone spilled some water on the floor and I slipped! Let me see it," and she jerked his arm towards her. Her green eyes studied the red welt for a slow heartbeat, and she appeared... pleased. But only for a moment. Her face was full of concern and contrition when she looked back at him. "It's not badly burned. Run cold water over it. As for the rest of you," she whirled to face the class, her beautiful features twisted in fierce and dangerous anger, "be more careful. This could have been a serious accident. If you spill any liquid, clean it up immediately. I could've broken my ankle and poor Thane," she looked down at him and her tone quieted, "poor Thane could have lost his hand. Well," she said, her voice returning to normal, "back to work, everyone."

As the flames burned and the students adjusted their safety glasses, Ms. Rasmussen pulled a box off the shelf behind her desk. It was dusty, and she smiled and held it for a moment. Then she wiped it off and placed it on her desk. "In this box I have several pieces of Field's Metal. Has anyone ever heard of it?" She paused, but no hands went up. "It is a most impressive alloy. It's a non-toxic mixture of bismuth, tin, and indium. There are many alloys that melt at low temperatures, even though the metals they are mixed from require much higher temperatures to melt in their pure form. These low melting point metals are called fusible alloys."

Several of the students were scribbling furiously, as Ms. Rasmussen was not writing on the board. Instead, her hands were resting on either side of the open box as she was intently watching the beaker and the flame in front of Remi and Thane. Remi was one of the desperate note takers-- Thane couldn't take his eyes away from the chemistry teacher, like a bird staring at a snake. His heart pounded against his chest and his palms felt sweaty. Something was wrong.

She reached her hand into the box and drew out what looked to be a silver straw. "Each of you will be given one of these Field's Metal wires. Place your thermometers into the water and the metal wire into your smaller empty beaker. Using the tongs, hold the smaller beaker partially submerged in the boiling water. Record at what temperature, both Fahrenheit and Celsius, the metal begins to melt. I will pass out molds to each team for you to pour your liquid metal into, and you will time how long it takes the metal to re-harden."

She walked to Thane, her heels clicking on the linoleum floor. Her intense smile was only for him. His stomach suddenly hurt, and he leaned away as she bent down to place the wire in the smaller beaker on the table. Ms Rasmussen turned, her back to the class, and spun around again with her hands full of the thin metal strips. The click of her heels and the clack of metal hitting glass traveled through the room. "All right, everyone, safety glasses on. Use your tongs to hold the small beaker half submerged in the water. Will the water boil first, or will the metal melt? Make sure your thermometers are in the water so you can keep track of the temperature."

The soft hum of voices and tinkling of metal on glass rose in the classroom. Remi put the thermometer in the water and made a notation of the temperature. Thane took the tongs and gripped the smaller beaker, lifting and placing it into the water. Remi was looking at him, little glances he wasn't sure if he was supposed to notice. Her forehead was furrowed. Thane was still feeling on edge, and Ms. Rasmussen was sitting behind her desk, staring at him, discomfiting him.

Remi whispered, "You don't have to take care of me."

"What?" Thane said. This made him feel worse.

Remi didn't look at him. She was focused on the tiny numbers printed on their thermometer. "I didn't give you much of a choice about being friends. We don't have to be. I know I can be pretty annoying."

"No," Thane objected. "That's not--" Thane had no idea how to talk about his feelings. No one had ever wanted to listen.

Remi said, still staring at the numbers. Thane was sure she had them memorized by now. "You're going through a lot right now, and I don't want--"

"Shut up," Thane blurted. "We're friends, so deal with it." He snapped his mouth closed and gulped. He waited for her to smack him or walk away. She did neither, but the corners of her mouth turned up and she glanced at him.

"Why is ours taking so long?" Remi said. Thane blinked. Other teams were making excited exclamations and pointing, blown away by metal that melted in warm water. Students were listing numbers, their partners writing notes.

"A hundred forty-three degrees Fahrenheit, sixty-one Celsius."

"One hundred forty-six degrees Fahrenheit, can you see the Celsius? It's too small..."

"Sixty-three degrees Celsius, you need new glasses..."

Thane looked at their thermometer. It read one hundred forty-seven degrees, but the silver straw wasn't melting yet. "Maybe ours is thicker than theirs?"

"Density shouldn't make that much of a difference to melting point," Remi responded. "Ms. Rasmussen's still staring at you."

Thane nodded. "I'm trying to ignore her. Take the tongs?" Remi did, and Thane peered at the numbers. "We're up to one fifty-four."

Remi made a note. "Something's got to be wrong with ours. Maybe we should ask?" Thane shook his head. "But if something is wrong--"

"It's melting. One hundred fifty-eight degrees Fahrenheit, seventy degrees Celsius."

Remi's pencil scratched along her paper as she wrote down the numbers. Ms. Rasmussen bounded up from her desk. "All right, I'll hand out the molds now. I suggest that the bravest partner hold the mold while the other pours; after all, you'll be holding molten metal in your hands." Her mouth was stretched in a manic smile as she handed out novelty ice cube trays in various shapes like fish, stars, and flowers. Holding the last tray, she stopped next to Thane and Remi's table and held it out.

The shapes were lightning bolts. Thane heard Remi's gasp as he stared at the tray. Then he raised his eyes to meet Ms. Rasmussen's and took it from her, his hands steady. "Thanks."

Ms. Rasmussen raised one too-thin eyebrow. Then she went back to her desk and flipped open her magazine again, ignoring them all.

"I can't believe she did that!" Remi hissed, glaring at their teacher.

"I'll hold it, you pour," Thane responded. Remi seemed about to protest, but Thane cut her off. "I'm not giving her the satisfaction of handing this thing to you." Remi tightened her grip on the tongs and raised the beaker of silver liquid. Drops of water falling from the glass hissed into steam as they hit the granite while Remi moved her hands until the silver metal was above the tray. She tilted the tongs and the molten metal inside spilled over the edge of the beaker, flowing down into the tray below and filling the contours of a lightning bolt.

"Ow-ow," Thane yelled and threw down the tray on the table, grabbing his leg halfway up the thigh. Remi jerked the beaker upright but most of the liquid was already out. Ms. Rasmussen was instantly at his side ripping his hands away. A small circle burned through his pants and there was a widening red mark on the skin underneath. His teacher seemed elated, then struggled to control herself.

"It's just a small burn, go to the nurse," she said using a cloth to wipe away the metal residue, and walked away to check on the other groups. Thane started out of the room as quickly as he could until he heard Remi whisper his name. She was pointing at the table. Hardening metal leaked from the upright tray. There had been a hole in the mold. Remi and Thane's eyes met, her eyebrows bunched together and his face carefully blank. Then he continued to the nurse's office.

Nurse Hamilton was an energetic, round-faced young woman who felt that excessive cheer made up for her lack of medical knowledge. "What did you say you were working with?" she asked again.

"Field's metal." She stared at him blankly. "It melts in hot water." Still blank. Thane sighed. "Hot water and metal in Chemistry class."

The nurse frowned. "What kind of chemicals?"

"Just metal and water."

"Was anything toxic or dangerous?"

Thane thought back through Ms. Rasmussen's lecture. "No, Field's metal isn't toxic."

She brightened. "It probably just burned because it was hot." She applied some burn ointment and wrapped it in gauze, then went and made a note on a form sitting at her desk.

"Am I good to go?" he asked.

"Hmm?" she looked up. "Oh, yes, you're good. We'll mail a copy to your parents." She smiled at him while he turned to leave. "Thane?"

He stopped and turned back to her, waiting. "Do you want me to look at your knuckles?"

"My knuckles?" he asked, startled. How had she known about that? He'd only told Remi, and he somehow doubted Nurse Hamilton knew the possibly insane Brennan Tayler.

"From punching Jeran. He said it was you. Was it not you?"

"Oh. No, it was me. They're fine," he said, and shuffled his feet. He hated getting lectured, but sweet Nurse Hamilton wouldn't be in the same category as his dad.

She smiled at him, larger than before. "Good for you, Thane. The experiment explains the burn on his jaw, too. Well, I'll see you later."

Thane nodded and smiled back a little. "Thanks Nurse Hamilton." She beamed and shooed him away.

Thane started to walk, hiding his limp. Fourth period was already half over and he didn't feel like trying to catch up. Going to his locker, dumping his books, and waiting for the bus seemed like the best option. This had been an awful day, but at least it was almost over. His parents weren't home yet and the girls were with Mrs. Knotts, so all he had to do was make it home.

"Thane!" Mr. Hoffman tried to modulate his voice so it came out slightly less than his usual echoing boom. Thane flinched, and he mutinously considered not stopping. But he sighed, and turned around. "Just the man I was looking for. Step into my office for a bit."

Mr. Hoffman followed Thane into his office, a small, cramped room filled with stuff. Masks, rugs, and pictures hung so thick it was impossible to see the walls. Bookshelves overflowed with books and papers. Thane sat in the chair in front and stared at his hands while Mr. Hoffman carefully maneuvered his way behind his desk to sit down. They sat in silence, Mr. Hoffman's smile bearing down on Thane until Thane felt trapped, like a wild animal in front of a train.

"You've had quite an exciting few days," Thane had to look up to make sure it was still Mr. Hoffman in the room with him. The voice that spoke was calm and kind, nothing like Mr. Hoffman's trademark booming exuberance. He was waiting for an answer, and Thane shrugged in response. Mr. Hoffman still waited.

"I guess," Thane finally answered. Mr. Hoffman nodded, his brown hair showing grey at the temples. Thane looked around the room to avoid looking back at Mr. Hoffman, who was still waiting.

"I have to talk to you about what happened today, Thane," Mr. Hoffman said. Thane stared at his lap again. "After Jeran went to the nurse, he told me how you sucker punched him because you're jealous." Thane slumped further down in his chair. If he protested, the yelling would start.

The assistant principal continued. "The bell had barely rung before your friend Remi was in here telling me what Jeran said to you, and then she told me about the experiment in chemistry class and your injuries. She accused Ms. Rasmussen of hurting you on purpose." Mr. Hoffman's chair creaked as he leaned forward. "Thane, those allegations are serious. Ms. Rasmussen will get a formal complaint filed in her teaching record for negligence and failing to maintain safety standards."

Thane snorted softly, and the balding man continued. "Yes, it isn't much, but with the teacher's union backing her and frankly, with her face, I doubt anyone interviewing her would bother looking at her record. But it is what I can do and so I will do it. As for the punch, this school has a zero tolerance policy for violence and for bullying." Mr. Hoffman looked sternly down at Thane, who shrank back into his chair. "Therefore, since he was bullying and you were violent, I'd say the two events cancel each other out."

Thane's head jerked up in shock. The smile lurking in the corners of Mr. Hoffman's mouth exploded full onto his face. "That kid really annoys me. Oh," Mr. Hoffman looked at Thane a little sheepishly, "I didn't say that." Thane smiled a little. Mr. Hoffman noticed the smile. "You're off the hook this time, Thane. But only this time. If he gives you more trouble, you let me handle the punishment, okay?"

The bell rang loudly, shattering the moment between them. Mr. Hoffman sat up and leaned back, his usual jovial smile back in place. "Glad we talked, Thane. You should probably go catch your bus!"

Thane blinked. "Um, yeah. Thanks, Mr. Hoffman. Bye."

"Bye, Thane," Mr. Hoffman said as Thane stood and hurried out the door. Mr. Hoffman's voice came over the PA system, asking if Ms. Rasmussen would please come to his office.

Thane was all mixed up inside, feeling grateful to the assistant principal but uncomfortable about how close he'd come to being in trouble. He was glad that Remi had stood up for him but he wasn't sure he could handle the attention being around her brought. His leg and wrist stung, and his knuckles were throbbing from the punch. He slowly wove his way through the crowd in the hallways back to his locker and saw Ms. Rasmussen gliding through the horde of high-schoolers like a queen in a parade, the masses moving aside to let her pass.

Remi ran to him the moment she saw him. "She did it on purpose," her voice exploded into the noise and traffic of teenagers. "There was a hole in each of them!"

Thane pulled her out of the middle of the hallway. "What are you talking about?"

"The molds. I looked at the tray she gave us, and there was a hole poked into every mold so that no matter which one we'd used, it would've leaked on you!" Remi was livid, and Thane wished she could be livid more quietly. "So I offered to help clean up and I looked at every other tray. Ours was the only one with holes! And remember when she fell? And how no one cleaned it up? I checked and there was no water on the floor. She made that up and she deliberately burned you! Twice!"

"Why would she do that?" Thane asked.

"I don't know. Maybe because you embarrassed Jeran and he was one of her favorites? Maybe she's still mad that your mom is prettier than she is.

55

Maybe," and Remi slowed down to emphasize each word, "she's a crazy bi-polar shrew and it's past time for her to be committed. There she is! Let's follow her," and she ducked down behind a passing group of girls and started walking away from the office. Thane turned around and saw Ms. Rasmussen, whose long red hair and height made her recognizable from a distance. Remi looked back at him and waved with her hand. "Come on!" she hissed, and Thane resisted rolling his eyes and followed her.

They tracked Ms. Rasmussen out to the faculty parking lot. Remi grabbed Thane's hand and pulled him behind some bushes and they crouched, watching her. "Why are we doing this?" Thane whispered, and Remi glared him into silence. The leggy redhead took a compact out of her purse and checked her makeup while standing next to a two-seater red convertible with a BMW logo on the grill. She put some powder on her nose and forehead, then shut the compact with a click. Ms. Rasmussen smiled her best snake smile at the bushes where Thane and Remi hid.

"See you tomorrow," she called and waved before getting into her car and revving the engine.

"Quick, get her license plate number!" Remi ordered. "Maybe we can call in a speeding tip to the police or something."

Thane pulled a pen out of his backpack and jotted down the letters and numbers of the plate onto his hand. The BMW drove away, the late afternoon sun glinting off the chrome plaited Z3 on the trunk. "Nice car," Thane noted.

"There's no way she affords that on a teacher's salary. She must be into something else, too. Probably something illegal. Did you get her plates?" Thane nodded. "Let me see." Thane held out his palm to her. Remi squinted, trying to read his handwriting. "P-Y-R-O-4-I-C," she read, then snorted. "That fits. I was right, she is crazy."

"I'm missing something here," Thane said.

"Pyrophoric," Remi said. "It means someone who loves fire."

"I thought that was pyromaniac."

"Whatever. It's something about fire."

"So she burned me twice because she likes fire?" Thane asked, incredulous.

"Maybe," Remi agreed. "Why didn't she get hurt?"

"What?" Thane asked. He hadn't followed that.

"When she pulled your wrist through the fire. She was holding on to it, which means her fingers went through the flame too. Why didn't she get burned?"

Thane paused. That was an excellent question, and he had no idea what it might mean. But he was sure it was something bad. "I hate today," Thane groaned.

Remi nodded in agreement. "We'll have to be really careful in class, check everything--"

"Not that," Thane interrupted, pointing. "That was my bus."

CHAPTER 4

Thane trudged slowly down the hill. Since he wasn't trying to catch the bus, he was taking the route directly home instead of going past the middle school. Grey puffs floated in front of his face with every breath and his nose and the tips of his ears stung in the late autumn chill. His stomach started to ache. The playground in the city park was empty of people and filled with dead leaves that rustled and crunched as he cut through. His leg throbbed in time with his heartbeat and he wondered why the burn on his thigh hurt more than the one on his wrist, even though it was smaller.

Main Street was just ahead, over a hundred years old and only one lane wide. It was lined with old Mom and Pop shops; antique stores, a bike shop, a bakery, a library, a book shop, two or three handcrafted knickknack shops, and a few cafes. There were usually some people on Main Street shopping or taking a walk, but there were almost never cars since the street was one way going into town instead of out towards the freeway. Thane thought that Main Street was a symbol for the whole town: boring, stale, and outdated.

A group of middle school girls passed him, giggling, as he walked by the library. Thane's eyes blurred and he shook his head to clear them. An old man walked an even older dog, pausing to look into the windows of the shops. An athletic looking couple went into the mountain biking shop, and a man wearing a flat cap read a book while sitting on the bench in front of the Chinese restaurant. Thane limped past, drawing concerned glances as he did.

"You kick a wall now, kid?" the man in the flat cap asked. Thane groaned, and didn't stop walking. Brennan Tayler stood up, closed his book, and followed. He caught up to Thane in three strides and strolled comfortably alongside him. "Rough day?"

"Leave me alone." Thane snapped. He was starting to feel sick to his stomach and sweaty.

Brennan tsked. "That's hardly a kind welcome to the guy who fixed your knuckles."

"I wouldn't have broken them if you hadn't provoked me." Thane's breathing grew labored, and he felt dizzy.

"You needed to be provoked-- whoa!" Thane stumbled and pitched forward and Brennan caught him. "Thane, what's wrong?" Thane opened his mouth to answer, and instead felt his stomach contract and he dry heaved on the sidewalk. Brennan held his arm under Thane's shoulders to keep the boy from falling. "Shredding holes!" Brennan said, "We need to get you inside."

"Not going... with you," Thane panted.

"Yeah, sure, we'll keep it public," Brennan assured, and steered Thane across the street. The Leaf and Dagger, a used book store, had been there since Main Street was first opened. Thane had never been inside. The windows were shaded so the light inside was faded and the air was dusty and thick with the smell of old paper. The cashier was in his mid-twenties, wearing fake glasses, suspenders, and a fedora. He seemed nonplussed at the sight of Brennan half-dragging Thane into the store. "Passing through," Brennan said, and the twenty-something hipster jerked his head toward a door on the far wall. Thane staggered another few steps and then dry heaved again.

"When was the last time you ate, kid?" Brennan asked.

Thane groaned in response. "Don't... food. Uhhhnnnhh."

"Right, my bad." Brennan opened the door and pulled Thane through. The musty air disappeared and the smell of grease, wood, and something bitter assaulted Thane's nose. Brennan dragged him another few feet then hauled him up by his armpits and set him on a stool. Thane's forehead thumped onto the wooden bar in front of him, and he tried to steady his breathing and make the world stop spinning.

"What's that, Brennan?" Thane barely registered the voice was female. The wood grain was rough against his forehead, and he tried not to move. "Did you do that to this poor boy? Is he for me?"

"Found him like this. Couldn't leave a pup this sick on the side of the road, he'd get hit by a car," Brennan answered, sounding glib, but Thane could feel Brennan's hand's on his wrist, undoing the bandage. "What's this?"

"Burn," Thane whispered.

"From what?"

"Fire."

"What fire? Did you breathe in smoke?" Brennan rewrapped the wrist and felt Thane's face. "You're burning up. How long have you had a fever?"

"I'm cold, don't got fever," Thane growled weakly.

"Did the fire burn you anywhere else?"

"The other burn's from metal," Thane was groggy, and felt sick again. He wished he'd eaten lunch so he'd have something to throw up. Then maybe he'd feel better.

"Metal?" Brennan was surprised. "How did you get burned from metal? Where?"

"Chemistry class. My leg." he moved his hand toward it, then let it drop. "Can I sleep now?"

"No!" Brennan snapped. Thane could hear Brennan looking for something, jingling keys and rustling paper. "There they are."

"Dibs if it makes him die faster," that smooth female voice said.

"What?" Thane said, trying to raise his head. Then he felt a sharp prick on the back of his neck, and another on his leg. "Ow!"

His body flooded with heat, and his stomach rebelled again. He lost his balance, falling from the stool and cracking his chin against the bar on his way to the floor. He grunted and convulsed, his eyes rolling back in his head. His knee spasmed and his shin bashed into something hard. Pain flashed up his leg, and heat followed. The pain and the warmth chased each other through his limbs and across his chest, finally settling in his stomach and lungs. Breathing hurt, his lungs protesting the stretch and the air inside them feeling super-heated. Thane gasped, curling around himself, trying to keep his lungs from exploding outward through his ribcage. Then, like a balloon, he deflated. The heat, pain, and tension drained out of him until he lay limply on the floor, drenched in sweat.

Thane never wanted to move again. He would die on this back room floor of some old bookstore in the most boring town in the world. He'd been an idiot to ever trust Brennan, and he wondered if Remi would ever know that she'd been right, Brennan was crazy.

"Kid? Thane?" Brennan's voice was concerned.

"I hate you," Thane mumbled. "I'm dead, and I hate you."

Brennan burst out laughing. "Well, I guess I can see your point of view. Get up!" and Brennan hauled Thane up and put him back on the stool. Thane put both hands on the counter to steady himself. "You'll need some food. Raven, get my boy here a Philly with onion rings and something cold to drink."

"I like it better when they die." Thane's eyes were drawn to the unknown speaker, and he felt Brennan's arm snap into place across his back to keep him from falling over again. She was black. The color black, like a crayon or his backpack, but with faint red stripes sliding across her skin. Her hair hung most of the way down her back and it was silver and red in a complex pattern. Pointed black and red ears poked up out of it. When she spoke, her teeth were crimson and her eyes were silver, with no other color and no black center.

Thane shoved Brennan away with as much force as he could. "This is your fault!" he shouted, and stood up. "You went crazy and dragged me with you!" He was wobbly on weak legs, but he still took a swing. Brennan knocked it aside easily. Thane stepped closer and swung again at the other man's stomach. Brennan took the hit without flinching. Thane's ineffectiveness made him angrier, and he pulled back and punched as hard as he could right at Brennan's face.

Brennan's hand shot up and caught Thane's fist with plenty of room to spare. "I've been patient, and you're no longer trying to puke on me," Brennan's hand flexed and Thane's arm lowered involuntarily. "I've put up with your whining and accusations. But I have already had a bad day." Brennan's arm tensed and moved forward, and Thane was pushed back until he felt the stool behind his legs. "All my instincts are screaming that I need to be miles away, but I've been ordered here, to check on you. So you are going to sit down," Brennan swept his leg behind Thane's legs, forcing his knees to bend and his backside to smack the top of the stool, "and answer my questions." Brennan held Thane's fist in front of the boy's face, then let it go with a slight shove.

"You're not--" As Brennan's hand opened, Thane's retort died. The man's middle finger ended jaggedly about halfway up, and where the index should have been the palm ended in a slant, as if the finger had been a plant torn out by the roots. "Wha-- what happened?" The red-haired man wiggled his remaining fingers, gazing at his hand with a sigh.

"Courtesy of Rip," he said, and slumped down into the stool next to Thane. The ebony and scarlet colored woman placed a tall glass of amber colored liquid on the bar in front of him, and he nodded gratefully. "I swear you could blow his head off and it would only give you time to start running before he came after you again."

"I like Rip," Raven purred. "There is always such lovely carnage and chaos when he's let loose." She shivered, sighing, and went through a door behind the bar.

Thane spun to look at Brennan. "Do you swear I'm not crazy? Did I hit my head?"

Brennan chuckled. "I'm not qualified to answer that first one, but I can tell you that Raven looks a little different than your average bar tender. So take a few breaths and calm down."

"But what is she?" Thane insisted. "Does she have some horrible disease?"

"Don't say that where she can hear you, kid," Brennan warned. "This is a lot to take in, but that's no reason to be rude."

Thane took a deep, slow breath in through his nose, and exhaled out his mouth. "Brennan. My chemistry teacher attacked me twice today. I almost died five minutes ago. Please."

Brennan sighed. "Yeah, okay. I'm being evasive because I'm going to get in trouble for bringing you here, but I needed somewhere to heal you. I have to find out why your tracker failed and get back to my team. I'm off my game here, because all my instincts are only telling me one thing. This is not where I should be. So I'm hurrying and taking shortcuts and you're the one who has to suffer for them. Sorry for that. It would be best for both of us if you chalk all this up to a bad fever dream and swear you'll never try to find this place on your own. Then maybe Andrus won't shoot me."

Thane latched onto that. "This is all a bad dream?"

"Add confusing and overwhelming to bad, and you've got it."

"All right. I can't look for a bad dream."

Brennan grinned at him. "I like you, kid. I hope for your sake you never have to see me again after today."

Thane tried to smile back. "I don't know. I've never had an imaginary friend before. I must really suck at it if you're the best I can do."

Raven entered with a large white plate and set it in front of Thane. His eyes widened. It was heaped with huge onion rings and had the biggest sandwich he'd ever seen, with greasy steak and gooey cheese overflowing from the sides. It smelled incredible, and Thane realized he was starving. He reached out with both hands.

"Wait." Brennan's arm appeared between Thane and the food. Brennan looked at Raven, expressionless while she set down a huge tankard of something so cold that water beaded on the outside. Thane tried not to stare at Brennan's hand; it was pretty easy, considering how hard he was staring at the food.

"Fine," she sighed, and reached into the fried rings, plucking out a long needle. Brennan still waited, barring Thane from eating. Raven smiled and pulled something like a fish hook out of the sandwich meat. "That's all."

"By your Oath and Song, there is nothing else that will cause him harm?"

"There's twice his daily calorie needs and a lot of fat and grease," she sneered. "But by my Oath and Song, the rest is just food. And milk. He's a baby, after all."

Brennan moved his arm and went back to his drink. Thane didn't move. "Eat, kid, its fine," Brennan said. "Never trust a Sang Evarish without getting their oath, but they can't break it without losing their Song and they won't risk that. Besides, Raven's cooking is worth a little danger."

There was a long moment of silence as Thane considered. "It will get cold if you wait much longer, and then it isn't worth eating," the black and red woman said, and that decided it. Thane started eating, one small bite of the steak. The moment it hit his tongue he felt like he hadn't eaten in weeks, and began stuffing the rest in his mouth.

Brennan let Thane eat for a few minutes, taking small pulls of his drink while Thane chewed. The slate grey tankard took two hands to lift, but the milk was thick and cold and tasted fresher than any milk he'd ever had. The sandwich was three quarters gone and only a few onion rings remained before his rapid pace slacked off to something close to normal.

"You're a good cook," Thane said, and Raven's face twisted into something between a grimace and a snarl.

"Be nice to the kid, Raven. He's new." Brennan said.

She hissed and stalked to the other end of the bar. Brennan snorted and turned to Thane.

"So how'd you get burned?"

"The burner in chemistry class."

"You were goofing around with it? That's not smart, kid."

"My teacher fell. She grabbed my arm for balance and pulled it through the flame." Thane tried to sound belligerent, but it was hard through a mouthful of meat and cheese and bread.

"Huh. What about your leg?"

Thane's chewing slowed while he took a minute to consider his response. "We were studying the melting point of metal. Some spilled on my leg."

"You were melting metal?" Brennan straightened and looked at Thane. "What kind? How?"

"With water. It had a really low melting point and we were supposed to learn about it."

The other man's eyes narrowed. "Were you keeping track of the temperature?"

"Yeah." Thane picked up the last few fries and put them in his mouth.

"Did it melt at one forty-four degrees or one fifty-seven degrees Fahrenheit?"

"How did you know that? Most everyone else's was around forty-four, but ours was one fifty-seven." Thane jumped when Brennan slammed his drink on the counter.

"That explains the fever and vomiting. You were poisoned. The fumes from Wood's Metal cause flu like symptoms and the toxins burn the skin. You're lucky I was ordered to check your device when the transmissions stopped. Those healing darts saved you a week of the flu and a bad burn on your leg." Brennan took a swallow of his ale while Thane processed.

"She called it Field's Metal, not Wood's. Wait, check on my device? What device? And what are healing darts?"

"Healing darts are these," Brennan fished around in his pocket for a moment and pulled out a small oval shaped dart. It was about the size of a quarter with a short hollow needle on one end. "I poke you with one of these and squeeze, and the medicine enters your bloodstream. They can fix just about anything, given enough time and juice."

Thane's gaze traveled from the healing dart to the hand that held it, with the glaring absence of a finger and a half. "So why didn't they fix your fingers?"

"Ah," Brennan said. He looked down and took another drink before continuing. "The darts can heal anything your body would heal on its own. That's what Raven meant about you dying faster. If whatever was making you sick was stronger than your body, then you would've died on the floor here rather than in a few weeks. Of course medications and doctors can help," he paused, taking another drink, "because the darts accelerate the pace of the illness or disease too, to get it over with faster. So sometimes we can't take the darts because we need the normal medical treatment to weaken whatever's wrong with us first so we would get better anyway. It just takes too long. That's why we're not prancing around blow-gunning people with cancer or HIV or whatever. It could just kill them where they might've lived otherwise." Brennan took a last long drink and set down the empty glass.

"So if there had been too much toxin in my system, you would've killed me?" Thane said thinking it through. "But if you'd taken me to a hospital and gotten me treated, I could've lived? You were gambling with my life because you didn't want to wait to find out?"

"Felt like the right thing to do," Brennan winked.

"Yes, your lack of fingers inspires confidence in your instincts." Thane retorted, and pulled out his cell phone. Brennan grabbed it from him.

"No calls."

"I have to call Remi. She needs to know about the metal poisoning."

"You can call your girlfriend later. Now is not the time-"

"She isn't my girlfriend, she was my lab partner." Thane emphasized the last two words. "She's going to get sick too, she could die," and he tried to grab the phone back.

Brennan paused, thinking. "You can text her. Briefly. But she'll be fine, kid," and he held out the phone.

"How would you know?" Thane said, taking it back.

"Did she get burned too?" Thane shook his head without looking up, texting rapidly and pressing send. "I know she'll be fine because you're fine, and the metal actually touched you. She'll probably just be out of school with the flu for a few days."

"Is that what your instincts tell you?" Thane said sarcastically, shoving his phone into the backpack by his feet.

"My instincts got my fingers torn off instead of my whole arm. Even with that, Rip put me in the infirmary for over three hours. I could've stayed another two if the general hadn't jerked me out of there to send me here. I like it better when we draw to be on the same side in training. Rip is decent enough, but that daemon inside him wants to see the world burn..." As he spoke, Brennan got a strange look on his face, an odd, haunted expression. He looked down at his empty glass, and then over to where Raven stood, calmly wiping the counter with a wicked grin.

"What did you do, you evil blood beast?" Brennan demanded. Raven's grin widened, each crimson fang gleaming.

"In vino veritas, mercenary. You only asked about the boy's food, not yours." Her grin turned feral, a sharp toothed snarl that gave Thane his first experience with primal fear. "You take too much pride in the secrets you hide and the weapons you use to keep us enslaved. When you forget the rules, it's your fault, not mine. Besides, you said you fought Rip this morning, which means you nearly died. Which means..." Raven's chuckle was throaty and malicious.

Brennan's already pale face drained of what little color it had left, although he kept his expression neutral. "Moirai," he whispered, and glanced around the room.

"You poisoned him?" Thane's voice cracked up an octave and back down. Raven gnashed her teeth at Thane, and he cringed.

"She's not gonna kill him," a deep male voice slurred. Thane's eyes darted around looking for the speaker, but there wasn't anyone else. A wet belch drew Thane's eyes to Brennan. The man's lips were moving as he silently cursed, and he leaned forward, running his fingers through his red hair. As his head sank lower, Thane caught a glimpse of... someone... sitting on the other side. The boy leaned back.

"Raven's not dumb. She knows she kills somebody in here Sanctum would revoke her license and send her to jail. Unless it wasn't her first whoopsie-- then they'd just unravel her Song," the speaker leered at Raven, who hissed, snake-like, back at him. Another sloppy burp exploded out, and he raised a tankard of ale to his lips and let it slosh around.

The speaker was... unexpected. Less than four feet tall, he was clearly a fully grown male with a few days worth of dark scruffy stubble covering puffy checks and slack jowls. His bulbous nose was slightly red, and his head was slick bald. Black bushy eyebrows were over watery eyes and although he wore no shirt, it was hard to see the rolls of fat on his chest and round belly underneath the thick masses of body hair. His only clothing was a large loincloth, so dark and dirty that the original color was hard to guess. His legs were also incredibly hairy, and the calloused feet were bare, with long jagged toenails.

Then there were his wings. Glistening and iridescent, they rose out of his back like dragonfly wings. With every move shining diamond dust shook from them, making the air around him shimmer and shine. Some of the glittering motes wafted into the tankard of ale, and the little man used filthy fingernails to dig them out. Rows of dirty, cracked teeth showed as he grinned at Thane's stare. Deliberately, he flicked the ale soaked particles into Brennan's hair, using his other hand to scratch himself.

"She just dropped some slippery tongue in his drink. Makes him like talking. Right, sweetie?" and he smiled, still scratching.

Raven gagged. "You knotted discordant hairy beast!" she spat. "You have one use and one use only, and it does not require your mouth!"

"Hung like a grizzly, that's all the women care about," the little man leaned on one hip and grunted. Loud, smelly gas ripped out, knocking Thane back and forcing Brennan to cover his face with his sleeve. The hairy small man sighed in satisfaction. "There's another batch nearly done, dearie. One, maybe two more, and this'll be the bubbliest ale this side of the weave." He took another long pull of his tankard and scratched his belly in satisfaction.

"You frothing stupid fairy! Warn me before you do that, some of it almost got in my mouth," Brennan snapped. "Come on kid, we've got to get out of here before she shows up."

"Brennan, what was it like tapping Moirai's barrel?" the Beer Fairy leered. "She must've been very grateful to you to go slumming it with a disgusting human. Why, it's like a fairy tale!" and his cracked and stained teeth became visible as he grinned. "Why fight it? It's kismet."

A low growl started deep in Brennan's throat. "Don't-"

The Beer Fairy blithely continued. "You could say it's destiny."

Brennan's lips curled in a snarl. "say-"

"It's fate!" the grubby pixie crowed, and Brennan launched himself from the stool onto the counter where the fairy sat, his eight and a half fingered hands grasping for the fairy's throat.

Before his fingers had connected with the flabby begrimed neck, the smaller man vanished with a puff of lavender smoke and a nutty smell. Brennan soared through the space above the counter, upsetting the half empty tankard, and smashed into the colored bottles that lined the wall behind it. The Beer Fairy reappeared sitting on a table further back in the room, laughing so hard his eyes streamed with tears. Raven yowled and grabbed Brennan by the shoulders, digging her clawed fingers into his flesh and threw him back over the counter. The full weight of Brennan's hurtling body slammed into the Beer Fairy's belly. With all of the momentum of Raven's throw behind it the man, the fairy, and the table crashed to the ground.

"You bent my slogging wing!" the pixie man shrieked, grabbing the broken table top and swinging it at Brennan. Raven leapt over the counter and dove into the brawl. Brennan tried to crawl backwards on his hands and feet to escape the fairy's assault but Thane could tell there was no way he'd get far enough away in time. Luckily Brennan's hand slipped in the spilled ale and he sprawled flat on his back. The table top sliced through the air over him, connecting with an audible thump into Raven's torso as she tried to pounce on the prone man.

Raven screeched, the Beer Fairy cursed and belched, and Brennan dodged and threw things. The noise from the fight was too loud for Brennan's voice to carry, but Thane saw the other man's lips as they formed the words.

"I hate today."

Thane totally understood. Brennan tossed an empty tankard over the hairy man's shoulder and it smacked against Raven. She pounced on the Beer Fairy, giving Brennan time enough to stand and hurry over to Thane. "Let's go somewhere we can talk," he said, and opened a door on the other side of the room. Thane would have hesitated, but Raven's snarls and curses propelled him forward into darkness.

CHAPTER 5

The other side of the door was not the back parking lot that Thane expected. Instead he emerged into a warm forest, the trees so dense that sunlight couldn't get through. Something wet touched the back of his neck and he spun around and punched, panicked.

He hit Brennan in the stomach. The red haired man doubled over, wrapping both hands around his waist. "Shredding holes, kid, what was that for?"

"Something touched me," Thane said, his eyes wide and feeling unhinged. "Where is this? What happened?" He kept his hands in fists, ready to be attacked at any moment.

"Don't hit me again. It wouldn't be worth it, because then I'd have to get up and kill you, and the general would saddle me with Jaeger for the next three cycles. Then I'd have to kill myself and you'd still be stuck with me." Brennan gingerly sat up while he spoke. "What happened is we went through a door and we are near Iguassu."

"Where?"

"Brazil. All a bad dream, remember?" Brennan sat on a nearby log and gestured for Thane to sit too. Thane shook his head.

"You owe me answers first, old man."

"You sucker punched me, boy. I don't owe you anything."

"You dragged me to a bar, nearly killed me, almost got me poisoned, then I almost got poisoned again by fairy fart, then you got into a bar fight, pulled me through a door and told me I'm on another continent." Thane retorted, and Brennan looked at him with raised eyebrows.

"A little dramatic, are we?"

"Don't care. Are you going to answer me?"

"Maybe." Brennan looked at him. "It depends on the question. Some questions I can't answer because I swore to protect those answers. Some I just won't know."

Thane considered. "Fair enough. But you have to be honest."

"My being honest won't be the hard part. You believing any of it will."

Thane ignored that. "What the crap is a beer fairy?"

Brennan laughed. "It isn't 'a' beer fairy, it's the Beer Fairy. There's only one of him, thank the Weaver. He's technically not even a fairy- those are much smaller, about the length of your hand, and don't look very much like people at all. The Beer Fairy's actually a sprite. He is one of the oldest of old ones- you've probably heard of him under different names. Have you studied much mythology?" Thane shrugged. "The Beer Fairy was at the height of his popularity in ancient Greece. They called him Dionysus, and he was worshiped as a god."

Thane snorted, and Brennan chuckled. "Yeah, that's what I think, too. He wasn't very good at being a deity, but there's no one better at throwing a party. The dragons used to have him at all of their best ones. He invented alcohol, and then alcoholism, and then after a few centuries the children of men outgrew him and other, more mature gods took their interest. I think he likes it better this way."

Thane stared out at the trees and vines for several long moments. He didn't know why, but he was sure Brennan was wrong. Brennan was silent too. "So you're telling me," said Thane in a quiet voice, "that mythology is real. That magic is real." His voice turned mocking. "If I don't clap, do the fairies die?"

"The fairies don't care if you clap or not," Brennan's response was calm. "And it isn't just fairies. Mythology as a whole, no. But the roots of the stories- the creatures that exist beyond our sight and understanding, yes. The fairies, the satyrs, the daemons, yes. Dwarves, giants, werewolves, yes."

"Dragons and vampires and unicorns, too?" Thane's voice was scathing.

"No. No vampires. Don't be stupid."

"Vampires are the stupid ones here?"

"Vampires showed up in fiction as a way for people to explain what was going on around them. Lots of shadow creatures feed off the life essence of others and none of them are damaged by garlic, crosses, sunlight, or holy water. People made that up so they would feel less powerless. Who would be afraid of an undead being that couldn't come in your house unless you invited it and you could take out with a pencil and a squirt gun?" Brennan made a dismissive gesture. "No. The Sang Evarish are the closest thing in the real world to vampires, and they're close like a tyrannosaurus is close to a chicken. You saw Raven at the pub. She's a Sang Evarish. Some people who've seen them in the past called them 'elves', but never say that to her face. It's a mortal insult."

Thane shuddered at the memory. "Why was she so mad at me? I said she made good food!"

Brennan chortled. "Sang are shadow, kid. Never say that anything 'good' comes from them unless you want to be a good meal for one."

"Shadow?"

The other man paused. "That's... again, that's a really long explanation. We divide the magic or mythological creatures into three categories: shadow, shade, and fae. Shadow creatures are evil, shade are chaotic, and fae are generally good. Collectively we call them Shae."

"Shae?"

"Yes. Shadow, shade, and fae. Shae."

"Who is we?"

Brennan was quiet for a moment, drumming his fingers on the log. "The group I belong to is called Sanctum. They're the people I work for, who both protect the Shae and protect humans from the Shae."

Thane sat, sifting through hundreds of questions. "Are you, um, a shae?"

"Not a Shae, just Shae. And no. I'm human, one hundred percent pure."

"And Raven is shadow."

"Yes."

"The Beer Fairy?"

"Shade. Can you imagine him as anything but chaotic?"

Thane gave Brennan a blank look.

"Chaotic. It means without order. It means he'll do whatever he feels like whenever he feels like it without regard for consequences. Not without reason or logic, but with an underlying premise of selfish intent. Understand?" Thane nodded.

"Chaotic means no logic, Beer Fairy is chaotic, and chaotic is shade, check. What is a Moirai, and why are we hiding from it?"

Brennan sucked air in through his teeth. "Moirai isn't an it. She's my ex."

"And she can track you?" Remembering all that had happened, a question flashed to the forefront of his mind. A question he had asked, but Brennan had dodged. "Wait. What transmitter?"

"What?" Brennan stiffened. Thane turned to face him.

"You said the general sent you here because my transmitter stopped sending a signal and you were supposed to figure out why. What transmitter?"

"Thane, I was drugged, Raven was trying to get me in trouble--"

"Raven's drug made you talk, not made you lie," Thane cut him off. "You're asking me to believe a lot here. You lie, I walk."

"Where will you go?" Brennan shot back. He indicated the jungle all around them. "You going to find a monkey and ask it for food? You're stuck here until I decide to take us back. You don't know how to work the doors."

"You're right," Thane said. "Your boss would be pretty mad if I ended up somewhere I wasn't supposed to, right? Especially since you can't track me now?" Thane started to stand up, getting ready to run.

"Fine!" said Brennan, making a placating gesture and also rising. "When I shot you with a healing dart in the hospital I also inserted a tracker. It's tiny and painless, so you'd never notice. Sometimes lightning strikes are random, sometimes they're not. We just wanted to protect you in case it wasn't random, or prove that it was so we could get our tracker back and move on."

"I did notice," Thane said. Brennan looked skeptical. Thane pointed to the joint between his second and third knuckles. "It was right here, like a tiny marble. It was hard and it moved when I pushed on it." Brennan looked dumbfounded.

"Did it break when you pushed on it?"

"No, it seemed fine."

"Hmm," Brennan said, and paused. "Can I look at it?"

"How?"

"I can take it out and run a diagnostic on it. Is that all right?"

"What, you'll put it in without telling me but you'll ask to take it out? Great ethics."

Brennan grinned. "Just don't sucker punch me again." He pulled a zippered bag from his back pocket. In it was a small grey box with an LED screen on the front and a pair of tweezers with a button. "This shouldn't hurt, but it might," the man warned, and he held the tips of the tweezers next Thane's hand and pressed the button. Thane felt something move under his skin and the strangeness of it made his muscles twitch and spasm. A tiny silver sphere slid out and onto the tweezers. Brennan pinched them closed gently and placed the sphere into the little grey box. It hummed for a moment, and then the LED screen showed three numbers.

"What happened to it?" asked Thane, curious.

"Shorted out," said Brennan. He looked at Thane appraisingly. "Want to go home?"

The young man paused. Did he? "I have more questions."

Grinning, Brennan said, "I bet you do. Later, okay? It's been a long day, and I still need to get you home before I report to the general. Telling him the transmitter shorted out isn't going to be good enough. He'll want to know why, and he'll send me back here to find out. You can ask me more questions then."

"And you'll answer them," it was more a challenge than a request.

"Depends on what they are. But I'll do my best." Brennan held out his hand. After a moment, Thane shook it. A sharp prick stung the center of his hand. He flinched and jerked his hand away, glaring at Brennan. "It's the other part of the deal, kid. I'll answer your questions and you let us keep tracking you. You've proven you can find the trackers and maybe even short them out, but that only makes you more interesting." Brennan stepped to the closed door and then looked back at Thane, something weighing on his mind. "Kid," he began, and then trailed off. Thane didn't move, just waited.

Brennan tried again. "Thane, I will do my best to answer your questions, but the answers won't make much sense without context. If I said there was a whole world out there that you'd never seen, that wouldn't scratch the surface of everything you might need to know. And knowledge without context can be dangerous. It can even be a lie. So when I answer your questions, don't take those answers at face value. Find out where the answers fit before you try to use them. Do you understand?" Thane shrugged.

"So you'll answer my questions, but I shouldn't go do something stupid because I might know the what but not the why?" Thane surmised. The other man looked surprised.

"Who knew you were smart?" said Brennan. Thane rolled his eyes.

"Adults always think they're so funny. Just open the door already."

"Are you thinking about home?" Brennan asked. Thane nodded. "Well cut it out. I need you to think about the back room of the Leaf and Dagger. You left your backpack on the floor and I have to walk you back through the front in the next hour so the cashier can lock up."

He focused on his memories of the Leaf and Dagger, the feel of the wood grain, the smell of grease, and the size and shape of the room. "Ready?" Brennan asked. Thane nodded. "Good." Brennan turned the knob and pulled the door open.

"You great galloumphs spill your drinks and wreck the tables, and now you're going to track mud all across the floor I've just spent an hour cleaning?" a tremulous voice said. There was a large wet spot on the floor of the Leaf and Dagger where a very small, very old person was mopping. The top of her head was barely as high as Thane's knees, and her wrinkled hands were shaky, the fingers bent with age. Thane blanched, looking down at his feet.

"I'm sorry, ma'am. I'll help clean it up. Is there another broom?" he offered, contrite. Her wispy white hair held up in a high bun reminded him of his Grandma Whitaker, who'd died when he was Lanie's age. The tiny woman turned to look up at him with surprisingly lively blue eyes.

"A polite young one! Will the Weaver add wonders? Don't worry, mud won't do this floor any harm," a smile lifted the corners of her mouth as she looked at him. "Go on, now, get your things. This is a time of day when growing boys should be eating dinner! What's your name, child?"

"Thane Whitaker, ma'am."

"Well Thane Whitaker, I'm Temperance Blythe Minerva Cottle, and I am pleased to make your acquaintance." She smiled again, and Thane smiled back. "Should you ever be needing help of a little sort, you can call on me."

Raven looked thunderstruck, and Brennan's jaw dropped open. Thane glanced at them, wondering what the big deal was. "Thank you, Ms. Cottle. It was nice to meet you," Thane responded, but he thought shaking her hand might break it, and unsure of what else to do, he bowed.

The tiny old woman laughed delightedly and clapped her hands. "Oh, you're a treasure, young one. Off you go!" and she turned back to her mopping.

Thane stepped carefully around her and retrieved his backpack. He slid it onto one shoulder and started towards another door, then halted and looked back at Brennan. The red haired man was still standing with his mouth open looking down at Ms. Cottle. Thane cleared his throat, and Brennan shook his head as if to clear it.

"One more to the right," he said, and Thane turned and opened the door one over from where he stood.

"Finally," the hipster cashier said in a nasal voice. "I need to close up."

"Sorry," Thane muttered, and walked toward the front door. Brennan followed him, giving the lone bookstore employee a grin and a jaunty wave.

"Whatever," the twenty-something responded, and locked the door behind them. Brennan put his flat cap back on and nodded to Thane, then walked away. Thane watched Brennan as he sauntered up Main Street and saw a young woman step out from between two buildings to join him. She handed him something that looked like a clip board, and glanced back over her shoulder at Thane. He started, feeling silly at being caught staring, and turned to walk the other way.

The phone in his back pack buzzed and he jumped.

Remi had texted him back several times in response to his terse message, "See a doctor, it was Wood's Metal. Been poisoned. I'm fine, whole story later." The first message was skeptical, the second was that she was sick, the third was that her doctor had told her she would be out of school for the rest of the week. It was the last that really caught his attention.

"Don't go back to chemistry without me. We need to stick together-- neither of us is safe alone. Tell me what's going on!" He needed to talk all this out with someone. He'd already promised Remi that he'd tell her everything, and he trusted her to listen and help him reason through this and figure out what to do next.

And she'd probably feed him. That thought brightened his mood even more. Thane pulled out his phone and wrote a text. "Need to talk. Can I come over?"

Her response was immediate. She must have been waiting. "Sure, need a ride?" He was grateful she asked and responded in the affirmative. "Calder will be there in ten minutes. Aren't you even sicker than I am?"

Thane paused. "I'm fine. I'm not sick anymore. It's part of all that stuff we need to talk about."

The phone rang. "Why aren't you sick? What's going on?"

"You won't believe me--"

"I don't care. Don't leave anything out. Thane, Ms. Rasmussen poisoned us. On purpose. If you know something, I deserve to know it too."

She thought he knew something about their chemistry teacher. In the excitement of everything else, Thane had nearly forgotten the molten metal dripping on his leg. "This is bigger than chemistry class. And I don't know if Ms. Rasmussen has anything to do with it." Thane noticed the people on the street had gone quiet, listening to his conversation. He shot them a dirty look, and they hurriedly resumed walking. "Look, I'll tell you everything when I get there, I promise, but I can't talk here."

"Ten minutes," she responded, and they hung up.

CHAPTER 6

The Kendall Air Force Base lay west of town and was surrounded by a high chain link fence topped with barbed wire. The front gate was an imposing edifice of bricks and iron bars and armed guards who held their rifles and stared straight ahead. Senior Airman Calder rolled down the window and flashed a badge, saying, "I have Thane Whittaker, civilian, minor, as a guest of Remi Gage." Thane saw the gate guard raise his eyebrows and glance at him in the backseat.

"Doesn't look crazy enough for that," the guard commented.

Senior Airman Calder shrugged. "The kid runs really fast."

"Does he know?" the guard asked.

"Nope," replied Calder smugly.

"Enjoy the ride, kid," the soldier said and waved them through.

The gate opened and they drove through it. Thane had to try not to flinch when it closed. "Know what?" Thane asked Senior Airman Calder.

Calder glanced at him the rearview mirror. "What you're getting into."

Thane looked back at the guarded gate. Calder noticed, and commented, "Running is still an option. We're not at the top of the hill yet, so say the word and I'll take you home. I can tell Miss Gage that you weren't feeling as well as you thought."

"No, I'm fine." Remi lived at the top of the hill?

Thane could see the military part of the base behind him as Calder turned left into a group of houses. There were several blocks of simple clean yards and modest homes. After that were nicer houses, and then Calder turned and the road inclined upward. Thane felt his stomach drop and stay behind.

The road ran straight past another block of houses and then turned, curving to run alongside a wall. Calder turned into an opening in the wall, driving under an arch with a bronze eagle in the center. A sprawling two-story house rose before them. Thane felt himself growing smaller as the house loomed large in his vision. Calder pulled the car onto the circular driveway and stopped in front of the porch steps.

They both got out of the car, and Calder mounted the steps first and stopped at the top blocking Thane's way. At that moment, a huge black truck pulled under the archway. Senior Airman Calder's posture stiffened and he saluted, even as his mouth twitched in a smile. The truck was polished and waxed to shining, and the early afternoon sun shone on the chrome F250 above the driver's wheel well. The windows were all tinted darkly, and one of the three garage doors ground open. The truck disappeared inside, and the garage closed behind it like the mouth of a monster swallowing its prey.

"You're about to meet Remi's father," said Calder, lowering his salute and answering Thane's unasked question, "General Gage. He recently requested transfer here because he wanted somewhere safe to raise his daughter, of whom he is very protective." The Senior Airman gave Thane a wicked smile. "As per protocol, when Miss Gage requested an in house visitor General Gage was contacted. He authorized the visit provided that I detain you outside until his arrival. He wants to meet you." Calder's eyes narrowed. "He wants to meet you before Remi knows you're here. I may be telling her that you were too sick after all."

Thane's stomach must have found its own way up the hill because it began to twist and knot in his gut. Here was another adult to push him around and make himself feel tougher by making Thane feel small. And this one could keep Thane from talking to Remi. Thane felt his jaw clench at the thought. He needed Remi, needed to talk to someone who wouldn't think he was making it up. If that meant submitting to her father's verbal abuse, well, he'd had lots of practice with his own parents and he doubted someone else would be as good at knowing exactly how to hurt him most. Magic was real. He'd survived being poisoned. General Gage could do his worst and short of being shot, Thane would not budge. And Thane half expected that if he did get shot, Brennan would show up with more healing darts before Thane could finish bleeding out. The thought was more comforting than he wanted to admit.

The front door clicked as someone turned the knob. Senior Airman Calder snapped back into attention, his salute sharp. Thane squared his shoulders and lifted his chin, watching as the heavy oak front door opened. Filling the doorway was a giant, with enormous muscular arms, a neck thicker than his head, and a vicious snarl on his face as he glared down at Thane.

Or that's what Thane had expected. The real General Gage was man of medium height and thinning brown hair that was gray at the temples. He stood with the confidence of bearing that only comes with decades of military service. Something about the way he held his shoulders, not hunching but with a suggestion of a hunch, gave Thane the feeling that General Gage was carrying a heavy weight and had been for a long time.

Gage was looking Thane over at the same time. Thane wondered what he thought. "At ease, Calder," the general said. Calder crisply finished his salute, placed his hands behind his back, and stood with his feet apart. "You must be Thane Whitaker," Gage said. It wasn't a question, but Thane nodded anyway. "Calder, you're dismissed. I will call you when Mr. Whitaker is ready to leave." Gage eyed Thane again. "Stay close." With a final salute, Calder spun on his heel, marched to the car, and drove away.

Once Calder had driven under the arch and out of sight, Gage's face relaxed and he smiled. "Come in, Thane," he said, and stood back holding the door open. Thane climbed the steps and entered the house.

The front room was large and had windows along two walls, filling the room with sunlight. The furniture was sparse and in light colors, as was the carpet and decor. Thane liked it. The room felt bright and welcoming. Remi's father walked past him and sat down on one of the square stuffed chairs that faced the windows, and indicated that Thane should have a seat also. Thane picked a chair that faced at a right angle to where Gage was. From here Thane could look into the kitchen and partly down one hallway, where a stack of dark cardboard boxes were a stark contrast to the white walls.

"We still have a lot to unpack from the move," Remi's father commented. "We've been on base for maybe two weeks now, but I'm gone so much and Remi shouldn't have to do it alone. Besides, she's been so busy with school and making new friends..." Gage trailed off for a moment as his gaze turned to Thane. "Which brings us to you." Thane met Gage's ice blue eyes for a moment, then looked down at his own hands. "Tell me about you, Thane."

"I'm Thane, I'm in tenth grade..." Thane said. He couldn't think of anything else.

"How old are you?"

"Fifteen, sir." Thane thought it couldn't hurt to be extra polite.

"You're the same age as Remi, then. And in her grade. Why did you decide to be friends with my daughter?"

"She didn't give me a choice," Thane said, surprise making him blunt. He cringed. "Not that didn't want to be her friend, I mean..."

General Gage laughed. "Remi's tenacious, and when she decides something, heaven and earth can't make her change her mind. So she chose you as a friend. All right, fair enough. And I understand you're in chemistry together, you were lab partners, and you're the one who alerted her to her present condition." Gage waited for Thane's confirming nod. "So what I really want to know is why your teacher isn't in custody for malicious endangerment of minors and why you're not sick and my daughter is."

As he spoke, his entire demeanor changed and Thane saw the snarling giant simmering underneath the surface. The man who would order armies and soldiers would leap to obey. "Well?" Gage demanded. Thane quailed, cowering in on himself. Reflexively he raised one arm halfway to his face waiting for the blow that usually followed when he was asked that question with that tone. Nothing happened. Thane risked a glance up toward Gage and saw Remi's father studying him, his posture, his expression.

"Ah," Gage said. Thane didn't respond. He held onto his tension and kept looking down and away, although he did lower his arm. Gage spoke mildly now. "You aren't in trouble here, Thane. Remi was very clear this chemistry teacher of yours was the only one to blame for her illness and that you were a victim as well. I do need to know what happened and what is being done at the school about this. When I phoned them, I was told that Ms. Rasmussen and Mr. Hoffman were in conference and that the matter was being handled. Please, son, tell me what happened in chemistry."

Briefly, Thane outlined the events in chemistry class, starting with the experiment. He didn't think telling Remi's father about punching Jeran was a good idea. Gage's expression grew fiercer with every word, but he did not raise his voice again.

Only when it was clear Thane was finished did Remi's father speak. "So why, then, is Remi still sick when the metal actually touched you?" Gage asked mildly, "and how is it you figured out that it was Wood's Metal instead of Field's?"

Thane was thinking furiously, trying to find a plausible answer that wouldn't also be a lie. "Because the metal touched me, it affected me more rapidly," he began. Gage listened. "I got really sick really fast, and didn't make home before I was too weak to keep going. I went into a book store on Main Street and a man asked me if I was all right. He's the one who figured out what the metal really was and told me, and he treated the burn on my leg. He made me throw up, and I collapsed on the floor. I thought I was going to die," Thane shuddered and gagged a little at the memory of writhing on the floor, being a week's worth of sick in just a few minutes. "Then he fed me something and I felt better. I guess because I got so sick so fast and so much that I got it all out more quickly. It was awful," Thane added honestly.

Thane could tell Gage knew that wasn't the whole story, but Remi's father seemed satisfied. "Well, I suppose I can be grateful that my girl is only feeling like she has the flu. You should find that man and thank him, for all of us. This could've been a lot worse for you two if he hadn't figured out what was going on. Did you get his name?"

"Um, it was something like Brandon?" Thane replied. That was true, if not the best answer he could have given.

Gage smiled. "I suppose you were a little preoccupied at the time."

"Yes, sir. Not dying takes effort." Thane smiled back, a little.

Remi's father chuckled, the laugh lines on his face showing. "It does, some days more than others." Gage's face grew serious again. "So what will happen to Ms. Rasmussen?"

"Mr. Hoffman said there would be a reprimand put in her file," Thane said, "but it would be hard to prove she did anything on purpose and if there was a board of inquiry they would side with her because of the union and she's good looking." Thane tensed, expecting General Gage to lash out. Instead, the General smiled a grim smile.

"Is that the way it is? Well, there are other recourses." He stared out the window, lost in thought. Thane waited quietly, relieved to have the General's attention away from him. "I have a few things that I can do on my end, but I can't be with my daughter during the day and this chemistry teacher seems unbalanced to me. I know you won't understand, Thane, because you're too young, but in the end I'm going to be accountable for Remi because she's my daughter. I am responsible for her, physically, mentally, and emotionally, and someday there will be a reckoning." The monster was there, lurking in his eyes as Remi's father looked at Thane. Thane tried not to let his shiver be too visible.

"But I'm not always around." Gage continued, leaning back in his chair. "You two will need to watch out for each other. Soldiers go into battle knowing they are stronger together. You and Remi will have to be the same way. And if you are going to watch out for each other, then you will be responsible for her physical, mental, and emotional well being, and you will be accountable to me." Gage's eyes flashed and Thane had no doubt that Gage would also hold a reckoning. "Can I trust you with her until I can find a more permanent solution to the problem of Ms. Rasmussen?"

Thane hesitated, weighing his need for Remi's friendship against the danger he might be putting her in and his ability to protect her. Remi wanted to know everything and Thane needed someone to keep him grounded in all this madness. He might be putting her in danger, but Thane had survived his childhood. He would keep her safe. Lifting his chin Thane looked the General in the eye, then nodded. Gage held out his right hand and Thane shook it.

"Daa-aad," Remi's voice floated down from upstairs. "Are you finished interrogating him yet? He's here to talk to me, not you old man."

"Be patient, princess, I'll send him right up," Gage teased back. He stood and Thane quickly rose too. "Let me get her a drink and you can take it up. Her room is the open door at the end of the hall. The door is open for a reason," Gage said while he filled a glass with ginger ale and ice. Thane nodded, understanding.

Gage handed him the glass. "Go on up. But don't tire her too much; she didn't get all of her being sick out at once. We need to get her better." Gage gave Thane a comradely grin. Thane smiled back and took the glass, then turned and climbed the stairs.

The room at the end of the hall was a cacophony of purples, greens, and browns. If the room hadn't been so large the colors would've been dizzying. Remi was propped up in bed on a pile of purple and green pillows, somewhere between sitting and lying down. Thane brought her the ginger ale and she took it with a grateful smile.

"Sorry about my dad," she croaked. "He's over protective, especially since I'm all he has."

"You sound sicker than you look," said Thane, then realized that could be taken badly. "I mean you don't look sick."

Remi smiled at him. "I feel like I ate whatever's been growing in my locker. Why are you okay? I'm glad you're okay, but can I be okay too please?"

"That's a long story." Thane took a deep breath and lowered his voice. "Remember Brennan Tayler, that guy I met at the hospital?"

Remi's eyes widened. "The guy who healed your knuckles. You saw him again? And he healed you?" She grimaced dramatically. "Why are you the one with all the luck?"

"Not as lucky as you think," Thane began, again remembering the agony on the floor of the back room. "But there's more than we knew. I ran into Brennan while I was walking home."

Thane told her everything, as quietly and quickly as possible. He didn't leave anything out, not the bar behind the book store, not the healing darts, not the Beer Fairy. She had lots of questions.

"If the healing darts are so great, why don't they make them available to everyone? Why be so secretive?"

"She tried to poison you? And you still ate the food?"

"You've got to be joking. A Beer Fairy? Who farts to make beer? That's the stupidest and grossest thing I've ever heard."

"Rip ate his fingers?"

"Brennan has an ex?"

Thane begged her to keep her voice down. "I don't want your father kicking me out yet. There's more."

Thane told her about going through the door into the jungle. He went into detail about punching Brennan, and she laughed out loud in approval. "He deserved it," she announced, and that made Thane feel warm. He told her the threat he made and the questions he asked, and all of Brennan's answers as well as he could remember them.

"So they're all real? All the fairytales and myths?" she asked.

"I guess. Well, not vampires. Brennan said vampire stories were too stupid to be real."

"The man who told you about the Beer Fairy said that vampires are stupid?" Remi said with a raised eyebrow. Thane agreed.

When he told her about Brennan re-tagging him, Remi looked incredulous. "Are you serious? After all that, he still tricked you into being tracked again?"

"He said it was part of the deal for getting answers," Thane explained. "But I don't like it either. I almost didn't tell you anything because I thought they might be listening, and I didn't want to get you involved in all this."

"No!" Remi grabbed his left hand and held it in both of hers. "Thane, you have to tell me everything. Everything! Where you're going, what happens, everything you learn about magic, all of it! I hate not knowing what's going on." She was so vehement that Thane was taken aback.

"But what if it puts you in danger too?"

"If I'm in danger, wouldn't it be better that I know from who and why?" she argued. "It isn't like not knowing gives me some shield of ignorance. Every time my dad leaves..." she scrubbed her eyes with her shoulder, not releasing Thane's hand. She was crying, and that terrified him. "I never know. Not where he's going or why or when he'll come back. I hate not knowing. It makes me sick," and her red eyes overflowed with tears.

"I'll tell you everything," Thane said, panicked.

"Promise me!"

"I promise!" Thane would've promised anything. She was crying.

She rubbed her face on her shoulder again and let go of his hand to reach for the tissues on her nightstand. Thane looked away, his heart pounding like he'd been running. He heard Remi wipe her face, blow her nose, and take another drink, the ice rattling and sliding in the near empty cup. They sat in an absence of words, both breathing heavily.

"Ugh," Remi said, "being sick always makes me so emotional." Thane risked a glance at her, and was immeasurably relieved not to see she tears. "Did Brennan tell you anything else?"

"Not that I can think of, but I still don't know what he's after or why they're tracking me." Thane started to rub his palm in distraction.

"We need to find out more about Sanctum," Remi stated. "They seem to be the core of all this. What did Brennan say about them?"

"They protect the Shae and protect us from the Shae. Raven made it sound like Sanctum was some sort of secret police; she said they had weapons and secrets and used them to keep the Shae in line."

"And she was the bar tender? From what you've said, it sounds like someone needs to keep her from killing everyone. Shadow, shade, and fae. Evil, neutral, and good. Which is Sanctum?"

"I wish I knew." Thane clenched and unclenched his right hand carefully. "And I wish I knew what they wanted with me. I'm nobody."

"You're not nobody! You survived the lightning bolt without a scratch. You punched Jeran, you escaped from the bar, and most impressive of all, you survived meeting my father." She grinned at him, and Thane felt that warmth flood inside him again. He smiled back. "Speaking of my father, I think I hear him coming upstairs."

Thane hurried and stood up from her bed moments before General Gage came through the open door. Remi's father was carrying a tray with steaming soup that smelled like chicken and spices. There was another glass of ginger ale, cold enough that water was condensing on the outside, and the two rolls on a napkin filled Thane's nose with the smell of warm bread. His stomach growled loudly enough that both Remi and her father laughed. Thane flushed.

"There's more downstairs in the kitchen," Gage said, setting down the tray on Remi's nightstand.

She groaned and looked away from the food. "Give him that, I'm not ready to eat anything yet." She fell back dramatically onto her pillows. "I don't think I want to eat anything ever again."

"But you look so much better," Gage began, and then stopped and looked more closely at her. "When did you put makeup on? You weren't wearing any when I left--"

"Dad," Remi cut him off and emphasized, "I always look like this."

"Sure, whatever you say," Gage said with a small smile. "Come on, Thane, I'll get you a plate downstairs. I'll be back up to check on you, princess, but for now I think visiting hours are over." Gage smiled at them both but put his arm around Thane's shoulder and steered him towards the door.

"I hate when you call me princess. Don't talk about me," Remi croaked.

"Just rest, little princess."

"I'm serious, old man! No talking about me, promise, or I will follow you downstairs and cough on everything you try to eat!" Her voice was weak and her throat was raw, but her jaw was set and her eyes were steady.

"No talking about you, I promise." The General said. Remi looked at Thane, waiting.

Gage nudged Thane. "Oh, um, me too. I promise."

"Good. My dad never breaks a promise." She glared at Thane to make sure he was paying attention. "Never."

"We're going now, you're resting and eating your soup," Gage said, steering Thane out of the room. "And then you can sleep." Remi's father shut the door behind them.

Down in the kitchen, Gage served up more soup and rolls while Thane sat at the counter. "Do you have chemistry tomorrow?" Remi's father asked.

Thane nodded.

"Well, if Ms. Rasmussen did do this on purpose, she won't be expecting you in class. She'll assume that you're sick. If she is doing this deliberately, going back alone could be dangerous," Gage paused, setting down a large bowl of steaming soup and a plate of warm rolls with jam in front of Thane. The steam tickled Thane's nostrils with the smell of chicken and oregano. "On the other hand, if she switched the metals on purpose, you showing up for class would be a huge surprise." Thane stopped mid-bite, half his roll in his mouth as he looked at Remi's father. The older man had his back to Thane, stirring the pot of soup and turning off the stove. "It is possible that it was all some elaborate accident, I suppose, but if you did show up and she was surprised, then we would know." Gage put a large glass of milk on the counter by Thane's bowl and met the young man's eyes. "It would be better to know, don't you agree?"

Mouth full, Thane nodded. It made sense. And the idea of acting like nothing happened and showing Ms. Rasmussen she hadn't fazed him appealed to Thane. He nodded again and swallowed, and picked up his drink.

"I'm feeling pretty good, and I do have homework to turn in. I should probably go to school tomorrow." He tilted the bowl up to his lips and slurped.

"If you say so," Gage said. "And you would be welcome to come visit Remi again tomorrow after school and give her the homework she missed. You can tell us both how school went."

"Okay," Thane swallowed again, and reached for more without finding any. Startled, he realized he'd already eaten the whole bowl of soup and both rolls. Gage tossed him another roll, and Thane caught it and took a bite.

"We'll see you tomorrow, then." Gage smiled and pulled out his cell phone. He dialed, and held it to his ear. "Senior Airman Calder, Mr. Whitaker is ready to be taken home. And you are now authorized to drive him home from school.

It seems he gets into trouble if he has to walk." Gage winked at Thane, who was finishing the last bite of the roll. "However, the restriction regarding my daughter remains. He is allowed inside only if I am present." Gage listened for a moment longer, then ended the call.

"Thanks for the rides," said Thane. Having an option other than the bus or walking was nice.

"You're my daughter's friend," General Gage shrugged it off.

A horn sounded outside. "There's Calder." Gage walked Thane to the door and opened it for him. "You have a cell phone, right?" Thane nodded. "If you need anything tomorrow, call Remi. I'll send someone. Otherwise Calder will pick you up from school and bring you here." The last sentence was spoken loudly enough for Calder to hear where he stood by the car. The Airman's eyes went wide, but he still saluted sharply.

"Yeah, I'll see you tomorrow," Thane said, and got in the car. Calder got in just after and drove away. Thane slouched in the back seat, feeling tired.

"You're going back?" Calder was incredulous.

"Yeah, so?"

"Nothing." After a pause, Calder spoke again. "Look, General Gage is one of the most brilliant military minds of our time. And the thing he cares most about is his daughter."

"So?" Thane challenged.

"So if he wants you hanging around, he has a reason." Thane thought about Gage sending him to chemistry tomorrow to see if Ms. Rasmussen showed any guilt and silently agreed with Calder. "Make sure you know what the reason is before you get too involved."

"Calder, I'm not worried about General Gage," Thane retorted. He meant it, too. Compared to Sanctum and their tracker and their still unknown motives and allegiances, Remi's dad didn't seem to be much of a threat. If Thane was honest with himself, he would even admit he liked General Gage. Gage seemed nice, and he honestly cared about Remi. Thane could think of so many things that were worse than caring about your child.

"Whatever, kid. Maybe you are crazy enough." Calder said, and they drove the rest of the way in silence.

CHAPTER 7

Thane wondered briefly how his dad was doing. He was walking to school in the late morning sunlight, skipping his first two classes. The lightning strike had been five days ago on Monday, and today was Friday. Thane tried to remember if he had ever gone this long without a blow up from his dad before. The only time he could remember was when Grandpa Whitaker had taken Thane camping for a week when he was nine.

"You're special, son," Grandpa Whitaker had said, resting his hand on Thane's head while they roasted marshmallows in the dying coals of their fire. Young Thane had huddled close to Grandpa Whitaker for warmth and tried to touch the orange glow with his skewer. The black sky above had tiny points of light far away, and crickets sang in the darkness. "You hide it well, but someday everybody's going to know just how incredibly special you are."

Thane arrived at school near the end of lunch so no one would know he was there and warn her. Not that he expected anyone to notice him or thought that Ms. Rasmussen had spies watching for him-- the thought was ludicrous. But then again, he'd met the Beer Fairy so apparently nothing was too ridiculous to be real.

About five minutes before the first bell rang Thane slipped into Ms. Rasmussen's empty classroom and, after a moment of deliberation, sat on his newly acquired front row stool and tried to look bored while the other students filtered in. Cressida Rasmussen entered the classroom like an empress, the three most aggressive class lackeys giggling and fawning over her. Her green and gold eyes swept the classroom with possessive confidence. Thane couldn't keep up his facade of boredom. He couldn't help it. He had to know, and so couldn't do anything but stare at her until her eyes connected with his.

Her eyes widened and her pupils constricted. Thane had been prepared for surprise, but that wasn't the expression that flooded her perfectly symmetrical face. Her nostrils flared and the self-satisfied smile lifting the corners of her mouth instantly twisted into a snarl, while the rest of her froze in mid-step, one heeled foot not quite resting on the floor.

"No." Her voice was quiet, but so intense that Thane felt it cut through his rib cage and lodge in his spine. The giggling minions froze, and her word smothered every other sound in the room to silence. She did not blink and her eyes did not waver from Thane, or his from hers. His hands were slick with sweat, his stomach was clenched so tightly it seemed it was trying to climb inside itself, but his gaze was steady. Instinctively he knew that to flinch or look away was suicide, even though every memory inside his mind screamed at him to flee, to be invisible again.

"Thane!" she said. The heat in her voice could've been mistaken for warmth or affection, but Thane heard the threat and something else. It sounded like fear. "It's so good to see you." He watched as her eyes traveled over him, taking in his uninjured left wrist, and her gaze paused where the burn on his leg had been, hidden beneath his jeans. Without moving her eyes or changing expression, his chemistry teacher pushed her three attendants towards their tables. "Sit down, and take the rest of these whining parasitic amoebas with you," she hissed. The girls gasped, insulted. One started to whine.

"But Cressa, you said--"

"Shut up." Cressida's eyes broke from Thane and latched onto the girl, who cringed away. Thane fell forward slightly as if something he'd been leaning on had moved.

"Is something wrong?" Mr. Hoffman's cheerful voice smothered the threat like cool rain on fire as he strode through the open doorway. Ms. Rasmussen breathed quickly and changed her entire demeanor in an instant, meeting the assistant principal with a playful smile.

"No, just starting class," Cressida said. She reminded Thane of his mom when his mom wanted something from a man. A lifetime of watching her get her way had taught him a lot about manipulation. Next to his chemistry teacher, though, Gwen Whitaker looked like an amateur. Even though the postures were the same-- deep breath in, shoulders pushed back, one hip raised and slightly forward, head tilted-- but Thane always felt like his mom was using her charisma as a tool. Ms. Rasmussen was a weapon.

Mr. Hoffman took a long pause, seeming to consider her words carefully. Thane was watching him and so was prepared when Mr. Hoffman's eyes flicked to meet his. Thane shook his head slightly. No. Mr. Hoffman jerked his chin in acknowledgement and his eyes swept the classroom. "Remember there is a zero tolerance policy here for bullying." Mr. Hoffman again locked eyes with Ms. Rasmussen. "From anyone."

She smiled charmingly and her eyes narrowed. Mr. Hoffman gave Thane's chemistry teacher one more hard look, then left and shut the door behind him. From his seat Thane could see through the window cut into the door that Mr. Hoffman had only taken a few steps and was standing in the hallway nearby, ostensibly as a monitor. Ms Rasmussen must've noticed also, because she ground her teeth for a moment before facing the class with a huge smile.

"Let's begin today's lesson, shall we? Everyone take out your books and turn to chapter nineteen, section four." She waited patiently while everyone pulled out their books and started flipping pages.

Thane was thinking rapidly. Deep down he'd believed the metal poisoning was accidental. After all, what could Ms. Rasmussen possibly get from poisoning him? After talking to Remi and Brennan, he had thought maybe she'd played a mean prank and would be surprised when he showed up. Maybe even embarrassed. But Cressida Rasmussen hadn't reacted in any way that would've made sense. The expression that burned in her eyes had been a familiar one to Thane, one he'd seen in the eyes of his father hundreds of times right before he felt the fist. Calling it anger seemed weak. Naming it fear was inadequate. It was both, and greater than either one.

"How are you feeling?" her voice purred near his ear. Thane started. Ms. Rasmussen was bending down next to him, moving so quietly he hadn't noticed. She rested a hand on his thigh and squeezed the spot where the molten metal had landed. Instead of flinching, with deliberate motion he took her wrist and lifted her hand up, pointedly looked at the fingers that should have burned in the fire along with his wrist, and then dropped her hand without glancing at her face.

"You may heal quickly," she hissed. "But the fire and metal did damage you. That tells me enough." She straightened and returned to the front of the class. Thane stared blankly at her back. What was she talking about? Told her enough for what? He turned a few more pages in chapter nineteen until the big bold letters in the middle of the page announced "Section 4."

"Electrical Conductivity," his chemistry teacher said the words as though they were a prayer, or a call to battle. "Electrical conductivity is the ability of different types of matter to conduct an electric current. Electrical conductivity is due to the presence of electrons or ions able to move through the material of interest. And you all look bored to death. How about an example?" and she smiled the way a predator reveals its teeth before the kill. Thane's muscles clenched and adrenaline rushed through him, his fight or flight response activating. "Johanna. Please come here."

Johanna paled and stood up. She went to the front of the class where Ms. Rasmussen was pulling several objects out of a cabinet and laying them on her desk. A long piece of wood, a bar of metal, a large jar, and finally she held up a thin metal stick with two prongs, a black handle and a button. It took Thane a moment to identify it.

"This is a cattle prod," Ms. Rasmussen announced, holding it up by the handle. "Pushing this button generates a high-voltage, low-current electrical shock. If something conducts electricity, the current passes through it to whatever else it may be touching. If an object is non-conductive, the current does not pass through. For example, Johanna, please select one of these items." Johanna released a breath and picked up the wood. Ms. Rasmussen's smile deepened. "Good girl. Wood is non-conductive," and she jabbed the cattle prod into the other end and pushed the button. There was a buzzing noise and the wood blackened in two small spots, but Johanna was unaffected. Cressida nodded, and Johanna put the wood down and fled back to her stool.

"Metal is highly conductive," Ms. Rasmussen continued, "and so no one should be holding that. Instead," she put a light bulb against the other end of the metal bar and then activated the cattle prod. The light bulb flickered, and a slight "oooh" sound came from the class. "It's almost like magic," she laughed, enjoying their attention. "Even water is conductive. Jeran," she lifted the large empty jar off her desk with one hand, letting the prod dangle in the other, "will you fill this with water?"

She took a few steps forward until she was standing slightly past Thane. Thane twisted his head to watch Jeran slowly rise and walk forward to take the jar from her hand. It must've been heavier than it appeared, because he bobbled it and had to grab it with two hands to keep from dropping it, face flushing red as classmates giggled nervously. Music began singing in Thane's mind, a wild song that was somehow familiar. In addition, Thane could hear a small hissing sound and a burning smell tickled his nose. He glanced down towards the source.

Ms. Rasmussen was holding the cattle prod against his calf and pressing the button with her thumb. Two holes were burned into his jeans as the prongs brushed his skin, sending a high-voltage low-current of pure electricity into his body. And it didn't hurt. He did feel a cool rushing, like water in a stream, sliding through the insides of his legs and arms, and even across his chest. The sound of the song filled his ears as this strange sensation filled his body, flowing into every part of him and filling it. There was a popping in his right hand and he felt a flash of heat. His brain was screaming at him that this was wrong, very wrong, and he needed to stop it, jump up, move away, something, anything! But he was mesmerized by the sight of those two tiny prongs flashing with blue light, resting on his unharmed flesh through holes burnt in his jeans.

She wasn't looking at him and didn't know that he'd noticed the cattle prod. The sound of flowing water cut off as Jeran finished and the sensation of being filled stopped as Ms. Rasmussen moved back to the front of the room. Jeran brought the heavy jar forward and placed it on her desk. She pulled Jeran into an embrace that was completely inappropriate for a teacher and a student, her eyes looking over his shoulder and straight at Thane.

"You delightful boy," she purred in Jeran's ear, her green gold eyes locked onto Thane's brownish ones. "Things can finally get interesting around here."

The rest of Ms. Rasmussen's lecture was a blur. Thane could not concentrate. Energy crawled through him like ants under his skin, tickling and teasing, and the song that sang wild in his mind made him want to do... something. He gripped the edge of his table with both hands trying to keep still. Every few minutes, Ms. Rasmussen would glance at him and smile triumphantly. Thane found himself smiling back. The prickling vibrations of the power were distracting and uncomfortable and unending, but they felt good in a painful way.

"Thane, could you stay after class?" Ms. Rasmussen asked as the bell rang. Papers shuffled and zippers closed, and the class left the room chattering excitedly, all infected by their teacher's mysteriously elated mood. Thane's hands were shaking as he stood sideways in front of her desk, backpack slung over one shoulder. As the last student passed through the doorway, she walked to the door and closed it, and to his surprise, locked it and leaned against it, her back blocking the window so no one could see in. Thane felt a flash of trepidation, which instantly transformed into wonder as an arc of blue light jumped from his thumb to his index finger.

He lifted his hand up to his eyes, trying to do it again. Nothing happened. Ms. Rasmussen laughed, startling him, and flashes of white and blue danced along his fingertips. "You darling boy," she purred, staying motionless against the door while devouring him with her eyes. "I would never have guessed it was you. That clever witch gave you a disguise no one would have suspected. She made you ordinary." She spat the last word like a curse. "I should have realized when I met your mother. What did they promise you for your silence? For your cooperation? Even the strongest of Shae magic couldn't keep you locked in such an unattractive frame without your consent. Poor child," and her eyes filled with pity, "what lies have they been telling you?"

"Shae magic?" hearing her say those words jarred him enough to forget about the bright sparks, although being called unattractive hurt. "What do you know about Shae?"

She laughed again, rich and warm. "Little one, I am Shae." Ms. Rasmussen smiled, "And so are you."

"No I'm not--" Thane began angrily, but his fingers lighting up again cut off his words. Was he Shae? Is that why Brennan kept showing up, why Sanctum was tracking him? What else could explain... "You're doing this. Not me. Why? What could you possibly hope to get through me?"

"You have everything backwards, Thane," she said his name like a caress, gentle and slow. "I want to help you. I want to give you answers, to teach you how to use the wonderful gift you've been given, to show you how to rise above these bleating sheep. I want to take you away from all that is boring and mundane and show you what magic, what power, really is and how to take it. I want you to come back where you belong."

"Where do I belong?" he whispered, desperate for the answer and afraid to hear it.

"With me." She smiled again, warmly, but still didn't make any move towards him. Instead she was almost perfectly still, her hands behind her back and pressed against the door, blocking him from leaving while also staying far away. He took a step towards her and she flinched.

"You're lying." He was sure of it. "Why?"

Ms. Rasmussen snorted. "I'm not the one who's been lying to you. Seriously, what did they have to say to keep you like that? I didn't even notice you were in my class until last week. It must drive you crazy staying so utterly bland that no one can even remember your face."

"This is just what I look like!" Thane exploded. "No one told me I had to be like this, I'm not in disguise, this is who I am." He saw her cringe away from him, her eyes wide with fear, and realized that the arcs of electricity were no longer confined to his fingers, but were sparking and wrapping up and down both his arms. The music in his head was so loud it was hard to concentrate. Thane took another step towards her and heard someone pounding on the door.

"Ms. Rasmussen, unlock this door!" Mr. Hoffman's voice thundered from the hallway, fist banging against the door and jiggling the handle. Ms. Rasmussen continued to bar Thane's exit, but shrank away from him as he drew closer.

"Let me out." Thane's voice was quiet, but cracked up an octave on the last word. His teacher shook her head.

"I need to explain, you can't leave," she pleaded.

Thane didn't bother trying to convince her. He reached out with his left hand, crackling with visible energy. She held her position until his fingers were close enough that the electricity caused the hair on her arms to rise, and then bolted. Thane's brownish eyes met Mr. Hoffman's blue ones through the window glass.

"Thane, are you all right?" Mr. Hoffman bellowed. "Unlock the door."

Thane nodded, and reached down to the metal handle to turn the lock. His fingers neared the thin bar and he heard Ms. Rasmussen giggling behind him. "You don't listen in class, either."

He turned to look at her as his fingers touched the knob. "What--" there was a flash of blue white light and the door shuddered, shattering the window as the music exploded in a huge crescendoed note. Thane spun back in time to see Mr. Hoffman's body hit the floor with a thump.

People screamed as the class who'd gathered outside scattered down the hallways or collapsed to the floor in fear. One girl sat with her arms wrapped around her knees, rocking back and forth and sobbing, "he's dead, he's dead," while another girl had whipped out her phone and was talking to someone on the other end.

"Yes, at the high school, Mr. Hoffman just fell, he isn't waking up, send an ambulance--"

Thane was staring, dumbfounded, while Cressida whispered behind him. "You killed him," she said. "You'll have to come with me now, unless you want to spend the rest of your life in jail for murder." She placed a hand possessively on Thane's shoulder.

"Shut up." Thane whispered, then again, more fiercely, "shut up!"

"Thane!" a male voice shouted from down the hallway. Ms. Rasmussen removed her hand and backed away. "Thane!" Brennan came pounding into view, running full tilt towards the door. He grabbed the handle and jerked the door open, then snatched Thane and hauled him into the hallway by the front of his shirt. Brennan jerked Thane down to his knees next to Mr. Hoffman.

"How long as he been unconscious?" Brennan demanded, feeling for a pulse. Thane didn't answer. "How long?" Brennan demanded, shaking Thane a little.

"Less than two minutes," the girl who had called for the ambulance answered him. Brennan switched his attention to her.

"What happened?"

"We were trying to go to chemistry but the door was locked and Ms. Rasmussen was blocking it. Mr. Hoffman told her to, but she still wouldn't open the door. She finally moved out of the way and we saw him," she gestured to Thane, "standing in the window. He tried to open the door but she must have booby-trapped it or something because there was a flash and the glass broke and Mr. Hoffman fell. I called 911, but they won't be here for another few minutes."

"He doesn't have a few minutes," Brennan stated flatly. "I'm not finding a pulse. Go to the nurse's office and find me an AED defibrillator." She nodded, and took off running. "The rest of you go somewhere else and get out of the way." Brennan barked. The other students left, one of the larger boys picking up the rocking girl and carrying her. Brennan had not released his grip on Thane's shirt and now turned back to him.

"You need to restart his heart, now." Brennan said urgently. Thane tried to process that, but couldn't. Brennan shook him again. "Now is not the time to fall apart. This guy's going to die unless you restart his heart. You have to shock him again, and you have to do it now."

"I," Thane whispered, looking down at his hands. There was no more light, no glowing. "I can't. I didn't-- she did it, not me, I'm not special..." Thane's fingers trembled.

"Crisis later, kid, I need you now!" Brennan tore open the front of Mr. Hoffman's button down shirt and grabbed one of Thane's hands, pressing it onto the prone man's bare chest. Nothing happened. "Argh!" Brennan yelled in frustration. "We have less than a minute before restarting his heart is pointless."

"Can't you use a dart?"

"It won't do anything because this guy isn't ever getting better on his own. He needs voltage direct to his heart, and you are the only one who can do it. So do it!" Brennan was yelling in Thane's face.

Thane quailed. "I can't," he said, trying to pull his hand out of Brennan's grip.

Footsteps came thudding down the hallway, and the girl and Nurse Hamilton came into view. Brennan tore the red box the girl was carrying out of her grasp. He pulled out the paddles and engaged the power with expert swiftness and placed the paddles directly on Mr. Hoffman's chest. "Clear!" he shouted, and the prone man's chest rose and fell with the jolt. Nurse Hamilton, already on her knees, checked for a pulse.

"Nothing."

"Clear!" Brennan yelled again, and again the chest rose and fell. The girl was crying silently, and Thane felt wetness on his cheeks too, although he wasn't sure if that was from sweat or tears or both. Nurse Hamilton held her fingers pressed deeply into the flesh of Mr. Hoffman's neck.

"There's a pulse," she whispered. "Oh thank God, there's a pulse."

Brennan threw the paddles aside and rocked back into a sitting position, resting his head on one bent knee. His breathing was ragged. They all looked up at the sound of sirens wailing in the distance, getting louder. Brennan glanced at the girl. "Go meet them and bring them here. And be proud of yourself-- without you, he would have died." She nodded and took off running again. Nurse Hamilton kept her fingers on Mr. Hoffman's neck, keeping track of his heartbeats. Thane stared at them all, numb, Brennan's words floating through his mind.

CHAPTER 8

"Without you, he would have died." Thane stumbled to his feet and walked away. Dimly he heard Brennan yelling after him as his jerking legs carried him forward and outside. Once the doors closed behind him, he started running. "Without you, he would have died." Thane slowed to a stop his stomach twisted and heaved, puking out the small lunch he'd eaten. He spat bile and wiped his chin with his sleeve, his whole body trembling now with shock, fatigue, and cold. "Without you, he would have died."

He ran again, through the park. Leaves crunched under his feet as he pelted through the creek bed. Thane wasn't thinking about where he was going. "I almost killed Mr. Hoffman," the thought came unbidden and unwelcome, with the image of the body laying still and pale in the hallway juxtaposed with the memory of Mr. Hoffman in his office talking to Thane, saying he wouldn't get in trouble. His stomach twisted again and he gagged, but nothing else came out. "I stopped his heart," the flash of light and the sound of Cressida's giggling, and watching through broken glass as Mr. Hoffman's body hit the ground.

"What am I?" Thane whispered to the cold. It did not answer. The blaring of sirens sounded behind him, seemed to scream at him, shouting "mon-ster, mon-ster, mon-ster!" into the frigid air. Thane flinched and ran through a doorway. Why couldn't he have stayed invisible? Thane wished, and wished desperately, that he'd never gone outside in the storm, that he'd never made his father angry, and that he'd never missed the bus. He wished he really was invisible, so Mr. Hoffman would never have seen him, never have picked him out of the hallway to help Remi find her locker.

A voice said, "Can I help you?" Thane looked up, startled. The hipster behind the cash register was watching him.

"No," Thane said, and backed away. Sirens wailed in front of the bookstore and Thane ran into the back room.

"Not you again," Raven sounded annoyed.

"Sorry," Thane said, and wished he was anywhere but here. He turned around and went back through the door.

But it must not have been the same door. Pale grey sand stretched out before him, alternating between round small hills and low waves. The sky was a darkening blue, and the yellow and orange strips of light on the distant horizon showed where the sun had barely set. Turning his head slowly Thane saw the same landscape to his right, and then his left. A breeze ruffled his hair and blew sand across his shoes. He seemed to be standing partway up one of the larger dunes, which gave him a better vantage point so he could clearly see all the emptiness surrounding him.

Sweat was pouring down his face and he pulled his hoodie off and dropped it. He had no idea where the door had brought him, but he wasn't in any hurry to get back. Not now, and maybe not ever. "Without you, he would have died." And without Thane, he never would have been in danger.

Thane turned to look behind him, and he lost his footing in the sand and landed on his backside with a muffled thump. He didn't bother to get up and sat in the still warm sand, staring back at where he'd emerged.

Laying at a steep vertical angle in the dune was a wooden door with a black handle. The loose sand from above was sliding down it like a small waterfall, partially obscuring it. Strange geometric shapes and whirling lines where carved into the unpolished surface, sometimes complimenting and sometimes crossing the wood grain. Thane rose to his feet carefully, brushing sand from his shirt absently as he studied the door. He wondered if he could make it take him anywhere-- he needed to keep running if he didn't want Sanctum to find him.

Thane reached out to touch the black door handle and jerked his hand back. It was burning hot, baked all day in the desert sun. He could wrap his hoodie around his hand to protect it and then figure out where to go next.

Falling down had made his hoodie slide away on the sand. Thane saw its dark shape about four feet lower on the dune than he was. He took some wobbling steps towards it, but the sand he dislodged pushed the hoodie even further away. Thane bent his knees and did his best standing long jump. If his feet weren't in the sand while he moved, the sand wouldn't get pushed, he reasoned. He made it about three feet through the air before his feet came down in the sand, which unlike the hardwood floors of the school gym, did not stay still and solid under his feet. The small particles slid forward, carrying his feet out from under him and he flailed his arms wildly trying to regain his balance.

The sand was only pushed forward inches until it formed a ridge as high as his shins, stopping his feet and legs while momentum pitched him forward. He landed face first on the side of the dune. His inertia pushed him another few feet down before stopping, scraping his face in the sand. Thane placed his hands on either side of his head and pushed, hissing at the pain. He froze when something hissed back. Keeping every other muscle still, Thane moved his eyes cautiously towards where the sound had come from. His hoodie was less than a foot from his left hand, and an equal distance on the other side of it a snake's head rose out of the desert.

The snake's body was the same color as the sand, with a regular pattern of darker spots along its back that were only visible for a few inches, as most of the snake's body was buried. The triangular head had two yellow eyes with black slits that were staring at his face. Thane held perfectly still. So did the snake. They stared at each other, unmoving and only a few feet apart, as the last rays of sunlight faded and the air around them started to cool.

Thane was positive the snake was venomous and only hadn't struck yet because he'd startled it. What would it feel like to die? Would it hurt? Thane imagined what it would be like if he let the snake bite him. It would be easier for his family if he wasn't there. There wouldn't be any more fighting, no one to screw everything up, and no one could see you if you were dead. The idea made him ache deep within. He didn't want to be dead, but he didn't want to be everyone's problem, either.

"Coward," Remi's voice sounded in his head. "It isn't everyone else you're worried about, it's you. You think it would be easier to be dead because you think living is too hard. Don't pretend like this is noble or self-sacrificing. You're a coward. Get over it and find a way to move on."

"But how?" he asked her voice in his mind. "I'm tired of being angry and scared and trying to be out of the way. And it isn't working anymore. I can't find a safe place to hide."

"So stop hiding," Remi's voice changed, deepened and sounded older. "It's only yourself you're hiding from. You're trying so hard to keep from finding yourself that no one else can find you either. That's why you feel alone. Get found."

Looking fixedly into those slitted yellow eyes, Thane felt his panic leave particle by particle like sand blowing away in the wind. Underneath where his fear had been he felt something else. In that hollow, empty space he held deep inside where he hid his despair, anger, and loneliness, Thane felt something move. A dark, free feeling, unlike anything he had ever felt before. It felt powerful. The expression on Thane's face changed until instead of anxiety, he was looking at the viper with a challenge.

It tensed. Thane tensed. And then Thane acted. His left arm shot out, grabbing the hoodie and pulling it up. At the same moment, the viper shot forward, but with the extra distance it had to go to get at Thane's face, it didn't make it. Instead it flew face first into the hoodie, which Thane wrapped around it like a bag. The viper's large fangs bit through the fabric and held on, venom dripping down and staining the dark fabric black. Thane held on to the ends where the snake could not reach him, and used the sleeves to tie the makeshift bag closed.

There was a heartbeat of silence. "Yes!" Thane crowed, dropping the bag and pumping both fists into the air. "Yes!" He jabbed a finger at the writhing cloth. "Take that! Woo!" Then he rubbed his face with both hands and winced as the sand on his hand rubbed into the soft skin of his face. "Argh!" He wiped his face with his arm and tried to shake the sand off his hands without causing more damage. Air hissed through his teeth as he winced and an answering muffled hiss came from under the fabric.

Thane glanced at the bag. "Guess you're not having the best day either," he said to the serpent. He grabbed the hoodie by the ends of the sleeves and carefully raised it up. The viper had retracted its fangs and lay in the bottom of the bag near where the pocket would be. Thane considered what to do with the snake now. Although the viper could easily bite through the fabric, Thane doubted it would be able to chew a hole large enough to get out if he left it. He certainly didn't want to untie the sleeves and set it free here because it would bite him at the first opportunity, and he couldn't take it with him. Back home it could snow any day and he knew it wouldn't survive there.

Thane didn't want the snake to die-- it hadn't done anything wrong, and attacking him had been more self defense than anything. In fact, he felt more affection for the snake than loathing, as his battle with the snake had made him feel invincible. He'd never felt that way before and wanted to revel in it and was grateful to the little serpent for it.

Looking out over the desert as the stars appeared in the night-dark sky, he had an idea. Thane loosened the knot on the sleeves until he had a small hole at the top of the bag. He didn't look in-- it would be too dark to see anything and he didn't want to give the viper something to strike at. Instead, he got a firm grip on the slackened knot and began to swing the bag around. Faster and harder he spun in a circle, and then released it at the moment when he hoped the angle and the force would be greatest. The thick hoodie flew through the air in a high arc, over and away across the waves of sand. Thane hoped the snake would be too dizzy and distracted to make its way out for a while, and that it couldn't find its way back to where he was.

"You're an idiot." Brennan's voice was harsh, and right next to him. Thane recoiled, falling back down into the sand. If he looked pitiful, Brennan didn't seem to care. "Do you have any idea how many bad things could've happened to you, going to the Leaf and Dagger and then using a door on your own?" Brennan sat down next to him in the sand.

"Why are you here?" Thane asked.

Brennan snorted. "You shorted out your tracker again. Lucky for you and your assistant principal, I was coming to see why."

"Is Mr. Hoffman going to be okay?" he whispered, almost hoping that Brennan wouldn't hear.

"Yeah," Brennan said, and a tightness in Thane's chest loosened. The young man took his first deep breath in over an hour and exhaled. "The paramedics said it was a close thing, but when they took him to the hospital he was awake and talking. He was very concerned about you. I promised him I'd make sure you were all right. He'll have to stay in the hospital just to be sure, but he'll be fine." Thane took several short gasping breaths, his back shuddering, and put his face down between his knees so the other man wouldn't see the tears streaming from his eyes and dripping off his nose.

If Brennan knew Thane was crying, he chose to ignore it. Thane was grateful. Brennan sat for a few minutes before continuing. "The police are asking everyone questions about what happened. That teacher of yours was found calming and comforting the other students in the cafeteria, playing the martyr and concerned benefactor. She told the police that you were threatening her with the cattle prod and she locked the door to protect the students in her next class from coming in."

That shocked Thane enough to actually jerk his head up and look at Brennan. Brennan's mouth was set in a grim line. "She also said that you made her move away from the door and electrocuted the door handle with the cattle prod. When the police questioned the nurse, she mentioned that you'd gotten in a fight with another classmate earlier in the week and that you'd gotten two burns that same day in chemistry. Of course your lovely chemistry teacher told the police, while batting her long eyelashes, that you getting injured was accidental but your friend accused her of hurting you on purpose. What if you were out for revenge? It also doesn't help," Brennan continued, ignoring Thane's visible mounting panic, "that the police are familiar with your name because of some domestic disturbance complaints from your neighbors. So right now it looks to the police like you're an abused teenager who may have turned violent, and I'll admit, if all I knew was the story I heard in there," jerking his head back to indicate the school, "I'd believe it."

"But it isn't true," Thane whispered to the ground.

"Your dad doesn't scream at you and you didn't punch someone and get burned twice in Chemistry?" Brennan retorted. Thane's mouth worked silently, unable to protest. "That's what makes this the most effective kind of lie, Thane. Most of it is true. Most of it can be verified, which makes the rest seem credible and likely." Brennan leaned his head back. "Your teacher has an agenda, and it involves you. I wish I knew what it was."

"She mentioned Shae magic," Thane remembered. Brennan's head shot up. "What?"

"When we were alone in the room, she mentioned Shae."

"Did she say anything else?"

"She said she was Shae, and," Thane paused, swallowing, "and that I was, too, and that everyone else had been lying to me and that I belonged with her. Is she from Sanctum?"

"No," Brennan was clearly concerned. "No, she isn't. And she can't be Shae, she's not on the registry. She would've popped up on the list for Payson when I was assigned to come check you out. But she wasn't-- the Shae population here is one of the smallest anywhere, and there has never been a Song or Weave event here in recorded history. She can't be Shae, but then, how would she know about it?" Brennan mused.

"Her fingers didn't burn." Thane's statement got Brennan's attention again. "When she pulled my wrist through the fire, her fingers went through too but they didn't get burned."

Brennan blanched. "Did she say anything else to you?"

Thane thought back. "She kept asking what lies they told me to make me look like this, but she never said who they were. And when Mr. Hoffman was trying to open the door, she laughed and said I didn't listen in class. She didn't try to stop me," Thane took a deep breath, trying to say the words without seeing the memories, and spoke the rest in a rush. "Then she called me a murderer and said I had to go with her unless I wanted to go to jail. Then you showed up and she disappeared." Thane put his face in his hands again. "I can't ever go back."

"Things aren't that bad, kid." Brennan said. "You know what?"

Brennan paused, waiting. Thane didn't respond. The silence stretched out between them, Thane's ragged breathing slowing down and Brennan making no move to get up. Almost two full minutes passed in silence, until a flash of annoyance cut through Thane's self pity. "What?" he finally snapped.

"I can still play piano," Brennan answered. Thane turned his head enough to see Brennan wiggling the remaining fingers of his right hand.
Thane's skepticism must have been obvious because Brennan amended, "Not as well as I used to, but I'm not giving up on it. Life is going to keep beating up and breaking us down because that's what life does. But how we respond, well, that's up to us."

"You responded by forgetting to make sure Raven didn't drug you and getting into a bar fight." Thane retorted, anger coloring his voice.

"Well, yeah, but," Brennan paused, and Thane heard him take a deep breath. "Losing my fingers didn't make me happy, but it isn't going to stop me from doing what I want to do. You're losing something big right now too. Bigger than my fingers. You're losing your confidence in what is real in the world and what isn't. All the ground you thought you had under your feet is being pulled away. I get that. I went through it. But it's up to you what you're going to do about it." The red haired man leaned back and Thane turned his face toward the ground, thinking. "Would you rather not go to jail?" asked Brennan. Thane's head whipped towards him, fear making him angry.

"What do you think? Don't patronize me," he shouted, smacking away the hand Brennan tried to lay on his shoulder. "Don't tell me it's going to be all right or that I can decide what to do. I can't--"

"You can." Brennan's voice cut through Thane's tirade. "And you do have somewhere to go, if you would shut up and listen." Brennan waited but Thane stayed silent, hands trembling with cold, fear, and anger. "You aren't going to jail. You're fifteen, this is your first offense, and there will only be charges if Mr. Hoffman decides to press any. I don't think he will. What's going to happen is that the police will question you and then remand you into the custody of your parents. Then you'll go back to your life and Ms. Rasmussen will be free to take another crack at you. That's your first choice."

There was a long pause as Thane mulled over everything Brennan had just said. It wasn't jail. It wasn't even that bad, just a few weeks of more embarrassing attention for his family and then everything would go back to normal. Oh, and his chemistry teacher might try to kidnap or kill him. That was a factor too.

"What's the second choice?" Thane asked, his voice raw from crying, vomiting, and getting sand in his throat.

"The second choice is that you stand up and take control of what's happening to you. It requires that you acknowledge that you are not a normal teenager, and that you accept the world is not as you always thought it was. The second choice says you start taking responsibility for things that happen to you, and because of you." Brennan had been looking up and away, but now he turned his gaze to Thane and met his eyes. "The second choice is Sanctum."

"What do you mean?"

"Thane, you have an affinity for electricity. If you choose to come to Sanctum you can learn to control your affinity so that if you come in contact with a charge, like the lightning or the cattle prod, you can decide how and where to get rid of it. That requires you accept that there is more to you than you've always thought, and you are not the person you've always believed yourself to be. Some people cannot handle that because you have to stop thinking of yourself as human." Brennan watched Thane carefully for a reaction. Thane was too numb to have one.

"There's another price," Brennan continued after a moment of silence. "In exchange for your training, Sanctum will require you to register with them. And they may occasionally call on you for assistance, if they ever need someone of your specific talents. Lots of people have small affinities like yours so it's unlikely that they would call on you, but it's possible."

"So more grownups trying to control me and decide where I can go and what I can do. Pass." Brennan shook his head.

"It's more than that, and less than that. If you want to join Sanctum full time and be a part of their mission that's up to you, if you qualify. If you don't, Sanctum helps you, logs you, and lets you go. It's in their best interest that Shaefolk know how to control their powers and understand their affinities. Uncontrolled Shae magic leads to public displays and inquiries. Sanctum protects the secret of the Shae in exchange for the Shae protecting the world from the Weave unraveling."

"I don't know what you're talking about," Thane sighed, feeling suddenly exhausted and wiping sweat from his forehead.

"They are long explanations, and I don't have time for them now." Brennan stood up stiffly, and held his hand down to Thane. "But I promise, if you decide to come to Sanctum, I will answer your questions as completely as I can."

Thane looked at the outstretched hand, the one with all the fingers. "If I choose Sanctum, what will you tell the police, or my parents?"

"The police are waiting for you to come home. If you decide you want to take control of your affinity, someone from Sanctum will be waiting at your house as a representative from Child Protective Services. They will not allow the police to take you anywhere, and will recommend to both the officers and your parents that you undergo a week of counseling at a special facility for youth facing unique challenges. That facility is Sanctum, but they'll leave that part out. Then your parents will sign some consent paperwork and first thing in the morning a car will arrive to take you to the airport. I will meet you there and take you to Sanctum."

"My parents are home?" Thane asked.

"Your father was discharged about an hour ago. Shredding holes, doesn't your mother tell you anything?" Thane reached up and gripped Brennan's hand. Brennan hauled the younger man up to his feet and helped to steady him when Thane's legs proved too stiff to balance on their own.

Thane shrugged, choosing not to answer that. "So my choices are stay ignorant and wait for someone else to try and use me, or give up everything I know to go somewhere I've never heard of with people I don't know to teach me how to control something I still don't believe in?" he summarized.

Brennan grinned. "Pretty much, kid."

A movement next to his head caught Thane's attention, and he watched as the desert breeze blew the sand around his feet. The memory of watching Mr. Hoffman fall through the shattered glass replayed in his mind, and then repeated but with Remi's body hitting the ground. Then Lanie. Thane swallowed, his skin slick with sweat and his heart numb with fear. But he'd beaten the viper.

"Only for a week?"

"One week. You'll be back by next Sunday."

"I'm not joining up. This is just to keep everyone safe."

"I get it, kid." Brennan's face was somber. "Go home. I'll make sure someone from Sanctum is there when you get there."

CHAPTER 9

Snow was falling thick and fast when Thane arrived home. He'd tried to send Remi a text that he couldn't come and would tell her more later, but his cell phone's screen was cracked and it wouldn't turn on. Another casualty of the electrocution. Thane walked slowly up the stairs to his front door, noting that his father's car was in the driveway and blocked in by the police, and that a third car, a comfortable squarish blue sedan was parked on the street just past the driveway. He assumed that was the Sanctum car, and wondered who they would've sent. His front door was locked so he rang the doorbell.

The lock clicked and the bolt ground back before the knob turned and the door swung inward. Bert Whitaker stood there, looking at his son. He seemed smaller than Thane remembered, sort of shrunken and feeble. The son waited with his head down for the verbal tirade about to be unleashed. Missing the bus had merited a shouting match and a blow. What would having the police descend on the house earn?

"Yes?" Bert asked in a soft voice. "Can I help you?"

"Um, dad?" Thane lifted his chin, blinking a little. "I'm, I'm home. From school."

"You are?" Bert stared at him closely. "Are you Thane?"

"Thane!" his mother shrieked from the kitchen. "There are several people in here who would like to talk to you, so get in here!" Her piercing voice made both Thane and his father flinch together, and Bert smiled at Thane apologetically.

"I'm sorry, I'm sorry, Thane," he said softly. "I was in an accident-- they tell me we were both hit by lightning-- I'm still getting better. I don't have all my memories yet. I didn't recognize Harper, either. I think that scared her," Bert's face was so sad that Thane felt an unexpected stab of pity. "She started crying and ran to her room. I'm still working on remembering things. I hope," his eyes shone with tears that Thane desperately hoped wouldn't fall, "I hope you can be patient. Maybe later we'll call Grandpa Whitaker and go fishing. He used to take me fishing when I was younger. Maybe that will help me remember the last time you and I went."

"Thane!" Gwen's voice was shrill and angry. Bert cringed.

"We can talk later. You'd better go," his father urged him, and then went to sit on the couch. "I'll stay here so I'm not in the way." Thane's dad gave him a weak smile. Thane tried to smile back, but it must not have worked because his dad's lips twisted, and he looked down at his hands.

The weight Thane was carrying doubled, so fast and hard that Thane felt like the wind had been knocked out of him. In one of the lives inexorably intertwined with Thane's, he had become finally and completely invisible. He'd dreamed so many times, when his father was angry and screaming or cold and disapproving, that he could just fade into the wall so his dad couldn't see him anymore. Thane had spent years learning how to be unobtrusive, pass through unnoticed, so as not to raise his father's ire. The burden on his shoulders slid down and collected in a hard lump in his stomach. He had even once wished that Bert Whitaker didn't know who Thane was. That had been outside, in the icy rain, the moment before the lightning struck.

"Sanctum had better be able to fix me before I do kill someone," he mumbled. He shuffled slowly into the kitchen, his head down.

He was met with the sound of several people breathing. Thane's downcast eyes saw Gwen's manicured toenails peeking out of fashionable flowery sandals, her ankles crossed under the table. Next to those was a pair of black polished men's dress shoes, both feet flat on the ground under bent knees. Another pair of larger black shoes stood to the side and behind the others, the officers staying together to show solidarity. The fourth pair of shoes was a bright blue with pointed toes and high heels, showing off bare ankles and legs up to the crossed knees. He thought of how appropriate that all was; one shallow and frivolous, three who meant business. His eyes returned to his own old, scuffed sneakers. Technically a shoe for the young, but used hard and getting worn out.

"Are you Thane Whitaker, a sophomore at Payson High School?" one of the officers asked severely.

"Yes sir," Thane responded without making eye contact. He wasn't sullen or belligerent, he was tired and scared. That must've made an impression, because the officer's voice softened.

"Why don't you sit down, son?" suddenly today he was everyone's son. Why the change? "We have to ask you some questions about school today. About what happened with Ms. Rasmussen and with Mr. Hoffman."

"Questions you don't have to answer," said another unfamiliar voice, this one clipped and businesslike. The woman with the serious heels. "As a minor and without being charged with any crime, you are not required to cooperate with these men. Especially if you feel threatened or in danger, or you would be required to incriminate yourself in any way."

"I understand, Ms. LaPointe, that you are only doing your job. Please try to understand that we are only trying to do ours." The older officer standing next to Thane looked down at the woman sternly. She met his gaze calmly, without malice or aggression.

"Officer Barrigan, I understand your position. Please understand mine. This young man has undergone a terrible trauma, and not only today." She held up one hand and began ticking off events on her fingers. "He and his father were the victims of a lightning strike on Monday, a mere five days ago. On Wednesday, he was injured twice in his chemistry class as a direct result of the negligence of this same teacher who today maliciously subjected him to another electrical shock and then slandered him. Of all of these grievous injuries I have documented evidence. Where is yours?"

"Is all that true?" a shocked voice came from the doorway. The adult heads swiveled around, and even Thane didn't recognize Bert Whitaker's voice. Maybe now his dad would remember what a screw up he was and start yelling. Maybe then things could get back to normal. Thane heard his father's steps as the other man entered the room and drew close to the table. Bert's breathing was labored, and he stopped directly behind Thane's chair. "Thane, is she right? Did all that happen to you?"

Thane gave a half shrug and nodded. His dad placed his hands on the back of Thane's chair to steady himself and Thane suppressed a flinch. Cowering would only make things worse. "Then what are you people doing here? He doesn't need jail, he needs help! What's wrong with you?" The boy heard his father take a deep breath and then exhale noisily. Thane felt like laughing, more than a little unhinged at the irony of being defended by his father. Only his anxiety kept him quiet.

"Actually, Mr. Whitaker, that is precisely what we are suggesting. At least, CPS is." Thane saw her shoot a smug glance towards the seated officer. "There is an option provided by the government for youth in exceptional circumstances. The requirements for this program are very specific; fortunately, Thane meets them. This program would provide Thane with one week of counseling and cognitive therapy in order to enable him to better cope with his traumatic experiences. The government will subsidize one week of therapy," she emphasized, making eye contact with a reluctant Gwen, "and if additional therapy is needed, the cost of that counseling will be submitted to the minor's health insurance carrier and ultimately be the responsibility of his parents or guardians."

Thane blanched. Why was she giving them such a hard sell? Was she trying to make them say no? He needed to get away, get out of Payson and far from anyone he knew so that if his electrical conductivity went haywire again no one else would get hurt. He opened his mouth, but his mom cut in.

"But the first week is totally paid for?" Gwen pressed. "He could go away to this therapy and it wouldn't cost us anything?"

"The first seven days are completely covered by governmental funding," Ms. LaPointe confirmed. "Travel, room, board, and all therapy and counseling sessions are included for those who meet all the requirements."

"And Thane does," his mother challenged. "You would take him for a week and it wouldn't cost us anything and when he came back he'd be fixed?"

"Fixed implies he's broken, Mrs. Whitaker. Thane isn't. He is a young man whose circumstances are more traumatic and difficult to cope with than others." Ms. LaPointe answered as if she was repeating something she'd been required to memorize. "We cannot guarantee any results, as any counseling or therapy is only as efficacious as the person participating desires it to be." Her statement met with blank looks all around the table. She gave a frustrated little sigh. "He'll only get out of it what he's willing to put into it. It won't work if he doesn't want it to," she clarified, indicating Thane.

"Of course he wants it to, don't be ridiculous," Bert said. "But what about the police? What if that man-- Mr. Hoffman? What if he decides to press charges, what happens then?"

Thane appreciated him asking, because he was wondering that too. Ms. LaPointe answered in the same memorized monotone. "This voluntary therapy would take the place of any police custody, hearing, or judicial sentencing under federal juvenile retention laws. Essentially, if you agree to send him to therapy, no matter what anyone else decides, they can't touch him." Thane glanced up at the adults. Ms. LaPointe smiled at the officer across the table. He grunted disapprovingly, but could not object. His father still stood behind him, both hands resting on the back of Thane's chair, and Thane couldn't make himself turn to face Bert Whitaker, the man he'd electrocuted, who's memory he'd wiped, and who was defending him against the police.

"Because he doesn't remember who I am," Thane thought. "Because he doesn't remember whatever it is about me that makes him hate me. I wonder how long it'll be before he remembers, or if whatever is wrong with me will just make him hate me all over again." He slumped a little further in his chair, only barely listening to what was being said.

"...pick him up tomorrow morning, and we would return him the following Sunday morning," Ms. LaPointe was saying. Bert was asking questions, and Gwen didn't seem to be paying attention. "A car would be here at 9 a.m. I have a packing list and a list of prohibited items," and she produced some papers from her briefcase.

The radio on Officer Barrigan's belt jangled to life. "...eighteen in progress on Tatum Drive. Closest units, please respond." Barrigan and his partner made eye contact and the other man rose to his feet.

"Please excuse us." He shook hands all around, even Thane, and left, shutting the front door gently behind him. No one spoke for a few moments as the siren on their police car blared to life, and the sound of their tires screeching faded into the distance.

Ms. LaPointe pulled out a thick stack of paperwork from her expensive looking briefcase. "These are the forms I need to you fill out and sign for Thane." She slid them across the table to Gwen.

"Here, Bert, you do it," Thane's mom waved a hand over the stack before her. Bert leaned forward but Ms. LaPointe stopped him.

"I'm sorry, Mr. Whitaker, but you've been discharged from the hospital for less than twenty-four hours. Nothing you sign will be legally binding," Ms. LaPointe gave a Gwen a small, smug smile. "It has to be you, and I have to watch you do it."

"I think I need to lie down," Thane's father said, and Thane stared down at the table, listening as the shuffling steps grew quieter, and the door to his parent's bedroom opened and closed.

"I think we're all right to finish this, Thane," Ms. LaPointe said. More papers rustled and she pushed a white sheet into his field of vision on the table. "Here is the packing list, and the prohibited list is on the back. Why don't you go get started." It was an instruction, not a question, so Thane grabbed his backpack and the paper and went downstairs.

"How many pages are there?" his mother's whine echoed after him.

"AS MANY AS I COULD THINK OF," Ms. LaPointe's voice sounded inside his head. He froze on the stairwell and looked back over his shoulder.

She was still sitting at the table, pointing out missed lines and giving instructions to his mom. She glanced up at Thane and smiled without warmth or humor. "WELCOME TO SANCTUM, MR. WHITAKER," her words whispered jarringly in his mind, "I HOPE YOU REALIZE YOU'RE NOT PREPARED FOR IT."

He turned and fled into the basement.

Hours later he had finished stuffing his few possessions into his backpack. He didn't have as many pairs of socks as the list suggested-- he hoped no one would check. It was past dark now, and the house was quiet. Thane tried to check the time, but his phone's screen remained black and uncommunicative. He needed to talk to Remi. The Whitakers had disconnected their land line months ago, but it wouldn't have mattered if they did have another phone. Remi had entered her cell number into his speed dial, and Thane wasn't sure he'd even looked at what her number was. Even with a phone in hand, he would have no way to call her.

"Argh!" he groaned. He needed to talk to Remi because he needed someone to help him figure this out, and because he owed her an explanation before he disappeared for a week. The image of Remi crying in her room flashed into his mind. She cried because her father would leave and she didn't know where or if he was coming back. Thane had promised that he would not do that to her, and that he would always tell her what was going on. He wasn't going to break that promise.

Quietly, he slid open the window in his room. The window well was narrow, but he knew from experience he could climb out of the basement into the backyard. He pulled a black hoodie out of his suitcase and tugged it over his head. Pushing the screen out into the wet slush, Thane lifted himself out of his room and into the well. He straightened, keeping his back pressed against the house. He leaned out just enough to see the pink curtains drawn across the window to his sisters' room. Thane vaulted out of the window well and onto the fresh new snow, and ran softly through his yard and out onto the sidewalk.

He knew this was not the best plan. His feet crunched in the wet snow and his breath came out in visible puffs of white; sneaking around outside in the winter was not the best way to be inconspicuous. But he had made a promise, and that promise pushed him on; Sanctum was going to pick him up in the morning and this might be his last chance to talk to Remi. In fact, he realized, this might be a better opportunity than he'd thought. Brennan said that Thane had shorted out his tracker again and that was why he'd come to check on him, but neither Brennan nor Ms. LaPointe had inserted a new one. They were assuming he'd be there in the morning, waiting for the car like a good little boy.

Thane grinned, his first real smile in what felt like years. Sanctum wasn't tracking him. They would have no idea where he'd gone, and he could talk to Remi without being afraid they were listening. He could keep his promise and not be pulling her deeper into whatever this was. And tonight was the last night he had before he would be too far in to ever back out.

The houses fell away behind him as he entered the last open stretch of road, and the lights of Kendall base shone bright in the grey chill of the night. Thane slowed, considering. He didn't have anyone to vouch for him and no one expecting him to be there. What if they wouldn't let him in? He couldn't not get to Remi. Maybe he could sneak past the gate? He waited just outside the circles of light the street lamps and spotlights of the base created. If a truck came by, he could grab onto the bottom and ride it in. Or maybe he could create a distraction and run through the gate while all the guards were looking the other way.

"What are you doing, kid?" the gate soldier yelled. Thane jumped and slipped on the wet snow. He flailed wildly, barely keeping his balance. The gate guard barked a laugh. "Either keep coming or go away, but you can't hang out around here. Especially at night."

"You can see me?" Thane asked.

"Of course I can see you! You aren't that far away, you're wearing black against snow, and I have video feeds from the security cameras," the guard said. "Now tell me what you want or go home."

Thane hesitated. "I want to talk to Remi Gage."

There was no response from the guardhouse for several moments.

"Get over here," finally came, and Thane walked towards the two soldiers standing in front of the closed gate. As he drew closer, the guard on his left elbowed his companion. "It's that kid. The one that Gage likes. He is insane!"

Thane was getting really tired of people questioning his sanity. "So can I go in, already? Gage was expecting me hours ago."

"You're late to see General Gage?" the new guard was incredulous. The soldier who recognized Thane elbowed the other airman again. "We'll, um, we'll have to get you cleared," he stammered.

"Not it," called the first guard. The new guard swore under his breath and went into the guardhouse to use the phone, his face a little paler.

Thane could hear the other soldier stammering into the phone, "I know sir, I'm sorry sir-- no it isn't an emergency, but-- yes sir, but there's a kid here to see you- no sir, I didn't ask... yes sir." The new guard put his hand over the phone receiver, "What's your name, kid?"

"Thane Whitaker."

"Thane Whitaker." There was a long pause, the invisible voice on the other end of the line silent. Then a sharp command. "Yes sir!" the on duty soldier saluted into the phone, and hung up. He turned to Thane with slightly wild eyes. "Senior Airman Calder will be here within three minutes to take you to the General."

They stood there until headlights shone and tires squealed in the snow from the other side of the gate. A very annoyed Calder cracked the tinted window of the dark sedan. "Get in, Whitaker!" he barked. Thane walked through the gate, opened barely wide enough to allow one person through.

All the downstairs lights were on at Remi's house when Calder pulled the car through the arch, and Thane hadn't finished getting out before Gage had the front door open. "Dismissed, Calder!" the General barked, and Calder drove away while Thane was ushered into the house.

"Your hands are freezing," Gage observed after he'd greeted Thane with a firm handshake. "Do you want some hot chocolate? Sit down," and he indicated the chair Thane had occupied only yesterday.

"No thank you sir," Thane said, and did not sit. "I know it's late and I'm really sorry, but can I talk to Remi? It's important."

"She's asleep and with as sick as she's been, she needs her rest, son," Gage refused gently but firmly.

Thane was suddenly tired of everyone calling him "son," and that made him feel reckless. "General Gage sir, I know she's been sick. But I made a promise that I would tell her what was going on and this is my only chance to keep it. I'm," he faltered, unsure of what to say, "I'm leaving in the morning and I won't be back for a while. My phone is cracked and won't turn on, so I couldn't call her. And I don't know if I can use the internet when I get there."

The General seemed sympathetic but unrelenting, so Thane pushed on into dangerous territory. "It really bothers her when you leave and she doesn't know where you are or when you're coming back. She was telling me about it yesterday and started crying. I promised her I wouldn't do that, and showing up now was the only thing I could think to do to let her know. I didn't come this afternoon and I won't be around after tomorrow, and if she showed up for school on Monday and I still wasn't there she might think something really bad had happened to me. I don't want to do that to her. Do you?"

Remi's father was taken aback by Thane's blunt honesty. "She cried?" he said. Thane nodded. Gage was quiet for the space of three heartbeats. "What happened in school, why didn't you ride here with Calder after, and where are you going?"

"It's a long story."

"Tell me first, and then I'll decide if you need to wake her."

Thane sighed, frustrated. "Ms. Rasmussen electrocuted Mr. Hoffman today and his heart stopped. He's going to be okay, but he's in the hospital. The police thought it was my fault so I had to go home and talk to them. My phone broke or I would have called." He held out his cell for Remi's father to see.

Gage glanced at it. "I almost went to your house myself to find out what was going on. Remi convinced me otherwise. She was sure you would come here as soon as you could." The General paused, considering. "I suppose she was right. What happened with the police?"

"It would've been bad for me if Ms. LaPointe hadn't been there. She said she was from Child Protective Services and wouldn't let the cops force me into anything or take me anywhere. She told my parents I qualified for some government funded youth therapy thing for a week because I've had so many traumatic experiences recently." Thane ran his fingers through his hair, trying to remember to repeat only what Ms. LaPointe had said out loud and not in his head. "My mom signed the papers and they're coming to get me tomorrow morning."

"They?" Gage asked.

Thane shrugged. "The therapy people, I guess. They're supposed to train me to be able to deal with everything that's been happening to me lately."

"That sounds like a very good thing," Gage smiled. "All right, as a man of honor, I can't stand in the way of you keeping a promise to my daughter. And I'll admit I'm nervous at how furious she'd be if I didn't let you talk to her. Wait here, I'll call you when she's ready." Gage stood and walked upstairs. Thane sat down in the chair, looking out the enormous glass windows at all the lights on the base shining below and the reflection of the light on the low hanging clouds. The light seemed trapped, trying to break free into the night sky and held back by the heavy grey clouds. Thane's head drooped forward, and he jerked it up. He shifted in the plush white chair, scooting forward so his head could lean against the back while he waited. It had been a long day.

"Thane." Thane jerked awake, embarrassed. "She's ready for you. I was going to say don't keep her long, but I don't think you could if you tried. Go on up, I'll stay here. Remember her door stays open," and Gage jerked his thumb over his shoulder.

Remi was propped up in her bed again on the pile of purple pillows. She looked exhausted, her face puffy with illness and sleep and lines of black smearing away from her eyelids. Still, she smiled when she saw him and warmth ran through Thane's insides again. He smiled back.

"I can't believe you went to chemistry without me," she said. Thane's smile vanished. "I told you it was dangerous. What were you thinking? What happened? Dad told me that you didn't come back today because the police were waiting for you! Why," and she paused between each word for emphasis, "were the police waiting for you?"

"They thought I tried to kill Mr. Hoffman." He had the momentary satisfaction of seeing her mouth drop open. "But I went to test your theory."

Her mouth worked soundlessly for a moment before words came out. "My theory?"

"That she poisoned us on purpose. Without Brennan's healing darts, I wouldn't be better yet, like you. So if I showed up in class I could see if she was surprised or not."

"Because if she knew it was the wrong metal, she would be surprised to see you," Remi caught on instantly. "That's brilliant. But you're still an idiot for going without me. Was she surprised?"

"More like angry," Thane said. "She checked my wrist and my leg and then told me that it didn't matter anyway because she'd seen the fire and metal hurt me, and that was enough."

"Enough for what?"

"I don't know. But then she pulled out a cattle prod and started talking about electrical conductivity."

"A what?" Remi gave him a confused look.

"A cattle prod. It's this metal stick with two prongs on one end and a button on the other that shoots out electricity."

"Like a taser," she said, her face clearing.

"Yeah, but it's for animals. So she pulled it out and started electrocuting stuff. She really freaked out Johanna." Remi's face was grim, waiting for him to go on. "Then she asked Jeran to fill a jar with water, and stood next to me while she waited. She held the cattle prod against my leg and pushed the button--"

"What?" Remi interrupted, furious. "She tasered you? The other kids had to see that. Did you all tell Mr. Hoffman? They have to take action against her now, that's three times in one week you've gotten seriously hurt in her class..." coughing halted her tirade, and Thane hurried to refill the empty cup on her nightstand with water from her bathroom. She took the cup gratefully and drank while Thane continued.

"It didn't hurt." He said. She sputtered. "Sorry," Thane apologized, chagrined.

"What do you mean?" Remi gasped out.

"The electricity didn't hurt. Mostly it felt... good," he glanced at her face to watch her reaction. Remi watched him, fascinated. Encouraged, Thane kept going. "It felt like energy was pouring into me. I couldn't focus on anything else, couldn't concentrate. I have no idea what she said next until she asked me to stay after class. Then it got weird." Thane hesitated, looking down and feeling uncomfortable. This was a lot to take in, and what if Remi didn't believe him?

Remi's hand crept into his field of vision, and he watched her small fingers wrap around his hand. "Weird how?" she asked in low tones.

Thane took a moment to breathe before continuing. Her skin was soft, and extra warm from being in bed. It took some effort to pull his thoughts back in line. "She shut the door and locked it. Then Ms. Rasmussen said she found me and I had a great disguise and what lies did they tell me to keep me so ordinary," his words tumbled out. "Then she said she was Shae, and I was too."

"She knows about Shae?" Remi was shocked, not doubting. "Is she with Sanctum?"

"Brennan said she wasn't."

"Brennan showed up too? Is that how you got away from Ms. Rasmussen?"

"Not... exactly," said Thane. "I could see all the electricity bouncing around on my fingers and Ms. Rasmussen was blocking the door and mocking me and then Mr. Hoffman started pounding on the other side. She wouldn't get out of the way but she seemed scared of me, especially if I got close. So I walked towards her until she moved away from the door, and Mr. Hoffman saw me through the window. He told me to open the door so I tried to unlock it while he turned the knob--"

Remi gasped. "And with that huge electrical charge you were carrying around..." she closed her eyes for a heartbeat. "Ms. Rasmussen didn't try to stop you? She just let you electrocute Mr. Hoffman?"

"She seemed to think it was funny," Thane grimaced. "Then she called me a murderer and said now I would have to go with her or I'd go to jail." Remi covered her mouth with both hands and tears spilled over her cheeks, drips making darker purple circles on her bedspread. Thane froze, too afraid to move.

"Mr. Hoffman, he's... dead?" she said, her words muffled.

"No, no, he's fine, he's in the hospital, Brennan restarted his heart and said he was going to be fine," Thane was quick to reassure her. She inhaled slowly, then released it all at once and wiped her eyes.

"Start with that next time?" she asked, and Thane nodded. "Let me make sure I understand. She wanted you to leave with her." Remi's voice was cold enough that Thane shivered. "But she knew that we don't like her or trust her." Again he moved his chin up and down in affirmation. "So having filled you with enough of an electrical charge to stop a grown man's heart, she locked you in a classroom and refused to open the door, knowing that another class was coming and when they couldn't get in they would go get someone. Then when help arrived, instead of opening the door herself she manipulated you into doing it because she knew whoever was on the other side was going to be holding onto the knob and the electricity would jump through and maybe kill them, just to make you desperate enough to give her what she wanted; control over you."

Thane sat back, stunned. "That was all on purpose," he realized.

Remi shuddered. "I'm glad Brennan showed up. What did he want this time?"

"I shorted out my tracker again," Thane said, holding out his palm. "He came to see why."

"Why is obvious. You got electrically juiced with a cattle prod. What did you do?"

"I ran," she was silent all through Thane's retelling of wanting to be as far away as possible and going through the door. Her eyes were huge as he recounted sunset in the desert, and even though he downplayed exactly how he came face to face with the viper, she still giggled quietly and listened.

"Where were you? Where did the door take you?"

Thane reached into his pocket and pulled out a handful of sand. "I don't know, but I was covered in this." He showed her, and her mouth made a small "o" and she held out both her hands. Thane slowly poured the sand from his open palm into her cupped ones. She seemed a little awed.

"Can I keep this?" her voice was hushed.

"Sure," said Thane, "I've got plenty, it's in all my pockets."

"There's a little brown box on my dresser. Will you get it for me?"

She nodded behind him and he turned around and saw her bright purple dresser against the far wall next to an open door. He went back to the bed and opened the box, and Remi almost reverently let the sand slide through her fingers into it.

"Why do you want it? It's just sand."

"It's proof," answered Remi, brushing the remaining sand from her fingers carefully so it all fell into the box. "Proof that magic is real, that Brennan is real, the doors are real."

"Yeah," Thane looked down, wishing she was still holding his hand. The contact might make saying the next part easier. "That wasn't all. He thinks I have an affinity for electricity, since it's been twice now that I've had electrical currents running through me without being hurt. But both times someone else did. Did get hurt." He hunched his shoulders and stared at the floor. "Brennan said I had two choices. That I could ignore everything strange going on and to go back living my life and still be a target for Ms. Rasmussen, or I go register with Sanctum and they'll teach me how to control it as long as I promise to obey all their rules and help out if they need me." Thane didn't dare look up at her, but his palms started sweating as the seconds ticked by without her saying anything.

He couldn't stand it. Still staring at the floor, he tried to explain. "I don't like the idea of running to Sanctum to get their permission to live my life and I won't do anything illegal or to hurt people, no matter what they say. But I keep seeing Mr. Hoffman fall," his voice broke and he tried to steady it, speaking faster to get through all the words tumbling around trying to push their way out, "except it isn't always Mr. Hoffman. Sometimes it's you, or Lanie. Mr. Hoffman and my dad, they're adults, they'll get over it. You wouldn't. Lanie wouldn't. Then it would be my fault because I had the chance to fix it and I didn't." He held what little breath he had left, needing but not wanting to hear her answer.

Remi's hand crept back into his. He wrapped both his hands around it. "I'm a freak, Remi, and I need to learn how to not be in danger of killing anyone. So I'm going to freak school for a week."

"A week?" Remi punched him in the shoulder with her free hand.

He flinched, lifting his chin to face her. "Ow. Yeah, they're coming to get me tomorrow morning. I'll be back next Sunday."

"You moron," she said, "the way you were talking I thought you were coming to say goodbye forever. I couldn't decide if you were being self-sacrificing or a misogynistic jerk. Of course you can go to freak camp for a week." She smiled, and he smiled back. "But you have to tell me everything they tell you. They'll probably say it's all very secret and you can't tell anyone for their own protection, or something asinine like that. Being shielded by ignorance always keeps people safe, 'Oh, I'm so glad no one told me that bridge would collapse if I walked on it,' 'It's such a good thing that no one told us the lion was so hungry before we put our arms in the cage'." Remi snorted in disgust.

"I have to tell you everything," Thane responded. "You're the only person who wouldn't think I'm insane."

"I haven't ruled it out, but I believe you're telling the truth," she quipped. "Call me when you get there, to Sanctum."

"I can't," Thane said, pulling out his phone to show her the cracked and dark screen. "My tracker wasn't the only thing that shorted out. Cell phones are on the prohibited list, anyway."

"Prohibited list?" she raised an eyebrow.

"It was on the back side of the packing list," Thane explained.

Remi giggled. "You really are going to camp. Bring me back the bird feeder you make." Thane made a face at her, and they both laughed.

"Remi, Thane, it's one thirty in the morning, and Calder is here to take Thane home," Gage called up the stairs firmly, the sudden intrusion making them jerk their hands apart.

Thane tried to give her a brave smile. "See you in a week. Skip chemistry."

She smiled back, but her eyes were worried. "See you in a week. Don't get eaten by a monster."

"Monster spray is on the packing list." Thane resisted the impulse to hug her, and couldn't think of anything else to say. They held each other's eyes until a horn honked outside, and Thane turned and went downstairs. He would never admit to her that he was afraid. He didn't have to.

CHAPTER 10

The next morning started out like almost every other Saturday morning had for the last four years. Thane was jolted awake by a squealing little girl throwing herself on top of him at full speed. The only variant was where she landed, and Thane had learned through painful experience to sleep on his stomach.

"Daddy said come eat breakfast," Lanie said, grinning. He rubbed his eyes again and checked his phone to see what time it was. The shattered screen told him nothing. He groaned, and threw the phone across the room where it bounced off the floor and through the space between the framing boards into the dark beyond.

"Thane, breakfast! Hurry, they'll be here in fifteen minutes!" his dad yelled down the stairs, and Lanie bounded up into the kitchen. That answered the time question, and Thane stumbled out of bed and through the wall to the bathroom. It took him several minutes to get ready enough to go upstairs, and he dragged his backpack behind him, bumping each stair he climbed.

The kitchen was clean and smelled good. Thane blinked and almost went back downstairs to bed, because if he was dreaming he wanted to do it back on his mattress. Bert Whitaker stood next to the sink, scrubbing the last pan. "Eat, Thane, they're going to be here any minute," he said, using the washcloth to point to the table. There was a large pile of scrambled eggs and some kind of soggy bread with syrup sitting on a plate with silverware on either side. Thane looked at the food, his mouth starting to water, and back to his dad. Bert had turned back to the dishes, humming while he scrubbed.

"This isn't you," Thane blurted out. His father stopped, hands in the hot water red and puckered. "The lightning, it burned out parts of your memory, and now you don't know--" Thane couldn't push the words "you hate me" past the hardness in his throat and switched to, "this isn't you."

His dad slowly finished washing the last dish and put it on the drying rack. He turned off the water, and then rested his hands on the front of the sink, his shoulders hunching forward and down. "I know," he finally said. "I'm so sorry, Thane, I'm so sorry that I don't remember you. I don't remember what you like to do, I don't remember you being little, I don't know if you like French toast or not." That must be the soggy bread on the plate. Thane glared at it, angry and hungry at the same time. "I'm starting to get glimpses of Harper-- a birthday, a conversation, even something as small as a hug-- but still nothing for you. I'm working on it, I promise. I want to know you."

"No you don't," Thane said under his breath. If his dad heard, he pretended not to.

"You should eat before it gets too cold," Bert said, "And before they--"

A horn honking covered the rest of whatever his father was saying. Lanie went pounding past them to look out the front window. "It's a black car! It's at our house!" she yelled so everybody would know. "It must be the government! Thane, the government is here for you!"

Thane walked to the front room and opened the door. Ms. LaPointe was on the other side, waiting. "Are you ready? We have a tight schedule," she said without being bothered by social niceties like saying hello. Thane slung on his backpack to indicate he was good to go, and she turned on her heel and walked back to the car.

"Bye Lanie," Thane said to the only other person in the living room. She threw herself into his arms and he caught her and held her for a moment.

"Bring me a bear," she whispered in his ear. "A not smelly one that likes me best."

He hugged her tighter and put her down. Out of the corner of his eye he saw his father, standing in the kitchen doorway. Thane straightened and father and son locked eyes, neither one speaking. Bert lowered his eyes first, and went back into the kitchen with bowed shoulders. Harper and his mother were nowhere to be seen, which made Thane more relieved than sad. And that made him sad.

Ms. LaPointe was already in the car with the door closed, and the horn honked again. The rear side door opened, pushed by someone on the inside. Thane got in and sat. "So that's what your face looks like when you're not in the middle of something awful. It's surprisingly the same." Brennan Tayler sat in the seat next to him, grinning.

"Brennan!" Thane was surprised and glad to see him. "I thought I'd meet you at until the airport."

"Yeah. Change of plans. Our timetable is a little more crunched than expected, so I'm here now. You'll have someone else assigned to you once you get to Sanctum." Brennan's smile was easy and relaxed. "Buckle up, kid."

Grabbing the strap, Thane noted that the car had a partition between the front and the back like a limousine. It was closed so he couldn't see into the front seat. Ms. LaPointe had gotten into the front passenger side door, so it was probable someone else was driving. Thane cataloged that for later; he had other questions he wanted answered. "Where are we going?" he asked Brennan. "What are they going to do to me? What does Sanctum want? What is Sanctum?"

"Slow down, kid. You hungry?" Brennan produced a large bag that smelled like grease and meat. Thane took it and pulled out a breakfast bagel sandwich, fried hash browns, and a cup of fruit and yogurt. Putting that one back in, he started in on the rest and chewed quickly, the food still hot enough to burn a little.

Brennan allowed him to take several bites before starting to answer. "We are going to Sanctum's main training facility. It's kind of a long trip, but I'm not allowed to disclose the location. What Sanctum is and what they want is kind of a long story, and you won't understand Sanctum unless I tell you about the Shaerealm first."

Mouth full and grease dripping down his chin, Thane wiped his face with his sleeve and indicated Brennan should continue. The car picked up speed and Thane realized they must be on the freeway, but the windows were tinted on the inside so Thane couldn't see out. Brennan took a deep breath and leaned back into his seat. "Knowing where to start is always hardest. Sanctum's motto is 'Portamus oneris omnium planetarum in solum eventus,' which means 'The only burden we carry is the fate of all worlds.' Have you ever heard of the multi-verse theory?"

Thane shrugged. "No," he mumbled around half a bagel.

"Scientists will tell you that the multi-verse, or meta-universe, is the hypothetical set of multiple possible universes, including ours, which together comprise everything that exists or can exist. Universes all have physical matter, but each universe has a specific resonance range that all matter and energy operate within. We call it 'phase.' So every universe is slightly out of phase with every other universe, allowing them all to coexist without overlapping. The resonance that each universe has is like music, creating sound waves. If the sound waves of two universes overlap too closely, the sound gets canceled out, but if they travel together, it creates harmony. This is the Song. Here."

Finishing the last of the bagel, Thane reached out and took the large paper cup Brennan was holding out. The egg and cheese breakfast bagel had made Thane thirstier than he realized, and he gratefully filled his mouth with overly sweet orange juice. He grimaced, but drank anyway.

Brennan stretched his arms and put his hands behind his head. "Every person is a part of the Song, because the matter in your body is resonating within the frequency range of your universe. And as long as the universes stay separate and distinct, there's no problem. The thing that keeps them apart is called The Weave. Have you ever heard of string theory?"

Cheeks packed with hash browns and orange juice, Thane shook his head. Brennan sighed. "Essentially it says the smallest fundamental particles, the things that atoms are made of, are tiny string-like objects which exist in the normal four dimensional space-time, as well as many others. The properties and interactions of these strings with each other are based on their vibrations. So the most fundamental particles that make up everything are minuscule interconnected strings. These invisible strings all vibrate together to make a weave that encircles and defines our world. Quite literally the fabric of reality. Are you following me so far?"

Chewing and swallowing the last of the hash browns, Thane wiped his hands on his pants and thought it over. "There are lots of universes that resonate differently, like they are each playing a different note. Everybody and everything is made of tiny strings that vibrate to make that note, like plucking a string on a bass. All those strings connect to make one universe and that connection is called the Weave and the resonant sound they make is called the Song."

Thane had the satisfaction of seeing Brennan's jaw actually drop. "Threads and holes, kid, how did you know that? Even I was getting bored listening to myself. It took me months to wrap my head around all this."

"My AP Music class. We've talked about resonance and vibration on and off for months." Thane shrugged, trying to be nonchalant about it but inwardly exulted at having impressed Brennan. "Music is just math you can hear. But everything you said so far is just science. I thought we were going to talk about magic."

"It's the same thing," Brennan said, trying to regain his composure. "Science and magic, at their core, just mean something you can explain with physical laws and something you can't. Science here is magic to the Shae, because they don't understand it or why it works, whereas their magic to them is mundane but to us is inexplicable." Thane yawned. "Now I'm boring you?"

"No, just didn't get much sleep," Thane said, yawning again. "So where does Sanctum come into this?"

"That's where the magic comes in," Brennan said, modulating his voice to sound deeper and more mysterious. Thane rolled his eyes. "In a universe beyond our stars in a time we don't understand, a group of thaumaturgists set out to control the Song. They-"

"A group of what?" Thane interrupted.

"Thaumaturgists. Magicians. This group had studied the singing of space and time for longer than we can know, and found a loophole. They set out to create a golem that could pass through the weaves-"

"Create what?"

Brennan pressed his lips together. "A golem. A construct. An imitation person made from other elements like clay or rock or fire or whatever you can manipulate that can move around and follow your directions."

"Like a robot," Thane suggested.

"Sure, like an advanced robot. They built one that could change the tension in every string that composed her, thereby changing her resonant frequency. She could phase through the Weave. She also had the ability to access the Song and increase the tension of those around her until their strings would snap, and they would die. The power of their Songs would flow through her to her masters. She had no thought or free will; she was a tool, nothing more. They called her The Sylph and she did their bidding until no life was left in their world but each other."

Thane's eyelids were heavy, and he yawned again, blinking. "That's stupid. What was the point?"

"Power. With every life she took their power grew. So as the evil often do, those who created The Sylph turned on each other. They each pulled The Sylph with opposing wills and directives, and for the first time many thoughts were in her head. The combination of the billions of lives that had passed through her and the conflicting desires filling her combined to wake her up and she became self aware."

"Sentient," Thane said, thinking of Remi. He leaned back, resting his head against the top of the seat.

"Sentient," Brennan agreed. "And she the anger, fear, and pain she had experienced with every soul drawn through her drove her mad. The Sylph killed every one of her former masters and then looked to the stars, and on her first day of life she was the last living thing on her world. She wept strange tears of Song, and where they fell the Weave tore open. The Sylph peered into the darkness and outside the one note of her world she could hear the harmonies of the multi-verse. And so she left, being careful to travel with the sound and never cross it, moving between the universes in small spaces between the singers of the Song. The Sylph-"

"How?" Thane asked, lifting his head up.

Brennan was irritated. "How what?"

"How did she move between the universes? How could there be space between the sound?"

Brennan was dumbfounded. "I don't know if anyone's ever thought to ask that," he admitted.

"Well, how do you know the story?"

"From Sanctum. It's part of the advanced reading material."

"How do they know?" Thane pressed.

"She told them. During the Guardian Wars when our two worlds were colliding and everything was snapping and shattering from the dissonance and no one knew how to fix it or what was happening. The Sylph showed up in the middle of the battle and stopped it cold, and told everyone the story so they would know it was her fault." Brennan scratched his chin, considering. "She still shows up sometimes, or so I'm told. I've personally never met Sylphie."

"Sylphie?"

"Yeah, apparently she thought being called The Sylph was insulting because it sounded like a thing instead of a person, so she changed it after they established the Guardians."

"What are the Guardians?"

Brennan placed his palm on Thane's forehead. "You, my young friend, have an intelligent and agile mind. Now shut up." He pushed Thane's head back down against the seat. "I will get to the Guardians and the Wars and the Shae and Sanctum but only if you let me talk without interrupting me." Fighting to stay awake, Thane yawned widely enough that his jaw popped. "Or you can go to sleep."

"No, keep going," Thane tried to sound alert.

"Whatever you say. So the Sylph traveled in the space between the universes and listened to the Song. She filled the emptiness of her soul with the Song shared by the living of every world. Until in one distant universe the wrong star exploded." Thane's head lolled forward, and he jerked it up. Brennan looked at him, seeming to expect an interruption, but Thane just waited. "The explosion blew a hole in the Weave of that universe and it started to fail, the vibrations slowing and its Song dying. But the dying Song was going to pass too close to our universe and the Sylph knew we would be destroyed too."

"What? How?" Thane's words were slurred, but he fought to stay awake.

"The sound waves would cancel each other out. So the Sylph made a choice and moved us." Brennan held up a hand to forestall any questions. "I'm not sure exactly how. Not much, but enough that the other universe died without taking us with it. The problem was now we were too close to the Shaerealm. We wouldn't collide because we were moving the same direction at about the same speed. It's more like we were tangled together, their Weave and ours, and in one place particularly the Weaves intertwined so much the two universes opened to each other."

Thane couldn't raise his eyelids, and the inside of his head felt sloshy. His body slumped, shoulders rolling back, and his head slid to rest wedged between the door and the back of his seat. He wasn't completely asleep, but was far enough that he couldn't open his eyes or move his head. In this semi-conscious state, Thane heard a rap rap rap and then a whirring sound, like an electric window.

"He's out," Brennan's voice floated through his remaining consciousness.

"Finally." LaPointe sounded annoyed. Thane could feel the car slowing and pulling off the road. "He should've been out within seconds of drinking all that."

"I told you, the kid is tough," Brennan said, and the car came to a stop.

A third voice spoke up. "What is the ending of the story?" the accent the man had reminded Thane of villains in old movies. He heard Brennan snort, and the speaker defended, "You have to finish the story, or it is like hanging up without saying goodbye. It is rude."

Brennan sighed, then spoke in a rush. "So The Sylph became Sylphie and we used science and magic to establish the guardian stones that balance the resonant realities of our worlds. We didn't have the power to close the tears, so Sanctum was established to coordinate the integration of the inhabitants of the two worlds, and to establish and enforce ground rules, and generally to oversee the stabilization of both universes so that they could coexist. Happy now?"

"I've heard it done better. Although I don't think I've ever heard anyone give a better summary of the Weave and the Song than that kid. He made you look like an idiot!" the third voice was blissful.

Thane was fighting for every moment, his mind slipping in and out of awareness. The door he was leaning on opened, and he slid bonelessly out into a pair of waiting arms. The third voice spoke right next to his ear, "I am still unclear." The arms lifted him out of the car and set him gently on the ground without any effort. "There are millions of people with some Shae blood in them.

Why is this one such a priority, especially now when there are so many other Weave events?" Russian. The accent the third man had was Russian.

"Because his teacher, who may be a hidden Shae or may be insane, has discovered his affinity and is using him as a weapon. Thankfully this town has never had a Shae event before so no one is asking uncomfortable questions, but Thane has to learn to control his talent before she makes him kill someone." Brennan answered briskly. Thane got the impression Brennan did not like explaining himself.

"I wish we could just use the doors," LaPointe said, her clipped tone disapproving.

"You know Sanctum is on lockdown. Doors are all inoperable," the third voice said. "Full security measures in effect. Besides, you've got me." The final vowel was stretched and deepened and Thane could feel the ground underneath him shake.

"Just take care of him, both of you. I've got to go-- Turcato'll make me write all the reports if I'm any later, and I'm the only one who knows anything about how to talk to an effreet." Brennan's voice drew further away, and Thane could hear a car door shut. The engine roared to life, and the sound of tires crunching on gravel told him the car was turning around and driving away.

Someone was moving him, wrapping straps under his arms and rolling him over to fasten more around his torso. "His harness is ready," LaPointe said. "Put him on." Thane's last bit of fleeting consciousness must really have been a dream, because he felt something like enormous tree trunks wrap around him and lift him off the ground towards the sky. He thought he heard LaPointe's voice again in his mind, "STOP EAVESDROPPING AND GO TO SLEEP." And one last mental sigh, "I HATE FLYING."

CHAPTER 11

The air felt wrong. The light pressing against his closed eyes was bright, and Thane threw his arm across them to block it. His mind was sluggish, slowly beginning to take input from his senses and trying to process it. His body was prone and whatever he was on wasn't very soft or yielding. The tongue in his mouth was swollen and dry, and his stomach felt as though he hadn't eaten in a long time. Thane took in all of this information and allowed it to roll around in his mind without making sense of it. With effort, he opened his eyes.

The ceiling above him was white. He was lying on his back on a cot, rough blankets underneath him and a pillow pushed off to one side. He wore the same clothes, stiff with sweat and streaked with dirt. Thane pushed himself up to a sitting position and held onto the edge of the cot with both hands while his head stopped swimming. There was a second cot pushed against the wall opposite him, the blankets neatly tucked and folded and the pillow crisp and white on one end. Gingerly, he moved his head so he could look around the rest of the room.

There was an open door and a hallway to his left, and to his right there was a nightstand next to each cot. A window was open in the wall between the two beds and opposite the door. Through it Thane could see a bright blue sky. Hot and sticky air came in through that open window, but cooler air flowed from the hallway. He liked the cool air. Thane stood up and leaned against the cot to balance himself, and standing did a lot to clear his head. He walked to the window.

He'd wanted to close it, but the view outside caught his attention. Wet air pressed into his cheeks, and palm trees stood tall in the space between square stucco buildings. High overhead, an exotic red bird flew in lazy circles. Thane had never been anywhere outside Payson, where the air was always dry and it snowed from October to late March every year. Here tropical flowers bloomed in profusion, bright reds, pinks, oranges and yellows adorning the constant flow of green vegetation. It was hot. Thane tugged the black hoodie over his head, struggling a little with the stiff material. He managed to get it off and dropped it on the messy cot he thought of as his.

His battle with the sweater seemed to have drawn the eye of the bird, and it circled closer to Thane's window. Something about it was... off. Having no experience with tropical birds and little with birds in general, Thane couldn't quite pinpoint what about this particular animal was bothering him. It was flying closer, and Thane leaned out the window to get a better look at it.

It was moving faster now, the open-winged gliding from before being replaced with rapid wing beats. The four legs were tucked up close so they wouldn't interfere with its flight. The wings... Thane blinked. Four legs? Did birds have four legs? That couldn't be right. He looked up again to try and figure out what he'd mistaken for a second set of legs, but the bright red creature was only a few feet away now and Thane got one, good clear look at it the moment before it smacked him full in the face and wrapped its arms and legs around his head, digging in with sharp claws.

"Hyu are perfekt!" the creature said in a surprisingly deep loud voice. It had a body the size and proportions of an organ grinder's monkey, with large leathery bat-like wings that it kept extended. It pulled back so that it could look Thane directly in the face. The creature's head looked like an extremely old, wrinkly, bald man with vertically slit yellow and black eyes, and when it smiled it revealed four rows of bright white pointed teeth. "Is hyu a present? Did I order hyu on the internets?"

Thane screamed, as shrill and as high as any scream Lanie could have done. He started skipping and flailing around the small room, banging into cots and nightstands and waving his arms back and forth, both trying to get the thing off his head and being too afraid to actually touch it. "Get off get off get off get off," he yelled, wincing and yelping when one of his arms brushed against a leathery wing.

It seemed thrilled by his response, and began to climb all over his head, muttering. "Yes, yes, the dimensions hyu have are perfekt!" A long, scaly red tail wrapped around Thane's throat, tightening and loosening. Thane felt small pricks all over his scalp as the thing skittered around his head using sharp black talons to hold on. "But the shape! Is it exact?" The tail released Thane's neck and wrapped across his forehead instead, surrounding his skull and squeezing.

Thane screeched again, buffeting the creature with his forearms. Sharp pains stabbed his ears as it grabbed them both with black claws and bent upside down over his forehead to look him in the eye, vertical yellow slits widening. "Presents don't fight back! Hyu is doing it wrong!" and grinned, flicking out a forked tongue and whipping the end of Thane's nose with it.

"AAAAAAaaaaahhhhhhhh!" Thane yelled again, holding onto his nose and trying to rapidly back away. But since the old man devil red monkey was sitting on his head, it just came with him. He banged into the cot behind him and nearly fell, then climbed on top of it and tried to jump out the window. The window being too small, Thane merely succeeded in knocking down both nightstands and bruising his ribs, the red monkey devil man laughing joyously and continuing to climb all over and around him like a lizard on a sugar rush.

"There you are." The voice came from the doorway and Thane spun to see who it was, but the thing on his head crawled across his face and hissed.

"No, this is mine! Hyu can't take it!"

"I don't want it." It was definitely a woman speaking, but the way the words were pronounced made Thane think her lips didn't move quite the same way his did. This observation was suddenly vitally important. The scaled red tail slipped back around his neck and Thane redoubled his flailing, bouncing into walls. "Look at it, it can't even walk."

"It is perfekt and it is mine!" the thing insisted, tightening both claws and tail to counteract Thane's increasing desperation.

"Andrus wants you, Jaeger. Playtime is over."

"Aye need two more measurements," the red monkey replied.

"Now," the unseen female switched from patient to angry with nothing in between. Thane felt a whoosh of air as something shot towards him. He ducked to avoid it and saw a black streak pass him. The black motion flew towards him from another side and he jumped away, the cot getting tangled in his legs and making him almost fall. The thing she'd called Jaeger was still gripping his head, laughing maniacally. There was a low growl and something slammed into his shoulders, knocking him backwards onto the once clean cot. Jaeger moved to the top of his head, and Thane was suddenly face to face with a jungle panther.

"Stop. Moving. Human." It enunciated every word, punctuating with growls. Thane felt half extended claws pushing against the cloth covering his shoulders and froze.

The she-panther waited one heartbeat to ensure Thane wasn't going to flail any more, and released him, using her claws to extricate the demon monkey from his hair. From his vantage point, Thane got a very close and thorough look at her paws and her face. Paws wasn't the right term- she had opposable thumbs, like humans and primates, and her face was rounder and slightly flatter than a normal feline's. The most notable difference was her eyes. Her pupils were round and black, and whereas Thane thought most panthers had amber or yellow eyes, her eyes were a deep green with brown and gold flecks.

She finished removing the creature from his head and tucked it under one arm. "But Paka," it whined, "Aye was nearly done. One or two more measurements to be sure! It is mathematical perfektion!" Ignoring the monkey devil's complaining, she straightened on two hind legs and stalked to the door, tail lashing, every moment both efficient and graceful. The panther left without glancing back, ignoring the young human on the bed.

Lying on the cot, Thane stared at the ceiling. He didn't feel traumatized, he felt... unhinged. Nothing in his experience or knowledge suggested that what he'd just gone through could possibly be real.

"Aren't you up yet?" Thane sprang back, crouching in the corner on top of the cot and staring at the doorway. Standing there was a skinny young man about Thane's own age, maybe a little older, with dark brown hair. "I know the dose was a little much, but they said you were supposed to be tough. You look like you're going to pee your pants. You forget your teddy bear?"

"Are you going to fly into my face or grab my head or knock me down?" Thane asked.

"Not how I do things. Are you going to get up or what?" he answered. After a moment, Thane responded by getting off the cot and standing on the floor in a crouch, hands extended in front of him just in case. The young man watching him snorted. "I'm supposed to show you around." With that, he turned and walked away.

Thane stayed where he was. Was he supposed to follow? The brown-haired boy stuck his head back into the doorway. "Are you coming?"

"Yeah," Thane answered, hurrying to the door. The other boy was already several steps down the hall, and Thane broke into a run to catch up.

"These are the student dorms," his guide was already talking. Thane hoped he hadn't missed anything important. "Buildings eight and nine hold all the classes for everyone eighteen and under, if you haven't already graduated." He seemed smug about that, but kept talking. "You have to be sixteen to be admitted into Sanctum, unless there are remarkable circumstances. Only twice in the history of the school has a student been accepted younger than sixteen, and both of those students ended up being assigned to Omega Team."

"What's Omega Team?" Thane asked, looking around, but the other boy wasn't waiting for or listening to him, and Thane had to move fast to catch up again.

"Everybody's at lunch now, otherwise this building would be pretty full. No classes on Sundays, but the seniors have training exercises just like the teams. Training buildings are twelve through eighteen, but those are off limits to students. Student training missions are kept to building eleven, but you have to have a pass code and an instructor permission card to enter." There were two sets of glass double doors ahead, and Thane and his guide emerged into the warm sunshine.

Sidewalks crisscrossed ahead of them, leading to other identical brick and stucco buildings that sprang up at irregular intervals. The feeling of the place was similar to a college campus Thane had once been to on a school field trip, but it also made him think of the Kendall Air Force base. He could see groups of people gathered here and there, some eating lunch outdoors with friends, some in combat gear walking purposefully from one building to another.

A group of five teenagers, boys and girls, came walking down the sidewalk towards Thane and his guide. As they drew closer he noticed subtle irregularities, and some not so subtle. A short, quick boy with elongated ears was joking and laughing with an abnormally tall, thick-shouldered boy with a sloping forehead and protruding jaw. A girl with bright blue hair was texting and walking just above the ground, while the last boy and girl were flirting, she resting a three fingered hand on his chest while laughing. The boy Thane immediately resented, as his improbable good looks and athletic build marked him as someone Ms. Rasmussen would have as one of her pets.

As the group of teens passed them, the pretty boy sneered. "What's this, Twitch? Demoted to babysitter?" The other three laughed, while the giant looked puzzled. Thane's companion tensed, but then relaxed.

"Correllan, the test results are back from mid-terms. You're going to have to repeat Axial Era history, again. What's this, third time?"

Correllan's forehead wrinkled and he snarled, "You can't know that, the scores don't post until tomorrow."

Thane's companion stared him down, not bothering to respond. Already bored, the small boy darted on past them into the dorms and the hulk lumbered after. The blue haired girl hadn't stopped texting to look up, but Thane noticed that when she passed his guide her eyes flicked up to his and she smiled slightly. Correllan and his girl had little choice but to continue on with their friends, and the glass doors banged shut behind them.

"Your name is Twitch?" asked Thane.

The other boy shrugged. "Sure. It's the only thing anyone around here calls me, and it's been going on too long to change."

"How long have you been here?" Thane said. His companion started walking again.

"I'm seventeen. I've been here five years, four months, one week and six days," Twitch responded. Thane stopped, mouth agape and staring at the other boy's back getting further away. "I was twelve when I started at Sanctum." There was a small pause, then he added, "Okay, technically twelve years and ten months, so closer to thirteen. Happy?"

"But you said you had to be sixteen," Thane protested.

Twitch shrugged again without looking back. "I also said that twice students were admitted younger than that because of extenuating circumstances. I was one. Iselle was the other. Come on, I don't have all day to babysit."

Thane jogged up next to Twitch again, re-evaluating his first impression. Twitch was taller and thinner than Thane with pale skin and almost no muscle definition. And yet this seventeen year old boy had been admitted to a clandestine organization dedicated to rescuing and preserving two worlds when he was only twelve. There wasn't anything visibly different about Twitch, no horns or wings or slitted eyes, but Thane knew that didn't mean Twitch wasn't Shae.

"So what are you?" Thane tried to sound a little bored, like asking someone else what species they were was a normal part of his everyday life. Twitch didn't respond, so Thane elaborated, wanting to seem informed and confident. "Are you shadow, shade, or fae?"

Twitch snorted. "Don't ever ask anyone that unless you're trying to get killed. A shade won't care, but shadow or fae will be offended enough to gut you without hesitation. Shadow will enjoy it; fae will assume that you're shadow trying to trick them. Either way, there's a sixty six percent chance that the creature you're asking will kill you." He paused, eyes watching the empty grass to his left, then laughed. "Good thing he's only here for a week."

Thane looked at the grass, but there wasn't anyone else around. "Um, yeah, good thing. So since you didn't just try to kill me, you're a shade?"

Twitch snickered. "No, I'm human. Songless. I was a product of some of those extraordinary circumstances. You're a charger, right?" Thane gave him a blank look. "You have an affinity for positively and negatively charged particles, and you can push them in one direction or another, right?"

"I guess," Thane said.

They had reached another building by this point, which had a huge number 7 above the glass double doors. Twitch opened a door and walked inside quickly, and Thane, who was twisting his head all around trying to take in everything, ran into the closing door with his face. "Ow."

Twitch didn't notice, as he had already continued talking and moved rapidly down the hallway. "I have an affinity for technology, a purely human thing. The Shae don't understand computers or cell phones or pretty much anything with a battery, but I understand them without having to really think about it. My father was at a loss for what to do with me, and he had a unique arrangement with Sanctum at the time. So he bargained to have me admitted here and become their problem. It was a solution that turned out to be mutually beneficial."

"So you're on Omega Team?" Thane asked, remembering what Twitch had said initially about the two exceptions to admissions.

"Yes. This is building seven where all the students have their physical education classes taught by faculty members or military adjutants who share similar abilities or affinities. Gym class here is a lot more exciting than your typical high school. The pool is downstairs," he indicated a set of double doors with the word "Stairs" painted on the wall above them, "weight lifting is the entire first floor, the second floor is a track, and the third floor has specially designed rooms based on needs. Magic study and spell casting is building nineteen," Twitch pointed out a window on his right, "about half a mile that way. The distance from the rest of campus is deliberate."

Twitch kept a rapid, constant pace, and Thane alternated between looking around and trying to catch up. "But what is Omega Team?"

There was another pause, and a snort. "I can't tell him that," Twitch said, again speaking slightly off to his left, and then addressed Thane again. "Once you graduate and have a strong level of control over your specific talent, you're given the option to sign on as a member of the SMG within Sanctum or make a life for yourself out in the world. Most grads choose the second option, wanting more control and choice than being a merc would give them. But those who choose the SMG go through another two years of training before they're assigned to a team. Every team has a letter designation based on the Earth Greek Alphabet, starting with Alpha. Those with the best marks and highest rankings go there. Then Beta, Gamma, Delta, Epsilon, and so forth. Omega is the last one."

"So people assigned to the Omega Team were the lowest graduating members of their class?" Thane guessed. This time Twitch really did laugh, a loud guffaw.

"No." His head turned slightly left again, and he chuckled. "Yeah, I'd want to see his face after I told him that too," he said. "Every team has a specific skill set. Alphas are generally the smartest and the strongest. Beta Team is mostly reconnaissance, and they're specialists in stealth and recovery. Rho Team are all

155

techno-mages, experts in combining Shae magic with human technology. Tau Team guards tears in the Weave, while Omicron sweeps for new ones and Nu are the first response team whenever a new wave of Shae cross over, since they are authorities on the subtle vibrations of the Song."

They emerged again into the afternoon sunlight on the far side of building seven. The air conditioning of inside the building made the wet heat outside even more noticeable, and Thane wiped his forehead with his shoulder. "So what's Omega Team's specialty? I would've thought that you'd be assigned to Rho."

"Me too," Twitch admitted, and then turned his head slightly left again. "No, I'm not disappointed. This is better." He strode with long steps along the sidewalk, taking the first left turn between buildings. Movement in the sky made Thane flinch and duck, but it was just a small yellow bird, not the red devil called Jaeger. Twitch was nearing the smallest building Thane had seen so far, made of red brick and yellow stucco and only two stories. This time there was a single door made of steel instead of double glass ones, and Twitch had to enter a code and press his palm against a scanner before a click and a pop opened the door for him.

"This is building two." Twitch said, but did not elaborate. Thane stayed near him as the hallways were narrower and not well lit, and every door along the hallway had a card reader and scanner next to it. Halfway down, Twitch turned to face a heavy grey door and placed his right hand on the scanner. The blue light cast eerie patterns on Twitch's face. Instead of popping open, this door slid silently aside and Twitch entered the room beyond.

There were computers everywhere. Flat screen monitors larger than any TV Thane had ever seen lined the walls and formed a circle in the center of the open room. Keyboards, touch pads, mice, joysticks, and other things Thane couldn't identify filled the desks and tables under the monitors, but something was wrong. Only four of the thirty something computer stations were in use, and Twitch slid into a chair at one of the stations in the center circle. Thane saw him remove a small black earpiece from his left ear and replace it with a much larger one that also had a connecting eye piece that hovered about an inch in front of Twitch's left eye like half a pair of glasses.

Twitch's fingers blurred as he typed, entering in a complicated login code which he authenticated with a thumb print and possibly a retinal scan, Thane wasn't sure. Thane waited behind where Twitch sat typing in a language that used numbers and letters that Thane was familiar with but didn't make sense in that order. Thane's eyes wandered around the room, finally realizing what it was about the room that felt strange. Even with all the monitors and keyboards and other computer related equipment, there were no visible towers or cables anywhere.

"What?" Twitch said, his head tilting left and his fingers halting and hovering over the keys. "Still?" He swiveled around in his chair and stared up at Thane. "Why are you still here?"

Taken aback, Thane stammered, "You didn't tell me where else I was supposed to go."

"Building five," Twitch waved a hand as he turned back to his work. Thane cleared his throat and Twitch spun back. "What?"

"Where and what is building five?" Thane asked.

Twitch made an annoyed sound in his throat. "Building five is the cafeteria and mess hall. Turn right when you leave this room and go all the way to the end of the hallway. There will be a red door on your left with a push bar. Go out that door. Do not attempt to open any door that does not have a push bar. You'll be outside again. Go straight past building three and the landing area, keeping this building directly behind you. Once you pass the landing area--"

"How will I know--"

"It has signs. Do you read?" Twitch asked. Thane didn't bother to answer and Twitch went on. "After the landing area go right and building five will be the tall grey building in front of you. If you get lost, ask someone. Everyone knows you're new."

Twitch twisted back around and resumed his work before Thane could ask any more questions. Thane turned right once he'd left the computer room and went to the end of the hallway, careful to walk in the exact middle and therefore as far away from any of the other doors as possible. At the end of the hallway there were two red doors, one on the left and one on the right, and both had push bars. Panicked, Thane almost went back, but the door to the computer room had slid shut behind him and he doubted he could get it open again to ask Twitch for help.

Thane inhaled deeply and tried to think. Twitch had said the door on the left went outside. Thane held both his hands just over the push bar, held his breath, and ran. The bar went down, the door opened, and sunlight and humidity bathed his face as he burst out of building two. Two girls passing by jumped and the smaller one was so startled she squeaked, her tail sticking straight out behind her. Thane blushed, and they walked off, giggling. He overheard the tall one, who he noticed also had long pointed ears, whisper something about, "new kid," and his cheeks burned even more hotly as he stalked straight ahead.

He passed an enormous brick and stucco structure with a large number 3 and didn't bother to wonder what was in it. After a lifetime of perfecting his ability to blend in, to become so nondescript as to be invisible, that very normalcy made him stick out like a bonfire on a dark night here. He was frustrated and not a little freaked out, and now he was wandering around alone.

The landing area was obvious, a large cleared rectangle of pavement with painted lines. Helicopters were parked in a line on the side nearest building three, and long runways could be seen on the far end although Thane didn't see any airplanes. The side he walked along now was a carefully raked square of sand big enough for four houses. A line of trees marked the end of the landing area and Thane could see other buildings beyond, including the top of what must be the cafeteria.

A shadow passed overhead, and Thane cringed away. He looked up to see that same yellow bird, except what he'd interpreted as being small was instead far away. But it was getting closer, and bigger. Much bigger. He broke into a run, making for the trees ahead of him for cover. If whatever that was tried to land on his face it would crush him.

Again the shadow circled overhead, the beat of its wings creating the first cool breeze Thane had felt here. He heard people shouting behind him coupled with a large motor grinding and risked a glance over his shoulder.

The entire side of building three was opening. A vertical line split the structure down the center and was widening as the huge doors slid apart. People and things that were not people came out of the opening, shouting to be heard over the sound of the engine that powered the hangar doors. Behind them a variety of aircrafts could be seen.

All that Thane saw and processed in the second he looked back. The shadow was getting close, blocking out the afternoon sun almost completely. Thane reached the line of trees moments before a rush of wind engulfed him, and he blew along the ground like a piece of crumpled paper until his back slammed into a tree trunk.

He lay there facing the landing area with the wind knocked out of him and gasping for breath while his mind grappled with the scene before him. A metallic gold dragon settled onto the ground, four legs digging into the sand and wings that seemed to span the sky finishing a final backstroke. The behemoth shook its wedge shaped head as the people and not-people that had come out of building three swarmed around it. Thane blinked spots from his vision and realized they were a ground crew, undoing straps and unloading cargo from the dragon's back and belly. Once all the boxes and crates had been removed from the semi-protection of the golden underside the dragon settled down into the sand.

Thane shook his head and rubbed his eyes. This couldn't be happening. Sure, he'd been filled with electricity twice and discharged it into someone else. Fine, maybe he'd met a Sang Evarish and the Beer Fairy, but they'd both been more unusual than anything else. This was... bigger. Truly something fantastic, and something that could not be explained away by a skin condition or food poisoning. It was a good thing Thane had the wind knocked out of him because otherwise he would be hyperventilating. His breath came in strange small gasps and wheezes as he tried to make his lungs work again, his heart pounding and adrenaline flooding his system.

The gold dragon turned his head towards where Thane hid underneath the trailing boughs of the trees. It spoke, a growling, rumbling, deafening sound, but in no language Thane recognized. One of the men in the ground crew answered, shouting back so his words would reach dragon ears, and the sound of his voice carried to where Thane was as well.

"Don't know. Some newb. Hold still," floated on the wind, and the dragon made a guttural roaring sound. Through the petrifying fear, Thane thought it was laughing at him.

His pride rescued him. Managing to take a real breath, Thane righted himself against the trunk. He stood on shaky legs, and although adrenaline pulsed in his veins and his survival instinct screamed, he turned his back on the golden dinosauric creature and walked toward building five.

But he couldn't make himself leave the cover of the trees. The sound of draconic laughter filled the air behind him again. Thane had made it perhaps four trees down the line towards building five when the branches crackled. There was a whoosh, and immediately in front of him the dragon's face appeared, crunching through the low hanging boughs.

It was so sudden and unexpected that Thane couldn't check himself in time and crashed into the golden snout, bouncing off and landing in the dirt on his backside. He was bathed in the warm air of the dragon's breath as it chuckled, and the enormous head turned so one golden eye stared down at him. "If I had decided to eat you," the dragon spoke, the human words sounding strange and hollow resonating out of the enormous chest, "it would've happened the first time, before you even noticed I existed." The dragon's snout parted, revealing two rows of carnivorous sharp fangs, each longer than Thane's arm.

Thane did not pass out. He wanted to, but the instinct to survive kept him conscious and embarrassment kept him from screaming like a tiny girl again. The dragon dipped his head once in an approximation of a nod and withdrew, to shouts of "Gideon! Oi, get back here!"

The branches, crushed and mangled as they were, rustled and crackled back into place with the scaled head's retraction. The ground trembled a little as Thane watched the leviathan crossing the landing area towards the open side of building three, the enormity of the beast incomprehensible even though it was right in front of him.

Again, Thane used the tree trunk behind him to push himself to his feet and waited for his legs to stop trembling. He was grateful for the shelter of the trees so no one could see him while he collected himself. It took a few minutes, but eventually his breathing slowed and his heartbeat returned to normal. And it helped that the doors of building three closed with a resounding boom, hiding the gold dragon from view.

Thane brushed dirt from his pants and combed his hair with his fingers, getting the leaves and twigs out the best he could. He rubbed his hands on the front of his jeans and stepped out onto the sidewalk, trying to act like nothing weird was happening. "Besides," he told himself, "after chest bumping a dragon in the nose, I'm ready for anything."

For a moment, he thought he heard the dragon laughing again. But he didn't look back. His stomach was growling, and the cafeteria was in the building ahead of him.

CHAPTER 12

Lunch in the cafeteria was loud. The dense concrete walls of the immense mess hall caused sounds to echo in endless reverberation; the catcalls and raucous laughter of the soldiers and support staff, playful banter, angry growls, and overwhelming mutter of conversation filled the air. Thane's eyes were just as accosted as his ears. Visually the assembled lunch crowds were just as overpowering as the cacophony of noise.

Creatures of nightmares and visions wandered the open hall, sat at tables, even served the food. Ogres and trolls, their long arms gesturing and swinging, walked or talked with or saluted haflings, dwarves, and creatures Thane couldn't even identify. In one far corner there was a giant straight out of a bedtime story he remembered reading to Lanie, complete with a club that he swung and gestured with while holding an animated conversation with something that looked like a half man, half horse. Thane knew there was a word for such a thing, but his mind was too busy drowning in the deluge of the bizarre to remember what it was.

Humans were the dominant species by number, but often with some extra touch: horns, claws, snakes for hair, scales instead of skin jumped out to his gaze like characters in a surrealist painting. Thane thought the artist had rather overstated his theme. But even though the characters were unlike anything he'd ever experienced, the scene going on around him was comfortingly familiar.

He was in a crowded lunch room filled with groups of people to which he did not belong. No one was interested in talking to him or even acknowledging him, and his place in the social ladder was firmly at the bottom. That was exactly where he had maneuvered himself to be while at Payson High so as not to draw attention from any who might put him down to elevate themselves, and it was where he wanted to be more than ever right now. Quietly and without making eye contact, he stood at the end of the lunch line and waited without comment while those in front chatted and eventually collected their food.

His brilliant plan had a flaw. As he neared the front of the line, Thane noticed that each person or creature would fill their plate and walk between a set of guards. These great hulking beasts would run a scanner across the tray of food and then across the bearer's wrist. The scanner would beep and the creature would pass on to go and eat. Thane stepped out of line and turned back towards the tables.

Twitch had said something about there being no classes on Sundays, which meant that Thane had been unconscious for nearly twenty-four hours. The last time Thane had eaten was breakfast yesterday, and that had been drugged. But no matter how hungry he was it didn't seem worth risking the ire of the trollish lunch ladies who guarded the food.

There were two tables in the very back that were empty, and they were pushed further apart from all the other tables in the cafeteria. A bubble of empty space surrounded them as if even though they were empty, these creatures of legend and fable wanted to keep their distance from whatever would sit there. It seemed like the perfect place to Thane since assuredly whoever would sit there would have eaten already and left.

He made his way carefully through the horde, sliding sideways and keeping his eyes down, plotting his course based upon which groups had the loudest speakers or made the largest gestures and avoiding them in favor of passing by quieter or more subdued ones. It worked just as well here as it would have in the high school. No one bothered him because he didn't look worth bothering. Even in his own mind, Thane repeated, "I'm not here, don't see me, I'm not here," over and over. It was the work of only a few minutes before he reached the abandoned tables and slid onto a bench.

This wasn't so bad. His stomach was growling and he was starving in an abnormally large cafeteria full of people and other things eating, but even this wasn't an unusual experience. There had been times during every school year that his parents had neglected to give him lunch money either because they forgot or as a punishment for something he'd done wrong. Those times he'd skipped the lunch room all together, or if he'd been really desperate, he'd volunteered to help the lunch ladies clean up and snuck food off of returned trays. It amazed him how much the other students threw away.

Glancing over his shoulder at the trolls serving the food, Thane thought they probably wouldn't be very welcoming to an offer of help. So he'd tough it out. So what? The only problem he couldn't figure out was what to do when the bell rang, so to speak. When they stopped serving lunch and cleared everyone out, where was he supposed to go? He could probably find his way back to the student dorms, but even then he had no idea which room he'd come out of and he couldn't just open every door and look for his hoodie.

The raucous conversations suddenly quieted. The overall noise didn't cease but the volume decreased significantly, especially near the empty tables where Thane sat. He tensed, his survival instincts saying he should run. The idea that something big enough and dangerous enough to quiet this particular room was coming his way made him momentarily glad he hadn't eaten anything. Was it the dragon? Could the dragon even fit in here?

"Hyu go splat better than any fat man aye haf ever seen!" The red old man monkey, Jaeger, flew overhead a group of people walking towards where Thane sat. The sound of its voice caused panic in Thane, and his eyes darted around for a place to hide. The only thing that presented itself was the table and he dove underneath it. The group that Jaeger entered with came directly to the tables and sat down. He was suddenly surrounded by the knees, legs, and feet of individuals he desperately wanted to avoid. Thane wished there was a door in the floor that would take him back to the desert. He missed the viper.

Voices above him spoke, giving him some impression of the person attached to each pair of legs. One was obvious, black fur showing underneath knee length brown leather pants. The black panther woman that Jaeger had called Paka was sitting on Thane's right by his shoulders. Her lower paws were bare, and she seemed irritated by something as her claws kept extending and retracting as she flexed her feet. Thane adjusted as slowly and quietly as possible so his shoulder was out of reach of those two inch long blades.

Thane recognized the careful enunciation of Paka's voice when she spoke. "You had no idea I was behind you, Turcato, so don't pretend that you didn't wet yourself when the effreet attacked. Bleck," she made a spit hissing sound, "I hate getting slime in my mouth."

Someone down by Thane's ankles responded. "Of course I knew you were there, cat. How else would I have known to duck?" The human male voice sounded tired and annoyed; this was apparently the continuation of a long argument.

"You didn't duck, you dropped like a stone," a lilting woman's voice drifted musically through the air, starting above and to the left of Thane's hips. Those legs were pale, muscular, and shapely, and visible from the knee down because of twin slits in the dark green skirt she wore. "That shadow filth would've taken your head off if Paka hadn't intervened."

More voices drew near, and the people around the table shifted to make room for the latecomers. They must have brought the food, because Thane could hear the sound of clanking trays and shuffling plates, and for several minutes the only conversation was about distribution of sandwiches, pizza, pasta, chips, sodas, and a litany of other things that made Thane's mouth water and his stomach grumble.

"Fat man is hungry!" Jaeger crowed. The man by his ankles shifted in his seat.

"I am not fat, it's all muscle," the man responded.

"Fat man has extra rumbles, aye heard them," Jaeger insisted.

Thane froze. "I'm not here, there's no one here," he thought, repeating the litany.

"Whatever, you insane rat bird," the man said, and Thane could hear spoons and forks scraping against plates and the sound of chewing. He started breathing again. The three people who joined the others all sat beyond Thane's head. After a few minutes of chewing and eating, the flow of conversation picked up again.

"Has your eye returned to normal, Rip?" the woman with the musical voice asked, and the banter over the table quieted. Rip? The man with the demon inside who had torn Brennan's fingers into so many pieces that the medics couldn't find enough of them to put back together? Thane didn't just stop moving, he tried to stop existing. There was a deep throated grunt from somewhere above him that he was too terrified to pinpoint, and the conversation resumed.

It took Thane several minutes to resume normal vital functions like a heartbeat and blinking his eyes, so he missed some conversation on the other side of the table top. The woman with the lilting voice was speaking with Paka, the feline's deep and purring alto making a fascinating counterpoint to the golden soprano. The complimentary tones they spoke in comforted Thane as he started to relax, until the context of their conversation sunk into his consciousness.

"I dislike evisceration, it is unnecessarily messy. I prefer merely halting the function of a vital organ, a well placed projectile through the eye, severing the brainstem, things of that nature," the woman spoke.

Again, Thane was grateful his stomach was empty. Who were these people, and what would they do if they found him? He needed a way out, and he needed one now. There was a small gap ahead and slightly to his left where the last two people had sat down. Thane wiggled his body like a worm, trying to push himself forward without allowing any part of his body to deviate to the right or left. Maybe if he broke out from under the table and hit the ground running he could disappear into the crowd before the blood thirsty demon infected friends of the red devil old man monkey could catch him.

He was almost there. The break between the chairs was just ahead of him, and he readied himself in a crouch. Mentally taking a deep breath, he counted, "Three, two, one--"

"Has anyone seen Twitch?" The man in the chair to his left spoke.

"He's supposed to be babysitting your pet charger. Andrus pulled him from the effreet assault after the stunt he pulled with the car speakers and that internet video with the cats." the man at the far end of the table, one with the middle eastern accent, was speaking when Thane popped up between the chairs.

"Brennan?" Thane said, inches away from the red haired man's face.

"Aayee!" Brennan yelled, falling off the chair and landing on the floor. Paka hissed and jumped on the table. Jaeger flipped backwards in the air, ramming into a man's face. A beautiful woman with an angular face and pointed, elongated ears dropped her fork onto her lap and stained the front of her tunic. An olive-skinned man at the end of the table rose to his feet and drew a gun in the same motion, and a girl that Thane thought he'd seen before didn't seem to react at all, continuing to eat. The sullen man's hand flashed out and grabbed Jaeger around the throat and threw him across the room without effort and without changing expression.

"Turcato, put it away, this is the kid," Brennan said from the floor. Thane was holding statue still, hands in plain view and looking slightly down and away from the man holding the weapon pointed at him. Turcato lowered and holstered the weapon so quickly that Thane didn't quite see the movement; the gun was pointed at him with a threat and a promise, and then it was put away and inert. "Thane, what in all the worlds were you doing under the table? And where is Twitch? He was supposed to show you around and then meet us here with you."

Sheepish, Thane didn't want to admit he was hiding under the table because he heard Jaeger coming. So he skipped the first question in favor of the second. "Twitch showed me around and sent me here. He's in building two in the computer room."

"Of course he is," Brennan put his face in his palm for a moment, then looked back at Thane. "Did you get any lunch? No," he didn't wait for Thane to answer, "you don't have any way to get past the staff. Twitch was supposed to feed you, too. I'll go and get you some lunch, you can wait here and I'll be right back."

"That's okay, I'll go with you," Thane said quickly. Brennan looked at him, eyebrow raised. Thane made a slight, pleading gesture with one low hand.

"I will go," said girl at the other end of the table. She spoke with a soft French accent that only barely changed the way her words sounded. Brennan looked at Turcato, and Turcato nodded to her. She rose, lithe and smooth, and walked towards the dwindling food line. Watching her walk away, Thane remembered where he had seen her.

"She was with you when you took me into the bookstore, wasn't she?" he said to Brennan.

"Yeah, that's Iselle. She's very useful." Brennan said. Hearing her name triggered a memory for Thane of something Twitch had said, adding it to a conversation with Brennan in the back of the Leaf and Dagger.

"That's Iselle, Rip is here, Twitch is supposed to be with you... is this Omega Team?" Thane asked. Turcato blinked and looked back from Thane to Brennan.

"You told him about Omega Team? That's privileged information, Tayler. You can't be bragging to every civilian contact you make about the SMG. What else did you tell him?" Turcato's voice was harsh and angry, and he remained standing.

"I wasn't bragging, Turcato, I was drugged." Brennan's response was cold.

Paka sprang down off the table. "Your debriefing report did not mention you being drugged. Have you been hiding anything else from us, luck man?"

"Because you always include everything in your reports to Andrus and the Council, little slave pet," the woman with pointed ears interjected. Paka hissed at her, claws extended, and the woman rose to her feet. "Here, kitty, kitty," she crooned.

Paka growled and sprang, but her trajectory was interrupted by Jaeger's return. "It is hyu! My present!" he cackled, his beeline flight at Thane knocking Paka off her attack. The cat woman used her tail to slap the red monkey in the face as he flew past, causing him to yowl in pain. But it didn't stop him from latching onto Thane's face again. "Aye only haf two or three more measurements, but hyu are perfect! Aye thought aye would haf to build another hat, but hyu are perfect!"

Jaeger swarmed around his face and his head, chittering with excitement, while between the red arms, legs, wings, and tail, Thane caught glimpses of the cat and the elf circling dangerously, Brennan and Turcato shouting at each other from opposite ends of the table, and Rip breathing heavily and holding his head in his hands. Thane forgot to care about the devil monkey grabbing his hair and ears while staring at the face of a man who was quite literally struggling against an inner demon. His fingers were splayed out so Thane could see the moment when his closed eyes opened. They were black. Thane had never been particularly religious since his parents didn't ever take the time to bring them to church, but at that moment he closed his eyes and prayed for a miracle.

"You will all sit down and shut up now." The voice was so laden with authority and command that it cut through the cacophony like a bullet through paper and shut it down. Turcato and Brennan snapped their mouths shut and returned to their seats. Paka and the tall woman immediately detangled themselves, ignoring scratches and bruises and other inflicted wounds to sit back at the table. Rip placed his hands on either side of his plate, palms down, and blinked rapidly. The black substance that covered his eyes drained away. Jaeger clung more tightly to Thane for a moment, and then sighed and released him, springing from Thane's head and landing lightly on the back of Brennan's chair.

Jaeger left Thane facing the off white table where the combatants now sat expectantly. The individual they were all waiting on stood directly behind him. Thane could feel the hairs on the back of his neck prickling. As curious as he was to see who had the clout to have his orders obeyed instantly and without question by a group such as this, he was terrified to see what sort of monster had the power to be obeyed instantly and without question by a group such as this. The late afternoon sun shone down through the clear glass roof of the mess hall, and Thane was engulfed in the shadow of whatever was waiting behind him.

"Aren't you going to say hello, Thane? I thought we'd left on good terms," General Gage said. Thane spun around so quickly he lost his balance and grabbed onto Brennan's chair to steady himself, feeling his stomach unclench. General Gage's consistently calm and mild demeanor, the way he spoke to Thane instead of at Thane, and his solid, anchoring presence as well as his connection to Remi made Thane feel like he had an ally, and a formidable one.

"General Gage," Thane said, stepping forward and shaking the hand of the sturdiest and substantial person he knew. "It's good to see you sir. How's--"

"Your family's fine, son," the general cut in. Gage squeezed his hand slightly and gave him a significant look. He didn't want Thane talking about Remi. Thane could understand that, he wouldn't want any of these people knowing where he kept the things he cared about either. Gage released Thane's hand and rested his palm on the boy's shoulder, deftly coming to stand next to him while turning Thane around to face the Omega Team.

There was a long silence while Gage did not yell, or even glare. Out of the corner of his eye Thane watched as the general made eye contact with each individual, holding their gaze until they looked away. When and how each team member broke the eye contact was vastly different.

"General sir," Iselle said, her quiet voice downplaying her accent even more as she came to stand just to the right and behind Thane. She was holding a tray piled with every kind of food the cafeteria offered, slices of pepperoni pizza, cheeseburgers, and a myriad of other inviting and delicious scents massaging Thane's nose. His stomach growled loudly, and Paka growled back at it. The tension of the moment snapped as Brennan and Turcato both laughed and the graceful woman poked the panther.

"I don't think he was talking to you," she said.

Paka bared her teeth in an approximation of a smile. "Too bad, that was the closest any of you have come to saying something intelligible."

The banter and chatter resumed more naturally. General Gage steered Thane to the second table, the one that remained empty. Iselle followed and Thane kept glancing back at her, curious. She wasn't large or imposing, and there was nothing visibly different about her, no horns, wings, pointy ears, fur, tail, scales, or any of the thirty or forty other variations on standard human that Thane had seen in the last three hours.

She placed the tray down on the table. "I am going to stay the same no matter how long you stare at me," she said. Thane started and heat rose in his cheeks.

Gage spoke. "What was so urgent that you left your team, Ms. de Lasser?"

Iselle de Lasser stood in a manner that suggested standing at attention without actually doing so. "The boy was starving, general."

"Someone else could have fed him. Young Mr. O'Malley was assigned to do that very thing. You should know better by now than to leave them after an encounter like the one they had this morning. They nearly fell apart," Gage said. Thane was having a difficult time processing the conversation. Iselle's head hung down slightly, but Remi's father didn't rant or raise his voice, did not insult or belittle. He was honestly asking for an explanation and making sure she was aware of the consequences. Hearing an adult talk like that was like passing through a door and seeing a whole different world. Which he had done twice in the last week.

"The boy was starving and Brennan offered to go get him food, but the boy was loathe to allow Brennan to leave and we were unsure what the troglodytarum would do if someone tried to pass without food and without an access code." Iselle spoke quietly and with careful enunciation. So careful that Thane was positive she'd been teased about her accent, and teased harshly. He knew what it felt like to be so beaten down that diminishing yourself became a part of your personality. He might have even liked her if she hadn't kept calling him "the boy." And troglody-somethings? What did that mean?

Gage cleared his throat. "I see that the situation was more difficult than your team was prepared to handle. In the future, send someone else. They need you." He stopped speaking and waited for her to look up at him. "We all need you." The corners of her mouth lifted marginally, and Thane wished fervently he had been the one to earn that praise and make that smile.

"May I bring you some lunch, sir?" she asked.

"No, thank you. Go and finish yours, and remember you have a second debriefing before the Council this afternoon. Do what you can to help your team be ready." He said this to her as though it held greater significance than the words alone would imply.

She dipped her head and went back to sit with her group, sliding into her place among them seamlessly. Thane watched her, interested and confused by their interaction and by what her purpose in Sanctum could possibly be. What talent could she have that Gage valued so highly?

"Are you going to eat?" Remi's father interrupted Thane's preoccupation. Gage was already sitting and indicating the empty chair place to him where Iselle had placed the food. Haughty and defensive as she may have been, she was excellent at choosing lunch.

Thane picked up a slice of pizza and began eating before sitting down. It was barely warm now, the grease on the cheese congealing and the crust going hard, and it was delicious. Thane ate the entire triangle in four bites and moved on to the cheeseburger. The bun, lettuce, tomato, burger, and cheese were all the same temperature, but it was juicy and dripped with ketchup and a little mustard. Normal conversation was in full swing at the table next to him, everyone finishing the last of their meals with full bellies and healing wounds.

"Hey!" Turcato shouted as Jaeger snatched his pudding and flew away.

"Fat man does not need pudding," Jaeger crowed.

"I am not fat!" bellowed Turcato as he lunged for the small flying devil, and the rest of the table laughed. Iselle gave a small smile at Turcato's fruitless lunging and swinging, but did not look directly at anyone sitting near her.

"What is that?" Thane asked General Gage, pointing to the other table.

Gage looked at where Thane was pointing, and then back. "What, specifically?"

Valid question. "The red monkey flying devil thing? The thing they call," Thane tried his best to say it, "Yay-grrr?"

Thane was relieved to see a smile spread across Gage's face. "Jaeger is an imp. They're like small flying demons, but they are constrained to one physical form."

"It's a demon? So it's evil, um, shadow?"

"No, imps are shade. They are chaotic by nature, and fascinated by shiny things and by technology. Out of all the Shae the imps are the best at adapting to science, and none more than that one." Thane listened, remembering Jaeger's reaction to Gage's stare. The imp had met the man's eyes, then looked down, locked eyes, looked up with the vertical black pupils expanding and contracting, locked eyes, and looked down again and closed his eyes. Watching the exchange had been hard to follow, it had happened so fast that Thane's eyes were dry afterwards as he hadn't wanted to blink.

"Give me my pudding back, you winged rat," Turcato stated flatly, loud enough that the few other remaining mess hall patrons turned to stare. Jaeger chittered and swooped down to a nearby table and rose back into the air, gripping a pilfered salt shaker and fork.

"What about the cat?" Thane asked, wanting to take advantage of Gage's talkative mood.

"Usiku Paka. Sanctum discovered her fighting as a guerrilla soldier in the Congo. When we tried to recruit her we found out that she was a slave and the only way to get her out was to purchase her. We asked them what her name was and they said slaves don't have names; they just called her black cat." Gage was staring into the distance, lost in the memory. "As the entire exchange was in Swahili, they said she was usiku paka. We tried to discover her name once we got her back, but she refused to tell us. Paka was the only thing she would respond to, so that's what stuck. Felidae are surprisingly stubborn."

When Gage had engaged Paka after the argument, the panther had bowed her head humbly, but her green eyes stayed locked on his, burning with defiance and pride. The human and feline held each other's gaze for two full heartbeats before Paka chose to let her eyes fall, acknowledging Gage as the leader. During those heartbeats Thane had surreptitiously searched for a place to hide. "Felidae?" He asked around a mouthful of fries and ketchup.

"Cat people. There are at least three breeds that we know of; Leonae, Pantera, and Feronin. They are very similar and very different. Paka is a Pantera, and also chaotic. But less so than Jaeger," Gage amended.

Mouth too full to get any sound out, Thane nodded emphatically. Remi's dad chuckled looking at Thane's stuffed cheeks.

"Fat man wants pudding!" Jaeger yelled, and he turned a crank on a conglomeration of spoons and forks and a knife and parts of the salt and pepper shakers. A blob of chocolate hurled through the air and exploded in Turcato's face. Turcato roared in shock and tried to wipe the sticky pudding from his eyes.

"How did you make it explode?" asked the woman with pointed ears, although Thane got the impression she didn't really care. Gage nodded towards her.

"Kari Loren is Eltucari, an Evarish," Gage continued. "Even though she's a Fae and therefore is incapable of taking an action that would be evil, she's arrogant and condescending. But she does her job well and since she was assigned to the team they haven't had to replace anyone else. That in itself is a minor miracle." That fit. When Kari had met Gage's eyes, it had only been for a moment before she dipped her chin once in a small show of respect and looked away. Not down, away.

"She looks like an el--" Thane began, but Gage cut him off.

"Don't say that where she can hear you," the general leaned in and whispered. "Calling an Evarish an elf is a mortal insult, and one that they won't forgive." He spoke so quietly that Thane had to strain to hear him at all.

Thane had managed to clear half the tray and was starting to chew. The pizza, burger, fries, onion rings, and hot dogs were settling comfortably in his stomach, and his abdomen no longer threatened to cave in on itself. He swallowed. "What about R--" Thane stopped himself, "Turcato? The guy on the end?" He wasn't sure he wanted to hear about Rip, or about the daemon Brennan mentioned haunted him from the inside.

"Turcato Peshawar is from northern Iran. His talents are less obvious than Paka or Jaeger. Around here, we call Turcato and those like him lashers." Gage tilted his head from side to side, the vertebrae in his neck popping audibly. "In the realms of Shae there are creatures that don't have physical bodies but exist as spirits."

"Like ghosts?" Thane said, then swallowed.

"Yes and no. These spirits are more tangible, more powerful, and more present than a standard ghost would be. Like the Felidae and like most of the species of Shae, the Ingenium are divided into three categories; the Djinn, the Garuda, and the Simurgh. And like other Shae, they are fae, shade, and shadow. The Ingenium themselves can't survive here in their pure form because our Song is too different. So those that found themselves trapped here, rather than slowly drifting apart, found human hosts to inhabit and used those physical bodies to protect and contain their own."

"They possessed people?" Thane asked, scraping the last of the ketchup off one of the plates with his finger and licking it.

"Quite the opposite. The Ingenium have will and desire, but they lack a distinctive personality. Inhabiting a human caused the spirit and the soul to mesh, allowing the Ingenium to continue and the human to have access to the Ingenium's ability. Their children were given the abilities of their parents, but to a lesser degree because the Ingenium don't alter a human's basic DNA the way having a baby with a Shae creature would. Instead a particle of the Ingenium itself is transferred along with the chromosome, and eventually the entire Ingenium will leave the host and transfer to the child. As most families have more than one child, the Ingenium spirit disperses equally between them and so lessens the power of each one. The Ingenium are empathic, telepathic, and telekinetic respectively, and they are the most prevalent of all the Shaeblooded."

"No way," Thane said.

"Way," said Gage. "Watch."

Turcato was standing now, watching Jaeger. "Fat man loves pudding but can't fly," Jaeger taunted. Turcato roared, and Thane saw a napkin rise from the floor behind Jaeger and whoosh towards the imp. Jaeger was focused on Turcato, so when the used cloth appeared over his eyes he was not prepared. With Jaeger distracted, a chair shot like a bullet from the floor, scooped up the imp from behind, and propelled it into Turcato's waiting hands.

"Hyu are my favorite fat man," Jaeger's sincerity and glee were obvious, and Turcato's face turned another shade of purple. He sputtered and tightened his grip, and Jaeger laughed harder.

"You... you..." suddenly Turcato reversed his grip so Jaeger was under his arm and gave the imp a solid noogie and burst out laughing. "How did you make it explode?"
Jaeger launched into an explanation so fast that his words were unintelligible, but his delight was unmistakable and the imp scrubbed at his fat man's face with the used napkin while he spoke.

"That's incredible," Thane said, "what about Brennan? What can he do?"

"Brennan will have to tell you his own story. Even I have a hard time believing that one, and I have been asked to not only believe in, but lead the unimaginable against the unforgivable." For a moment that passed by so quickly Thane wasn't sure it happened, Gage looked old and vulnerable. Then the indomitable general stood, and everyone at the other table quieted.

"Omega Team, you have a debriefing with the Guardian Council in twenty minutes. I suggest you compare reports and choose a speaker. Thane, we still have a few more questions that need to be answered about you before we can begin your training. Paka, please escort Mr. Whitaker to testing and processing room One Six. Then rejoin your team before the debriefing starts. I will not be present for it," Gage raised one eyebrow, "but I'm sure I will be hearing about it afterward. I hope that comes from you, and not as a summons from the Council. Again. Dismissed."

Gage patted Thane's shoulder and strode out of the mess hall, confident and purposeful. Brennan and his companions picked up their trays and walked to the trash cans near the doors, cleaning off the trash and placing the trays in a large bin. "Just like at school," Thane muttered to himself and followed their example. His sarcasm was forced and fell flat, even in his own ears. He was trying not to care that he was going to be alone with Paka, the strange alien cat person whose humanly developed curves and furry tail made him feel uncomfortable in different ways.

She waited for him at the door while the others left. Brennan hung back for a moment to cuff his shoulder and tell him not to worry, which only proved to Thane that there was something to worry about. "What's a troglody, um, trog--" Thane whispered.

"Troglodytarum," Brennan whispered back. "The Shae serving lunch. We rotate."

"The trolls?"

The corners of Brennan's mouth turned down. "You shouldn't use those storybook names. They're insulting and perpetuate unflattering stereotypes."

Paka shooed Brennan away. "I will watch after the cub, you go and help Iselle tend the others," the panther woman said, her teeth and tongue making light hissing noises every time she pronounced the "s" sound. Brennan smiled and walked away to catch up to where Iselle waited at the building's exit.

"Come, cub." Paka said, going in the opposite direction. Thane cast one longing glance after Brennan, told himself to man up, and followed her. He kept his chin up and shoulders squared and tried to imitate Gage's self-assured stride.

"You can stop being afraid of me," Paka said, not looking at him. "I have been ordered to walk with you, and that is all."

"I'm not afraid of you," Thane said, his brave assertion undercut by his voice breaking on the word "you." He cleared his throat, trying to play it off, and lifted his chin higher and made his back even more stiff and straight.

"Stop that before you hurt yourself," she snapped, turning to poke him in the chest. He flinched before she made contact, but her paws were velveted, claws safely away. "Fear is a smell, not a stance. Yours burns my nose. I am a slave and so will never disobey my master, and my orders are to deliver you to the testing facility." She spoke the last word slowly, her difficulties with human speech making it hard to pronounce. "But I have noticed humans do not believe a slave can have honor. You believe in deals, where we each must benefit. So let's make a deal, cub..." she eyed him expectantly, waiting.

"Um, Thane," he said.

"Thane. This is a good name. We will have a deal, Thane. I will not touch you with fang or claw, and you will not pull my tail nor never," her intelligent emerald eyes glittered, "ever call me kitty. If these things happen, our deal is over. Agreed?"

The conditions startled Thane enough that he almost laughed. Almost. Fortunately his sense of self preservation dominated his sense of humor. "Agreed," he said, holding out his hand.

She sniffed it. "Bleck. When did you last wash?" Thane flushed and Paka bore her teeth in her approximation of a smile. "Come. They will be waiting in room One Six, and the longer they wait the more difficult they become."

"Room sixteen?" Thane asked.

"No." Paka did not explain, but instead walked through the doors into the late afternoon sun. The moist air made Thane feel sticky all over and wearing the same clothes since Friday didn't help.

"After this, can I take a shower or something?" Thane asked.

"Thane cub, I did not mean to injure your pride," she sounded contrite. "I am sure that those with less advanced noses do not smell your stink at all."

"No, that wasn't-- I do stink?" self-conscious, Thane's cheeks flushed and he tried to slow down his pace so he would be further away from the cat woman and her advanced nose. She looked at him with lowered eyebrows and an annoyed curl to her mouth.

"Your face is really expressive," he blurted out, off balance and discomfited by her gaze and knowing that with her face towards him she could smell him even more powerfully. "Is that a Shae thing or because you're like a cat human or what?"

Her gold-flecked green eyes held him as she stared, silently. Thane wondered if calling her a cat human was the insult equivalent of kitty and was getting ready to run when she shook her head and resumed walking. "You are unfamiliar with felines."

"My dad thinks pets are a waste of money," Thane said.

She bristled at the word "pet." "Let us travel in silence, cub," she suggested.

"Okay."

"Starting now."

"Okay."

"If you respond again I will feed you to a troglodytarum."

Thane opened his mouth to agree, then snapped it shut as her statement penetrated his skull. Paka watched him with one raised eyebrow, then gave him a wicked smile and turned her back to him.

CHAPTER 13

Paka's fur shone outdoors, and following behind her, Thane noticed it wasn't uniformly black. It had intricate patterns of grey that he suspected were only visible in direct light. He focused on following those patterns with his eyes, and not thinking about whatever tests they were going to give him. He doubted it was with a number two pencil and a bubble sheet. A shadow crossed overhead.

"Argh!" he yelled and ducked.

"Where?" Paka whirled around, claws extended and crouched in front of him, ready to repel attackers. There were none. Thane's cheeks were red as he scanned the area and saw some kids playing frisbee on a field of grass. A plastic disc the size of a dinner plate. That's what was coming to get him. Thane stood sheepishly while Paka, who had better training, stayed in a defensive crouch and waited.

"It's nothing," Thane said. Paka remained in her crouch. "It, oh," Thane put his face in his palm and rushed through the rest. "It was the frisbee. It flew over my head and scared me." He peeked through his fingers and saw her straighten, natural weapons retracting back into her paw pads.

"Do you always spook so easily, Thane cub?" she asked.

He shrugged helplessly. "I thought it was Jaeger."

"Ah," Paka stretched the sound with a long exhalation. "Yes, Jaeger seems to have taken an unusual interest in you. He does not often notice anything that isn't made with gears and noise." Thane stood with his head hung down. How was he going to survive this if a toy tossed in the air could throw him off so much? He felt... not sick, really, more like brittle. Like if one more thing hit him he'd shatter.

A deep rumbling sound came from the panther's throat. It wasn't a growl; there was no anger in it. Thane looked up at her through his fingers. "Little one," she said, stepping close and nuzzling his shoulder. He froze. "Your situation itself is strange. Most with affinities or talents of Song have quiet awakenings, moments of happiness or peace in the company of pack family who is prepared. The magic of Song runs in bloodlines, so there are teachers to guide and protect. We hide our existence because the Guardian Council says it is best, and so those who know nothing of our world of two worlds never have need of knowing. And then sometimes there is one such as you."

Paka placed her velvet paw flat on his chest over his heart, still making the low thrumming sound. The vibrations from it passed along her arm and into Thane's chest, and he felt a flush of warmth and sympathy. His eyes were suddenly wet, and he resisted the urge to throw himself into the arms of this strange companion. What was wrong with him?

"I am one such as you," she said, keeping her hand on his chest. "I was torn from my family as a cub too young to hunt. My parents were killed and their pelts sold, and I was taken as a curiosity. I had many masters in my first years until I grew too large to be cute. Then I became a soldier, pressed into the service of a war lord. And now my masters are the Guardian Council of Sanctum and I am still a slave among the free. I had no pack to hunt with, no family to teach me the ways of my people. Those were taken and I cannot have them back."

Tears were streaming down his face, but tears were creating narrow trails of darker, wet fur on her cheeks too. "I can choose to belong. I run with a strange pack now. We have no blood or belief to bind us. We fight. But we choose to be our own pack, and that makes me strong. You must find such strength, find such a place to belong and choose to be a part of it. Without that, even if you find it, you will forever be afraid. With it, you will still be afraid, but can act for yourself despite it."

Thane looked down at paw she still held on his chest. "How do I find it? How do I know where I belong?"

She arched an eyebrow at him and halted her thrumming. "We begin by finding out what you can do and where you come from. Come, we must hurry now to make up for time spent weeping." She smiled to show she meant it kindly, and then turned and ran. Thane sprinted after her, struggling to keep up. Paka glanced at him once in surprise as he gasped for breath and kept his feet pounding alongside her.

They had left the other buildings behind them and Paka directed their impromptu race towards a structure that was different from the others. This one had a separate fence around it and was only one story tall, with towers built high at each corner. There was a smaller landing area on the south side of the fence with a tunnel that connected it to the building.

"What is that?" Thane panted, ignoring the stitch in his side.

"Building six," Paka replied, the "s" sound even more prevalent when she was breathing heavily. "It is for placement determination."

"It looks like a jail," Thane observed. Paka did not answer, but lengthened her stride and pulled ahead. Reveling in the freedom, Thane increased his stride also, and put on a burst of speed to get along side her again. The panther woman growled and dropped to all fours, shooting ahead so rapidly he could never hope to catch up. But he still sprinted all the way to where she was waiting at the door.

"You," he panted between each word, "cheated. If you'd stayed on two legs like I have to, I would've had you."

"Never," she said, her breathing almost back to normal already, "I was toying with you." Still she treated him with more deference than before. "This is where your testing shall be. I will take you to room One Six, but once we pass these outer doors you must not talk unless you are asked a question." She paused and he opened his mouth to say he understood, but remembering her threat earlier, closed his mouth and nodded instead.

Paka gave him her strange smile, and pushed open a heavy steel door. They took a few steps inside before the huge door closed behind them with a boom. There were no other people, and no sound at all. It was an uncomfortable sensation, like his ears were underwater, and the air was thicker and almost hard to walk through. They passed several rooms whose numbering system made no sense. Two Four was next to Five Five Nine, always with the words written out and not the numeral.

Thane and Paka were more than halfway down the length of the hall when the panther stopped. She turned to look at him and then indicated the plate next to a door. One Six. Paka turned the handle and pulled the door open, indicating Thane should enter. He looked through the doorway and back at Paka, who pointed him inside again more emphatically.

He went in. The room was mostly dark, with a pool of yellow light in the middle coming from a spotlight on the ceiling. He glanced at Paka again, who saluted a farewell gesture with her fist and then shut the door. Thane stared at the closed door, hating it for cutting him off from someone who was starting to feel maybe like a friend. And then he noticed there was no door handle on the inside.

Thane moved quickly around the room, always in the edges and darkness and staying as far as possible from the circle of light. The walls of the room had a strange texture that was unlike anything he'd seen or felt before. Foam pyramids as long as his forearm covered every inch of each of the four walls, with their square bases overlapping. From what he could see of the ceiling in the dimness, it was covered in those foam pyramids as well. The foam and the thick carpet on the floor were the same ivory color. There didn't seem to be anything in the room other than Thane and the pyramid walls and the light shining down.

If he hadn't been facing the door he wouldn't have seen her come in. The opening and closing of the door made no sound in this thick, heavy air. She again wore business-ready high heels and a knee length skirt with a matching suit jacket. Ms. LaPointe opened her mouth and spoke to him, but Thane only heard a muffled murmur.

A flash of irritation crossed her face, and she made a few notes on the clipboard she was holding. Thane watched as she touched her ear and spoke again, still without being about to hear any of the words. An overhead light, bright and large enough to illuminate the whole room, burst on and air rushed by his cheeks and ruffled his hair.

"Ah, that's better," LaPointe said. She made a few more notes on her clipboard and then glanced back at Thane. "Omega Team was called before the Guardian Council again and somehow whenever that happens I end up with more paperwork." She seemed truly put out, but Thane's survival instincts said that it wasn't him causing her the grief. He was just the one in the room with her. He decided to mitigate.

"I'm sorry if I'm a problem, ma'am," he said, standing up.

She waved him off. "Working in the soundproof chambers and dealing with the Omega Team give me individual headaches." Thane was distracted by her comment. This is what soundproofing looked like. Thane ran his fingers along the edge of the foam, wondering how it worked. Why would the room need to be soundproof? "Name?"

He was engrossed enough in his contemplation of the wall that he almost missed the question. "What?" He was confused. She knew who he was.

She sighed. "Please be thorough in answering and speak clearly. Full legal name, please."

"Thane Reed Whitaker."

"Current age."

"Fifteen." She waited expectantly. "Years old," he added.

She continued shooting questions at him, parents' names, his address, birth date, grade in school, all the while making notes on her clipboard. This was nothing like the test Thane had envisioned. This was more like the questionnaire the desk nurse had wanted him to fill out at the Emergency Room, and he had no idea how she was fitting all of this onto one paper.

"Age of awakening event."

"My what?" The question caught Thane off guard.

LaPointe peered at him over her glasses. "Your awakening event. The first time you accessed your Shae ability. How old were you?"

"Fifteen." She gave him a dirty look. "Years old."

"I don't have time for this," she grumbled, and then to Thane she said, "Look. You either have a Shae affinity or you don't. If you do, your awakening event happens usually in kindergarten, when you're old enough to start sorting out how you feel and who you are and what your relationship is to the world. If you're particularly powerful, it will happen sooner. If the blood is very weak or diluted, your awakening will be a year or two later. Maybe. Your awakening event does not happen when you're a teenager."

"Well mine did," Thane felt a hot flush at her doubt. He wouldn't lie. "I missed the bus so my dad was yelling at me and I went out in the rain and he followed and I was so sick and tired of him and he was going to hit Lanie and we got struck by lightning and I pushed it all into him." He had started out belligerent, frustration making him forget to be cautious. The truth came out, the one he'd walled away and hidden without even looking at it because it made him a monster. He'd pushed the lightening into his dad. Ms. Rasmussen had used him as a tool to kill a rival, but he'd tried to kill his own father.

LaPointe sniffed. "Fine. With electrical affinities it can be hard to determine. You could've been moving electrical charge your whole life and not noticed. I'll leave it blank for now. Do you have any special talents or skills that come naturally?"

"No," Thane said, trying to decide whether her complete lack of sympathy was offensive or reassuring. He had admitted something awful to her and she hadn't so much as blinked. But then, if she hadn't so much as blinked, how awful could it have been?

"All right, just a few more. Have you ever generated an electrical charge or merely conducted those already available?"

"The second one, I think."

"Good, those are easier to deal with. What is the greatest amount of voltage or current you have moved without assistance?"

"One hundred million," Thane answered, remembering what Dr. Bicknell said about the lighting.

LaPointe paused, lifting her pen off the clipboard. "What?"

"The lightning bolt. The doctor who examined us said it was probably about a hundred million volts," he explained. "He's a lightning specialist."

She was staring at him, lips pressed together. "That doesn't work with the rest of your answers. It's a fairly solid contradiction, actually. An affinity talent of your level should be able to move at maximum one million volts. And that would be fatal. The record for your affinity type is one point two million, and that was two working together before they burnt out. Don't," she stopped him before he could ask how they were recording or why they would run that test, "it was for a mission you are not cleared to hear about. But this is a problem. We'll have to do a physical scan to verify."

LaPointe stepped back. "Stand in the center of the yellow light," she said. Thane hesitated, uncomfortable, but then complied. She pressed her earpiece again and spoke into the tiny microphone. "Run physical analysis scan, room One Six, blue level." The overhead light turned off and Thane was left standing in the middle of the spotlight in an otherwise dark room.

"What--" Thane began, but LaPointe cut him off.

"No talking. Hold still."

The light surrounding Thane became brighter. He squinted, but the light coming through the cracks of his eyelids intensified enough to hurt, so he finally gave in and closed his eyes. The air around him grew warmer. Thane could feel tiny vibrations across his skin, like the memory of butterfly wings brushing him. Then the sensation stopped, the yellow light dimmed, and the bright white light filled the room again.

Before Thane could ask what had happened, a computerized female voice filled the room. "Physical Analysis Scan complete." Thane felt the hairs on the back of his neck prickle again. What would the scan have discovered? What sort of monster was he?

Ms. LaPointe was apparently as curious as he was, because she pressed her earpiece again and said, "Read results of analysis, clearance LaPointe level Bravo one two Alpha."

The two or three second pause the computer took in processing the request stretched in Thane's mind to be unending. What if he was shadow? That would explain why his father hated him and his mother couldn't stand him. They could sense the evil in his blood. Were they right?

The voice responded with mechanical intonation, the words disjointed, "Analysis result, human, male, adolescent."

"What?" LaPointe and Thane said together.

"I'm not Shae at all?" Thane asked, afraid to hope but doing it anyway.

"This isn't possible, there is a glitch here somewhere," LaPointe was flustered, and Thane could tell she was not a person used to being flustered. Her hand flashed up to her ear, and she spoke to the computer again.

"Run verbal diagnostic without scan, room One Six, blue level," she said, and the room was plunged into full darkness. Thane had expected a lighting change this time, but not like this.

The computer spoke into the darkness. "Please state your full legal name."

Thane groaned to himself, but responded. "Thane Reed Whitaker."

The computer took him through the entire series of questions LaPointe had asked with no variation. No variation in the questions, but the computer also did it without the condescension, pithy comments, and outright disbelief LaPointe had used, and Thane found the second time through to be much faster and less painful.

"Verbal diagnostic complete, room One Six, blue level," the computer stated, and the room filled with white light again.

Thane's head were starting to hurt. He rubbed his eyes with the heels of his hands and heard LaPointe speak again. "Results of verbal diagnostic, clearance LaPointe level Bravo one two Alpha."

This time even LaPointe tapped her heel and checked the time as they waited for the computer's response. Thane didn't know what to think. How could he be human after Ms. Rasmussen's test, after stopping Mr. Hoffman's heart, after the lightening? If he was only human, he could go home. He could tell Ms. Rasmussen that he had no Shae magic. Maybe they would even give him a certificate to show her or something. Then she would leave him alone. He could go back to class, back to the basement, and back to being invisible. He wasn't as excited by the prospect as he thought he should be. But the alternative was losing himself to Sanctum and the Shaerealm and whatever was hiding in him.

"Verbal diagnostic result, dragon-blood, blue, humanoid, male, adolescent."

"What?" LaPointe said, sounding puzzled. Thane was too shocked to make any sound at all. Dragon-blood? He shook his head, both trying to clear it and denying what he'd heard. That can't have been what the computer said.

"That can't be right," LaPointe echoed his thought. She reached for her earpiece again. "Computer, combine the two results from testing in room One Six into a single result file, Thane Whitaker."

"Unable to comply," the automated female voice responded.

"Explain."

"Results do not fit parameters for one individual." LaPointe gazed at Thane for a long moment after the computer had finished, but didn't say anything.

"What's going on?" Thane blurted. His calm facade had completely worn away, and now he was doing his best to not hyperventilate. That feeling of being about to shatter was back.

LaPointe met his gaze and responded coolly, "When I figure it out, I'll tell you." She made a long note on her clipboard and then pressed her thumb against it, and the paper made a soft beeping sound.

"But what are you testing for?" he demanded. "We know less now than we did when we started, and the computer doesn't think I can be one person!"

"We don't know what you are and we're trying to figure it out."

"How many options are there?" It was finally happening. After being awake in Sanctum for almost half of one day, Thane was going to have a nervous breakdown.

LaPointe stared at him calmly, waiting for his breathing to slow and seemingly uninterested in how his brain was about to explode. "If you're not going to read the initiate information packet we give you, why do you think I'd answer your questions?"

"I wasn't given any information packet. I don't know what I am, I don't know what you want from me, and I don't know why this is happening to me." Thane said, allowing his self pity to get the better of him. He sank down onto the floor, putting his head between his knees and trying to focus on not flying apart. Long breaths in and out felt like a miracle.

LaPointe was unimpressed. "Then there must be a reason, and on that reason I have not been briefed, and so I will leave it to those who have been given responsibility for you." She checked her watch again.

Thane wished from his position on the floor that she would be upset, just a little. Then he wouldn't have to do all the panicking on his own. Her being so calm made him think she wasn't grasping how serious this was, and the only way he could help was to be distressed enough for both of them. "I do understand the gravity of the situation., LaPointe said, "I am calm because I am always calm, as those I work with tend to be--" she searched for the right word, lifting her hand as if she could pluck it from the air. "Irrational."

Deliberately not raising his eyes from the floor, Thane tried to focus. "You've talked to me in my mind," he thought at her, and suddenly remembered those last fleeting moments of consciousness the morning they had drugged him. "Twice. Can you hear what I'm thinking?" That last thought had an edge of panic, and wonder.

"Yes," she said, "I can, but only if I'm focusing on you directly. It isn't obvious unless you're feeling something very strongly or you're trying to be heard. My telepathy is imperfect, but useful. Exhausting at times, but useful."

"You're an, um, Ingen-something?" Thane asked out loud, thinking back over the conversation he'd had with General Gage in the mess hall.

"Ingenium. Yes. My specific Shaeblood is Garuda, but several generations back, thankfully."

"Why thankfully?"

"The Garuda are shade, and so the impulse for chaos can be... difficult." Thane cataloged Ms. LaPointe's appearance; tight bun, power suit, business heels, and her always business-like manner. Maybe she wasn't cold and distant to the point of inaccessible. Maybe it was like Iselle's accent, or his existence. A personality flaw they were each trying to compensate for. The thought was a sobering one.

"Why is the room soundproof?" he asked, rising to his feet and trying to distract himself. His internal calm was returning with the knowledge that the unflappable Ms. LaPointe had a problem of her own to deal with.

She glanced up from her clipboard. "To mute the Song. Occasionally we have to test hostiles in order to properly maintain security around them. It is easier to do if they cannot access their Song and cause problems."

"Oh," Thane said, taken aback by the simplicity of her answer. She was making notes on her clipboard, and now that he was standing and the light was steady, he noticed with surprise that it wasn't a clipboard at all, but a touch screen with information that scrolled through and an open messaging window. The last message typed was "We have a problem in One Six. Get him here now."

The door to the room opened and General Gage entered. "Hello, Thane," he said, warmth in his voice and holding out his hand. "I understand you're giving our system some trouble."

"I don't mean to, sir," Thane said, shaking Gage's hand and the apprehension that gripped him faded in the general's solid and confident presence.

"I know you don't, son." Gage released Thane's hand and looked at his face, searchingly. "You look like a cornered bear." Internally, Thane sighed. His anxiety must not have disappeared as much as he thought. "I know you've had a lot thrown at you very fast. And thus far you've been given little to go on and less reason to trust. We have very strict rules about what and who we give information and access, but once we are able to determine where you fit in to our secret world, you will be told everything that it is safe for you to know."

Gage put his hand on Thane's shoulder, and the weight of it was warm and heavy. "Remi tells me you haven't had a lot in your life you can trust. You should know something about me; I have never broken my word. I cannot afford to do so. Lives depend on my team being able to trust what I say, and so I never speak any word that is not true. I promise you, Thane, that we are trying to help you and you can be safe here."

It couldn't be possible. There was no where that was safe, no one that was trustworthy, and no one that wouldn't hurt him eventually. Thane looked at these beliefs, written on the windows of his mind through which he saw the world. He thought about Grandpa Whitaker, and the stroke that had taken him away and punctured Thane's heart. He thought about Remi, his first real friend, and how she was guaranteed to move away. He looked at his window again, where was written that everyone will either hurt you or leave you, and they can hurt without leaving, but they cannot leave without hurting. That was so deeply ingrained in him that it felt etched on his soul. But Gage wouldn't lie.

Deep inside, Thane touched it again. Behind the walls of fear and loneliness that he held together through experience, that power moved toward him. Dark and primal, that strength offered him freedom, if he would only take it. There was so much of it that Thane knew if he released it, it would overpower him and he would be gone. But he knew it was there, that he hadn't imagined it, and that was enough.

He opened his eyes and met General Gage's gaze. "I am willing to try, sir," Thane said.

General Gage ruffled his hair, eroding Thane's pride in how manly his response had been. "Atta boy. So, Teresa, what is it that I had to come and see for myself?"

LaPointe pressed her earpiece, face impassive. "Computer, read back results of most recent physical analysis, room One Six level blue, authorization clearance LaPointe level Bravo one two Alpha."

The computerized female voice responded, "Analysis result, human, male, adolescent." General Gage raised both eyebrows and looked at LaPointe. She held up one finger, indicating she wasn't finished yet.

"Computer, read back results of most recent verbal diagnostic for room One Six, blue level, clearance LaPointe level Bravo one two Alpha."

There was a pause, and the automated voice spoke again. "Verbal diagnostic result, dragon-blood, blue, humanoid, male, adolescent."

LaPointe turned to the general, her expression one Thane had seen many times on the faces of his sisters and his mom. It meant "See? I told you," more politely than saying it out loud.

"Get Twitch in here." Gage ordered, and LaPointe typed into her touchpad again. Moments later a voice came through the speakers that was not automated, and certainly not female.

"Yes General Gage sir?" Twitch's voice came from several corners of the room, making it hard to know where to look. Four of the pyramids on the wall opposite the door lit up, and small white lines connected the pinnacle of each one to form a square. A picture emerged of Twitch sitting at his computer terminal in building two, grainy, but discernible.

"You were supposed to come here, Twitch. The computer in the testing facility is glitching," General Gage was stern and disapproving.

"It would take me eighteen and a half minutes to get there, and another four minutes to pass the security checkpoints. I can both see and hear you just as well as if I was there and I can access all the computer systems here. Besides General, you agreed I needed to be here once I showed you the situation I was tracking. What's wrong with the testing programs?"

Gage drew a deep breath and pinched the bridge of his nose. "We are running multiple tests in room One Six on the same individual and getting contradictory results. The computer won't even allow that the results are for the same person," he said without further comment about how Twitch chose to interpret his orders.

"What tests did you run?" Twitch sounded curious, and a little excited.

"A verbal diagnostic and a physical analysis scan, blue level," LaPointe answered after a look from Gage.

Twitch turned to his monitor and started typing. He twitched at irregular intervals, his head moving to the left and his eyes unfocusing as if he was listening to someone. He muttered, "I know," and "obviously," and "check that system," off and on for the next minute or so before looking back at the three people waiting. "The computer is fine. Must be user error."

Teresa harrumphed and Gage raised one eyebrow. Twitch swallowed. "I mean, the program is running perfectly. Have you run a phasic screening?" Twitch asked. Gage looked surprised. So did LaPointe. Twitch took their silence as a no. "I am initiating a phasic screen now. The computer will read the results without a prompt as soon as the test is finished. Thane, stay where you are. General, Teresa, take two steps away." Gage remained in place, glaring toward the screen. Twitch noticed, and twitched. "Please." Gage was impassive. "Sir," Twitch added, and Gage took two slow, deliberate steps sideways.

The bright light ceased, and again Thane was bathed in the yellow circle of the spotlight. The floor under Thane's feet changed, glowing red, and white lights shot up in a cylindrical shape around him. The crimson carpet slowly changed to yellow, the color moving in a line, and then the yellow was replaced by blue. Thane felt his skin tingling and his body hair standing on end all over. The butterfly tickling sensation of the last scan had been almost pleasant. This felt more like being pricked by tiny needles. The columns of white light began to pulse, and the blue coloring of the floor began to bleed up into them, like a drop of food coloring into clear water but upside down. Once the columns were more than half converted from white to blue, they began to tighten around him, drawing closer. Thane subconsciously held his breath as the columns of light penetrated his body, but they didn't feel like anything. The light coalesced along his center, one pillar of light exactly over his head which got brighter until Thane had to close his eyes. There was a flash bright enough to be seen through his eyelids, then darkness.

In the silence and darkness, Thane felt his heart beat twice before the automated female voice spoke into the dark. "Phasic ability level five detected. Phasic distortion currently at sixty-two point two five percent. Phasic saturation blood and bone. Phasic resonance blue-dragon, shifter level four. Compilation of three most recent tests now possible. Continue?"

No one responded. Thane opened his eyes but the room was still dark. The computer repeated, "Continue with merge for test subject results?"

Gage finally spoke. "Confirm merge. Return test room to status two." The lights came back on, and Thane could see the others again. They were all staring at him, Twitch O'Malley with wide eyes, Teresa LaPointe with narrowed ones, and General Gage's seemed... curious.

Teresa's voice exploded into the closed atmosphere of the room, angry and loud. "Level five? Blood and bone, with sixty shredding two percent? This can't be possible." She rounded on Twitch, shouting at the screen. "Is this some kind of joke? You rigged the tests to go from confusing to impossible? Well the joke is on you, techno-boy. I'll ban you from the nets. I'll revoke every computer privilege you have. I will have Gideon toss you out of Sanctum from the top of the security shield. I will--"

"LaPointe." Gage interrupted, his voice firm. Thane looked over his shoulder to where the woman in the business suit had been screaming at the image of Twitch. She wasn't yelling anymore. Instead her expression was steady, as was the hand she used to hold the gun pointed at Thane.

He'd never seen a real gun before, and this was the second one he'd seen today by looking down the barrel. "What--" he began, and she pulled the trigger. Almost at the same moment Thane's chest got pushed back hard enough to knock him to the ground. As he fell, a second impact punctured his thigh. His eyes stared up at the off-white pyramids covering the ceiling, trying to make sense of the last few seconds.

The only thing he came up with was that in a soundproof room, no one would hear if you screamed. Or if you got shot. Then Teresa LaPointe filled his remaining vision, standing above him and looking down. Still expressionless, she raised the gun again and squeezed the trigger. One more impact in the center of his throat. Then all was darkness.

CHAPTER 14

Thane was starting to hate being unconscious. This would have been the worst so far-- his whole body was stiff and ached like he'd been folded in half and shut in a trunk for several days-- but the discomfort and disorientation were lessened by how surprised and grateful he was to be waking up at all. He'd been shot, he remembered that. Shot three times, in fact.

With memory came awareness, and he began a catalog of pains. His chest was sore and breathing was difficult. Both of his sides were burning, and one had a sharp pain as well. An ankle throbbed and his right knee felt twisted. His neck was cramping and his head felt like someone inside it was hitting his brain with a hammer in a steady rhythm. A strange, constant low hum in the air drew his attention to how much his ear drums ached. The most pain came from his shoulders, both of which ached, burned, and were twisted uncomfortably behind him. Thane was pleased to note none of his toes hurt.

Focusing on his toes, Thane tried to relieve the suffering of his shoulders by moving them. Attempting this taught him two important things about his predicament. One, he was laying on his side a stone floor. Two, someone was nearby.

"Good, you're waking up." Gage's voice penetrated the veil of fog and agony hanging over Thane's mind. He tried to rub his eyes with his hand, but the dirt on them from the stone floor ground against his eyeballs.

"What..." he desperately fought to get his bearings, get his mind working again. Pushing with his feet, Thane tried to move in the direction Gage's voice had come from.

"Whoa there, son, don't go that way. Those bars are ionized. Anything that touches them will disintegrate," Gage warned, and Thane stopped moving towards him. Instead he froze, unsure if there was a safe way to go. He looked up through watery eyes, trying to make out his surroundings.

He was in a prison cell, two walls of stone and two of bars. General Gage sat outside the cell on a small wooden bench mounted to another stone wall. Thane wondered irrationally if they were in the dungeon of a castle, and then wondered if that was actually irrational. Still unable to make anything but small, weak sounds, Thane looked at the bars, then at the stone wall, and then at Gage.

Gage understood the question. "The wall is fine. The stone isn't active."

Thane crawled to the stone wall furthest from the general and used it to push himself upright. He slipped twice, bashing his foot against a loose floor stone. Now his toes hurt. His blurry vision could not focus on any one thing with certainty and his neck and throat felt as though they'd been chewed on, so speaking was impossibly painful. He turned his face in the direction he thought Gage's voice had come from and pushed out one small, wheezing syllable.

"Why?"

He heard the older man sigh. "I'm sorry, Thane. I had no way of knowing that your test results would be so... dramatic. It's protocol that whenever a Shae of half or greater arrives within our facility without a qualifying escort they are tranquilized and removed for evaluation." Gage sounded tired, and older than his years. "And it didn't help that you startled LaPointe so much. She has," there was a pause, "unusually strong feelings about dragons and the dragon-blooded. And with you being a blue, well, she overreacted."

"Not..." Thane tried to protest, but his vocal cords wouldn't function. Every word he tried to push through made his throat constrict, and his mouth wasn't producing enough saliva for him to swallow. Leaning his head back on the hard stone, he focused on pulling in and pushing out enough oxygen to sustain him.

There wasn't any other sound for what seemed to Thane like a very long time, and he wondered if Gage had left. But not very much; most of his thought was centered on the pain, and how to make it stop. Was he alone? "Help," he whispered, throat constricting again. Being still alive didn't seem like such a great thing anymore, and he found himself wishing he hadn't woken up.

"Help is coming," Gage said quietly. Thane heard a set of footsteps that started far away and were coming closer. His blurred and bleary vision was starting to clear as the tears leaking from his eyes removed the dirt and grime, and he could make out a second figure nearing where Gage sat. It looked human, but Thane couldn't be sure.

"Here they are, sir," Thane identified Twitch's voice, and the blurry shape was the right height for the computer genius. Twitch passed something to General Gage and made a movement approximating a salute. "You know this is against regulations."

"And you know she overreacted. Even with the resistance he showed to the tranquilizers during transport, one tranq dart would have been sufficient. Perhaps a second, if he started to regain consciousness before he was secure. She shot him three times, Mr. O'Malley. Three. We're lucky he woke up at all." Gage said. Twitch didn't respond. "You changed the count?"

"All the inventory records have been modified to match current inventory levels," Twitch said. There was a pause, and then he added a belated, "Sir."

"Thank you, Mr. O'Malley, you are dismissed." Gage stood and the blurry shape that was him moved closer to Thane's cell. The fuzzy humanoid that was Twitch didn't move. Gage spoke again. "I said you can leave, Twitch."

The blob on top of the fuzziness moved up and down, and the shape of Twitch grew smaller as he went back down the hallway. Gage's larger and progressively less blurry shape moved towards Thane and the bars that held him. Thane kept blinking, his vision clearing. When the general neared the bars, Thane could see him well enough to see the pity in his eyes-- and the gun in his hand.

"No," Thane wheezed, his words desperate and barely audible, "no more."

201

"I'm sorry, son," Gage said, leveling the weapon at him. "But we only have a week, and we can't waste any more of it." And he fired.

Thane and his consciousness were forcibly separated again. This time when he started to wake up, instead of allowing it to return gradually he grabbed it with both hands and yanked, unwilling to be caught half asleep and get shot or attacked in the face or taken away again. He jerked his eyes open and refused to allow them to close again, squinting as they adjusted to the light. Thane sprang to his feet.

Muscles and joints responded with agility. It wasn't until he was standing, ready to try and defend himself or dodge more bullets that he realized he wasn't in pain anymore. He recognized the feeling of strength and gnawing hunger that were the after effects of healing darts. That was what had been in the gun when General Gage shot him. Why hadn't he said so?

And where was he? Looking past the bars, Thane saw no one was outside the cell. He didn't see any cameras or other monitoring equipment, either, but he knew better than to think there wasn't any. Not knowing where they were just meant he didn't have anywhere to direct his ire, so instead he shouted down the hall.

"No more shooting me! I am done with guns and being shot. I am hungry and I am sick of being in here and if someone doesn't let me out in the next five seconds I swear I will blow something up!"

"Knows how tae throw a proper tantrum, disnae he?" Thane bristled at the condescension in that voice and turned to glare at the speaker. General Gage was entering the hallway through a door at the far end and he was followed by a man Thane immediately disliked. The man was three or four inches taller than General Gage with a strong square jaw and a carefully shaved head. He had those effortless good looks and lean muscular frame Thane associated with arrogance and vanity, and his thick accent managed to be both uneducated and pretentious.

"He's had an unexpectedly difficult day," Gage answered.

Thane gave a hard, short laugh. "Yeah, you could say that. You invited me here because you say you want to help me. So I come, and you drug me. Then your devil monkey attacks me, my guide ditches me, I almost get shot, I get locked in a soundproof room, you tell me I'm not human, I get shot, then when I wake up what happens? Oh yeah, you shoot me again! After," and Thane spat this last toward Gage, "promising me that I would be safe."

Gage and his companion had continued walking as Thane spoke, and so the general was within a few feet of Thane now. The young man tried not to notice or care about the worry lines in the other man's face or the tiredness in his eyes. Gage didn't try to refute the attack.

The other man's mouth twisted up in a gleeful half smile that went all the way to the slight crow's feet at his eyes. "Good with snark, too. I'm sure ye deserve every last bit, general. I've nae doubt this lad's ready tae go back tae wherever ye plucked him and forget ye all, except maybe to piss on yer grave someday. I'm looking forward tae that pleasure myself. Maybe we can carpool," he said to Thane with a wink.

"Yes, because learning to talk like a leprechaun would be so helpful," Thane bit back, angry at this stranger for belittling General Gage. What right did this entitled prick have to mouth off to Remi's dad?

"I'll learn ye some manners, boy, if ye hain't got the sense ye were born with--" the man began, his Scottish brogue thickening, but cut off when General Gage laid a hand on his arm.

Gage's expression didn't change, but the tension around his eyes softened as he looked at the boy. "This is Charlie, Thane," Gage introduced the other man before they could exchange any more insults. "Charlie is... difficult to explain. But he is the most qualified," Thane noticed as Gage paused slightly, "person we can access to help with your situation. Charlie, this is Thane."

The square-jawed and muscular man studied Thane with clear and intelligent blue eyes. "Disnae look like much, does he?"

Thane bristled, but Gage spoke before he could. "He's sixty-two percent phased, Charlie."

Charlie blinked. Thane felt a little smug at catching him off guard. "Is that so?" Charlie asked, flippant tone gone. Gage nodded and pulled out the touchpad, handing it to Charlie. The two very different men stood in silence while the newest read through the test results. He muttered under his breath, but Thane wasn't close enough to make out any words.

"Come up, lad," Charlie ordered without lifting his eyes from the pad. Thane remained motionless. Charlie looked up, annoyance crossing his face. "I need tae look at ye more canny and yer too far away. Get closer." Thane did not acknowledge that the other man had spoken but stood, resolute, against the stone wall at the back of the cell. "Thrawn like a donkey, isn't he?" Charlie commented to Gage.

"Another reason we thought of you," Gage said.

Charlie smirked. "Well, I cannae tell ye jack now. So either get the kid tae move, or I'm considering my debt discharged and I'll be daundering off." And he held the pad out for the general to take.

General Gage made no move towards it. "Thane, please come stand nearer to the bars. You may remain out of reach, but we do need Charlie to tell us what he can about you."

Both Thane and Charlie snorted, which made Charlie laugh loudly and made Thane even less inclined to obey. Charlie added, "And if it's being shot ye've so concerned yerself with, it disnae matter where in the cell you stand." He held out both hands away from his sides. "I dinnae hold with guns, but I'm like tae be the only one here who disnae."

Not allowing his face to reflect how fast his heart was beating and trying to keep his breathing steady, Thane took five deliberate steps in the direction of

Gage and Charlie. He hated Charlie's nonchalance and how dismissive he was of General Gage, how he could stand there, ready to walk away, as if none of this mattered. Focusing on his anger made it easier for Thane to hide his fear, and he glared up at Charlie and blamed everything that was going wrong on this conceited, self-satisfied tool.

Gage raised an eyebrow as Thane drew nearer. "Careful, he'll bite," quipped Charlie, "isnae good tae get yer fingers close."

Thane had the sudden and vicious desire to grab him by the front of his shirt and pull him into the humming bars so he could watch the contempt dissolve along with Charlie's face. The thought shocked him enough to make him gasp, and pull him out of his anger. It was an evil, violent thought, and Thane hated himself for it. What was happening to him? Was knowing he had evil Shae blood in him enough to make him evil? If so, he would never go home again. Not to Remi, not to Lanie. He would stay in this cell and beg to be shot.

Something of his thoughts must have been clear on his face, because Gage interrupted his desire for dramatic self sacrifice. "You're all right, Thane. I know it's hard to believe, but Charlie does have his uses. He'll be able to tell us more about where you've come from and which of your parents is the dragon, and he'll be able to help you learn to control your Song."

"Which of my parents is what?" Thane asked. He couldn't have heard that right.

"These things are genetic, son. One of your parents has dragon blood; one of them is a dragon. We need to know which one, because the names you've given us don't show up in our data bases. You can't imagine how upset Twitch is about that." Gage seemed amused by Twitch's discomfort.

Thane was too busy re-evaluating his entire life to share the general's humor. It was his father. Of course it was his father. That explained the rage and the violence, and his constant disappointment in Thane. Bert had expected to share this gift with his son, and instead Thane had never shown any talent or skill. Of course his father was frustrated and discouraged. And if the Shae blood made you violent that made his father's dragon blood only more convincing. It would also explain why Grandpa Whitaker, who must also be a dragon, was so convinced that Thane was special.

"It's my father," Thane said. "My father is the dragon."

"He's told you this?" Before Thane could answer, Gage was on his headset. "Get me Twitch. Robert Whitaker is a pseudonym. We need to figure out a list of possible alias and associations so we can trace--"

"Disnae make sense." Charlie had been silent through the exchange, studying Thane with penetrating blue eyes and humming quietly. Now he broke in, his tone certain. "This is one of mine, but at least four back. When I sing Giselle's Song, there's some resonance within. But the lad's all blue." Charlie and Gage shared a serious look, neither one afraid but with enough weight that Thane understood there was something to be afraid of. "How's yer mum cried?"

Thane glanced at General Gage, who said, "Your mother's name."

"Oh," Thane said. "Gwen Whitaker."

"Gwen? I dinnae ken a Gwen. He almost puts me in mind of..." Charlie trailed off and shook his head. "What's your mum's maiden name?"

"Go ahead, Thane," Gage prompted when Thane didn't answer.

"I don't know," Thane admitted. He'd never asked, and if he'd heard it anywhere he hadn't paid attention.

"Get him out of that box." Charlie demanded. Gage nodded. "We have a lot of work tae do with this one."

"So you're in?" Gage said the words lightly, but Thane recognized the tension around his eyes. Remi would do that too, when she was trying to joke about something she found very serious.

"I am. This one is at least partially my blood. And besides, ye dafties are all awful at dealing with dragons." Charlie gave Gage a wicked smile, which Gage obviously failed to appreciate.

The humming ceased and the bars retracted with a grinding noise. Thane started and shrank away, worried that it was another test. "This has been a rough day for you, son, and I'm sorry about that," Gage said. "You've been through a lot, more than any person should have to deal with. However, nothing, not being shot, drugged, or Jaeger's strange fascination with your head has been as bad as what I'm going to do to you next."

Thane tried to rub his suddenly sweaty palms on his pants without the men noticing. His heartbeat doubled in speed which such force that it hurt, and his mouth was so dry that he had to try twice to speak. "What," he cleared his throat and swallowed, "what's that?"

"I am assigning you to Charlie for training." Thane waited to hear the rest of the joke. There wasn't one.

"Wait, you're serious?" Thane said.

"As a streak o' lightning!" Charlie said cheerfully. "Dinnae worry, laddie, I'm not dancing for it either. Seeing as I do owe these scaffies a favor or two and you being a result of my loins a century or so back, I suppose I can be making the sacrifice. I'll need tae be assigned a food card and some guest quarters, preferably near the girls dorms?" and he elbowed the general suggestively.

Gage sighed, putting his face in his palm. "God save us all," he mumbled. Then more directly, "All that will be taken care of. In the meantime I suggest you get going. We do have to return him in one piece with enough training to not be a danger to himself or others for at least another year, and there's only a week to do it."

"Why a year?" Charlie asked.

"He's only fifteen. He can't be admitted to Sanctum until he's sixteen."

"When's yer birthday, lad?" Charlie asked.

"August seventeenth," Thane answered sullenly. He did not like being assigned to Charlie and was determined to let them both know.

They didn't seem to care. "It's a glaikit rule," Charlie argued. "The lad is sixty-two percent phased. Those are yer figures, not mine. Putting him back in the civilian word is suicide at best--"

"I don't think that's best," Thane interjected.

"And at worst it's a series of deaths and injuries by electrocution that gets smart people or important people curious." Charlie went on as if Thane hadn't spoken, "That's the sort of attention that wilnae be good for any of us. Yer Guardian Council is like a Scot's best grannie when it comes tae cleaning up messes."

Gage winced. It wasn't a large wince, but it was the first wince of any kind Thane had seen from the general. Apparently Scottish grannies were really awful about cleaning. Or about messes; Thane wasn't sure how the comment fit together. And although he would never admit how much the idea of permanently attending the Sanctum school terrified him, it did seem less dangerous than letting Ms. Rasmussen play with him whenever she wanted. He didn't like that she knew so much more about what was going on than he did.

"Regardless, we currently have six days for Thane to understand and control his abilities. And we have you. So we will work with what we have, and that will have to suffice for now." Gage said.

"Yer daft, I'm out," Charlie stated flatly. "You cannae put that kind of pressure on me nor on the lad, tae be learning sommat that takes a hatchling a good score to get right and giving us six peerie days. Then what? Ye'll be booting him back intae the world with just a prayer they'll be no need tae call the cleaners? Ye Sanctum puddocks have enough on me without me seeing the lad down the road just enough tae cut him bleeding afore ye throw him back in the shark tank." Charlie crossed his arms and stared, unblinking, into Gage's eyes. "Get one of yer Omega monkeys tae do it. I'll not."

A little hope had risen in Thane's chest when the bars had vanished. An idea, tickling the back of his mind, that there might really be a way out of this, that he could learn to control himself and not be at the mercy of others any longer. That maybe, if he got it no matter what, maybe his father would ruffle his hair and tell him he was special like Grandpa Whitaker had. A tiny hope that there was a place for him to belong, and a father who would finally choose him for a son. Now that it was there, Thane was desperate to hold onto it.

"I can do it," he said. Charlie snorted, and Thane felt a flash of heat in his chest and his hands clenched in fists. "Maybe you couldn't, but I can. Or are you scared to teach me? Scared that I'll be stronger than you? I am sixty-two percent phased," Thane repeated the phrase, not knowing what it meant but remembering everyone reacted to it.

"Ye aren't going tae be stronger than me, tadpole," Charlie's blue eyes glittered dangerously. "And it isn't myself I'm scared for. If ye had any sense ye'd run screaming from these Sanctum types and never stop. That's what I tried tae do, the first time they started nipping me."

Gage cleared his throat. "And instead, here you are, on the receiving end of several favors it is now in your power to repay." Charlie looked down at Gage sharply. He was only a little taller than the general, but at that moment he was using the height to as much advantage as he could squeeze out of it.

"That cannae be what it sounds like," Charlie's voice was cold.

"Omega Team has several intensive and vital mission trainings scheduled over the next few days and none of them can be spared. No other members of Sanctum have either the requisite experience or the familiarity with this specific talent to do what must be done. I have been authorized by a majority vote of the Guardian Council to offer you a deal," Gage said, "once. You accept full responsibility for the training and management for civilian Thane Whitaker, sixty-two percent Draconem Shade, for the next six days. In return for this service all debts and favors incurred by you will be canceled and considered paid in full."

Charlie sucked in a sharp breath between his teeth. "I want my record expunged. No more being tracked."

"I can't do that, but I can give you full immunity and we will redact everything from your file but vital statistics and census records." Gage managed to give the impression of standing impassively with his arms folded in a "take it or leave it" posture without actually moving at all.

"Done." Charlie held out a hand and General Gage took it. The two men, one dedicated to a cause greater than himself for the good of the many and one dedicated to himself for the good of the one, shook hands to seal his fate. At least for the next week. As Thane's parents had already signed his life away until Sunday he wasn't as impressed by their own self-importance.

"Yer mine now, laddie buck," Charlie said eagerly, rubbing his hands together. "Where should I take fresh meat tae start the pounding?"

Thane's stomach also had a question and asked it loudly, much to Thane's chagrin. The gnawing hunger had been growing steadily stronger and more insistent since he had woken the second time. Neither Gage nor Charlie chuckled, which went a long way in restoring his faith in General Gage and earning Charlie a little gratitude.

"The lad's right, I'm fair gutted myself," Charlie said. "Where's the mess? And are the Evarish still serving?" His leer was well perfected.

"No, I'm afraid that duty has been rotated. It is currently the responsibility of the Troglodytarum," Gage answered.

Charlie shuddered. "Bah. Trolls fash my appetite. Especially fae trolls- that's not natural."

Thane silently agreed. "The training facilities are in building eleven for students," Gage answered. "Pick one of those and I'll have food sent to you."

"Well and good enough." Charlie put one of his muscular and unbathed arms across Thane's shoulders. "Welcome tae the good fight then, lad! Ye can cry me Charlie and I'll cry ye tadpole, and we'll swim along."

Thane squirmed under Charlie's arm. General Gage chuckled. "It isn't all bad, Thane. Charlie's an oaf, but you need someone to think outside of the box. He's given lectures on dealing with the ancient shadow for our student classes, and was even a guest professor for a few weeks for our senior's philosophy course. If he had consented to be a part of Sanctum originally, he's old enough to have made it on the Guardian Council." Gage stretched his neck by tilting his head from side to side, popping the stiff vertebrae.

"I'm not sure if yer trying tae insult me or butter me up, Gage," Charlie said. "Now trot back to yer peely-waley Omega Team and let them play at their training games. The tadpole and I have a real road tae walk."

"Oh, after you," Gage said.

CHAPTER 15

"I'm doing this as a kindness, tadpole. That grants me some leniency. And ye ken the general- I am responsible for yer teaching. That means I got tae train ye as I see fit, wherever I see fit."

"I don't think this is what he meant." Thane glanced around, wiping his sweaty palms on his jeans.

Charlie had gone directly to building fifteen and was neither surprised nor deterred when the door outside was locked. He'd merely waited a moment until he spotted a small group of people heading into the building from a different direction, and walked to intercept them. Two members of the group were female, and it took less than a minute for Charlie to be chatting and laughing with them, one arm around each slender waist. The group leader entered a code onto a keypad next to the door and then placed his palm on a scanner. There was a flash of blue light and a small beep, then the door clicked open.

"Allow me, gents," Charlie said with a winning smile, and held the door open as the group entered. The group's leader scowled at him, but made no comment. Thane's new mentor motioned for him to follow them through, and closed the door behind himself. He gave the girls a jaunty wave and strode off purposefully in a different direction.

"Remember, ye belong wherever ye want tae be. They're the ones as need excuses," Charlie said, not looking back to see if Thane was following. He was. He had nowhere else to go.

They had climbed several levels of stairs and tried doors on every floor, some of which were open and Charlie dismissed and some locked or in use. When they reached the top there wasn't a hallway anymore, just one door at the end of the stairs. It opened easily when Charlie tried the knob. "Finally," he said, and strode inside.

Thane wondered what exactly his new mentor was planning. This wasn't a room so much as the entire highest floor of the building. The ceiling was so high and the walls so far away that it almost felt like being outside. It was largely empty, with only a few practice mats stacked against a wall and some exercise machines scattered throughout. Windows lined all four walls, and the early evening sun poured in the western side.

Charlie walked towards the center of the room, rubbing his hands and looking around. "Get on, tadpole, let's begin. I'm waiting for ye tae bring it."

Thane stood near the door. Charlie waited expectantly. Being watched was disconcerting, and Thane couldn't think of anything he could do that Charlie might be interested in seeing. So he stood there, silent, eyes down.

"Och." Charlie's eyes narrowed. "Right, then. Lad, the only thing ye have tae do is keep breathing till the sun goes down. That should tell me." Thane's jaw clenched and his body tensed, watching Charlie with lowered eyes.

The bald man circled slowly to the left, face and body relaxed. He ignored Thane, moving in a wide arc until he stood in front of the western facing windows. Blinded by the sunlight Thane couldn't see Charlie anymore. Strangely, he heard music coming out of the light, a wild, crackling song. Thane knew what the moment before being struck felt like, and threw himself to the right and landed behind the stack of practice mats. His dad being angry and throwing a punch was one thing; if Thane ducked or moved, his father would get more angry and that would only make the punishment worse when it finally arrived. Thane took the hit and waited.

Charlie wasn't his father so when the first blow landed, Thane wasn't there anymore. A blue and white ball of crackling energy shot through where Thane had been and sizzled when it hit the wall. Thane also knew from being stalked by Jeran and his friends that staying in the same place got you stuffed in your locker, so the moment he was out of sight behind the mats he was looking for the next place to go.

He still didn't know where Charlie was, but he knew he didn't have a lot of time to move. Thane crawled around the edge of the practice mats, so his back was pressing against the short end. If Charlie had moved away from the cover of the sunlight, Thane would be visible. If he moved the other way, Charlie would be able to see between the mats and the wall where Thane had been, but not see him now.

A quick glance around the room showed that Charlie was still somewhere on the western edge. Ahead of Thane was a small cluster of treadmills, ellipticals, and a bench press with weights. He leaned low to the ground and started to move towards them.

Behind him, the practice mats burst apart with a boom, one flying into Thane's back and propelling him forward. The smell of burnt plastic distracted Thane momentarily, but he used the mat as a shield and pressed forward until he was in the midst of the workout equipment. He'd moved far enough that he could see Charlie, standing with the sun streaming around him and casting a long misshapen shadow. He had a manic grin on his face, but the rest of him still stood relaxed, almost slouching.

"Not bad, tadpole." Charlie breathed in deeply through his nose. "But none too bright." Without moving his head, Charlie raised his hand and bolt of energy shot out towards Thane. It hit the treadmill and the machine whirred to life, the belt spinning and the display flashing. Thane backed away and tripped backwards over the bench press, falling onto his back as another sizzling bolt flew overhead and hit the weights.

The jolt of the electricity passing through the metal of the bench and into his leg pushed him back onto his feet. Thane ran, keeping his head low and hunched down, diving forward when he felt the hairs on his arms rise or when the music grew louder. He rolled, tucking his head to the side and hearing the lightning bolt hit just behind. Pulling on his momentum he was back on his feet and running full out around the edge of the room, heading for the next cover.

Stacks of chairs filled one far corner of the room, the kind that folded up. The kind that hung on rolling racks. Thane slammed into the back of the nearest one without stopping, his inertia enough to start the chairs moving forward but slowing his speed by half. A ball of blue energy hit a rack next to him, and another hit the one in front, but Thane was getting back up to speed. He used the rack as a barrier between himself and Charlie, pushing it faster. Pushing it into the sunlight between Charlie and the windows.

"That's the plan? Metal chairs?" Charlie taunted, sending more bolts into the rack that Thane was pushing. Thane ignored him, forcing himself up to full speed and angling slightly. Angling just enough so that when he let go, the several thousand pounds of chairs were hurtling directly at his brand new mentor.

Charlie laughed. "Tadpole, yer going tae need tae put yer feet on," and he stepped aside, allowing the chairs to roll past him. "I've spent centuries getting the better of every twalley who challenged me."

And Thane had spent a lifetime figuring out exactly where to hide so those who would hurt him couldn't find him. The heavy weight of the metal rack slowed and halted several yards further. Thane, standing on the metal bars and holding on to the hanging chairs on the side opposite Charlie, peered though the spaces and watched the older man staring into the slowly fading sun. Charlie had assumed that Thane was using his own trick of putting the sun at his back to prepare an attack, and that the chairs had been a first strike. Or that was what Thane was hoping. The chairs had actually been a way to flee and disorient, so Thane could hide again. He'd managed to push the rack of chairs near the wall again, and hoped that his heart wasn't pounding loudly enough for Charlie to hear.

"The sun will be gone in two minutes, boy." The older man stood, feet apart and hands spread wide. "I'll give ye one chance afore that. Take yer best shot." Charlie waited, facing where he thought Thane was hiding while Thane stared at his back. There was no way he'd fall into that trap. He'd seen it enough before to know that seemingly vulnerable stance was the most dangerous.

But he didn't know what he should do. He couldn't hide here much longer, and when the sun went down Charlie would know he wasn't using the sunlight as cover. Thane closed his eyes and tried to breathe slowly, in through his nose and out through his mouth to calm his racing heart. What next? Had he survived long enough yet?

"Boo." Thane's eye's popped open and saw Charlie's piercing blue ones staring back at him through the space in the chairs.

"Ee-yah!" Thane let go of the metal bars and fell backwards off the rack, landing on his backside on the wood floor. Charlie chuckled.

"Not bad for a tadpole, I'll admit. Ye actually made me lose track of ye twice. Full marks for scuttling and fleeing. But I didnae see any dragon in that." Charlie held out his hand to help Thane rise. Thane stood on his own, pretending not to notice the older man's outstretched fingers.

"I'm not a dragon," Thane said.

"Maybe not all, but more is than not. Ye dinnae look much of one, but for all their scavy rules, these Sanctum dobbers are rarely wrong." Without looking, Charlie grabbed one of the folding chairs from the rack behind him and flipped it open, spun it backwards, and sat down on it with his chin on the top of the backrest. "So there's more tae the tale than I've been told. I'm an old hat, but I'm not getting any dragon from ye at all. The infopad I read said ye had two affinity events. Tell me about them."

Thane did not feel inclined to be helpful. "My teacher zapped me with a cattle prod and I electrocuted my assistant principal through a metal doorknob, and my dad and I were outside in a rainstorm and got struck by lightning."

"Yeah, I kenned that from the report," Charlie said. "But reports are useful as the paper they're printed on. And they're all electronic. Ye tell me."

"I don't know what you want," Thane stated flatly. "I told you what happened."

"Why were ye outside?"

"I was tired of being inside."

"Why were ye tired of being inside?"

"I didn't want to talk to my dad anymore." The questions were making Thane remember the fight and his fear and that made him angry.

"Why dinnae ye want tae talk with yer pa?"

Thane didn't respond.

Charlie seemed to understand that Thane wasn't going to budge on this, and so switched topics. "All right, so what about this teacher? Got ye with a cattle prod- why?"

"Because Ms. Rasmussen is crazy," Thane said.

"Rasmussen?" Charlie cocked his head. "Leggy ginger?"

Surprised, Thane met Charlie's eyes. "Yeah. How did you know that?"

Instead, Charlie shook his head. "Och tadpole, ye sure know how tae make things interesting."

"But Brennan said Sanctum had no record of Ms. Rasmussen. How do you know her?"

"Sanctum isn't the whole of the Shae world, lad. Best get that through yer noggin now. Plenty of darklings flow through the crevices, and plenty more send messengers and agents. That's what makes the evil so enticing here-- it's flagging easy." Charlie rubbed a hand across his bare shaved head. "They cannae send ye back."

"Why not?" Thane wasn't sure how he felt about that. Sanctum was terrifying, but at least here he wasn't a danger to anyone else. But Remi and Lanie were at home...

"If Cressa is there, that means she was hunting. And if she was hunting and found ye, that means it won't be long afore he knows, too."

"Who?"

"Yer father." Charlie's mouth was set in a grim line.

Thane was confused. "My father already knows." He paused, considering. "Or he used to know. He doesn't remember me now, which is probably why he isn't disappointed in me anymore. But once I learn, maybe then he'll remember me and..." the teenage boy swallowed, unable to say the words "be proud of me" out loud. The idea seemed ludicrous, but no longer impossible. Saying it out loud might jinx it, and he wouldn't-- he couldn't-- risk that.

"Why'd ye claim that, lad?"

"It's got to be why he's always hated me. Because he's waited my whole life for me to show that I can be like him, but I never have been." Thane stared down at his hands, curling and uncurling his fists. He couldn't tell what Charlie thought because he refused to look at his new teacher. "But when the lightning stuck it burned out part of his memories, so he doesn't know me anymore, but after I learn how to be a... a dragon, like him, he'll remember but it won't matter because I can finally be who he's always wanted me to be."

"That man cannae be yer natural father," Charlie said. His voice sounded strange, like he was trying to be gentle but had forgotten exactly how. Thane's hands tightened in fists.

"Why not?" Thane's voice had no emotion, no inflection. He was too busy shutting down every feeling that was trying to burst through, shoving them back so they wouldn't overwhelm him.

"Ye said ye were both fashed by lightning and that it burned out part of his memory." Charlie waited for Thane's confirming nod. "Biologically speaking, yer father is a full blooded blue dragon. The man who was struck by lightning with ye has no blue in him or he would nae have been hurt. Therefore that man cannae be your biological father."

"He isn't my father?" the fists Thane clenched by his side were shaking, just a little. He was trying very hard to hold onto his calm, and it was trying very hard to shatter. "That can't be true." His fists shook harder. "He is my father, and he hates me because I can't be strong like him. I'm not a dragon like he is. That's why he hates me."

"Maybe it's because ye aren't his son," Charlie suggested softly.

"What would you know about it?" Thane whispered, digging his fingernails into his palms hard enough that a little trickle of blood seeped out. Thane ignored it. "You're supposed to be so good at this dragon stuff? Fine. Have fun with it. I don't have to listen to you. Hit me all you want. I'm leaving."

Thane turned his back on the man straddling the folding chair and walked towards the door. He thought he heard a sigh behind him, but kept walked. "Lad, get back here," Charlie said. Thane ignored him and kept going, the immensity of the room stretching out before him. "This isnae done for us." No response. Charlie's voice gained an edge. "Yer getting far left of yerself, boy."

The words barely penetrated the fog of anger and hurt and fear filling Thane's mind. From behind him, he heard the screech and squeal of protesting metal, and the mangled remains of a folding chair flew past his head and slammed into the door, imbedding itself into the wood. Thane stopped walking just as an enormous blue scaled tail lashed in front of him and hit the floor with a crack, sending pieces flying into the air.

"When I tell you to stay, little meat-sack, you stay," the low voice rumbled like thunder and Thane felt the vibrations in his ribcage. With his eyes he haltingly followed the tip of the tail back up to sharp-taloned paws, along the ridges of the back, past front legs and up the long neck to the wedge shaped metallic blue head. Eyes that moved between brightest sky and darkest midnight in hue watched him like a cobra staring down a little wounded bird. The jaws opened to reveal several rows of bright teeth and the serpent tongue flicked out again.

"You ask what I know about this dragon stuff?" The Scottish accent was gone, replaced by something older. "Know then, little hatchling, that I am one of the oldest, first sons of the dragon mother when sea and sky were learning their Song. When the Shae formed and the lands split, the dragons were the eldest. Of shadow, shade, and fae were we the first, and will be the last. And so never," the dinosauric head lowered and twisted until one bright and burning blue eye was level with Thane's face. The eye alone was larger than his head. "Never challenge my authority, for mine is the authority of the first. And you would hardly be enough to get stuck in my teeth."

Thane's chest was so tight that his lungs couldn't expand, and spots swam in his vision. The dragon shut his mouth with an ear-splitting snap, close enough that Thane could feel the whoosh of warm air against his face. It smelled foul, sulfur and burnt flesh and Thane gagged. His thoughts swam in circles, unable to reconcile the shiftless con man who had been sitting behind him with the scaly monstrosity that surrounded him.

"Are you ready to listen now?" the dragon rumbled.

"This can't be real," Thane mumbled, pressing the sides of his head with his hands and trying to hold his brain inside. The changing shades of blue in the dragon's eye still whirled, inches from his face. "Two objects cannot occupy the same space at the same time."

"Ha!" the dragon's bark of laughter exploded in Thane's eardrums, making his head hurt more. "But I am only one. This is the form of my hatching. But this," and the dragon paused as his head shrank, and the reptilian body that filled the room the size of two school gyms pulled back into itself. Floor boards bent and cracked as the tail retracted, dragging along them. Talons disappeared into shrinking limbs, and the sharp edges of scales blurred into the smoothness of skin. "This makes it easier tae go round the fences," Charlie concluded, brogue back.

The twisted chair fell to the floor with a loud clang as someone pulled open the door. Both Charlie and Thane's heads swiveled to look, breaking the tension between them. Teresa LaPointe stood in the doorway stiff-backed and stone faced. "You were instructed to use building eleven," she said. "I had to search for some time before locating you."

"Didnae ye ask the twitchy computer lad?" Charlie asked.

"After looking for a half hour, yes, I did resort to requesting that Mr. O'Malley locate you." Her glare gave Thane chills, but it seemed to roll off Charlie.

"Well then lassie, that's a fault of yer logic and not my location." Charlie smiled and winked at her. Teresa stiffened even more, her teeth clenching and eyes narrowing. "Have ye ever been told ye've got a face like a bulldog chewing a wasp?"

"I have been ordered to bring you dinner," animosity rolled from her and engulfed Thane as she bent down and picked up a tray that had been hidden by the door frame. "If you had been in building eleven as you were told, it would have been warm. It is likely inedible now."

"Busted down tae waitress?" the dragon shifter chuckled. "Ye must've really pissed off yer dear general."

She straightened, smoothing her skirt, and locked eyes with Thane. "I have also been ordered to apologize to you for using excessive force to subdue your potential threat earlier." Both her posture and her expression let Thane know that stating the order was the most she was willing to do.

If she had cried, or even appeared contrite, Thane would've forgiven her. Even awkward or uncomfortable would've gotten leniency. But arrogance and anger radiated from her, and he'd had enough of that for one day. He lifted his chin and met her gaze. "Noted," he replied, "I'll look forward to the apology."

LaPointe blinked. Charlie guffawed and slapped Thane on the back. "There's a light for ye yet, tadpole," he crowed, and Teresa spun on her heel and left the room, slamming the door behind her. "Oh, that was fun," the dragon man commented as he wiped a tear from his eye.

The sun was completely down now as Charlie and Thane sat next to each other on the floor with the tray between them. They chewed on cold bread and drank warm soda for a few moments of quiet, Thane staring into the darkness beyond the window. The stars were distant, far removed from anything happening in the life of one fifteen year old boy. Watching them and letting his mind wander helped and calmed him. He swallowed.

"So he's not my dad," Thane said.

Charlie grunted. "Sorry, lad."

"It's okay," Thane said, and saying it out loud made him believe it a little. He took another bite. "He wasn't much of a dad anyway."

"It's going tae be alright once the pain has gone away," Charlie said. "We'll make a dragon of ye yet."

They chewed and swallowed for a few more minutes before Thane spoke again. "You said if Ms. Rasmussen found me, then he would find me too. My father." Thane waited, hoping Charlie would hear the question and answer it without having to be asked. Saying Bert wasn't much of a dad wasn't a stretch. Asking who his real father was felt like accepting all of this insanity was actually happening and that Sanctum, the Shae, the Weave and Song were the truth and the world he'd always thought he lived in was the lie. So he waited.

"Aye, I did," Charlie responded. The dragon man took another huge bite of cold roast in a hardening roll.

"So," Thane groped, "who is she working with?"

"Yer father."

"The dragon."

Charlie nodded. "Full blue, same as me."

"But there are other kinds of dragons?" Thane wasn't sure whether he was stalling because he was afraid or if he still hoped Charlie would tell him the blue dragon's name without being asked. His body acted like fear with sweaty palms and clenched stomach, but it didn't feel like fear on the inside.

The dragon man chewed, swallowed, and belched before answering. "Och, aye. Dragons set the standard in Shae. We're the rulers, and all other creatures are made tae follow us. So because there be shadow, shade, and fae dragons there be shadow, shade, and fae of all races, Troglodytarum, Ingenium, Felidae, Maliales, Sidhe, and hundreds more, all races divided and warring because of difference in desires and instinct and we, the dragons, above all."

"So shadow, shade, and fae are good, selfish, and evil?" Thane asked.

" Chaotic more than selfish, ye ken-- you never know what the shade will do when a whim takes," Charlie smiled with fond memories.

"So blue dragons are the good guys." Thane hoped if he made it a statement it would be true.

"Threads nae!" Charlie guffawed. "We're the craziest of the bunch! We're the heart and soul of chaos, that's us blues." The dragon man turned to wink at Thane. "Ye cannae ken where lightning will strike, right laddie?"

Some deep hope within Thane shriveled and died. "So I'm not good," he said. "It isn't the world that's gone insane. It's me."

"Dinnae take the world's insanity away from it, that makes it black affronted," Charlie advised. "The world spins along madly and would continue tae do so without us. And ye, tadpole, are neither good nor evil, nor even truly chaotic." Charlie cuffed the back of Thane's head affectionately. "Too much human in ye tae be wholly Shae, too much Shae tae be human. No. Ye are something we haven't seen afore. Yer a son of the old ones."

"So," Thane paused, unable to say "my father" and instead substituted, "the blue dragon who is looking for me is one of the old ones?"

"Aye lad. Now I think we've pulled enough this day. Ye look like death on a pirn stick." Charlie yawned and stretched for emphasis, and Thane found himself yawning too. It had been a very long day.

Charlie spoke loudly into the air. "Twitch, ye muckle. Speak up."

A speaker by the door crackled to life. "What? I'm busy."

"Thane needs tae get tae his bunk, and I understand ye owe him for leaving him in the lurch earlier. I'm sending him outside towards the dorm. Make sure he finds his way." Charlie stood and began walking to the door. Thane rose and followed.

"Fine," Twitch said, and the speaker turned off.

"But what about--" Thane began, but Charlie cut him off with a gesture.

"No more tonight. I dinnae want tae fash yer young human-thinking brain. Sleep now, haste ye back in the morn."

Charlie walked him out of the building and down the sidewalk. The group they'd gone in with was coming out a side door, bruised and battered but animatedly talking. Charlie eyed the two women, and patted Thane on the shoulder. "Dorms are yonder, tadpole," he said. "Business calls me away." And Charlie strolled off after the women.

Thane didn't bother watching Charlie insinuate himself into the other group again. Instead he kept going towards the dorms, trying to keep from falling asleep on the grass.

"Long day?" Twitch asked right next to him.

"Aah!" Thane yelled, startled enough to swing. Twitch dodged the clumsy punch with ease.

"And they say I'm twitchy." Twitch slid into step next to Thane.

"Is every day like this here?" Thane asked.

"Only the good ones." Twitch smiled. Thane didn't.

CHAPTER 16

"Oi, newbie, breakfast!" the unfamiliar voice in the hallway shouted while fists pounded on the door. Thane blearily opened his eyes. He was on his stomach, face toward the wall and legs tangled in the cot's single blanket. Bright morning light streamed in from the now locked window and Thane's body ached. Gingerly he pushed himself to sitting, testing sore muscles and feeling out bruises. His clothes were stiff with dried sweat, dirt, and even some blood where his skin had been punctured by darts.

Conversations and footsteps flowed past in the hallway beyond his door. At irregular intervals someone would pound on his door with a variation on the order to breakfast. Thane's eyes closed and his head drooped. Maybe he'd get up in a half hour or so, after the initial breakfast rush. Nothing seemed worth getting out of bed for right now.

Nothing but that. Thane groaned and rose to his feet, grabbing his backpack and shuffling to the door. He pulled it open and stopped the first person he saw in the hall, a scruffy looking teenage boy with dark grey skin.

"Bathroom?" Thane asked. The boy looked surprised, then wrinkled his nose and pointed.

"Left at the next hall. Can't miss it." His voice was deep and rumbled. Thane nodded his thanks.

He found the bathroom easily. After his immediate need was taken care of, he went into the locker area. Two rows of lockers rose higher than his head with a long wooden bench running the length of the aisle in the middle. On the end where the showers were, well used and no longer quite white towels lay folded in stacks on a shelf. Opposite them were two large fabric laundry bins. The floors and walls were an ugly green tile, and it smelled like every male locker room has smelled since the beginning of locker rooms.

Thane peeled his filthy clothes off in the shower stall. As nearly as he could figure, he'd put them on Friday night to go see Remi and this was Tuesday morning. He left them on the floor at his feet while warm water washed over him, rinsing away the grime of days and waking him up. There was soap provided, so he spent several minutes scrubbing the top layers of sweat and dirt off until he could see skin underneath, and scoured his hair until his scalp stopped itching. Once he was clean he turned his attention to his clothes. He had so few that he didn't dare put these in the laundry because never seeing them again would be a problem. Instead he used the soap and his hands to wash them as best he could, and planned to leave them hanging up in his dorm with the window open.

"Perfekt head is here, aye smell it!" Jaeger crowed. Thane stuck his head out the curtain and saw the imp dashing back and forth around heads and flying up long aisle's of lockers. He did a spinning back flip in the air and landed on a someone's shoulders, putting his head upside down into the short man's face and baring all his pointed fangs in a manic grin. "Where is he? Where are hyu perfekt head, aye need hyu! Ah-hah!" Jaeger sprang back into the air, forcing the diminutive man to his knees.

Thane was trying to duck back behind a shower curtain and hide, but a red clawed hand tore the curtain away. "Come come come come come, we haf trainings!" Jaeger said, bat wings flapping and tail lashing through the air. The imp flew forward and latched on Thane's ears, spinning back to straddle Thane's neck with his legs and sit on his shoulders like a child. Or like someone riding a horse. "Ha!" Jaeger shouted, whipping Thane's backside with his tail. "Getty up!"

Skin stinging, Thane staggered forward and clutched his towel with one hand while trying to get Jaeger off with the other. "Bad present," Jaeger said, smacking his hand away with one pointed claw.

"Ow!" Thane yelped as Jaeger whipped him again. He started to run, the imp wearing his backpack while riding him and covered only by a dingy towel around his waist. Thane used his other hand to scoop up his soggy clothes from the floor while trying not to slip on the wet tile. The other boys backed out of the way.

"Go out!" one clawed hand pulled Thane's right ear hard, forcing him to turn his head to the right and stumble out the door into the hallway. Girls screamed as Thane burst from the locker room naked but for a towel and with the imp steering him by the ears. Thane's face flushed and his cheeks burned so red that he was sure they were the same color as the flying monkey devil currently driving him like a motorcycle. His embarrassment must have slowed him, because he felt the sting of Jaeger's pointed tail against his back again. "We are late, hyu must hurry!"

"I need to put pants on!" Thane begged, breaking into a run.

"Pants are irrelevant. You haf perfekt head, aye don't need pants. Run," and the imp squeezed Thane's ears with more force. "Now left," and Thane's head was jerked left. Ahead of him he could see the two sets of double doors that led outside.

"No, please," he slowed down. "Not outside. Let me get dressed..."

"Present, hyu worry too much," Jaeger said gently, and twisted Thane's ears with such force they felt like they were being torn off. He shouted in pain and saw red leathery wings emerge in his peripheral vision which then wrapped around his head, so he couldn't see anything at all. Then Jaeger's tail lashed again rapidly, leaving stinging welts along Thane's bare back. "Run!"

Thane ran. His arms were bruised by running into door bars and pushing through, and he felt the change from dehumidified air conditioning into the hot and wet outside. The sidewalk pavement was rough and burned under his feet, and the bright sunlight highlighted the veins that crossed inside the imp's wings. He stumbled and twisted his knee as Jaeger jerked his head right and the pavement gave way to uneven grass that cut his feet with sharp edges.

"Pit stop," Jaeger shouted, and Thane was pushed to his knees as the imp released his ears and eyes and shot off Thane's bruised shoulders into the sky. Thane hissed as his knee throbbed and clutched his towel, disoriented. Jaeger had taken his backpack but he still had the pair of wet jeans across his arm. Thane rolled onto his back and tried to keep covered with the towel while pulling on the soggy pants.

"Argh," he groaned, the jean material twisting and pulling against his skin. Putting on wet jeans was painful and difficult but the material pressed against his knee and kept it from swelling. He managed to get the pants on all the way and pushed himself into a standing position. The grey rectangle of building fifteen rose in the distance and he was surprised at how much ground he'd covered while blinded by the imp's wings. Thane started back and tried not to limp.

"Dive bomb!" Jaeger descended from the sky and landed with a heavy thud back on Thane's shoulders. "Perfekt head has pants, good, fine, hyu can stop whining about it. Now run!" and the imp wrapped his wings across Thane's face again and twisted his head to the right by the ears. The jeans provided some protection against Jaeger's tail but Thane's back was still bare and new welts sliced across the reddened and burning skin.

He ran, turning his head and changing direction instantly as he felt the pressure on his ears change. The faster he responded the less Jaeger would twist, and the imp chuckled with glee. "It is learning present! The internets are magical," the devil monkey chuckled. "Now halt."

Thane's head was jerked backwards and he skidded to a stop with the air pressure in front of his face compressed as though there was a wall. Jaeger released one ear and the air hissed, a blast of cold dehumidified air blowing on Thane's bare chest. He shivered. "Go," and he stumbled forward. There was a whir and hiss behind him, and the light that shone through the thin membrane of the devil wings vanished. They were inside and, based on the echoes, walking down a narrow hallway. The floor was cool under his feet. Thane kept moving as the imp twisted his ears and muttered numbers.

Thane heard a steady hum just ahead and a light glowed red through the thin wings. He slowed, or tried to, but Jaeger lashed him across the shoulder blades and he continued forward blindly. The hum grew louder as he passed through a warm sheet of light and then into deeper darkness. "Final member of Omega Team is present," the computer's automated voice announced. "Training simulation two nine three seven one may now begin. Training room locked down. Beginning in three,"

"Where have you been?" Twitch's voice hissed in the darkness. "We should've started a half hour ago. Gage is going to crap pixies if we don't get this right. You're team B with me and Iselle, Turcato leading."

"Two."

"Aye needed the hat," Jaeger responded. "Aye have to test the prototype."

"Shredding holes!" Twitch swore. "You didn't go and get that kid--"

"What's going on?" Thane whispered.

"One."

Jaeger's wings pulled away, and Thane stared. He would've sworn they had gone inside, but he was standing in high weeds outdoors near a warehouse. The air felt like early autumn back home, and the weeds were yellowed and burnt from too much sun. The squat building was not quite two stories tall with three windows on the side facing Thane. He looked around for Twitch but didn't see the other boy until he looked down. Twitch lay flat on his stomach and hidden in the tall plants out of sight from anyone in the warehouse.

"What are you doing?" Thane asked.

Twitch didn't answer. Instead, he held up a small earpiece. Thane looked at it, then at Twitch. The prone boy rolled his eyes and whispered. "Stick this in your ear and hide. If you're listening and you pray really hard you might survive the next twenty minutes."

Thane took the small black device and stuck it in his ear, hoping he could hear it over how loud his heart was pounding. Voices rang from the other side, mostly the hard Middle Eastern accent of the man called Turcato Peshawar. "--need to sweep around the building to ensure that none of the hostiles are laying in wait outside. Twitch, move left, no sound, weapon ready. Iselle take the back side, you don't fire unless fired upon. Stay hidden at all costs. Jaeger--"

"Aye finished it!" the imp shouted in triumph, and Thane felt something hard and metallic slam down over his head. The rim sat level with his eyebrows and a handle was squarely placed in the middle of his face. Dots of light shone through the bowl all around his head, and he felt the imp's quick hands as straps were drawn under his chin and secured in the back with clamps attached to each of his ears.

"Am I wearing a colander?" Thane asked. He felt Jaeger's weight as the imp settled above and slightly behind the bowl on his head.

"Run!" Jaeger yelled gleefully lashed Thane's back.

He could hear Turcato yelling in his ear, "You shredding imp, that was not the plan!" as he pounded across the field towards the warehouse. The clamps on his ear would tighten and pull to direct him exactly as the imp had done with his claws before.

"Fire!" Jaeger crowed and Thane felt something on his head pull back and then shoot forward. Into his field of vision a small oval flew through the air and into one of the three open windows of the warehouse. There was a muffled boom and a flash of orange light in the window along with chunks of debris.

"Ah-ha-ha-haha-hah!" Jaeger's laughter filled the air around him and more lines of burning pain lit up his back. "Run, run perfekt head!" and Thane's right ear pulled away from his skull. He swerved right and did his best to keep running, feeling Jaeger's weight swivel above him.

"Fire!" and Thane felt the pull and release of something from the top of his head again. Another small green oval flew into a window of the warehouse to his left and after a moment there was a second boom and flash of light. Thane's head bent and jerked as Jaeger leaned down to whisper, "Better run better now. They know."

"Who?" Thane tried to ask but his words were drowned out by gunfire. A spray of bullets hit the ground in front of him as Jaeger jerked his left ear with enough force to make Thane spin in place. Knee forgotten, Thane ran. More bullets followed but Jaeger directed Thane in a complex weaving pattern and Thane felt the pressure of something being pulled again.

"I sees hyu," Jaeger said, and the pressure released. Thane glanced back. Another small shape flew into the air, higher and further, landing on top of the building. A distant figure sprang to their feet and jumped off the edge the moment before the grenade exploded in sound and violence.

The figure spun in the air and landed on the ground behind Thane with a thud. It didn't move as Thane watched, running parallel to the warehouse. "You killed him!" the boy shouted to the imp on his head.

"Watch," the imp responded and allowed him to slow.

The figure remained motionless in the flattened weeds for one long breath. Then it moved. Pushing off the ground, Rip stood up and shook himself. Visibly broken bones popped back into place and cuts sealed themselves closed as the man's black eyes focused on Thane from fifty yards away.

"Now run," Jaeger instructed.

Thane sprinted. Gunfire sounded all around him with more explosions as Jaeger launched his grenades. Twitch sprang up from his place hidden in the weeds and opened fire directly at Thane. Bullets flew on either side making tinging sounds behind him and one line of burning hot fire traced along Thane's bicep, blossoming with blood. Thane tried to swerve but Jaeger anticipated, keeping him running straight at Twitch.

"He's trying to kill me!" Thane shouted.

"Stupid perfekt head," Jaeger muttered, and Thane ran past Twitch one step, then two. On the third step Jaeger swung Thane's head around and launched another grenade low and hard. Kari Loren swung her many dented sword from where she had been pursuing and hit the grenade with the flat edge. It sailed away towards the warehouse.

"Home run!" called Jaeger as the moment it took to hit the grenade with the sword gave Twitch enough time to shoot her in the face. She dropped, and Thane realized the tinging sounds the bullets had made were the Eltucari deflecting the shots with her sword. She'd been trying to kill him.

"That's one," Twitch said. Thane screamed as Paka rose from the grass behind Twitch and drove a short sword through his ribs. Panic took over and Thane spun and ran, ignoring Jaeger's attempts to steer. He got a small head start while Paka removed her sword from the fallen tech specialist.

The pull and release and pull and release from the top of his head was steady as Jaeger continued to fire while Thane pelted away from certain death. He ran towards the open front doors of the warehouse seeking cover from the blood mad panther woman behind him. He wasn't going to make it. Thane heard Paka snarl the moment before she sprang and tried to redouble his speed. It wasn't enough.

His head jerked backwards and he landed flat on his back while the panther tore the imp from the seat on his helmet. With the breath knocked out of him and his knee torn and shattered, he rolled over and tried to crawl away as the black cat held the imp pinned down by the wings with her front paws. He did not watch what happened next, but he could still hear the tearing sounds.

"You singed my tail, Helshvar," she growled.

Thane crawled into the warehouse. The wooden doors lay open at strange angles, hinges half blown off. Inside was one large room with crates in irregular stacks along the walls. A wooden spiral staircase at either end led to a wooden catwalk that wrapped around all four walls at the level of the windows. The floor was packed dirt and the walls were cement, all of which Thane noted looking for a place to hide. There was space between the stacked crates and the walls that would work. Chest aching and lungs stinging, Thane pulled himself with his arms until he was laying behind two large wooden crates.

His right leg dragged useless behind him, twisted knee throbbing and a dull stinging in his thigh. Thane leaned against the rough wood of the crates and looked down. There was a hole in his jeans with blood seeping out. He'd been shot. When had that happened? He couldn't remember.

Movement out of the corner of his eye distracted him. He huddled into a ball trying to be as small as possible behind the crates and peered between the cracks as a man slid into the warehouse on the opposite side. In the dimness the man looked familiar. The man continued his way along the wall, moving so quietly that Thane was concerned he'd lost his hearing. There was shouting and gunfire outside, but muffled and distant through the thick concrete walls.

Behind him, Thane could hear snuffling. He rolled his back along the crate until he was facing back the way he'd come in. Paka's feline head was visible in the outline of the sky beyond the doors. Her nose was near the ground, sniffing in the dirt. With a jolt Thane realized she was following the trail of blood his leg had left. She moved forward on four silent paws, body outlined by the doorway for less than one of Thane's too rapid heartbeats.

That less than one was enough. There was a crack and a metallic whooshing, and Paka was pinned to the wall by shards of wood and the thin strips of iron that bound the crates. "Turcato," Paka hissed, "if you attack, attack and be seen. Do not hide in shadow without honor."

Turcato made no response. Thane wouldn't have either. The strips of metal wrapped around the panther woman and bound her legs tightly against the slick fur of her body. Once she was immobilized, the wood that held her against the wall fell and she fell with it, landing in the dirt with a thump. Where she lay now she could see Thane's hiding place. Thane watched as she extended one claw to its fullest length and began scratching into the metal, shavings drifting to the ground.

This was no longer a good place to hide. Thane leaned to the side and crawled on three limbs while pressing himself against the wall into the shadows cast by the catwalk above. His right leg dragged behind him, bullet wound and knee protesting every bump and movement. He could hear the scrape of claws on metal behind, and in front he saw the outline of the man starting to climb the spiral stairs and head for the high ground. A shaft of light from a window showed Brennan's face as the man passed through it. Across the warehouse a crate rose into the air with a slight creak and began speeding towards the top of the stairs.

"Look out!" Thane yelled and Brennan instantly ducked and jumped over the railing as the heavy wood smashed into the highest section of stairs, causing the whole staircase to crumble and fall to the ground. Brennan rolled on the ground and stopped in a crouch behind the stack of crates just ahead of Thane. He had two large pistols drawn and trained on the boy's face.

"Kid?" Brennan mouthed in shock. Thane nodded rapidly. To his relief, Brennan lowered his guns. "What are you doing--"

The wall next to Brennan exploded inward and crushed the man between the chunks of cement and the wooden crates. Turcato stood in the center of the warehouse dripping with sweat and fist clenched facing the remains of Brennan. Thane's stomach rebelled and he vomited, noisily sick behind the crates.

Turcato heard and the crates that hid Thane from his view slowly dragged themselves out of the way. "What in the name of the guardians are you doing here?" Turcato demanded. In response, Thane threw up again and all the rest of his dinner from last night spilled onto the dirt. Turcato made a disgusted sound and held his hand out toward Thane. Thane felt himself rising off the ground and sliding away from the pool of vomit. "We need to get you out of here, the exercise isn't over yet--"

From his vantage point Thane saw Rip enter through the hole Turcato had made in the building and pick up one of the wooden crates. Brennan's limp body slid down to the ground as Rip hurtled the full crate toward Turcato. The Iranian man's attention had been on Thane with his back part way turned to the hole and the crate took him full in the side. Thane collapsed to the ground again as Turcato's body flew backward from the impact. Rip roared a challenge and threw himself towards the other man. A shining blue sword appeared in Turcato's hand as he turned to face his attacker. The two men rushed to meet each other and continue to destroy.

Thane was crying. Tears of pain and fear leaked from both eyes as he dragged himself towards the hole. It was closer than either door and he kept his eyes firmly on the wall, not looking at the battle raging on the warehouse floor nor at the glassy vacant eyes of the man he'd thought of as his imaginary friend. He dug his fingernails into the dirt and pulled himself forward by inches until he could see outside. There was no one else in sight. Thane counted the members of Omega Team in his head as he had seen them in the mess hall- Brennan was dead, Kari Loren, Jaeger, and Twitch were dead, Paka was captured, and Turcato and Rip were doing their best to kill each other right behind him. That left Iselle, and Turcato's instruction to her not to fire unless she was fired upon.

The sound of the violence in the warehouse increased, and Thane pulled his other leg underneath him to crawl faster. He made it to the grass and pulled himself into its cover when the entire building exploded in a rush of heat and light and sound. The bottom of his feet blistered and burned with the intensity of the blaze and pieces of concrete the size of cars flew past. One landed with a scream only a few yards beyond him, and several hit with thuds and thumps immediately behind.

Iselle's head rose from the high weeds only a yard or two away. She had been the one who screamed, and tears ran down her cheeks in a silent river. "Can you move?" she asked, her voice steady and her French accent soft. Thane shook his head. The crying so visible in her eyes was nowhere in her voice. "A large piece has landed on my leg. I am trapped. Rip is unconscious a few feet past you. If you cannot move, we may both die when he wakes."

Thane pushed himself back up onto his elbows, strange metal helmet askew on his head. Rip was indeed lying on his stomach only a few feet away, one shoulder dislocated and the arm bent across his back, the other arm and one leg pinned under a huge section of what used to be a wall. The daemon possessed man was not moving, but in his mind's eye Thane could see the man fall from the top of the building and only take a few heartbeats to get back up.

"What do we do?" Thane asked Iselle.

She sighed. "It depends on who wakes. If it is the man, he will recognize that we are not a threat and move on. If it is the daemon, we will die." Iselle said this simply, as though saying that one train would take you to New York and another would stop in Sacramento.

His hands were shaking. Thane needed his hands to stop shaking, needed his mind to stop watching the tragic comedy that was his life and start coming up with solutions. He flashed through elementary and middle school, the trips with Grandpa Whitaker and telling Lanie stories, the painful mire of misery that was junior high and lingered over meeting Remi. The lightning strike and waking up in the hospital flew by, and then jerked to a halt at Brennan in the Leaf and Dagger. "I swear you could blow his head off and it would only barely give you time to start running before he came after you again."

Thane's hands stopped trembling and his fingers flew to remove the colander from his head. The straps were difficult, but Iselle passed him a knife and he cut through them. Pulling it off carefully, he noted the miniature trebuchet attached to the top with a swiveling base and a padded chair. Underneath the chair were three grenades, pins in and tightly secured.

He removed one from the helmet with halting fingers. Keeping the pin tight with his thumb, he unthreaded the straps until he had two long pieces. "Tie these together," he instructed Iselle, and she obeyed without comment. Handing it back, their fingers touched briefly and he noticed her hands were cold and sweaty, like his. She smiled tremulously at him.

Now was the hardest part. Heart thumping so loudly he was afraid it would wake Rip all on its own, Thane rolled over his good leg and pulled himself towards the prone daemon shell. Rip's mouth was already open slightly, and Thane wedged the grenade inside. He tied one end of the straps to the pin and with slow deliberation moved away with the other end, leaving lots of slack. He scooted himself back to where Iselle sat, one leg crushed under a large piece of wall. She looked at him with dark wide eyes.

"If it's the daemon, we'll blow his head off. That should give us time to get away," Thane said. She nodded. "Is there any way to make sure it isn't the daemon?"

Iselle considered the question and a breeze started blowing. The gentle movement of the tall weeds and the silence all around them highlighted the disparity of the moment. The world sat in quiet peace while he prepared to blow up a man's head with a grenade Thane had wedged in the man's mouth. Then Iselle started to sing.

Dodo, l'enfant do, l'enfant dormira bien vite
Dodo, l'enfant do l'enfant dormira bientôt.
Dodo, l'enfant do, l'enfant dormira bien vite
Dodo, l'enfant do l'enfant dormira bientôt.
Tout le monde est sage dans le voisinage Il

est l'heure d'aller dormir le sommeil va bientôt venir.

As she sang, a voice spoke in the earpiece Thane still wore. It startled him and he flinched, pain shooting through his wounds. But the female voice wasn't familiar and the words were strange. It took him a few moments to realize that the voice was translating the song Iselle sang into English.

Sleepy time, the young one sleeps, the child will sleep very soon
Sleepy time, the young one sleeps, the child will sleep oh, so soon.
Sleepy time, the young one sleeps, the child will sleep very soon.
Sleepy time, the young one sleeps, the child will sleep oh, so soon.
Everyone is calm all around it's the time for all to sleep
Sleep will come soon.

As Iselle sang, her soft voice carrying with the breeze, Rip stirred. First his arms twitched, and then his chin, his jaw working back and forth against the hard object in his mouth. His eyes fluttered open and their solid blackness rolled before focusing on Iselle. She continued to sing, repeating the lullaby. Rip's chest heaved as he took a shuddering breath around the grenade and Thane tightened the slack. The dark orbs followed the line of the strap from below his nose to Thane's shaking hands, and then locked onto Iselle.

She completed the lullaby a second time, the voice repeating the lyrics in Thane's ear. Iselle placed her hand over Thane's trembling fist and pushed down gently, lowering Thane's hand and loosening the slack as she began again. Thane let her.

Rip closed his eyes and took another deep breath, stronger than the first, and his overextended shoulder rolled back into place with a hard snap. Iselle gripped Thane's hand, her palm sweaty and Thane's stomach trying to reject food that was no longer there. The prone man's eyelids lifted again, and white showed on both sides of clear brown irises that circled small black pupils. He spat the grenade toward Thane.

Rip took one more deep breath and spoke in a mild baritone. "Terminate training simulation two nine three seven one. Omega Team complete, victory team B. Notify medical staff non-elegant exit and request full contingent. Civilian on the field."

"Acknowledged," the computerized female voice answered. That was definitely not the voice translating for Thane. Iselle's song finished and she remained quiescent as everything changed. The outdoor field and ruined building disappeared. Bright fluorescent lighting filled the area and a ceiling appeared overhead. All the pieces of concrete vanished, freeing Iselle and Rip.

Red double doors at the far end of the immense room burst open and several people in white uniforms entered at a run. They spread throughout Thane's vision. Rip rose unhurt and waved them over, pointing to Thane. "He may need more than merely the physical repair," the mild baritone was musical. "Evaluation for trauma should be included."

The medic nodded and turned to Thane. Thane held the helmet straps in one hand and noted that the grenade on the other end was gone, although the helmet was still sitting next to him. That struck him as hilarious. Thane started laughing. The medic looked at him, concerned.

"Are you all right, kid?"

That was even funnier. Thane laughed harder, trying to keep pulling in oxygen while his sides were stretching from mirth.

"Kid? Thane, are you all right?" Brennan stood in front of him, crouching down to be at eye level.

Brennan was alive. Of course he was. Thane cracked up harder. Twitch came over next without even a hole in his shirt. Why should there be? By now Thane was laughing so hard tears were rolling down his face and his breath came in short hard gasps. He should have blown Rip's head up; maybe candy would come out.

The concerned and even frightened looks on the faces of the adults surrounding him told Thane he was going mad. He didn't care. Sanity here was too hard. Reality was too malleable. Laughing was better. Laughing meant he wasn't balled up in a corner sobbing. And if he was crazy maybe everyone would leave him alone.

He didn't see the gun or feel the puncture, but when the darkness started to creep across his vision he knew someone had shot him with a tranquilizer. Thane hoped it was LaPointe. He hoped it was LaPointe and she'd shot him seven times and he'd never wake up this time again.

CHAPTER 17

It must have only been one tranquilizer dart because Thane started waking up before they'd finished carrying him out of the room. He was on a stretcher with his right leg in a splint. The pain searing through his knee and burning lines all across his bare back made sure that he didn't think anything was funny anymore. He opened his eyes while trying to ignore the people around him, either carrying or on other stretchers.

Rip was walking next to him. Thane flinched and closed his eyes. When he peeked through slitted lids Rip was gone. Brennan strode next to him instead, and Thane's mind flashed to Brennan being crushed between the heavy crates and cement wall. And Brennan's lifeless body sliding limply to the ground. And throwing up.

"Hey kid," Brennan said, watching Thane's face. The medic carrying the front of the stretcher glanced back and frowned. Thane winced, but Brennan rested a comforting hand on Thane's arm. "Don't worry, he's just mad that I was right and you woke up before the infirmary." Brennan squeezed and released Thane's arm.

"What..." Thane's mouth tried to form words that his mind shied away from. He had to know what happened to prove to himself that he wasn't dreaming or insane. Again. But he was afraid to know what happened because what if knowing broke his sanity? Images flashed through his mind; Rip falling, Rip getting up, Twitch shooting Kari, Paka eviscerating Twitch, Brennan dying, Turcato fighting Rip, Iselle screaming, Rip falling, Rip getting up, Twitch shooting Kari, Paka, Twitch, Paka, Jaeger, Brennan, Turcato, Iselle, over and over in an accelerating loop.

"He is falling," Thane heard Iselle's soft voice near him, and a gentle hand stroked his forehead. He opened the eyes he hadn't known he was squeezing shut and stared up at her while the warm skin of her fingers gave him something to focus on.

Brennan swore. "Shredding holes, kid, how did you even get in here? Team training buildings are secured from all students, and once a training exercise begins the room is on lockdown. I don't think even Twitch could override that!"

"Jaeger," Thane answered, and swallowed. "Jaeger said he needed my perfect head."

Two stretchers over, Jaeger's head popped up. "Hyu have a perfekt head for the mobile launcher helmet! Mobile, responsive, accuracy of more than ninety-three percent..." and the imp lay back down dreamily, one shredded wing dangling over the side.

"Wait," Thane said. "Why is he still hurt and you aren't? I saw you--" and he gulped, bile rising in his throat as the images started again. Brennan crushed, Rip attacking, Iselle screaming, Rip falling. Iselle's soft fingers suddenly pulled his hair to bring him back and he blinked tears out of his eyes.

"It has to do with the simulation. When the training exercise has started, the location and weapons are all simulated. So is any damage we take. But it has to feel real," Brennan explained, placing his hand on Thane's arm again, "because we have to know how to actually use these weapons and exactly what damage they cause. But that's all faked. The damage we cause each other, though, isn't." Brennan held up his right hand. "Rip tore off my fingers by himself. Real damage. Turcato threw me into fake crates with a fake wall. Simulated damage. Twitch got stabbed with a simulated sword. So did Jaeger. But Paka shredded his wings with her physical claws. Damage that needs to be repaired, like your knee."

Thane lay back and pondered that. "Who else is hurt?" he asked. There were two more stretchers besides his and Jaeger's.

Brennan grimaced. "Rip broke Paka's front legs and Turcato overexerted his ability when he blew up the building. So Paka is going to the infirmary with you two, and Turcato is going to a separate kind of recovery room."

As if saying so had been a signal, the final stretcher in the procession turned down a hallway and the remaining three entered a small hospital ward. Beds lined both walls and curtains that when drawn could offer minimal privacy hung from the ceiling. Monitors and IV stands stood at the head of each bed with bags of liquid ready for use. Thane was taken to the third bed on the left side, while Paka and Jaeger were placed on the second and third beds opposite him. He hissed with pain as they laid him down on the crisp white sheets, the weight of his body pushing against the lashings on his back.

"Brennan, what was that?" Thane asked the red haired man as he sat on the second bed next to Thane.

The man sighed, running his remaining fingers through his hair. "That's a long question, kid." Medical staff bustled about, inserting IVs and taking x-rays of Paka's arms, Jaeger's wings, and Thane's leg. The pain of having his knee moved made tears prick in the corners of Thane's eyes, and he saw Brennan notice them. "But I guess you've earned the answers. That was a training exercise for the Omega Team. Every team in Sanctum is required to complete a set number of training exercises each week, unless we're deployed somewhere. All teams are part of the Shaerealm Mercenary Guard, the force that protects this world against incursions from the Shaerealm."

"Mercenary?" Thane asked. "You aren't soldiers?"

"Some of them are, like Gage," Brennan said. "We get a lot of military types in here and we base our internal structure off military rankings. But we're not soldiers. We're paid to fight, and some only do it for the money. Some do it for the cause. Most do it because they don't think they can do anything else. You only stay in Sanctum if you're dedicated or if you don't have enough Song to disguise yourself out there."

A huge man in a lab coat entered from the far end of the room. His face was flat with a squished nose and a sloping forehead, and his shoulders were broad and muscular. He stood towering over the other medics, peering at info pads through tiny spectacles that perched on his wide nose. He turned to Thane.

"Knee," his voice rumbled. Hands the size of boxing gloves gripped either side of Thane's injured knee and huge sausage fingers prodded. Pain seared up Thane's leg and he tried to jerk away. "No," the ogre man said, and one hand pushed against Thane's bare chest and forced him to lay down again. That one calloused hand felt like an anvil, holding Thane in place while the man manipulated Thane's knee with the other. Through tears and clenched teeth Thane noticed a small name tag on the breast pocket of the man's lab coat. It read, "Dr. Thunk."

"Cut," Dr. Thunk said to an assistant, indicating Thane's damp jeans. The tiny assistant nodded and produced a pair of large scissors. Starting at the ankle, she cut the leg of his pants along the seam until above Thane's knee, and then cut around to remove the pant leg. Thunk grunted and resumed the examination. "Torn ACL. MCL. Soft bone crushed. Needs re-make. Nanites." The assistant nodded and Dr. Thunk turned back to Thane. He leaned forward until his large flat face was only inches from Thane's. "No move," the ogre man spoke slowly and enunciated carefully as though speaking to a dimwitted child. He waited until Thane nodded, then crossed to Paka.

"What cause?" Thane asked, gritting his teeth against the pain in his knee. A medic started an IV in his arm and injected it with a clear liquid from a syringe. Brennan looked at Thane with a raised eyebrow. "They're dedicated to the cause. What cause?"

"The balance of all worlds," Brennan answered. "The Weave has weak spots and even a few holes into the Shaerealm. The Song of the Shae leaks through, and the more their Song vibrates here, the more the two Songs clash. If we don't try to control or limit the Shae Song eventually our world will shatter. Sometimes Shaefolk themselves come through, usually the violent or the crazy, looking for power. Sanctum uses the SMG to protect against those incursions and keep the balance, so both our world and the Shaerealm can continue to exist."

Whatever the medic had injected seemed to be working because Thane felt the pain recede. Across from him, Dr. Thunk had taken one of Paka's arms in both his hands and twisted, setting the bone with an audible pop and making the panther woman yowl in pain. Next to her, a medic was brushing a shimmering clear liquid across Jaeger's wings and sliding the pieces together like a jigsaw puzzle. The adhesive made the bits of wing stick in place and must have had some of the healing serum in it as well, because the torn membranes started knitting themselves back together.

"Can't you fix it?" Thane asked, his breathing more calm and his head starting to buzz pleasantly. "Can't you close the Weave all the way so Shae isn't connected anymore?"

"Initially we couldn't," Brennan answered, having to repeat himself twice over Paka's yowling. Dr. Thunk had set her other front arm and placed them immobile in slings. "We didn't have the power or the knowledge. Now we do, but the cost would be too high."

"What cost?"

Across the room, Paka hissed. "Idiot. Selfish, stupid cub. You do not think. The Shae have been in this world for centuries uncounted, mating and mingling with humans. Fully a third of everyone in this world has the blood of the Shae in their veins. Do you have any idea how many that is?"

Jaeger crowed and launched himself into the air. His wings were slick and shiny and his flying was rough, but his elation was pure and his voice was loud. "One third of the population of Earth is approximately two point three four billion people. On average there is a net increase of two hundred twenty-nine thousand people every day with an additional third of those having Shae blood, or seventy-six thousand people every day multiplied by three hundred sixty-five point two five days per year is a net increase of nearly twenty-eight million people every year at minimum!" He flew through the room running into medics and machines until Dr. Thunk cuffed him on the side of the head, knocking him back down.

"No. Move." Dr. Thunk locked eyes with the imp. Jaeger giggled, but stayed on the bed and curled up like a cat.

"His head is perfekt," the imp pointed at Thane with red eyes whirling and still giggling. "Aye built the launcher mathematically exact to average so it would fit the people, but he is not a people and has the only perfekt average head!"

"What difference does it make how many people have Shae blood in them?" Thane asked, ignoring Jaeger. A medic stood next to him with a comically huge needle. Thane assumed it was a prop or a toy until she jabbed it into his knee and pushed the plunger. He screamed and tried to flail, but before he'd gotten his arms in the air Dr. Thunk had an enormous heavy forearm across his chest.

"No. Move." The mossy green eyes stared into Thane's brown ones until the medic removed the needle with painful slowness. Thane cringed, but otherwise held still. Thunk nodded and patted the boy on the head with a hand that could have easily palmed a watermelon. "Good. Tech bugs fix. Sleep soon."

"Okay," Thane said. Dr. Thunk smiled and moved to Jaeger, picking the imp up with one hand that covered the red body from knees to nose and used his other massive hand to spread out one of the leathery wings and inspected the healing membranes. Thane moved his head slowly to face Brennan. "Tech bugs?"

"Nanorobotics. Nanites are microscopic robots that can be programmed with specific tasks and injected into your bloodstream. Torn ligaments don't fix themselves, so healing darts would be useless for your knee. The nanites can stitch your ligaments back together from the inside without surgery and then the healing darts can cover whatever physical damage is left," Brennan explained.

Thane decided he liked the sound of Brennan's voice. In fact, Brennan was a great guy and he knew everything. "You know everything," Thane said, unable to hear his voice slurring. His brain felt sloshy, like an object in one of those things with the thick liquid that you tilted back and forth and the object would move opposite the flow. "You're a great guy."

"And you are hopped up on morphine, kid." Brennan grinned at him. "We'll talk more later," and he rose to leave.

"Wait," Thane said, trying to think past the thickness and buzzing in his head to the question he'd been asking. "Why, um, why can't they close the Weave?"

"Because every person in this world with even a drop of Shae blood in their veins would sicken and die within weeks if we did. The less blood the longer it would take, but if we close the Weave and silence the Song, billions of people would die on this side and every human or creature with human blood in the Shaerealm would die as well. That number is also in the billions." Brennan wasn't smiling now.

It took a moment for Thane to connect the points of logic. Then the meaning hit. "Lanie," Thane whispered. "And mom, and Harper... and Remi?"

Brennan understood the question. "No, Remi Gage is pure human, like her parents. She'd be safe."

"One safe," Thane sighed, breathing more slowly. This was much more pleasant than being shot. Warm and sleepy and frightened for billions of people that were all Lanie, and every Lanie was singing a lullaby in French. Some part of his brain acknowledged that he was dreaming now, but awake enough to feel when Brennan squeezed his hand and then walked away. Thane stopped fighting sleep and sank through a world of spinning dreams into a restful darkness.

He didn't know how many hours later he woke up. Violent and terrible dreams had been tearing through his subconscious, interrupting his rest by beating his mind with memories of the battle that weren't real memories. Brennan being crushed over and over between the cement and the crates transformed into Twitch shooting Mrs. Knotts. Paka raked her claws down Remi's red wings as his one and only friend lay dying in the dirt before the warehouse. Turcato's blue sword of light flashed, and the pieces of Robert Whitaker fell like leaves in autumn. Harper ran a Gatling gun from the roof trying to shoot Thane while Ms. Rasmussen whipped him from behind, driving him toward death. Fleeing the bullets, he ran past where his mother lay in the grass with her leg trapped under an enormous block of concrete. She was screaming as Rip, with eyes of black fire, tore off her fingers one by one with his teeth.

Thane gasped and nearly choked holding in a scream, rising halfway out of the hospital bed. It was a strange sort of semi-dark in the infirmary, but no windows to give him any information about the time. Lights from the different pieces of medical equipment blinked or glowed, making strange shadows against the hanging white curtains. The beds that Paka and Jaeger had used were empty. No medics walked the aisles. It was quiet, and Thane lay back against his pillows, breathing heavily and shaking with sweaty palms.

"You're right, this is a hole attempt," General Gage's voice said from somewhere to his right. Thane turned his head and saw bright light seeping into the infirmary from a door that was imperfectly closed. "Five of the seven items confirmed. You're sure?"

"The projections were uncertain until the Bone of the Guardian was taken last night. Five of the seven confirmed." Thane recognized Twitch's voice. "The remaining two items will be difficult to obtain, but no more so than actually getting a Guardian Bone. This is a class seven. We have to tell the Council." Long pause. "Sir."

"I will decide when and what we take to the Council, Mr. O'Malley," the general's voice was firm, but not angry. "There have been escalating tear and hole events everywhere. Teams are deployed across the globe. Omega has not been called up, but that should change in days. If we take this to the council they will be forced to act and draw resources away from other more dangerous areas. Continue to monitor for now, and once six of the items have been confirmed I will personally inform the council." Another pause, then Gage continued, "we can always hope the last two items will prove too difficult. It's happened before."

"You're right, it is fishy," Twitch said, then added, "um, yes sir."

"We have counselors, Twitch, and your psych evaluations are covered. Go see Dr. Freeman for a session."

"Is that an order?" Twitch sighed.

"If it has to be. I need my team in top form, and that includes you." There was a pause as the door opened. Thane closed his eyes and steadied his breathing. Be invisible. Footsteps approached, growing louder, and paused at the foot of his bed.

"His records indicate he should wake up in three more hours," Twitch said softly.

"Make sure there is plenty of food here then. He's due for a healing dart in half hour, and he'll be starving." A pause, and Thane focused on looking very asleep. Gage chuckled. "Jaeger really pulled him out of the shower?"

"He ran across half the compound wearing nothing but a towel around his waist and Jaeger around his head." Twitch thought it was hilarious too, judging by how hard he was trying to laugh quietly.

"This kid can't catch a break," General Gage said, and Thane silently agreed. The final image of his dream, the one that had woken him in terror, replayed in his mind. It started with Rip tearing off his mother's fingers... Thane shuddered.

General Gage must have seen Thane's shudder. "You may want to schedule an evaluation for Mr. Whitaker with Dr. Freeman as well. He was... unprepared for this morning."

Twitch snorted. "Did you watch the vids?"

Gage must've nodded, because Twitch went on. "Then you saw the end. That kid stuck a grenade in Rip's mouth and was ready to pull the pin. That's dark, even for us."

"That's what we're looking for." Twitch made a surprised sound. "What similarities have you noticed between yourself and the other members of Omega Team?" Gage asked.

Twitch was quiet, presumably thinking before responding. "We're all strong individuals with enormous physical or intellectual potential." Gage didn't comment, so Twitch continued. "We have all suffered loss or betrayal, we have trust issues, and we each have an incredible capacity for loyalty."

"Exactly. It's like you've read the files," Gage said wryly. "We need every team to trust Sanctum first. We need them to be loyal to Sanctum first, and their team second. We need them to be able to save the world, because they might have to." Gage paused, and Thane lifted his eyelids slightly and peeked through the slits. The general had stepped forward and placed a hand on Twitch's shoulder. "But Omega Team is different. We don't need you to save the world, we need you able to destroy it."

A decade and a half of instinct and practice saved Thane from moving or making noise. Be invisible; they can't catch you if they can't find you. Twitch must have had a more noticeable reaction because Gage chuckled. "Don't look so shocked; that certainly isn't the plan," the general reassured the computer specialist. "What is the purpose of Omega Team?"

"Last resort," Twitch said, obviously a question he'd answered before. "Omega Team is called in when any collateral damage is acceptable as long as the objective is achieved."

Thane gave a mental blink. He couldn't have heard that right. But going through the statement again in his mind, he didn't see how he could've heard it wrong.

"...and Thane showed today that he would be a prime candidate for Omega Team. Have you read his file?" Thane was so distracted by the revelation of Omega Team's specialty that he'd missed the first part of the general's statement.

"Student files are locked," Twitch said. "It would be unethical to access them."

"Yes, because that stops you. I don't believe there's a file in our system you haven't accessed, Mr. O'Malley. I would hate to think I've been overestimating you all this time." Twitch snorted. "Hypothetically, then, if you'd read his file what would it say?"

"Hypothetically," Twitch stretched the word, "he has also suffered loss and betrayal and the results of his phasic screening indicate great capacity for destruction. Oh."

Twitch and General Gage started walking away, their voices fading with distance. "We still need to go over the vids with the team. The presence of one civilian should not--" and the click of the door closing cut off the rest.

Thane lay in the low light of the infirmary and tried to fight off the nightmare. Pieces of General Gage and Twitch's conversation echoed in his mind, "Omega Team must be able to destroy the world... Thane is a prime candidate... that's dark, even for us...Thane is... able to destroy...dark, even for us..."

The nightmare won. Rip was attacking his mother when Thane turned into an enormous sky colored monster and ripped the daemon man's head off. The monster that was Thane turned, enraged, and smashed the wall under Harper with a clawed fist. Then he dove through the hole he created into the warehouse and tore everything living with fangs and talons until bright blood saturated the dirt and the ground could hold no more. Dragon Thane roared in anger and anguish, and cold blue eyes whirled with every possible shade and variation of the color. Trolls and daemons fled in terror from something truly and wholly reprehensible, and Ms. Rasmussen laughed in delight while her whip continued to leave bloody gashes across his back.

That was the truth Thane had been hiding. If he made himself invisible, no one would ever be able to see the secret he held. Thane was a monster. The worst kind. The kind that would hurt those too weak to fight back. He thought they could fix him here, at Sanctum. And if they couldn't take the monster out of him they could teach him to control it. He'd been hopeful. Then when they put him to the test, he was the worst monster of all. "Dark, even for us."

He pulled his knees to his chest and wrapped his arms around them, ignoring the tension that put on his IV line. The bed vibrated with how hard he was shivering, cold from the inside out. If he didn't push the monster back, Ms. Rasmussen could use him to do more than electrocute one man. She could make him kill millions.

A medic came in the room from the other end, the sound of their scrubs rustling overly loud in Thane's ears. "Your heart rate is spiking, honey," she said, her voice smooth and southern and her fingers webbed. "Let's see if we can't get you to rest a little more." She filled a syringe from a jar of clear liquid and walked to his IV stand.

"No," he whispered.

"It'll be all right, sugar, sleep is good for you," her smile was genuine and her teeth the normal human variety.

"Please, no." Thane closed his eyes and opened them immediately as the image of his monster self flashed behind his eyelids.

Warmth slid under his skin as the morphine trickled through his bloodstream. His legs involuntarily relaxed and straightened. His head increased in weight until his neck could not hold it up any longer, and he fell bonelessly back onto the pillow. The medic smiled and left him.

"No, please, no more nightmares," he whispered, tears leaking over his cheeks. "I already know I'm a monster. Please don't make me see it again..." his words became whimpers, then silence as the medicine overcame his weakening resistance.

But something somewhere must have heard him. In that final moment of consciousness, Thane felt gentle warm fingers stroking his forehead. Someone must have felt a stirring of pity for him because he sank past dreaming and into restful and healing darkness.

CHAPTER 18

Something heavy landing on the foot of his bed jolted Thane awake. He threw his arms over his face, protecting his eyes and head from whatever was attacking him now. Nothing happened. Thane gingerly opened his eyes and peered between his arms to see his backpack sinking into the blankets by his feet.

The lights were on in the infirmary, the fluorescence too bright against the white walls, curtains, and empty beds. Squinting, Thane looked around and saw a scowling Twitch standing next to his bed. Neither boy spoke, Twitch glaring down and Thane waiting.

"You're bunking with me now," Twitch finally said. That explained the angry expression.

"Why?" Thane asked.

Twitch snorted. "Apparently Jaeger thought that you might try to escape by running back to your room. He booby-trapped it."

"What? How?"

A grin was trying to break through the older boy's scowl. "It's complicated, but the Guardian Council decided it would be better to just wall off the room instead of trying to excavate it. We're lucky Charlie set off the trap. He's one of maybe six people in the facility right now who could've survived." The grin won.

"Is Charlie--"

"He's fine. Mad as a Chaun at an amusement park, though. Jaeger's lucky Paka shredded his wings during the training. Charlie was going to tear them off, but Thunk wouldn't let him in." Twitch's grin was wickedly gleeful.

Thane paused. Dr. Thunk versus Charlie would've been something to see, and Thane was sort of sad he'd missed it.

"Why you?"

The scowl came back. "Punishment. I'm babysitting."

"I survived, which was more than you did," Thane retorted, stung.

"Because I was busy taking down Kari Loren before she took you down," Twitch shot back.

"She's good. She wouldn't hurt me," Thane said.

Twitch's eyes widened, then he laughed. "You-- you think that-- oh!" and he laughed so hard he couldn't talk anymore. Thane folded his arms across his chest and glowered.

"Brennan said Shae are broken into three kinds, shadow, shade, and fae, and that they're bad, crazy, and good," Thane getting more defensive as Twitch kept laughing. "General Gage said Kari Loren was fae. That means she's good. Why is that funny?"

"Stop, stop, I need to talk," Twitch gasped, holding his stomach. He took a deep breath, then another, and then turned back to Thane. "Kari Loren is an Eltucari, which is the fae of the Evarish. So yes, technically, she's good." Thane widened his eyes, raised his eyebrows, and gestured with open hands as if to say, "So?"

"So she might think that dying would be a good experience for you," Twitch continued. Thane's crossed arms fell lower, wrapped around his stomach instead. Brennan crushed, Twitch stabbed, Jaeger, Paka, Iselle... "She might decide that the slower and more painful the death the more you would learn from it, and that would be a good thing for your growth. Yes, I'm getting to that," he glanced away from Thane and then back. "Shadow are always going to go for the most pain, pleasure, or power. Shade will do whatever they feel like based on the moment they're in. Fae will act to bring about the most good based on what they value. And every race," the tech teen slowed to emphasize each word, "value something different. Fae are the least predictable of all. Drives Gage and the other songless crazy."

"Songless?"

"Nickname for the pure humans, like Gage, Brennan, me, and a few others." Twitch suddenly folded his arms across his chest and scowled again. "I'm not your shredding tutor. I have work to do. Our dorm is building four, room four oh four." The older boy snickered, then turned on his heel and walked back down the aisle between the beds and exited through the same door he had last night with Gage.

Thane waited until the door closed, then snatched his backpack and pulled it open. He didn't want Twitch to see how much having it back meant so he'd ignored it while the other boy was watching. Now he rifled through one of his few possessions and everything else was there. The outfit he'd been wearing was destroyed, the shirt and hoodie left dripping and messy in the locker room and the jeans in tatters from...

His mind jerked away from that. He focused instead on the gnawing hunger in his stomach. Hadn't General Gage said that there would be food when he woke up? Thane looked all around the room and saw nothing edible. He still had no idea what time it was, but he hoped the cafeteria might be serving something until he remembered that he had no code for getting food.

He wanted to get dressed. Lying on wet sheets in half a pair of jeans was not good for his comfort or his self esteem. Thane reached out and grabbed one of the white curtains and dragged it along the track attached to the ceiling until it surrounded his bed with a gap near the pillow. He tugged at the curtain, but it wouldn't go further. He shrugged and began to wrestle off the ruined pants as quietly as possible.

The half pants were down around his ankles when a door opened and shut on the furthest edge of the room. "Just a minute!" Thane called to the medic that was likely coming to check on him, since there weren't any other patients.

"Thane?" Iselle's accent softened the hard vowel sound.

"Ack!" Thane tried to jerk his pants off with both hands and knocked himself backwards onto the bed. His feet kicked out and tangled in the curtains, and he slid off the bed and onto the cold tile floor trying to extract them.

"Are you all right?" Iselle asked, alarm evident in her voice. Her footsteps grew louder as she neared.

"I'm fine!" Thane shouted, panicked. He tugged his ruined jeans the rest of the way off with his back on the floor and his feet in the air. "Don't come closer!"

"Oh, okay," she said. From his position on the tile Thane could see her feet under the curtain. She was two beds away and standing with bare feet. He wondered where her shoes were as he threw himself to his feet and grabbed a pair of boxers out of his backpack.

"The food will be cold if I wait much longer," she pronounced the last word like "long hair," her accent more noticeable in his discomfort.

"You brought food?" Thane paused in pulling pants out of his backpack and breathed in deeply through his nose. His stomach grumbled as the smell of bacon, sausage, melted cheese, and grilled onions wafted into his nostrils.

She laughed when his stomach growled again, the first happy sound he'd heard her make. "There was food, but you slept hours longer than your chart suggested and it was inedible before you woke." Thane doubted that but didn't comment. "I had it taken away and brought more. There is bacon, eggs, sausage biscuits with cheese," He jerked up the zipper and grabbed a shirt from the backpack, "pancakes with syrup and biscuits with gravy. I was not sure what you would like, so I brought everything."

Thane tugged his head through the shirt hole with his arms while pulling back the curtain. "Thanks," he said, eyeing the food.

The girl studied him for a minute, then smiled. "I like your shirt." Thane glanced down to see which one he'd put on. High on one side a beaver played a guitar in a yellow circle. Low on the other side was a duck playing a keyboard in a blue circle. It finished with green in the center where the circles overlapped and a platypus playing a keytar.

"Thanks, I like your... tray," he said lamely, unable to look anywhere but at the food. Iselle giggled. She brought it over and almost placed the tray on his bed before noticing how damp the sheets were. "Oh," she said, surprised and pulling the tray back up.

"My jeans were wet," Thane blurted, face scarlet. He realized that didn't make it better. "No, they were wet before Jaeger got me. No, I mean, I was in the shower with my jeans..." he trailed off, trying to say words that would make it better and not being able to think of any.

Laughing again, Iselle turned around and placed the overflowing tray on the bed next to Thane where Brennan had sat. Her laugh sounded like a song, rising and falling with pure tones. "You should eat before Charlie comes for you. He's twice angry at Jaeger, both for losing a day of your training and for the trap. You heard about that, no?"

"No, I mean, yeah," Thane said around a mouthful eggs, bacon, and biscuits. The food was the perfect level of heat so every swallow slid warmly down his throat but no bite was uncomfortably hot in his mouth. "Twitch told me. What time is it?"

"Almost one o'clock. I knew you hadn't eaten so I asked the kitchen to prepare you breakfast."

Something she'd said sunk in. "Losing a day? But it's only one. And the battle--" he swallowed, suddenly queasy and memories flashing; Twitch stabbed, Kari Loren shot, Jaeger shredded, Brennan crushed... he closed his eyes and shoved the images down before they could overwhelm him. "It only took minutes." And lives. Brennan crushed, Iselle trapped, Rip with the grenade in his mouth and nightmare Thane destroying the world under Ms. Rasmussen's lashings. His stomach lurched and he gagged but held his food down, shoving the images away and slamming them down in the pit where he kept the rest of his anger and fear.

Warm pressure wrapped around his hand brought him back from the edge of that darkness. The image of himself as the blue leviathan burning against his retinas faded as he heard Iselle's voice, her soft "r" and longer than normal "e" tugging at the fringes of his attention. She spoke for several sentences before the cadence of her voice and the gentleness of her unfamiliar accent was able to pull enough of his focus to actually hear her words.

"… vineyard in Bordeaux. Many men worked for my father. Two of them were the best. One was my father's foreman, who had apprenticed at the vineyard and stayed. One of them, Alphonse, was aveugle, was blind from his birth and had lived his whole long life in our valley. They both knew when the grapes were most ripe, and which vines were most heavy and ready for harvest. They brought the best and most sweet grapes to my father, who made cheap wine of their offering." Thane fought to breathe, and listened.

"A fever swept through our small village. Many were sick, some died. Some were left disfigured or maimed by the disease. My father's foreman became aveugle, the sight burned out of his eyes. He could not see even the smallest light. He would not leave his bed, and he ordered the windows to be shuttered and barred. He became bitter and angry, and was violent towards those who would try to help him."

Thane realized that one of his hands was shaking and that his other was captured within both of Iselle's. His fist was wrapped inside her almost timid fingers, while her thumbs stroked the knuckles and made small circles on the back of his hand. He didn't feel the flush of warmth and louder heartbeat like when Remi had taken his hand, but he felt the fear draining away and right now that meant more. With every word she spoke the memories and nightmares sunk deeper and further away.

"Alphonse continued to work, to bring grapes to my father. My father joked of making the old blind man the new foreman and letting the young blind man drive himself to l'enfer. Many did not think his jokes were funny..." she trailed off for a moment, and in Thane's mind the images flared back to life.

"My father's foreman tried to return to work, but could not find the vineyard," Iselle's quiet voice cut across the clamor in his mind and Thane's attention was drawn to her again. She was still looking down at his hand. "Two men, both blind, one made excellent and one made a fool. My father's foreman tried to kill himself, but could not find a rope to hang himself with. Could not buy a gun to shoot himself with. No one would lead to the river to drown himself. Any way he tried to end his despair was taken from him and he was made to go on. His family, people he loved, would tell him, 'Ce n'est pas le plus mauvais, it isn't so bad, think of Alphonse; he has been blind his whole life and he goes on. He never has had what you had. Aren't you béni, aren't you blessed to have had sight at all?"

Thane tensed. Was she giving him a lecture? Telling him to man up, at least he wasn't dead, just like his father had done? But that man was not his father. The anger tried to claw its way out of the pit and Thane felt those claws dig in and pull him down.

"They did not know they were being cruel." Her words stopped his anger, made the claws release and the fury fall back. "To lose something you did not recognize, that is nothing. To have something taken that we value, that destroys us. It is not what we lose, it is how." Thane's fear surged; he loathed pity, and was afraid to see it in her. When he glanced up at her, she was looking at him, but there was no pity in her face. Instead there was anger, and defiance. Perhaps even a trace of her own fear.

"You and I have lost much and had much taken from us. Things that all children should have were rarely ours, and we understood their value. And now you are having what few things remained to you ripped away." He shuddered at her choice of words and her thumbs stopped making their small circles. The surcease of motion drew his eyes back to hers, brown with flecks of gold. "When every way to forget your loss is taken, how do you move on?"

"I don't know," he whispered. Iselle smiled in such a way it would have wrenched his heart less if she'd cried.

"You must find something that is greater than your loss. Finding courage is not enough. Finding strength is not enough. You must find something that is worth fighting to keep."

"How?"

Her crying smile was still in place. "I do not know. Ask Charlie. He has lifetimes of knowledge in losing and finding again. And Thane," she released his fist, allowing one of her hands to hang down and touching his cheek with the other, "you hold so tightly to your anger and fear. You are feeding a beast that will grow too large for the cage you have given it. When its hunger grows too great, it will devour you instead. You must learn to move on."

"Am I interrupting?" Charlie's brash voice was both cheerful and suggestive. Thane started and pulled away. Iselle let him.

"No!" Thane protested. The moment it was out of his mouth he knew it was too loud. Charlie chuckled. Iselle slid away and lowered her chin, allowing her brown hair to cover her face and hiding her expression from him.

"Naught tae be ashamed for, a body needs tae find comfort after a fight," Charlie continued. "And I've heard ye went through a snorter." Thane couldn't tell if he was relieved or annoyed by the disruption, but he was surprised at how glad he was to see Charlie. With his drunk on life teacher, he knew all he had to face was random balls of lightning. "Ye fit like, tadpole? We've lost nearly two days to that thrice knotted imp, and although I am pretty impressive I'm not so good with miracles."

"I thought we had until Sunday," Thane argued.

"Aye," Charlie said. "Tis Wednesday now. You've been out since after breakfast yesterday."

"But..." Thane searched for any argument that might prove his point, but nothing presented itself.

"Well, me lassie doc," Charlie addressed Iselle now, who had risen to her feet, "what do ye think? Is he fit for standing?"

She looked at him with the same deliberately blank expression she'd shown General Gage during her reprimand the last time she'd brought Thane food. "The boy is physically fine and prepared for training," she said each word carefully to downplay her accent. Charlie grinned at her and bowed before turning back to Thane.

"There ye have it. Now roust ye and grab some food tae chew while we go. I've time lost tae make up with you," and Charlie hooked his hand under one of the straps of Thane's backpack and tossed it in one smooth motion before taking two steps towards the infirmary door. Iselle raised a hand, palm out, and stopped him.

"Physically he is ready. But he has suffered great pain and loss, and you are not prepared to handle the beast you are trying to wake within him," she said, barely louder than a whisper and with almost no inflection.

Charlie blinked. The centuries old dragon man and the teenage French girl locked gazes. Thane struggled to get his backpack on while shoving eggs through gravy and onto a biscuit. He was too preoccupied to see the end of their exchange, but when he looked up Iselle had left.

"That's what all the ladies say about us blues," Charlie quipped. Thane rolled his eyes and took several more bites. "Come tadpole, we've got the day ahead."

Charlie led Thane around to a window of building fifteen, which was propped open with a stone. His teacher smiled smugly. "Bear in mind tadpole, these Sanctum types rely overmuch on magic and tech. Old and simple ways find 'em dropping the wean," and he lifted the window with one hand. "After ye."

Thane stood next to the window, not in front of it, and peered into the room beyond. It was empty. He climbed through nimbly, years of experience leaving through the basement bedroom window making him very skilled at not making any noise. His feet automatically searched out clear floor space and it wasn't until he was standing inside the dim room that he noticed all the debris strewn around.

"Fair work," Charlie said, standing next to him. "Better than expected."

Thane assumed Charlie was teasing and didn't respond. Instead, he looked around the small room and noted the piles of broken equipment. There were two that would be large enough to hide behind and several smaller ones that would make a racket if disturbed. Even in the dim light, Thane made his way through the room without touching any of the messes on the floor but passing close to both of the hiding places in case Charlie decided to throw lightning. Bare feet making no noise on the carpeted floor, Thane made it to the door and waited.

"Again, tadpole, better than expected," Charlie observed and opened the door. Thane blinked. He hadn't noticed Charlie crossing the room, but the dragon man preceded him out the door and into the hallway.

There were no more side trips or tests on the way to their top floor training room. They walked in silence and Thane's mind wandered backwards over his conversation with Iselle. "How do you move on? Find something greater than the loss... ask Charlie." What could lifetimes of experience in losing and finding possibly be? Could it help him forget the nightmares, Brennan crushed, Twitch stabbed, Iselle trapped... but the thought of her made the trembling in his hands slow and helped him breathe again before his nightmare self could claw its way from the abyss inside.

"I watched the vid," Charlie said abruptly. Thane kept his head down, kept walking up the stairs. "I saw what the imp did tae ye, and I watched ye seeing the others killed, not knowing twas naught but a game. I dinnae believe it."

Thane hoped that if he never responded, never acknowledged the topic that Charlie would drop it and they could get back to training. He'd much rather dodge balls of electricity for the next three days. Ask Charlie. But Charlie wasn't done yet.

"It wasnae that the flying monkey dragged ye in tae a closed session. Or that they dinnae suspend the training once they kenned ye was in there," Thane didn't comment, but he catalogued the knowledge that they could have stopped the training but didn't. Brennan made Sanctum sound noble, but most of Thane's experiences here had eroded the idea. "What really got my head burling was that ye went through all that and never sparked. Not once."

Thane paused, his foot hovering over the next step. He hadn't realized that, had not considered using the power they kept telling him he had. He'd reacted while people all around him fought and died. That meant his choices were to either be a monster or a coward, and neither was a great way to live a life. In his mind he heard Ms. Rasmussen giggle. His stomach hurt and no matter how hard he pushed it away, the image of his monster self resurfaced.

"... and that's how we'll do yer training going on," Charlie concluded. "If naught else, ye've proved danger disnae bring it out for ye. And I can be flexible." Thane thought about asking Charlie say it all again, but decided he didn't care. In fact, he was done.

"So what d'ye think, lad?" Charlie asked, opening the door at the top of the stairs.

"I can't do this," Thane said.

"Right enough," Charlie agreed. Thane was surprised enough to look the dragon man in the eye.

"What?"

"If ye say ye cannae, ye wilnae. If ye believe ye'll fail, it's already done. I cannae help ye." Charlie shut the door and walked down the staircase past Thane. "I'll let Gage know so he can wipe my slate here clean. Pleasure meeting ye, son."

"I am not your son," Thane exploded. His voice echoed down the stairwell. "I'm not anybody's son. I don't belong anywhere or to anyone because I'm a freak!" The last word burst from his mouth with a ball of blue white light and discordant crashing of music. It crackled through the air and boomed as it hit the far wall of the stairwell. The lights went extra bright and then plunged into darkness as Thane heard the pop and crack of shattering bulbs overhead and felt small glass shards raining down.

"That's keech." Charlie's voice was matter of fact. Thane could hear the dragon man coming closer as bits of glass crunched under his heavier feet. There were no windows in the stair well and in the darkness it was hard to tell exactly where the other man was until Thane felt Charlie's hand push against his arm. The dragon man found Thane's shoulder with his hand and pulled Thane into a rough embrace.

"Ye've had a rough start of it, one cannae argue that, but ye're a blinding good lad and those plugged nancies who've been in charge of ye dinnae ken what they've been missing." Charlie's arms were wrapped around Thane with a hand resting on the back of each of Thane's shoulders. Thane stood there and didn't resist. Charlie smelled a little like pine trees and more like campfire, and Thane remembered feeling safe and warm huddled next to Grandpa Whitaker, who ruffled his hair and told him he was special. His shoulders sagged and he leaned into Charlie.

"Yer special, Thane," Charlie unconsciously echoed Grandpa Whitaker in Thane's memory. "Ye dinnae ken how much. But time has come tae stop running away. Ye have tae accept yerself afore someone else can."

Not being able to see Charlie and knowing Charlie couldn't see him let Thane feel safer in the embrace. In a motion he had not made in more than six years, Thane awkwardly raised his arms and hugged Charlie back. He felt Charlie's arms tighten around him. "How?" Thane mumbled.

"How do ye accept yerself?" Charlie asked. Thane moved his head up and down against Charlie's shoulder. "Shut yer geggie against the whining." Thane reflexively pulled his head back to look at Charlie's face, even though he couldn't see it. "Yer a dragon, not a sea slug. A member of the most powerful race of beings in two worlds, and ye're braying like ye've lost a limb. Try finding the sunshine." Charlie rubbed the top of Thane's head affectionately, and more glass tinkled and fell off. "Speaking of," he added, and released the boy from the hug but kept a hand on his shoulder. "Let's get intae the room. We've got work ahead." And the dragon man directed Thane back up the stairs and opened the door.

Even with the power off, the windows flooded the room with afternoon sunlight. Thane saw that the room had been cleaned and emptied since they were here last, with all the gym equipment removed. There was nowhere to hide and nothing but open space bathed in light stretching out in every direction. It was like walking from a cave into an outdoor arena. Thane stayed in the doorway.

" I take back the last two days being wasteful. We've learned quite a bit." Charlie said, striding in to the room past him. "We ken being in danger disnae find yer Song. Scared's nary a bit of a bother. It's angry that gets ye afire. Which tells me something; ye're used to getting the fist and fighting back dinnae work. The man who raised ye mistreats ye, and that's made ye do a runner afore ever learning tae stand up for yerself. I shot up this place trying tae get ye tae touch yer Song. Naught. Ye watched five people bite it and stuck a grenade in a man's gob tae save a mite of a lady, but dinnae light up once. It's angry that ye're no good with, where ye lose enough control tae spark."

"So you're going to try to make me angry?" Thane asked from the doorway.

"Aye right!" Charlie snorted. "Brawling angry is for berserkers. Ye try that for earnest, ye're twice as like tae hurt someone on yer own side. This will be the third time I've said this so unstop yer ears and let it sink past. Ye need tae find a place of calm where naught can touch ye, and sing yer Song from there. That's the only way ye'll be in control. Ye have tae learn tae ride the lightning."

Thane considered that. Being in control sounded too good to be true, but the image of the blue leviathan tearing apart those he loved terrified him in a way that his dad's-- no, Robert Whitaker's-- anger never had. But he didn't dare hope. He'd never dared hope, because if he did and it was torn away Thane knew he'd never stop bleeding.

"Manky threads tadpole, get in here," Charlie ordered. "Ye'd think I was trying tae feed ye tae a snake instead of offering power and glory."

A snake. Thane flashed back to the viper in the desert. There hadn't been anyone around to hurt or protect or hide from and he had felt invincible. That something deep inside, past anger and fear down where he lived and wanted to keep living. Thane remembered touching that something and knew he could do this. He could defeat the monster inside. He lifted his foot and walked into the sunlight towards his teacher in the center of the room.

"All we need are some inspirational power chords," Thane joked. Maybe it was the hug in the dark. Or hearing that his tightly held fear of not being wanted was stupid. Or Iselle's story about loss and moving on. It was definitely the memory of defeating the viper.

But Thane decided, for the first time in his life, to hope.

CHAPTER 19

"This is hopeless!" Thane groaned, his body sore and aching, his mind frustrated, and his heart dispirited.

"Again, but focus yer breathing," Charlie instructed. "Mind, in and out yer nose only. Breath is the first step."

Sighing through his mouth, Thane repositioned his feet so they were less than a shoulder width apart and his toes were pointed forward. He closed his mouth and breathed in slowly through his nose with his arms hanging down. As he breathed out, he brought his arms around in front, right hand in a fist and left palm flat. Bringing them together, left palm over right fist, he pushed his right hand forward and released the fist then brought both open hands back slowly and lowered them to his sides.

"Ye're too stiff, lad. Movement has tae flow from ye, not fight ye."

"I'm trying!" Thane wished Charlie would just shut up and stop watching. It had been six hours and so far Thane was still in the opening position of the Taijiquan kata Charlie was trying to teach him. The first position had ten steps, all with names like "starting posture," "starting form," "beginning position," and Thane's current sarcastic favorite, "standing quietly."

"Watch me," Charlie ordered. Thane obediently kept his eyes on his teacher as the muscled dragon man closed his eyes and breathed. The dragon man placed his feet comfortably and began moving his arms through the forms, one stance blending seamlessly into the next. Charlie had already taught Thane the names and positions of each movement in the form, some cool ones like "Step Back and Repulse Monkey," some that he felt silly doing because they were called things like "Fair Lady Works the Shuttles," and some that weren't names as much as directions like "Hitting your Opponent's Ears with Both Fists."

Charlie made them look effortless, as though the kata was more natural to him than walking. Thane felt ridiculous going through them, like the awkward kid dancing while the crowd pointed and laughed. Charlie finished with "Closing Posture" and exhaled slowly.

"So what did ye learn?" the dragon man asked.

"That you've never been laughed at," Thane answered sullenly.

Charlie barked out a laugh. "True enough, I've never had an issue keeping a lady's attention. Affections can be a mite slippery, but I only go in for that once a century or so." Despite the glib tone, an expression of deep sadness drifted across Charlie's features. Thane wasn't expecting it, and the depth of the pain staggered him. Even with all his personal experience with grief, fear, and loneliness, Thane would have to live several lifetimes longer before understanding that level of anguish.

Iselle's voice sounded in his memory, the flavor of her accent stronger in his mind. "Ask Charlie. He has lifetimes of knowledge in losing and finding again."

"It's about being confident enough tae let go," Charlie began to explain. "Tae let the movement do itself while ye're just being there because ye belong there. Och, are ye heeding me?"

"Um," Thane responded, not sure how to ask the question. "What do you know about Iselle?"

"Is that skirt what has yer head tummeling yer monkees? Dinnae ken ye had it in ye. But now isnae the time for a pull-over--" Charlie started, but Thane jumped in.

"No, she isn't-- I mean, that's not why I was asking. She said something about you and I was wondering how well she knew you." Thane stuttered.

"Not as well as I think ye're implying, imp," Charlie cuffed him on the side of the head. "Why, what did the bit o' fluff say?"

"She said you knew a lot about loss," Thane tried to pull all his thoughts together to make the question but it wasn't something you just asked another guy. "She said you had lifetimes of experience in losing and finding and..." he couldn't quite push out that he should ask about it, and so added lamely, "well, do you?"

Charlie's penetrating blue eyes flashed and the color in them started to spin. Thane took one deliberate and slow step away, keeping his hands down and visible. "When I first met Iselle, I thought she was someone else. She read me and called me on it and I knew it wasnae her," Charlie began, his brogue fading as his voice deepened.

His morphing seemed slow and controlled, so Thane pressed on. "Who did you think she was?"

Charlie snarled and his fingers elongated into sharp claws with a crack. "Ye have nae earned that story yet, hatchling."

That stung, and Thane's shoulders slumped slightly. Even in his changing state, Charlie must've noticed because he sighed. "Here's our bargain: go through the form and if ye do well, I'll tell the story."

"Is it about a dragon?" Thane asked, wondering if that was the catalyst for his teacher's shifting.

"No," Charlie said, neck stretching and the tanned skin becoming mottled with blue. "Like all good stories, it's about a woman. Opening Posture of Taijiquan." As the average sized man standing near the center of the room grew and spread into the immense sapphire behemoth that wrapped around all its edge, Thane placed his feet and inhaled through his nose. He closed his eyes as Charlie had done, and tried to focus on his breath and movement and sound. His right fist and left palm rose and joined in front of his sternum.

"This story begins centuries ago," the rumbling voice was so deep that Thane could feel the sound waves vibrating in his ribcage like bass notes. His hands moved forward, palms open, and fell to his sides. "I was young and had spent my first two hundred years thinking humans were playthings, pets to romp and tumble with. I'd learned early on to enjoy the company of female humans, though never as anything but a pleasurable way to pass the time. Wild Horse Shakes Its Mane."

Thane shifted his weight to his right leg and held one arm with his open right palm at shoulder height and his left palm open at the waist, inhaling through his nose. "And then I met my phoenix," Charlie continued, the cadence of his voice changing to something slower and wondrous. As Thane rotated the hands toward his center he pulled his left foot in and turned his torso to his left side and exhaled.

"She was stunning. Literally. The first moment I saw her, I was too overwhelmed to speak. Because of some unsavory dealings with the Guardian Council I was hiding as a slave, rowing in a barge on the river. We came around a bend and she stepped to the edge of a glided balcony. Her hair was shining and black as the space between the stars. Spending all that time in the company of human woman had given me an artist's eye for their beauty, and she was perfect. By that time I'd mingled with all the refugees of Shae and met the Fates and the Muses and none of them, not one, could light a candle in a room where she was. White Crane Spreads Its Wings."

Thane pivoted on his right foot, inhaling through his nose as his right hand came sweeping down in an arc and scooped in front. His left palm led his body at center as it turned and he exhaled, bringing his right arm up until it hovered above his head. "It was her eyes, more than anything else that captivated me. I had lived centuries, but her eyes had seen worlds burn and be reborn. She laughed to see us coming, but in her eyes at that moment was so much sorrow. I swore to meet her. Brush Knee to Playing the Lute."

Thane heard the direction and his body flowed while his mind was miles away and centuries past. "I knew she would never converse with a slave, and so I assumed another identity. I choose someone who would be a political asset and whom she wouldn't dare refuse an audience." Thane inhaled, shifting his weight from right to left and watched the story unfold in his mind. "At first she only saw me as a resource and used me in her maneuvering for power and place. But I had two advantages that I'd never had before when courting: passion and sincerity. And she was a challenge, because for the first time I met a female who wanted nothing to do with me romantically. Step Back and Repulse Monkey to Grasping Sparrow's Tail, left then right."

Thane stepped back, shifting his weight from his left to his right and moving his arms almost as though he was doing a breast stroke but backwards, pushing out with one arm in a slow and steady motion while drawing the other back. Charlie's voice reverberated through the room, a series of bass notes that pulsed with the intensity of the memory. "When she loved me it was as though I finally understood the heaven that humans aspire to. Her Song was so strong within her that I could feel it in the air, and my body vibrated with it. When she died that first time, I understood hell. Single Whip, Waving Hands Like Clouds, Single Whip."

"She died?" Thane's eyes popped open and he looked around to find the dragon's head. Charlie was staring out the window, gazing at the lowering sun.

"Keep going, hatchling. You are doing well."

Thane closed his eyes again and resumed his push stance. He peeked through one eyelid to see Charlie's gargantuan head staring at him, waiting. Thane snapped his eye shut again and swiveled his body, hands passing at eye level with palms out and then floating down on the opposite side. "Yes, she died." The sorrow in his voice was fierce and poignant, and Thane felt a sympathetic rush of grief as he inhaled through his nose and allowed his hands to float into Waving Hands Like Clouds. "When I found her it was too late, and

I held her body in my arms while I felt her soul and Song depart. I was crushed. I had never before been lonely, for what dragon could possibly need any other to feel complete? But after her, I was broken into pieces so tiny I could not fathom putting them back together. I was angry, and wrecked such destruction as this world has rarely seen."

His sorrowful tone turned musing. "That era was when I earned most of my black marks with the Guardian Council. So few of them at the time had any capacity for love or grief that they could not understand what I was experiencing. Many thought I had gone mad. They were not wrong. It took two Legions to bring me to heel, and then they imprisoned me without sunlight or Song for over a decade. And it did not matter. My sun had been extinguished and my Song destroyed. Pat the Horse on the Back and Kick with Left Heel."

Thane's arms and legs followed his sensei's instructions without any interference from his brain. He was remembering being inside that prison cell, hurt and alone, where even the walls could annihilate him. What would that have been like for ten years? His mind shuddered.

"Then a friend brought me hope," and Charlie's entire demeanor changed. His story had felt like a burden, a weight that bowed him down that sharing had only made heavier. But now even with his eyes closed, Thane felt sunlight breaking through clouds as Charlie's voice took on both joy and awe. "She said that my love was a true phoenix, a rarity among the Shaerealm and one of the few stories your people got right. In our world they had been flying creatures of fire, in shape and size similar to a swan or peacock. When they grew old their fire would consume them until all that remained was their jeweled heart, a deep autumn orange in color and about the size of a man's fist. That jewel was the egg from which they would hatch, again to grow and fly and fill the world with fire and light. That was how they existed in the Shaerealm, the only creature to be neither shadow, shade, nor fae, but faceted unto themselves. Snake Creeps Down, Golden Rooster Stands on Left Leg."

Thane inhaled and extended his leg, bent back, and allowed his snake arm to creep down to his ankle while the opposite arm rose in a diagonal behind him. He kept his eyes closed, visions of the snake and the rooster interspersed with the orange jewel. "In this world the Song is different, and the fire of the phoenix cannot sustain them. When trapped here the phoenix began to die and their fires could not burn hot enough. This rare wonder of our world became even more scarce. The Sylph saved them. She found the fires of their souls were compatible with human bodies and so merged them. Thus they became the phoenix souled. Right leg."

Thane's body repeated its previous series of movements on the opposite side. What would it mean to be phoenix souled? Thane kept his eyes closed and mouth shut and waited for the answer.

"When the body of a phoenix souled passes, the spirit has two choices. It too can pass on into the ether or whatever may come after, or it can stay until it finds another compatible body. They are reborn. And the surest way for a phoenix to choose rebirth here instead of traveling on is if the phoenix was truly loved. As my love was." Charlie made a sound deep in his long throat that sounded similar to a purr, a sound of pure contentment. "This was the news that she-- my friend-- brought. My love was a phoenix soul, and was even now being reborn. And I could see her again. The first time our eyes met again I felt her Song, and I knew I had been reborn. Fair Lady Works the Shuttles."

There it was. Thane's body moved without conscious thought as he considered Charlie's experience with losing and finding again. On one side an eternal torture, knowing that no matter how many times he found her and loved her that he would watch her die again. On the other, an eternal joy knowing each time he lost her that she would be reborn so he could fall in love with her again. Thane flowed from Fair Lady to Pick Up the Needle and Flashing the Arms, the three which individually made him feel silly but as part of the entire kata felt right.

Going into Deflect, Parry, and Punch, Thane realized that there was one vital question he hadn't asked. "Did you find her again?" Thane spoke the words without opening his eyes so he wouldn't see the expression on the draconic face.

"I did. And again and again. She is the reason why Sanctum always calls me whenever blue dragon blood is suspected. I have been more prolific than any other dragon in the history of either world by a factor of ten. She loves children. Apparent Close and Punch."

"How many times?"

"We've had nineteen lifetimes together."

"Have you found her now?" Thane moved through the deceptive posture and into Cross Hands. Charlie didn't respond. Hands crossed with the right underneath, Thane inhaled through his nose as he brought his hands up to just below his neck. Allowing them to roll, he sank down with bent knees and exhaled while lowering his hands, palms down. Then he rose and his hands drifted back to his sides until he stood, straight backed and loose muscled.

"I did it!" he shouted, pumping a fist in the air. "I went through the whole form, Charlie!"

"You did." Charlie's diamond head drooped and he did not look at Thane while acknowledging the victory. Thane realized Charlie hadn't answered his last question, and that meant he knew what the answer was.

"When was the last time you saw her?" Thane asked.

Charlie sighed, dragon sides heaving and the temperature in the room rising slightly. "Nearly fifty years ago." His bass voice trembled and he seemed to shrink in on himself. "It has never taken this long to find her before."

"But there are billions of people in the world," Thane said, trying to be comforting. "How can you possibly find her every time?"

"That is my greatest fear," the floor shook as the entire length of the scaly body quivered. "If she has lived and I didn't find her and she chose to move on past the stars. How would I even know?" Another tremor passed through the dragon and he collapsed inward, the huge bulk imploding. Charlie the man sat on the floor, legs crossed, and stared at his hands.

"How did you find her the other times?" Thane asked without moving towards the dragon man.

"Times my friend would lend a hand. Oft times Sanctum would. They're a bunch of twally scunners, but they do know the world is better off if I have my love with me." Charlie ran a hand along the bare skin of his scalp. "This time neither of 'em has been any use. I dinnae ken where she is, or how tae find her."

"What's her name? I bet Twitch could do a search."

"Her name changes every life. She's been a bairn on every continent in every walk of life." Charlie sighed. "Sometimes I think she's trying tae make it hard."

"Could she be looking for you?"

"If she's been reborn, it's likely she's looking for something but she wouldnae ken what. She disnae have memories of old lives, just dreams or flashes. I like tae find her while she's young so we can grow up together and I get tae spend more time with her afore she moves on again." Charlie stared stoically forward, shoulders square, but Thane had enough experience holding back emotion himself to tell that Charlie was bleeding inside. "And if she is out there, could be I've missed most of her life by now," the dragon man cleared his throat noisily.

"I'll help," Thane blurted out, moved by the story and Charlie's pain and his own success with the Taijiquan kata.

"Ye, lad? How?"

"I don't know, but I will. I swear I'll help you find her if it takes my whole life," Thane took several quick steps toward Charlie, wanting to ease the man's pain and trying not to think too closely about what he was promising. He held out his right hand to the dragon.

"Ye're a braw lad and ye do me proud," Charlie shook Thane's hand solemnly, then pulled. Thane fell forward and Charlie guided his arm until they were sitting next to each other in the shadow under the windows. "Ye may be generations far, but yer family."

"I am?" Thane asked, surprised. When Charlie had said, "This one is mine, but at least four back," to Gage, Thane hadn't made the connection. But if Thane was a blue dragon and Charlie was a blue... "So you aren't my father. But you are my grandfather?"

Charlie tilted his head back and closed one eye, scratching his chin. "Bit further afore that, but aye, I'm back there somewhere for ye. Ye have any granders now?"

Thane swallowed and looked down. "Not really. I had Grandpa Whitaker, but he, um, he isn't around anymore."

Charlie leaned back against the wall. "So ye have nobody in yer corner, then, and I've lost the ones in mine." There was silence for a few beats. The sun set lower, dipping down below the horizon. "If yer in need of one, I could be yer grandpa, tadpole."

It was suddenly hard to swallow around the lump in his throat. Thane had to try twice before his voice would make any sound. "That's fine by me, I guess."

"Aye, me too," Charlie said, looking out the windows across the room. Following his example, Thane leaned back against the wall and stared through the glass. The purple in the sky was deepening and tiny pinpricks of light shone in the far distance. "I think Iselle's taken a shine to ye."

"No way," Thane instantly responded, distracted. "She's too old for me."

"She's not more than sixteen."

"She's sixteen?" Thane mused. She seemed so much older and more mature than he was. She intimidated him and seemed inaccessible. An image of Remi laughing with him in the hallway flashed into his mind. "Doesn't matter. She's not my type."

"Well then, if ye've already got a lass on yer line..." Charlie trailed off with a smile. They sat with their backs against the wall in companionable stillness. Until Thane's stomach growled.

"Aye, couldnae have said it better," Charlie stood. "Let's get something tae warm the belly. We have all day tomorrow for training."

"Okay grandpa," Thane said, and the word felt strange in his mouth. Charlie shuddered.

"Just Charlie? Being cried a grandpa doesn't sit right on my shoulders."

"Yeah, saying it felt weird," Thane admitted. "Can you call me Thane instead of tadpole?"

"Aye, right," Charlie grinned. "Now off tae the mess, tadpole. I'll lead the way."

"Okay grandpa," Thane said, and Charlie rolled his eyes. Saying it was still awkward, but even teasing, something inside Thane that had always been cold and hard softened, and a bit of warmth pushed in.

CHAPTER 20

It was still dark when Thane's eyes popped open. He'd spent so much time asleep in the infirmary he felt wide awake now. It was also disconcerting to be sharing a room; Thane had slept by himself in the unfinished basement for as long as he could remember. He was afraid of it at first, the framed out walls were like the house's skeleton and the uncovered pipes making strange and loud noises. Eventually he'd found music in the sounds and grew to like the bare bones look of his own underground world.

Twitch's breathing was like sleeping in the basement for the first time, but instead of being afraid of the deep darkness this room was claustrophobic. Thane's new bunkmate made strange noises and cast unfamiliar shadows on the wall. He even muttered and talked in his sleep. Surprisingly Twitch turned out to be religious, saying the word "faith" frequently in conjunction with "monitoring" and "understanding." From the disjointed and occasionally nonsensical phrases, Thane gathered that Twitch believed God was monitoring him through faith and that faith explained everything else, and that General Gage would never understand faith.

That last comment was harsh, but Thane had already heard Twitch and General Gage argue twice. Charlie didn't care for General Gage much either, but Thane thought he understood the man better than either of them because Thane knew about Remi. General Gage was taking the safety of the world more seriously than any of them because he had more to protect in it. Thane could respect that, and the more he experienced the bizarre world of Sanctum that was General Gage's workplace, the more he respected Remi's father for trying to protect her from it.

Twitch moaned and rolled over so his face was to the wall. Pale yellowish light started to shine through the room's single window and Thane knew it would be sunrise soon. The clock on the nightstand was impossible to read because it was angled towards Twitch's bed, so the red LED numbers faced away from Thane.

It made him nervous. What had once been a standard issue alarm clock had been transformed into something that looked futuristic and not entirely stable. He'd wanted to ask about it last night, but didn't dare. As the light from the window brought the room from the darkness of night to the dimness of dawn one of the two cylinders attached to the alarm clock started hissing. Thane sat up wishing he'd asked.

The silver cylinder hissed as the lens on top swiveled, and a red guidance laser lit up. One red dot slid along Twitch's exposed back until it stopped on his upper arm. The hissing increased in volume and intensity. Thane tensed and then there was a whoosh from the second hollow cylinder. A familiar looking dart the size of Thane's pinky finger flew from the contraption on the nightstand and pierced the center of the red dot, puncturing Twitch's skin. The computer expert groaned and rolled over, pulling his blankets over his head.

Thane watched his bunkmate intently, but nothing else happened. The hissing sound ceased and for several minutes more there was no sound except breathing. Careful to make no noise, Thane slid off his cot and padded across the room on bare feet. He halted next to Twitch's prone body. Should he pull back the covers to check on the other boy? Or should he just ignore this particular weirdness and go shower?

It occurred to him that he could see the clock from here and he turned to check the time. The moment his eyes connected to the glowing red numerals, the clock changed from 6:59 to 7:00 a.m. Thane turned back and was nose to nose with an opened eyed and standing Twitch.

"What the threads are you doing?"

"Ack!" Thane jumped back. Clutching his chest he gasped, "But you were asleep."

"And now I'm awake. It's good to know your powers of stating the obvious are intact. But I repeat; what in the nine knotted threads were you doing? Because I am more than happy to kick you out of my room and leave you to be Jaeger's perfectly average lab rat for as long as he finds you useful--"

"I was checking to see if you were okay, all right?" Thane cut in angrily. "You were talking in your sleep all night and keeping me up--"

"What did I say?" Twitch's left eyelid spasmed and his hand jerked up and down.

"What? I don't know, you were mumbling," Twitch was intense enough to make Thane nervous. The older boy stared at him, clearly unsatisfied, so Thane added, "You were talking about faith. Are you really religious or something?"

Left eye twitching sporadically, Twitch barked a harsh laugh. "Yeah, I'm Irish Catholic. Why were you checking on me?"

"That thing," Thane gestured towards the alarm clock, "shot you with a tranquilizer dart and I thought maybe Jaeger booby-trapped it like my room and so I wanted to make sure you were still breathing." He said all that in a rush, and sullenly looked down.

Twitch looked at Thane incredulously. "You're an idiot."

"You know what? Next time I won't care if you're dead, how about that."

"It's a caffeine dart, not a tranq. It helps me wake up in the morning. I designed it that way."

"You designed it?" Thane asked. "Why?"

"It's a completely elegant solution to an inelegant problem with the wet works," Twitch began, and went on about the simplicity and efficiency of the device. Thane was surprised to learn it was nothing but a blowgun that was hooked up to a compressed air cylinder with a webcam and laser pointer on it for aiming. Twitch had spent three days perfecting it. The hardest part was the chemistry of a dart filled with caffeine equal to about three cups of coffee so it would wake Twitch up but not cause caffeine intoxication. Luckily coffee was available in the mess hall and the chemistry lab had enough water and activated charcoal for Twitch to extract the caffeine for his own use.

Thane had never seen the other boy so animated or heard him talk so much. Twitch was passionate about technology and its applications and was delighted when Thane asked intelligent questions. Talking about the alarm clock led to a discussion about other things Twitch had designed. Some were simple but brilliant, like the voice command protocol for the computers. Others were catastrophic failures, like trying to reprogram a car's navigation system so that it used the GPS coordinates of a different car.

"It would have been great for tracking," Twitch insisted, "the car's computer just didn't have the capability to track the other car in real time and still be able to tell you where you were. Teams ended up stranded using it, so they pulled the program. But even that was better than my first alarm clock."

By this time the conversation had lasted all the way to breakfast in the mess hall. Thane still didn't have a code for food, but Twitch went through twice and brought him muffins, jam, eggs, bacon, juice, and the special of the day, waffles. Thane started shoveling food in his mouth before asking, "What was wrong with the first alarm clock?"

"I didn't think of caffeine," Twitch admitted. "I found an old car battery and some cables in my dad's shop, so I tried to rig it to give me an electric shock every morning. I couldn't get the voltage consistent with the old battery," he looked sheepish. "My dad was pretty mad."

"How old were you when you did this?" Thane asked.

Twitch grimaced. "Eight?"

"What? Why?"

The fingers of Twitch's right hand began to tap a complex pattern against his right thigh. "I don't sleep well," he finally admitted. "I take medication to let me sleep, but the meds make it hard to wake up. I used to miss class all the time. My dad would freak out when the school would call and say I'd been skipping. He didn't know what to do with me until he sent me here."

"Your dad sent you to Sanctum?" Thane was shocked. "I thought you said you didn't have any Shae blood."

"I don't."

"Then why did your dad send you here? How did he even know about it?"

"My dad owns a custom vehicle shop. The kind of place you take your car when you want to install extra huge speakers all around or rims that spin on their own or a really intricate paint job. That's the front, anyway. My dad's really good at it, so years ago Sanctum started bringing him their vehicles when they need to be modified."

"Modified?"

"Like gun turrets or Song-proof glass or big and tough enough for a troglodytarum to drive, stuff like that." Twitch shrugged, his right hand still tapping. "When I started reprogramming the cars computers, Sanctum owed my dad enough favors that they agreed to take me here."

Thane swallowed his second bite of his third waffle. "So your dad knows all about this stuff?"

"Yeah," Twitch sighed. "I'm the only kid in the world who gets to go away to magic school and still has to go home for Mass."

Thane snorted. "There are worse things." He took a pensive bite of a jam filled muffin.

"Yeah," Twitch agreed, the heavy statement drawing their conversation into silence.

"Tadpole!" Charlie's cheerful voice broke through the gloomy lull. "Ye fit like?"

"Sure, grandpa," Thane said, swallowing. Twitch's face was priceless, his mouth hanging open and his eyes wide.

Charlie grimaced. "Still not liking that name, lad."

Thane grinned at him. "You give me a better one and I'll do the same for you."

"Noted." Charlie smiled at Twitch. "Morning Twitch. Off tae watch the matrix?"

Twitch blinked and looked past them off to his left. "What? Threads, I have to find Gage," and he practically flew out of his seat and ran to the door.

"Did I say something amiss?" Charlie asked, surprised.

"I don't know," Thane said.

"Come on," and Charlie turned to the exit.

Thane picked up his tray and then piled Twitch's on top of it, struggling to balance both as he followed Charlie from the cafeteria. The troll on duty at the trash can gave Thane an evil glare at the uneaten food on both trays.

"Food doesn't grow on trees," it growled at him.

Thane blinked. He settled for an apologetic smile instead of arguing, and then hurried to follow Charlie back to building fifteen. How would they get in this time?

Charlie placed his palm on the scanner next to one of the side doors of building fifteen. The line of white traced his palm up and down and then the rectangle turned green and the door clicked, opening a few inches on its own.

"They gave you access?" Thane asked.

"Aye, days ago," Charlie responded. He glanced over his shoulder at Thane and smiled. "But the legal way just isnae as fun. Those granny grey hips on the Council need tae be shaken up once in a while afore they're full of naught save bum and parsley."

Thane hadn't been in their top floor training room in the morning before. The sun was already hot and the air sticky outside and the air conditioning in the building was churning to keep up with the rising temperature. Light shone in from every window wall and the room which had given Thane the feeling of a Roman arena now felt bright and cheerful.

"Right, tadpole, let's start with yer form. Breathe in through yer nose." Charlie instructed. Thane closed his eyes and began.

They spent all morning going through the form over and over. At first Charlie kept up a running commentary of suggestions and critiques, but as the hours passed, he quieted. Thane stopped paying attention to Charlie after about four hours, instead immersing himself and all his thoughts in the movements and flow of the kata. Then he sank deeper, forgetting the movements and focusing only on his breath. In for a slow set of heartbeats, and out for an equal length. Breathe in, pause, and breathe out.

"Hark now," Charlie's words floated across the top of his consciousness like drops of oil sliding over a deep pond, his voice the deep resonance of the dragon. "In that space between your palms there is energy, a glow that sparks and crackles. It sings with power and lightning."

From the void where he was, Thane heard the Song. The rumble of thunder and the movement of electricity ran in counterpoint, one deep and abiding and one sparkling and high. Moving ever between them was a tenor humming, a steady vibration that sang the first and root note of the chord. Thane allowed that melody to sing in his mind until it was set and clear and surprisingly familiar. This music had flowed through him before.

"Imagine a glass sphere between your hands," Thane did, lost in the music of his mind. "Now let the lightning Song flow from your hands into the sphere and watch it expand like a balloon. The ball will grow until the Song is contained inside. Let the Song lead."

The Song that filled Thane's darkness drifted through him like waves until he could feel it pouring out his palms. He imagined the glass ball drinking in all the sound and expanding as the Song filled it. But it wasn't quite right; the music felt incomplete. It had high, mid, and low, but it needed rhythm and counterpoint. Thane dug deeper into the Song and added his heartbeat as a driving beat and the rushing of his blood as a counterpoint. The ball in his mind's eye grew greater than the space between his hands, so he pushed it forward.

"Tadpole..." Charlie's voice lost the some of the dragon's lower tones.

The music filled Thane, the Song of life and lightning acting as a barrier between what Thane's ear's heard and what his mind could process.

"That's enough, tadpole," Charlie said more loudly.

The rumble of thunder and hum of electricity folded Charlie's words into their Song and played more intensely. The ball still expanded in Thane's mind, the music never ending and so the ball would never be full.

"Thane!" Charlie shouted, and the edge of panic in his voice was discordant enough to register, but not distract Thane. The music rushed out of him, pulling away strength and weakening his defenses. It demanded his attention and his power, drawing away the tightly held lid on his anger and fear. Memories flooded him and were pulled into the music, whirlpooling around him and submerging him.

He was drowning. Every time Robert Whitaker yelled at him, beat him or locked him in the basement flashed past his eyes, the pain and fear of the memory grabbing him and spinning him. Anger flowed over the edge. Millions of memories of his mother ignoring him or manipulating him dug their claws in and jerked him the other direction. Bitterness and resentment colored the flow of his music, the snapping and crackling increasing in volume while the bass of thunder intensified. Mocking and laughing from classmates because of his clothes or lack of any of the coolest newest things, Harper's blackmail, Lanie's tears, Grandpa Whitaker's swung fist after the stroke, and Ms. Rasmussen making him electrocute Mr. Hoffman crashed in waves against him and sucked him under, making the music dark and violent.

And underneath everything, so far inside the music that it plucked the strings to make them vibrate, something stirred. Not the deep power he'd felt before. Like the plates of the earth shifting to change the face of the planet, the pieces of Thane's soul that he had never acknowledged moved and rose. Covered by anger and fed with fear and hatred, he'd refused them. Ignored them. Pushed them away. But the Song pulled them out and set them free.

"No," Thane shouted, discordant and jarring. The leviathan, the monster slated to destroy the world, crawled out of the abyss in which he had imprisoned it and began to devour him from the inside. "No!" He tried to fight the music, to shut it away, but it was too powerful. He couldn't even open his eyes.

"Thane," a voice whispered in his hear. In the midst of his overwhelming internal struggle, he barely felt the hands that came to rest on each of his shoulders. The voice was quiet and dissonant, directly at odds with his Song of power and anger, lightning and violence. "Remi said she's running away with Jeran."

"Huh?" Thane opened his eyes and immediately shut them again as shining blue and white light burned against his retinas.

"Hold!" Charlie yelled, "Dinnae lose it or we'll all end sidey ways-"

And Thane lost all control of the Song. He felt the crackling energy as his hands released it. Something hard hit him from behind, knocking him prone and lying heavily across his back. There was a sound so loud his ears couldn't contain it and his mind couldn't comprehend it, and a wall of concussive force tore the weight off his back and pushed him several feet away on his stomach. The moment he stopped moving he was showered in shards of glass and bits of metal.

"Weaver's boads," Charlie swore. His voice sounded like it came from somewhere under water and far away, and Thane shook his head trying to clear it.

"What happened?" his words sounded warped and strange too. Charlie was standing on the opposite side of the room next to a very large hole where the wall used to be. Thane placed his palms on the floor and pushed, ignoring the slivers of glass that sliced his palms. He got to a sitting position and looked around the room.

"Why," Charlie began, sound stretching and shaping in bizarre ways in Thane's ears, "I suppose ye did."

"What?" Thane was dumbfounded. "How?"

"Yer electricity ball. Yer Song fair exploded out of ye and intae the wall," Charlie said, running a hand along the wall and assessing the damage. Sirens began wailing outside, sounding like alien ships to Thane's traumatized ears.

"Who stopped me?" Thane's clouded mind struggled to make sense of what Charlie was saying. He couldn't have done this. He was only imaging the ball while doing his kata. How could an imaginary ball do damage? He remembered drowning in the Song. Who brought him out of it? Who would have used Remi's name?

Thane's heart dropped into his stomach. "General Gage!" he shouted, spinning around awkwardly on his hands and knees. That had been the general's voice. How could he not have recognized it? The lightning Song must have taken over for General Gage to sound so dissonant against the Song. He frantically searched the debris, his eyes still fuzzy and his head sore and throbbing. Where was Remi's father? The first likely shape turned out to be twisted metal in a pile. Remi's tear stained face popped into his mind, "I hate not knowing where he is or if he's coming back. Promise me..."

"Argh!" Thane threw another large piece of broken rebar and window frame behind himself. "General Gage! Can you answer me?"

A warbled sound filtered in through his abused eardrums. It could have been a groan. Pushing unsteadily to his feet, Thane tried to figure out which direction it was coming from. As his eyes slowly cleared he saw movement about fifteen feet away and noticed a short path through the debris, as if something had landed in it and pushed it back. Thane wobbled closer as quickly as he could and saw the prone figure of a man in a uniform laying in the wreckage, like a broken toy after a fire. "General!" Thane called. There was no response. "Charlie, help," Thane called over his shoulder.

"Cannae just now, tadpole," Charlie yelled back. "Mite busy here."

"Charlie, General Gage could die," Thane screamed. "I need help!"

"Ye'll have tae do it, tadpole," Charlie called back calmly. "Ye managed tae knock out one of the support beams and if I let go this side of the building will collapse, followed by the rest of it."

Thane froze. He had no idea what to do. He thought back to Brennan kneeling over the unconscious Mr. Hoffman and checking for a pulse. Brennan had put two fingers somewhere on Mr. Hoffman's neck-- Thane tried it. Nothing.

"That's my Adam's apple, son," General Gage's voice was raspy. Thane jerked his hand away.

"General Gage sir, are you all right?" Thane asked loudly.

"I can't hear you. My head's still ringing from the blast," Gage lifted a shaky hand and patted Thane on the arm. "Glad I got to you before it got any bigger." He coughed. "Could've taken down the whole building, otherwise." He coughed again and gasped, trying to adjust his position.

"Don't move, sir," Thane pleaded. "I'll get help."

"That would be nice," the general said quietly. "I think I landed wrong."

Thane tried to keep his panic in check. "Twitch," he called in a shaky voice. There was no response. "Twitch!" he screamed, remembering how the computer tech almost magically appeared on a screen in the testing room. "Twitch! We need help!"

Gage's hand brushed his arm and Thane looked down. "I think... the blast... knocked out communications in the building." He was gasping and his breathing was becoming steadily more labored. The sound of the sirens around the compound grew clearer. "There should be...rescue crews. They'll start from the bottom and... sweep. Maybe you," the general was wheezing now, "could go get them."

"I'll be right back," Thane promised, and stood up. He took one moment to breathe in and choose to ignore the pain in his twisted ankle and the myriad of cuts and bits of glass wedged in his skin, then ran. He burst through the door into the stairwell and began leaping down the stairs two and three at a time, catching himself on the railings to minimize impact and increase speed. "Help!" he shouted, his voice echoing down in the darkness. "We need help! General Gage is hurt!"

There was no answer. There was no other sound besides the pounding of his feet and the echoes of his words. "Rescue crews! The general is down!" he screamed. He came down too hard on his ankle and it gave out, pitching him forward. Thane fell, arms pinwheeling, and landed hard with his ribs impacting the edges of the cement stairs. He bumped down two more stairs before rolling to a stop on the next landing. "Help," he wheezed, breath knocked out of him and fiery pain in his side.

From far below, he heard a door slam. Distant voices traveled up the empty stairwell, indistinct and tenuous. "Rescue crew!" Thane's mind screamed, but the weak sound that came out was barely more than a whisper. He could hear footsteps echoing on the stairs as the rescue crew pounded up from one floor to the next. In moments they would disappear through a door to search a floor below and General Gage might die before they entered the stairwell again.

"Argh!" he yelled, and below he heard a door bang open. The rescue crew was leaving the stairwell. He frantically looked around, but there was nothing to see in the darkness. His ankle throbbed and pushed against his shoe, trying to demand his attention when he really didn't care about it. Thane reached down and ripped his left shoe off, nearly blacking out with the pain. He threw it down the empty space in the center of the staircase.

"Ow," the exclamation floated back up to him though the darkness. Thane's chin jerked up. He could hear voices below speaking to each other, but the sound was too far away to make out the words. Then someone loudly called, "Is anyone there?" back up the stairs.

Thane was still too winded and wounded to shout back. Instead, he took off his other shoe and threw it down after the first one.

Another distant yelp answered his efforts. Voices shouted orders, and after a few moments Thane could see lights bobbing on the stairs below him and drawing nearer. He gripped the banister more vehemently and banged on it with his hands so they could tell where he was.

After being in the darkness for so long, the lights worn by the rescuers were blinding. "I have a visual," a thickly accented voice announced the moment the first light entered the section of stairs directly below Thane. "It is Thane Whitaker. Are you alone?" The Russian accent and the voice were familiar; it was the man who had been in the car on the way to Sanctum, the one he hadn't seen and whose name he didn't know.

"General Gage is hurt. He's on the top floor, he needs a medic," Thane said as loudly as he could. The light drew closer to his face as the person wearing it bent down, but it was shining directly in Thane's eyes and he couldn't see anything in the blackness around it. "Please hurry, he may be dying."

"Who may be dying?" the disembodied Russian voice asked.

"General Gage!" Thane screamed. The light jerked back.

"Priority one medical emergency, top floor, full crew now!" The accent thickened as the voice barked orders. More footsteps came pounding up the stairs and lights flashed past Thane, giving his strained eyes blurry glimpses of the rescue crew. At least two of them ran past on all fours-- was one of them a lion?-- and another had a huge misshapen backpack. The last one was enormous and the stairs shook as he lumbered past with impressive speed.

"Hey!" Thane called to the Russian, who was still on the landing next to him. The other man couldn't hear Thane over the sound of the rescue crew climbing the stairs, so Thane reached out and grabbed in the dark. "Hey!" he found the man's clothing and tugged on it.

"Eh? Is there something else, man child?" The light on the man's head swung back towards Thane, blinding him again.

"They need to be careful. Charlie says the building might collapse but he's holding up the wall." Thane wheezed.

"What was that, repeat please?"

"Charlie said the building might collapse!" Thane's lungs were starting to work again, and this time it came out loudly enough that the people on the stairs could hear him. "He's holding up one of the walls!"

For an instant there was silence as everyone froze. Then the rescue crew pounded up the stairs with redoubled speed. "Go, go, go!" the crew leader shouted, and then spoke rapidly. "This is Alpha Team rescue crew in building fifteen. Floors one and two have been cleared but we have a priority one emergency on the top floor. Please send additional crews immediately to check other floors. Structural failure is imminent. Twitch, remove yourself the comm line! This is an emergency!" The man was quiet for a moment, listening. "Yes, he is here." The light swung back to blind Thane again. "Are you injured?"

"I'm fine," Thane said reflexively. The light turned away.

"He is fine. Yes, he is right here. I will only transmit that information if you remove yourself from the emergency line immediately." There was another pause, then the light turned back to fill Thane's eyes. "Twitch says you are lucky idiot and to don't be touching his things if you get back to the room first. You are fine?" Thane nodded. "Then let us go," and the light turned to face upwards and the Russian began running up the stairs.

Thane took a deep breath and suppressed a wince when his lungs pressed against the cracked ribs. His ankle would not allow him to put weight on it, so instead he used the railings to pull himself forward and up while he hopped on the other foot. His progress was frustratingly slow, and not just for him.

"Do you have lead in your shoes?" the crew leader called back to him. Thane didn't answer, just kept working on making it up the next step. "Zavyazannyĭ temy," the man spat, and then Thane heard him coming back. The yellow headlamp shone full in Thane's eyes again. "If you need help, you ask. When you try to be brave hero all on your own then the mission is in danger. We are in teams because we are stronger as team. Now I ask one time more. Are you injured."

"Yes," Thane answered through gritted teeth.

"Where?"

"My ankle," Thane said, then added, "and my ribs."

"Thank you," the man said, and then grabbed Thane's arm and pulled. Thane flew forward in the air and the team leader swung him around. His momentum slowed just the right amount so that when his chest landed on the man's back it was gentle. "You are backpack. Like backpack, you hold on for yourself. Da?"

"Yes," Thane answered, and adjusted his position slightly so he could grip the man's waist with his knees.

"Good. Tell me if you need help to stay on. Needing to pick you up again would be problem. Adjusting so you don't fall is not problem. Da?"

"Yeah," Thane answered.

The man began running up the stairs. The rest of the rescue crew was already through the door at the top, and Thane had to focus on holding tightly as the man bounded higher. Thane's weight didn't seem to bother him at all and he made it through the door at the top in seconds.

"You sit here now, da?" the Russian said, flipping off his light in the sun filled room.

"Okay," Thane said, and slid off, landing carefully on his unhurt right foot. He saw the Russian for the first time as the blond man smiled at him with perfect white teeth, and then turned and ran to where Charlie stood. The man was built like an ultimate fighter. Thane was momentarily intimidated. No wonder he'd been carried like he weighed nothing.

The floor underneath him trembled. Thane lost his balance and leaned into the wall. Halfway across the room the heads of the people bending over General Gage popped up and turned to look towards Charlie and the Russian.

"How much time?" yelled a man with long ears that tapered to a point and long feminine hair. Thane noted he was the one with the bizarre pack, which looked even larger and stranger in full light.

"Another ten minutes afore it's done pure," Charlie called back. "This wall's tatties o'er the side. If we leave in the next five minutes we'll make it down afore the building does. How's his mightiness?"

"We need another six minutes to get him stabilized," the voice was a low baritone and very cultured, but the face was that of a lion with a golden mane. "He has suffered extensive internal damage. If we attempt to administer healing darts now, he will bleed out." Thane's heart seized in his chest painfully.

"We dinnae have that kind of time, Haider," Charlie shouted. "We wait six minutes and we'll all be working for the Weaver."

"Then none of us will get out," responded the man with pointed ears. He and the lion man stayed focused on their work, while the other three people gathered around Gage exchanged looks. They returned to assisting the lion man, and there was a tense lack of conversation for several moments.

"The rest of the building is clear," announced the Russian. He was standing next to Charlie now, both of them with their hands plunged inside the wall. Thane had no idea what they were doing but both men seemed strained and the tremors that ran through the building were growing more frequent and more intense.

"It's going tae go!" Charlie shouted. "Cannae we leave yet?"

"Two minutes," the lion man responded. "Figure it out or we all die here."

"What about the boy?" someone asked, and seven pairs of eyes turned to where Thane slumped against the wall.

He cringed under so much visibility. "I'm fine," he said.

"Travis, you take him," the Russian instructed.

"But Gideon, I am assisting Haider to stabilize General Gage," the long haired man argued.

"The general's life is in question. He may die anyway. The boy will not," Haider, the lion man, responded. Travis nodded and stood, walking towards Thane with a grace and balance that belied the unsteady floor and surrounding chaos.

Thane shrank back. "No, I'll stay here. This is my fault. I won't leave General Gage," he protested. Travis didn't respond. Instead, he held out his hand to Thane and waited. "I'm not going to run away while everyone else dies," Thane's voice shook.

Travis spoke. "Dying here defies everything these people are trying to do. We work and fight and bleed and die every day to save the lives of others. Would you invalidate our sacrifice simply because you're stubborn? Do you think General Gage would be pleased with that?"

Thane's bravado deflated. He reached up and took Travis' hand, allowing himself to be hauled up. The other man pulled Thane's arm across his shoulder and helped the boy hobble over to where Charlie and Gideon the Russian stood in front of the hole. Thane stared at Charlie.

"Dinnae look so fashed, tadpole, I'll be fine and so will this big lout," Charlie said, indicating Gideon. "And we'll pull the rest of these noble self-sacrificing loons out. Mind me, Thane," and Charlie locked eyes with him, making sure he was listening, "we'll be fine. And that was the most glorious electricity ball I've yet laid eyes on. Ye are special. Hold ontae that." With a wink, Thane's adopted grandfather turned back to holding the building together with his hands.

Travis took a few steps back and scooped Thane into a fireman's carry. "Hold my neck," he instructed, and ran at the wall.

"Wait, what?" Thane exclaimed, and then with a leap Travis hurtled through the enormous breach and beyond it into empty air. And then they were falling.

"Ahhh!" Thane yelled, wrapping his arms tightly around Travis.

"Let go!" Travis demanded.

"No way! You're the one who decided to fling us out a window!" Thane yelled back.

"You are impeding my wings, boy," Travis said.

"Wings?" Thane was surprised enough to loosen his grip. Travis pulled a string and the rough fabric on his back floated away. Immediately the strange shape of Travis' pack was obvious. It wasn't a backpack; he had huge wings the length of his body that had been loosely covered by a canvas. They snapped open and caught the wind, turning their headlong plummet into a controlled glide.

Since they had already fallen two stories there wasn't much space left for them to fly. Travis banked his wings and they cornered left, sweeping away from building fifteen and out to an open space beyond where people were gathering. Some were on stretchers, some were treating the injured. Most were just gawking, and several of those were teenagers. Spreading his wings to their fullest, Travis slowed their descent and landed running. As soon as both feet were firmly on the ground he slowed and put Thane down.

"You can lean on me, if needed," Travis offered but Thane shook his head no. His eyes were glued to the building they'd just left. How long had it been?

The entire structure trembled and a loud rumbling sound filled Thane's ears. "Alpha Team is still inside," someone yelled.

"Get them out," ordered someone else.

The building collapsed. The roof exploded outward and the walls buckled in on themselves, covering an area several feet beyond the walls with dirt and debris. "No," Thane cried and tried to hobble forward. Travis restrained him. "No," Thane whispered, in his mind a dual image of Remi crying in her bed and of General Gage lying on the floor asking him to go and get help.

"Showoffs," a nearby voice snorted, and Thane's head jerked up. In the sky above the destruction flew two dragons, one Charlie's blue and the other the gold dragon that Thane remembered from his first day. Each was the size of a large house. Between them they carried what looked like a misshapen rectangle. Beams, wire bundles, and pipes were exposed underneath it and they carried it gingerly as though it could fall apart at any moment. It didn't click for Thane what exactly it was until Travis laughed.

"If they were just going to pull up the whole floor, I didn't need to strain a wing getting you down here," he said good-naturedly. Thane blinked. That was the top floor?

"Tadpole," Charlie's voice was the deep and carrying resonance of the dragon but the cheerful and cheeky tone of the man. "Told you we would get him out. Haider insists we take him straight to the infirmary, but our dear general is nearly stable and asking for you."

"Tadpole?" one of the onlookers said curiously. "Who's tadpole?"

Thane flinched. A nickname like that would make you visible. He hoped fervently that no one would figure out Charlie meant him.

"Travis," Thane said quietly, "Could you take me to the infirmary? I should get my ankle looked at."

"And you should probably find out what General Gage wants, right tadpole?" Travis smiled at him.

"Probably," Thane grimaced. "We're on a tight schedule." Only three more days. Thane stumbled and Travis caught him, but didn't comment. It was lunchtime on Thursday. LaPointe had promised his parents he'd be back Sunday. Less than three days, and he already had to spend at least the next few hours in the infirmary. What was he going to do? If he didn't learn how to control his powers, Ms. Rasmussen would be free to abuse them again. And next time he was sure whoever she targeted wouldn't survive.

"What's your hurry, kid?" Travis asked. "You're trying to run on one leg."

"I don't have a lot of time left," Thane answered. The phrase echoed in his mind. He didn't have time. It was all running out.

CHAPTER 21

Thane lay in another white bed with white sheets surrounded by white curtains. This was a much larger facility devoted entirely to medicine and healing, with medical research taking up the top three floors. It was designated building one, and Thane thought it was interesting that the first building in Sanctum was the hospital.

The golden lion named Haider read Thane's infopad silently to himself. After a few moments, he shook his mane and looked at Thane with liquid brown eyes that held startling intelligence. "You, young man, present quite a read," he said in his low baritone. "We've done x-rays of your entire body to ensure that you didn't receive any additional damage in the explosion or your trip down the stairs. Oh, pardon the pun, that was unintentional." He grimaced in a very human way before continuing. "Your bones are more dense than the average for a human your age, more dense by half. If someone else had fallen down those stairs or been in that concussive blast their skeletons would've shattered. You escaped with some bruising, three cracked ribs, and a grade III ankle sprain."

Thane stared down at his hands, listening to the lion man but not really understanding. Maybe other people just weren't as used to being beaten up as he was. Haider seemed to be waiting for a response, so Thane shrugged.

"Hmm," Haider said. "I bet you don't get sick very often."

Thane thought about it. Once there had been an epidemic of chicken pox at his elementary school and he'd stayed home one day with a queasy stomach and a few itchy spots. His mother had sent him to the basement and brought him down soup. She'd even stroked his hair and sang to him, although that felt more like a dream than a memory. Other than that instance, though, Thane couldn't remember ever being sick except when Ms. Rasmussen had poisoned him. He shook his head.

"If I hadn't heard you speak in the gymnasium earlier I would be worried that you couldn't talk at all," Haider observed.

Thane shrugged.

"Now that we've verified your injuries we can fix them," Haider explained. "You are one tough kid. No internal bleeding, no concussion, minimal damage to optic or auditory functions." Thane gave him a confused look. "Your eyes and ears," Haider clarified. "You have some soft tissue damage to your ankle and three fractured ribs. Do you want to sleep while the healing takes place? I can give you a tranq dart as well."

"No," Thane answered. "No, I want to be awake." He paused, trying to think of a good way to say what he really wanted, something that would be an eloquent argument. Instead he blurted, "I want to see General Gage."

Thane tensed, expecting a sharp rebuff and blame for the general's current condition. Haider did press his mouth in a grim line, but didn't look angry. "I expected you would. He's sedated, but he is stable and healing. With the extent of the damage he should sleep for another two hours before he can receive visitors. You should be good to go in about a half hour. I'll let Charlie know so he can come and get you, and then I'll leave instructions with the medical staff for you to bring the general his dinner. Agreed?"

It sounded like a good plan. "All right," he said, and Haider smiled at him again.

"Good lad," and the lion man held out his forepaw. Thane looked at it. "Shake my hand, boy," Haider said, and Thane hurriedly grasped the paw with his own right hand. They shook firmly, then Haider pulled a white card out of his pocket. "For the cafeteria," he explained. "They'll scan the card once your tray is full. The General should be quite famished." Thane took the card and pocketed it, nodding. Haider administered the healing darts; one in his right side, and one just above his left ankle. Then he patted Thane on the head. "Be careful, tadpole."

"Yes sir," Thane responded and tried to smile. Haider gave him a full toothy grin, which was not nearly as reassuring as he might have thought it was. Then the lion man padded away on silent paws.

Thane leaned back onto his pillows, feeling the pull and itch as his bones and cartilage knit back together. If these people were right, he wasn't alone. It was a nice thought and even if he didn't really believe it, he allowed the idea to comfort him while he waited for his body to heal and for his great-great-great-great grandfather to come and get him.

Either the half hour passed quickly or Charlie was impatient to come and get him. Whichever it was, the blue dragon man entered the room earlier than Thane expected. "Tadpole! How did ye enjoy yer first flight?"

"Don't call me tadpole," Thane said, exasperated. "It's a stupid nickname."

Charlie paused to think. "Would ye rather be Tadpole the Mighty, Destroyer of Buildings?" he asked in mock seriousness.

Thane threw a pillow at him. "No."

Charlie caught it deftly and threw it back. "Tadpole it is, then. Put yer feet on. I'm sure yer gutted through, and the mess is only serving a bit longer."

"Can we take it somewhere else to eat?" Thane asked. Charlie looked at him expectantly. Thane realized he was waiting for a reason. "I don't want everyone in there staring at me or whispering about how I'm the destroyer of buildings. Or calling me tadpole," he muttered under his breath.

"Aye. Yer not a center of attention type. Sure lad, we can eat elsewhere. Ye have someplace in mind?" Charlie began walking and Thane followed.

"No," he admitted. "Just somewhere away from people."

"Hmm," Charlie pondered, rubbing the ever present stubble on his chin. "I think I ken a place. Ye want me tae leave ye there and get the food myself?"

"Yeah," Thane felt some of the tension leave his shoulders. "Thanks."

Charlie took him to the only hill Thane had seen anywhere on Sanctum's campus. It was small and on the edge past building nineteen, and Thane could see a shimmer in the air about ten yards past it. He sat on the far side of the hill so all of Sanctum's buildings were hidden from view and he was out of sight to anyone in them. His knees were bent and he wrapped his arms around his legs, resting his chin and gazing at the shining air. The distortion went in both directions and quite a ways up. The further away it was the less visible it was, so when Thane lay back in the grass and stared at the afternoon clouds he couldn't see it.

He heard footsteps and smelled food before Charlie came around the base of the hill. "Soup's on!" he shouted cheerfully, handing Thane an overflowing tray. Thane had never been fed so much or so consistently in his life, and he decided that being in Sanctum wasn't all bad. Today's menu was cheeseburgers and chicken strips with fries and chips and several pieces of fruit that Thane nudged off to one side.

"I could hear yer stomach rumble a mile off," Charlie teased.

"Healing dart," Thane explained around a mouthful of cheeseburger. He wolfed down the food without paying much attention to it. Instead he was thinking about questions he didn't know needed to be answered before he came here, and about the first and only grown-up who ever cared about him and stood up for him.

"Grandpa Whitaker," Thane sat fully upright and dropped the chicken strip he'd been eating.

"Grandpa Charlie, but really just Charlie, all right, tadpole?" Charlie answered.

"No, that wasn't-- if he isn't my dad, then Grandpa Whitaker wasn't my grandpa, either," Thane said. The realization was like lead lining his heart. It made his chest hurt. Grandpa Whitaker, who protected him and loved him.

Grandpa Whitaker who took him camping and told him he was special. Had he known that Bert wasn't Thane's father?

Thane hadn't asked Charlie about his real father yet because he was afraid of the answer, and afraid of all the answer might mean. He'd been holding on in the back of his mind to the idea that this was all a dream and he would wake up with everything back to normal. That he didn't have a very visible, very dangerous super power. That he wasn't a monster inside. He didn't want to know who his biological father was because then he would have to deal with the consequences of knowing. And he had no idea what those consequences might be.

But Grandpa Whitaker. This was like losing him all over again. Like going into that small room with the weird smell and finding the stranger wearing Grandpa's face. Except this time it felt like Grandpa had been a stranger all along and Thane had been more alone than he ever knew.

"Tadpole, ye fit?" Charlie's voice was concerned, and Thane realized he was clutching his chest.

"Charlie, who is my father?"

The dragon man sighed. "I've been waiting for ye tae ask that question. Dreading it, really." Thane's stomach dropped. It was bad news. Charlie sighed again. "I cannae tell ye, Thane."

"What? But you said you knew! You said he'd sent Ms. Rasmussen to look for me. You even knew what she looked like," Thane was agitated, and his voice cracked.

"Knowing and being able tae talk about it are different things, lad," Charlie began, but Thane interrupted.

"That's an excuse. If you knew you could tell me."

"I cannae," Charlie insisted. "It's against the rules."

"What, so now you're following the rules?" Thane was almost shouting. "You disobey whenever you feel like it, but when I want something you shut up? That's--"

"Not Sanctum's rules. These dobbers couldnae make a worthwhile rule if it meant putting out a fire," Charlie said disdainfully. "Nay, THE rules. The rules of Shae and of dragons. I cannae tell ye without violating dragon law, and no one does that." Charlie looked Thane in the eye, and Thane glared back.

"I thought you were chaotic!" Thane demanded. "Doesn't that mean you do whatever you want?"

"What I want is not getting my Song revoked by a thunder of dragons," Charlie replied. "Dragons dinnae talk about each other. Period. Rule number one. Every dragon lives his own solitary life, and if our paths cross we pass by each other and dinnae interfere. Gideon is the only dragon that lives and works with Sanctum. I am here under duress, and there isn't another dragon in the worlds that'd come near us and make it three." He crossed his arms stubbornly. "For our worlds tae continue tae function, dragons don't mix, and we dinnae go blethering about it."

"But why?" Thane was annoyed at how whiny his voice sounded when his heart was in a tightening vice.

"It's the rest of the rule. We all plot and scheme against each other tae gain power and dominance in the dragon hierarchy. But we never confront each other directly. In centuries past, we would use humans or Shae as go betweens tae attack each other, and those attacks escalated intae direct confrontation. It almost destroyed our worlds."

Charlie let out a long, slow sigh. "So we held a meeting. A logistical nightmare, but through the Guardian Council of Sanctum and a few other high ranking mages the dragons formed a pact, and then we all swore an oath. 'By the strength of the Weave and the sound of my Song, I will never speak the name of another dragon'." Charlie glanced at Thane. "So ye ken tadpole, it isnae that I wilnae, it's that I cannae. I dinnae have the ability tae say his name out loud. I've only been able tae speak ye this much because as greater than half dragon, I can treat ye like a hatchling."

Logically it made sense. It didn't stop Thane from feeling betrayed and angry, but he knew better than to keep arguing. Instead he turned back to his food, peeling the breading off of the chicken and throwing it into the weeds. "Fine," he said into the silence that stretched between them.

"Tadpole, I do want tae help ye-"

"I said it's fine," Thane interrupted.

"Shut yer geggie," Charlie shot back. "Ye need tae be listening."

"You aren't telling me anything."

"I'm trying tae tell ye everything, ye dafty," the dragon man growled. "I cannae tell ye his cussed name, but I'm not the only person what knows it. There are other people in this facility who know or could find out. Meanwhile, ask me something else, something that isnae about him directly, and that I can talk about."

Thane felt a surge of hope again and a little guilt for being so angry at his predecessor. What else could he ask? "Why would he send Ms. Rasmussen to look for me?"

"That's too much about him. Ask about her."

"About Ms. Rasmussen?" Thane stopped, and then realized there were some very important questions he should ask, questions that Remi would have asked already. "Who is she? Why didn't her fingers get burnt in the fire when she burned my wrist? Why would she help my father look for me?"

"Now yer thinking, lad. Cressida Rasmussen is a little fish with big ambitions. Once upon a time she learned she had red dragon blood in her veins. Not much, mind, only a wee bit. But enough tae give her a basic immunity tae fire and a taste for power. Her folks used their dragon granted charisma tae work their way intae politics, so little Cressa went tae the best schools with the worst grades, even though she really was a smart bit o' fluff. They even had enough influence and cash tae keep theirselves off the Sanctum records, not wanting anyone tae blow the whistle on their not being entirely human."

"How do you know all this?" Thane interrupted. It sounded like Ms. Rasmussen, entitled, bratty, and condescending, but why would Charlie know?

"I'm getting tae that, tadpole." The blue dragon man took a long drink. "Cressa did a semester abroad during university. She traveled the continent and came across me in France. The dragon-blooded have an affinity for each other, so she was drawn tae me but didnae ken how. Once I found out she knew all about Shae and Sanctum I told her who I was. Being a full blooded dragon is better than being a rock star. Dear little Cressa made her interest in yours truly plain, but as I was searching for my lady phoenix I had tae decline. That ginger lass is just the wrong side of hot and crazy. She went on her way and I went on mine, and we didn't cross paths for a few years more."

Here Charlie paused and looked at Thane expectantly. Thane couldn't think of any questions to ask, so instead he ate the last fried chicken finger and waited.

"All right then. She hunted me down about three years later while I was in Turkey--"

"How did she find you?" Thane asked with interest and a mouth full of chicken. Charlie sighed.

"Money. She dumped loads of the green intae tracking me down. She may have even bribed someone in here to tell, I dinnae ken. She found me in Turkey--"

"Why were you in Turkey?"

"It disnae matter tae the story. Shut yer geggie. She asked me how ye would find a dragon who didnae want tae be found. I told her tae do whatever she did tae find me. Cressa'd already tried that. I asked who she was hunting and she said it was the son of the man she loved. She-"

Thane lost the thread of the story as that revelation sank in. Ms. Rasmussen was trying to find him because she was in love with his father? Thane wished he hadn't eaten quite so many french fries; the thought of Ms. Rasmussen being his stepmom upset his stomach. His fa-- Bert-- was volatile, but predictable. Every day with Ms. Rasmussen was like playing Russian Roulette. You were never sure when the gun would go off and if it would miss you or shoot you in the face. Or make you shoot someone else.

"Ye ain't listening tadpole. I'm speaking all this out loud for yer benefit," Charlie admonished. Thane tried to pull his attention back from the terrifying image of stepmom Cressa and focus on the story again. Charlie waited an extra beat to make sure he had Thane's attention before continuing. "She said he'd promised tae have Cressa back if she found his son. But that didnae seem tae be enough-- she'd tried tae get admitted tae Sanctum but she didnae have power, only an affinity resistance. They denied her. All her money couldnae get her in and she was in a fair fit about it. That kind of bitter eats at yer soul. I'd stay away from that fountain of crazy, and I'd recommend ye do likewise."

"I've got two and a half more years at that school and she teaches chemistry for all three grades." Looking across the grassy field to the shimmering wall, those years seemed impossibly long.

"Cressa wants more. She's got a longer plan than just giving ye over tae dear old papa. I dinnae ken what she's after, but she's playing a deeper game." Charlie scrubbed his scalp with his hand. "Yer place is in here with the other Shaelings. They cannae send you back."

"I have to go back."

"Why?"

"I promised." Thane said it and hoped Charlie would understand.

Something in the way he said it or the look on his face must have been enough, because Charlie sighed. "Aye then, tadpole. But I dinnae have tae like it." The dragon man stretched, his muscles standing out against each other. "Let's get back tae work. We have tae find a new room."

"Can we be done for today?" Thane was hesitant to ask, but he couldn't shake the memory of the monster within crawling up to take control and destroy. That feeling of being swept away, of everything about himself that made him him being pulled out and sucked down... he couldn't seem to get over that. Everything that had happened after had clouded it or pulled focus but here, laying in the sunlight, all the distractions burned away.

"Ye fit, tadpole? Ye've just lost the bit o' color ye had." Charlie glanced at him and then up at the sky.

"You're losing your eyesight, old man," Thane retorted lightly. He didn't know who his father was, but if he was willing to set a psychopath like Cressida Rasmussen after him Thane could be fairly confident he wasn't one of the good guys.

If only Thane could be sure who the good guys were. "Tadpole, I'll make ye a bargain. I'll find us a new space tae play, ye take the rest of today and get yer head back. Square?" and Charlie held out his right hand.

Thane took it. "I'll be ready tomorrow. How early?"

"I'll find ye at breakfast." Charlie stood up and brushed grass off his pants. "Dinnae blow up anything else without me," he grinned a wicked grin, "I enjoy the mess."

"Whatever, grandpa," Thane forced his lips into a smile, fervently wishing that Charlie would believe it. The dragon man gave Thane a jaunty salute and sauntered off back over the hill. The boy finished off the rest of the food on the tray, staring at the sky while chewing. Not blowing anything up was a significant part of his plan, but not all of it. He still needed Charlie's training, because he needed to know how to discharge safely if Ms. Rasmussen decided to electrocute him again. Thane needed control, not power.

And he needed to talk to General Gage. After apologizing for nearly killing him, Thane was going to ask Remi's father who his own father was. He could only hope that General Gage hadn't promised not to tell, too.

CHAPTER 22

The door swung silently open as the medic allowed Thane to pass. Haider had been as good as his word, and the medical staff was expecting Thane and the general's lunch to arrive together. He walked into the private hospital room where General Gage sat propped up in bed with several pillows and attached to monitors. "Thane, good to see you son," Remi's father said. He turned to the medic and added, "You can leave us."

The door shut soundlessly and Thane stood alone with the man who had nearly died saving him. He had so many things he wanted to say; never wanting to use his affinity again, how he felt unbalanced and like part of him was missing after getting lost in the lightning Song, apologizing for blowing up the building, wanting to know who his father was, and more. It all jumbled together and got tangled, so the first thing that came out was, "So, Remi and Jeran... that wasn't true, right?"

General Gage laughed, and then winced as the motion jostled something that hadn't quite healed yet. "No, that wasn't true. I needed to rattle you enough to pull you out, and that was the best thing I could think of." Remi's father grimaced. "That would've jerked me out, too. That kid really annoys me."

Thane grinned, and brought the tray over. "Thank you," General Gage said. "These healing darts always make me hungry enough to eat like a pixie."

"A pixie?" Thane was confused. "Aren't they pretty small?"

"Like hummingbirds," said Gage, picking up an apple. "And also like some birds they eat three times their own weight every day."

"Wow," Thane was impressed.

"Flying is hard work," General Gage took a large bite out of the light red fruit. "Mmm, honey crisp. Best kind." While he chewed he looked at Thane musingly. Thane felt uncomfortable; scrutiny always made him want to hide, but being studied so by General Gage affected him differently. It made him want to sit straighter, to do something impressive or say something witty. He knew he wasn't good at any of those things though, so he waited. That, he was good at.

"Haider sent me copies of your x-rays," General Gage began in a conversational tone. He took another bite and chewed. "In almost every image there is evidence of remodeling from hairline fractures. Your bones are thicker than pure humans. It would take someone significantly larger and heavier than you to have done this damage, and based on the remodeling, the fractures happened over the course of years. You can look, if you want."

Thane took the infopad General Gage offered and used his finger to scroll through the images. Every image had at least one part circled with a note written next to it. "Hairline fracture. Remodeling indicates at least 6 years old." "Significant bone bruising. Thickening of bone indicates injury is 9 years old." "Multiple radiating fractures from a single impact point. Injury occurred no less than 11 years ago."

Seeing this journal of his life was like a hand squeezing around Thane's heart. He couldn't reconcile these images with his last memory of his... of Bert. The man who wasn't his father. Thane wondered if Bert even knew, or if he suspected that Thane wasn't his son. That could explain some of the animosity. But if he had known, he didn't remember anymore. Thane thought of the last time he'd seen the man, standing in the kitchen with his head bowed and apologizing. He had broken that man, in a more complete and thorough way than any of the x-rayed injuries he carried had damaged him.

"Have you talked to anyone about this, son?" Gage asked. "These bones didn't heal evenly, which tells me they weren't seen by a doctor. And your body language, the way you speak, and your refusal to look me in the eye tells me more. Thane," and the man waited until Thane looked up at his strangely sympathetic face. "This is not okay. Being treated like this is not okay. You didn't do anything to deserve this and it isn't your fault. Things like this," and he indicated the x-rays, "usually come from people we should be able to trust. When we can't it makes us feel like we can't count on anyone, like we're completely alone in this world. That's a lie. Do you know why I joined the Shaerealm Mercenary Guard?"

Thane shook his head.

"I was in the Air Force as a Captain, with an excellent career ahead of me. When Sanctum approached me I refused, thinking that I had everything I needed where I was. I thought their motto about carrying the fate of all worlds was self- aggrandizement. Then I met Meagan Quinn." His eyes took on a distant look, and his mouth curved in a strange little smile. "She was... unique. She was the one who explained to me that Sanctum has one motto, but the SMG has another. Have you heard it?" Thane shrugged, unsure.

"Nigerrimus mendacium nos semper nuntiavit est ut solus. The darkest lie we're ever told is that we are alone." General Gage focused on Thane, his intense brown eyes demanding Thane's full attention. "You are not alone. Not every person can be trusted, but that does not mean no one is trustworthy. Your instincts will tell you, and when you feel the urge to open up to someone, do not hesitate. Sometimes you'll get burned, but sometimes you'll find a place to be safe. And that's worth getting burned now and again."

Thane had been carefully still during the general's speech, unsure how to respond. But as General Gage turned back to his food Thane's mouth opened against his will. "How do you say that again? The SMG thing?"

The man turned back and smiled, and Thane was surprised at how much kindness and wisdom Remi's father smile could have. "Nigerrimus mendacium nos semper nuntiavit est ut solus; in English, 'The darkest lie we're ever told is that we are alone'."

"The darkest lie we're ever told is that we are alone," Thane repeated quietly. General Gage nodded, and his smile faded.

"Twitch, can we go radio silent on this room? Thane and I need to talk off the record, authorization Gage one seven alpha nine." Gage spoke into an earpiece that was sitting on the table next to his hospital bed. He must have received a confirmation because he pushed down the button on top until it blinked and went out. The general held the small comm tech in his hand for a moment before putting it back down on the end table and taking a deep breath.

"We need to talk about a few things, Thane," Remi's father began, looking Thane in the eye. Thane acknowledged the eye contact and then looked down. "We haven't had a chance to talk, just you and I, since the first day you arrived and that day was... busy." Thane snorted his agreement. It wasn't the kind of day you forgot having. "I appreciate your discretion. I'm sure you have questions for me about why Remi doesn't know about all this."

Thane blinked. He hadn't wondered about that at all. It seemed normal for Remi's father not to tell her anything about what he did. It honestly hadn't occurred to Thane, but rather than admit that to General Gage, he shrugged noncommittally.

"Still a man of few words. I can appreciate that. Thane, I didn't keep this all a secret from her by my own choice," Gage explained. It seemed very important to him that Thane understand. "When I was originally approached for this assignment I was sworn to protect and withhold any information about Sanctum and the Shae and everything connected to them. No one who was not of direct Shae heritage or working within Sanctum could know. Not civilians, not spouses, not children."

"Your wife didn't know?" Thane was surprised by that.

"Oh, she knew. She was a part of all this too," Gage responded, a hint of grief coloring his voice and his eyes looking at something far away Thane couldn't see. "In some ways, that's been the hardest part of all this."

"That she knew?"

"That Remi doesn't." Gage's eyes snapped back into focus on Thane. "I can't tell her, even though I've wanted to. Thousands of times across hundreds of days I want to tell my daughter every detail about what the world is really like. But I swore an oath, and a man has nothing if he doesn't have his word. Wouldn't you agree?"

Thane nodded. "Yes sir." Then he paused, considering. "If she needs to know, wouldn't the oath allow you to tell her? Isn't there a protection clause or emergency clause or something?"

"There is," Gage readily admitted, "but only if she is in immediate and mortal danger." Remi's father sighed, and the grey in his hair seemed more pronounced. "Bouncing her around from school to school was a way to keep her off the radar and away from trouble. If there was a Weave event or a Song breakthrough in an area close to where we lived, we moved. You might consider me paranoid," Gage said, as something of what Thane was thinking must have shown on his face, "but it's so easy for the Song to get out of hand. Even a Master Singer can't always control the secondary effects of a Song. Like knocking down a building, for example."

Thane flinched and looked down again. "I've been meaning to thank you for that," he began.

Gage jumped in before Thane could get further. "You've already been doing a great thing for me, son," he said, and Thane felt a glow of warmth in his stomach. "You are my loophole."

"What?" Thane was confused. "How?"

"I read the report Brennan turned in after your lightning incident, and I took more than usual interest in it since you were in my town and the same age as my daughter. There was more in the report to indicate your Shae status than merely the lack of injuries you suffered. And Brennan liked you and thought you were worth watching, and I've learned to trust his instincts." Gage finished eating the apple and started alternating between a pear and the onion rings.

Brennan liked him? That took Thane off guard and made him feel that good warm feeling inside again. He couldn't imagine what Brennan might have liked about him during their first meeting-- Thane had been emotional, unbalanced, and belligerent. But Brennan had liked him. It was an odd sensation, hearing that people thought you were worth watching. He stood straighter.

"Then Remi came home from school upset because you weren't there, and I made the connection that her quiet friend Thane and Brennan's tough hospital kid were the same person. You. And suddenly I had a choice: I could try to block you from her, force her to find new friends," Gage shook his head, and Thane tried to imagine anyone forcing Remi to do anything. It was not an easy picture. "Or I could wait until after I'd met you and decided for myself what kind of person you were."

There was a long and heavy silence while General Gage ate more of his lunch. Thane wanted to know what the general had thought of him on their first meeting, but refused to ask that question out loud. It felt desperate for approval. The lull stretched while the older man leaned back in his hospital bed and ate his lunch and the young man stood uncomfortably.

"You can sit down, son," General Gage indicated a chair next to his bed. "You standing there watching me eat is a little discomfiting."

Thane went to the chair and sat, trying to be patient while Remi's father chewed his food. Grownups who wanted to talk to him were rare, and Thane wasn't sure what the protocol was. He didn't want to offend the general by saying the wrong thing or speaking when it wasn't his turn, so he continued to wait.

"I liked you," General Gage said, rewarding his patience. "I still do, which makes it even harder that I've put you in such an awkward position."

"What's that, sir?" Thane asked. He couldn't imagine what General Gage was talking about... unless he was going to tell Thane now that he couldn't be friends with Remi anymore. That to keep Sanctum from Remi, he had to keep Thane from Remi. Thane felt his heart beat quicken and wiped his suddenly sweaty palms on his pants.

Gage sighed, and Thane thought his head would explode with tension. He wanted to scream, "Just tell me and get it over with!" but instead he waited, head down, hands at his sides.

The general swallowed and wiped his mouth with a napkin. "I need you to help me protect my daughter."

"How?" Thane asked. He couldn't help it, he had to keep the conversation moving. These long pauses and drawn out silences were starting to make him edgy.

"Look, son, I would never ask you to lie-" Gage began, but Thane interrupted.

"That's good, because I won't." He met the general's eyes as he said it, and then looked away again.

General Gage smiled. "I'm glad. That means I can trust what you say. And you can trust what I say, too. I want you to tell my daughter everything. Thane," and the aging father waited for Thane to look at him and then held his gaze while he continued, "I need you to tell Remi about Sanctum. About the Shaerealm. About all of it. She needs to know so that if something were to happen she'll be able to understand what's going on and protect herself. I swore an oath, but you," Gage pointed at Thane emphatically, "you can tell her. And you can keep her on her guard. The greatest evils this world has ever faced have all been from the shadow. Disasters and mayhem follow the shade. Even the fae definition of goodness changes with each race and circumstance. None of them can be trusted. She needs to know that."

He lowered his hand and leaned back against his pile of pillows, looking very old and careworn. Lines and wrinkles that Thane had never noticed became glaringly obvious as General Gage's expression slowly changed from vehement to lonely. Most people might have mistaken that expression for solemnity or seriousness, but Thane was so familiar the feeling that he recognized it instinctively.

"Are you all right, sir?" Thane asked, hesitant.

"You need to tell her about everything, except me," Gage answered. He stared into the middle distance as if looking at someone standing in the room that Thane couldn't see.

"Why?" It didn't make sense. "Wouldn't knowing that you were involved in all this make her more safe?"

"No, it might make everything even more dangerous for her. I'm good at my job," and he smiled a grim smile at the invisible person.

"Why does being good make it more dangerous for her?" Thane asked, glancing around the room to make sure there really wasn't someone else there.

"You can't be good at a job like this without making a few enemies. And when you're on the right side, it means that your enemies are even less predictable and willing to cross the line." General Gage's lonely expression became fierce.

"But wouldn't knowing make her more cautious?" Thane argued. "You said yourself that ignorance isn't protection. What if you aren't around? You can't protect her all the time--"

"I will keep our daughter safe!" General Gage thundered, turning viciously towards the chair. The tray flew off the bed. Thane threw his arms up over his face and shrank into the cushion at his back. He kept his palms open and facing out, feeling bits of food pelt his legs and forearms.

"I'm sorry. That outburst wasn't meant for you, son," Gage said quietly. "It's an old argument, but all I have left is my half. And my Remi." Thane peeked through his arms and then lowered them. The general had one arm across his chest with his hand in a fist, and the other elbow bent with his face in his palm. Thane remembered the first impression he'd had of General Gage, of a man carrying an increasingly heavy weight on his shoulders.

Thane didn't answer, but he did sit back up in the chair and let his arms fall to his sides again. "The truth is, Thane, that Remi isn't going to be safe the moment anyone outside of Sanctum finds out she's my daughter. If she doesn't know herself, then she can't tell anyone else, accidentally or on purpose. And if she never knows, then..." Gage sighed, rubbing his face with his hand, "then she'll never know that I kept this from her. She feels about secrets the same way you feel about lying. If she found out I was hiding something this big she might never speak to me again." His hand stopped, and for a moment the man was both very old and very fragile. "I don't think I could deal with that."

Thane felt a surge of protectiveness for General Gage. The general was involved in this for one reason; to save the world. And he only wanted to save the world so that he could make it safer for Remi. Thane was awed at how much this man cared about his daughter. Awed, and envious. "How can I tell her without talking about you?" he asked. He was looking for advice, not confrontation, and Gage smiled waveringly at the young man.

"Talk about me all you want. Every team handler is given the title 'General,' so when we have strategy meetings I'm usually referred to as 'General Omega.' If you need to use a name, you can use that one. It's as true as any other name for me here."

"I'll do my best, sir," Thane promised.

"Thank you, Thane," Gage said earnestly. "This means more to me than you can know." The general sighed. "Family is always the hardest thing to deal with, and the most important. You'll learn that, someday."

"Actually, on that topic," Thane began nervously. General Gage looked at him and waited. Under the scrutiny Thane almost chickened out, but he knew he wouldn't get a better set up than this. "It's about my father."

"Ah," understanding blossomed on General Gage's face. "Yes, Charlie mentioned to me that the two of you had talked about Robert Whitaker not having an electrical affinity. As he has no blue dragon blood in him and you are more than half blue..."

"He can't be my biological father," Thane concluded. He was proud that he said it with no waiver or break in his voice, so he'd hidden the pain in his chest well. "What I was wondering was, who is?"

"You should ask Charlie. He's the dragon authority," Gage answered.

Thane hesitated. "I did. He said he can't talk about it. Some kind of dragon rule."

Gage's eyes glittered as if he'd found something important. But he kept his voice nonchalant. "He did? Yes, I think I've heard of that. Dragons are very secretive, so they share as little as they can. Even golds like Gideon, who are supposed to be on our side, reserve their first loyalty to the Thunder Alpha."

"The what?"

"Different groups of animals have different names. A pack of wolves, a herd of horses, a murder of crows, and so on. The head of a group of animals is called the alpha. A group of dragons is called a thunder, so the head of a group of dragons is a thunder alpha. So the Thunder Alpha is the leader of dragons. We don't know who or what type of dragon he is because the holder of that title is a tightly kept secret." Gage explained as Thane nodded along.

Thane tucked away the information for future use, but right now there was only one name he was cared about learning. "So there's more than one dragon law about who they can't talk about, and Charlie can't tell me who my father is because of dragon law. He said I should ask someone who isn't a dragon but who would probably know." Thane waited, but Gage didn't volunteer any information. "So, um, do you know?"

"No." Thane felt his hope crumble, and Remi's father looked sympathetic. "I could take a few guesses, but no, I don't know for sure. The possibilities are limited because there are only seven full Shae dragons this side of the Weave, but I couldn't narrow it down."

"But if there are only seven," Thane allowed a small bit of hope to creep back, "couldn't we just go through them and eliminate some based on color or age or location or something? Then maybe I could find the rest and just, I don't know, ask them?"

General Gage looked at Thane, frowning. "We could if I had access to those files on the Sanctum database. I don't. When the old ones crossed over before the Guardian Wars they kept their identities secret with vehemence. After the Guardian Council made the pact to close the wars the dragons released the names and basic statistical information of the seven as an act of good faith, but with the stipulation that the file never be opened except in the case of direst need. I'm sorry," and he honestly looked sorry, "but one boy trying to find his father wouldn't count."

Thane shrank in on himself slightly-- their view of him was a little too close to his own opinion. "Oh," he whispered, looking down at his hands. They had crept into his lap and were curled up in fists next to each other.

"You are something of an anomaly, in fact," General Gage continued as if he hadn't heard Thane's small word. "Because of the dragon's stance on interbreeding and because of certain differences in the physiological makeup of humans and Shae, Sanctum made a strict rule against the children of dragons marrying or copulating with each other. You are the first in the history of either world to be more than half dragon."

"And less than half human," Thane whispered to himself. Inwardly he looked down to where he kept the leviathan hidden away and shuddered. "Am I a monster?"

"What?" Gage was clearly startled.

Thane met Gage's eyes and repeated the question, determined to hear the answer. "Am I a monster?"

"It doesn't matter who your parents are, son," Gage answered, keeping his gaze steady. "What matters is what you choose to do with the time you have here. Look around," and the general made a sweeping gesture with his arm. "There are nothing but monsters here. Every child's nightmare and the villain of every fairytale lives in this compound. The difference is that humans have something that no one in the Shaerealm has-- the ability to choose. In the Shae, when you're born a shade you live as a shade, and there's no good or evil, there's just being and doing what you do to survive. Fae and shadow are the same way. It wasn't until they crossed over that we assigned the labels of 'good' and 'evil' to what they do and how they act. Humans are the only ones with any morality code."

"But I'm not human," Thane said. "So what am I?"

"You are Thane." General Gage pointed his finger at Thane's chest. "There are monsters inside all of us screeching or whispering to try and wheedle their way into control, but they never win unless we let them. Even the smallest bit of human blood gives us the ability to choose. Are you a monster?"

"No," Thane said, but it was weak and unconvincing.

"If you believe you are, then you are. If you believe that it's a part of you but not all of you, then there's hope. Which is it?" Gage waited with his arms crossed.

Thane took a deep breath. "Hope," he answered, and Gage smiled.

"Good answer, son."

Thane smiled weakly back at him, and then suddenly laughed.

"What's so funny?" General Gage asked.

"The first day I met Remi she asked me about my family and if my dad gave me lectures," Thane grinned. "The way she asked made me think her dad was really good at them. I was right. But I've never had a real lecture before, so I've got nothing to compare it to. It's better than--" he stopped himself, not wanting to say the rest of the thought out loud. "Better than what I'm used to," he finished.

The expression on General Gage's face wasn't laughter. Not even close. Thane was afraid that he'd offended the man and rose to leave. "I should go," he stammered.

"Thane, I will take care of that," General Gage sounded resolute.

"Of what?" Thane asked.

"You won't be mistreated anymore. I'll see to it."

"Oh, no, don't worry about it," Thane said hurriedly. "It isn't so bad, and I don't want to get anybody in trouble." Gage's expression darkened with every word, so Thane added, "Besides, I kind of already took care of it."

"How?" demanded the general.

"The, the lightning. When it hit us, I was wishing he didn't know me. It worked." Thane coughed, trying to hide his emotion. "I think I need some water," he said.

Remi's father nodded at him. "Oh. I should probably rest for a few more hours. I'll be out of here by tomorrow and I'll come check up on you."

"Okay," Thane said thickly, and hurried out. "Oh," he said, sticking his head back in the room, "I'm sorry about the building."

"Alpha Team did just as much damage getting me out of there as you did," Gage said kindly. He had a strange expression on his face, something tender and hard at the same time. Thane didn't know how to respond, so he nodded again and shut the door. He was no closer to finding out who his father was, but at least he knew two things for sure.

One, General Gage was not a man he ever wanted to have mad at him.

Two, he didn't have to be a monster if he didn't want to be. Not because it wasn't inside him, but because he could choose what to do about it.

That part of him that had been missing since he'd been swept away in the lightning Song was back again, and he felt more complete. And even better, he'd just had an idea. Knowing it must be close to dinner, Thane walked quickly and unobtrusively back towards building five. He needed to find Twitch.

CHAPTER 23

"No shredding way," Twitch said. Thane was sitting next to him at one of the two tables frequented by the Omega Team. Six of the eight team members were there, with Brennan and Jaeger absent. When Thane had approached them with his tray, he'd done it obliquely, coming in from the side and trying to catch Twitch's attention without being seen by any of the others. Twitch was oblivious until Iselle nudged him and pointed out Thane.

Rip sat on the far edge of the second Omega table, the odd man out. Thane was trying especially hard to not be noticed by Rip. But as he drew near, the daemon ridden man stood and picked up his tray. He'd walked right past Thane on his way out, pausing as he'd come along side the boy.

"I'm sorry," Rip had said, his gentle baritone all the more incongruous knowing what lurked inside him. "I lost control of him. I don't usually; that day was hard enough for me without having to deal with a training." Rip had turned to look at Thane, but Thane was carefully keeping his eyes down. He'd heard the man sigh and say, "I hope you can forgive me," as he walked away.

The statement had startled Thane and he looked up, but Rip had already left the cafeteria. Forgive Rip? Thane was the one who'd put a grenade in the man's mouth. Sure it was fake, but Thane didn't know that until later. He sat down at the table Rip had just vacated and tried to get Twitch's attention so he could explain his idea and ask for a favor.

"No shredding knotted way," Twitch reiterated. "Those files are encrypted at top security levels. Even the file paths are encrypted. I shouldn't even know about these files, and yes I know I shouldn't be talking about them!" he snapped off to his left. He turned back to Thane. "I can't help you. If I even go near those files we'll be setting off all kinds of alarms and getting attention that we just can't get. Fly under the radar, don't get caught, no physical evidence. Trying to read those files breaks all my rules." The older boy bit into his churro decisively. Thane didn't respond.

Thane wasn't answering because he was disappointed. This had been his only idea. Gage had inferred that Twitch had broken into every file on the Sanctum servers-- Thane just wanted to know what Twitch had read in the one about dragons. But Twitch must have misinterpreted Thane's silence for something else, because he kept defending himself.

"Of course I can't try to break into those files! It would take days, and you're not going to be here that long. Even if I found the information I couldn't give it to you. No, dead drops are too obvious and traceable," he was talking to his left shoulder again, "I couldn't do that. No, even if I found the information anything on the nets would be suspect and too easy to follow. It could even lead them back to you. I can't let that happen. Sure, I could probably figure out a way to do it, but I shouldn't. Too risky. Information that sensitive is protected at the highest levels. I wonder what it says?"

Twitch was so preoccupied with his conversation with himself that Thane took two of the four churros off his plate and ate them. And then some chicken wings. They were spicy, so Thane opened the can of lemonade Twitch had and drank it. "And why do you care so much?" Twitch asked, suddenly looking at Thane. Thane coughed into the lemonade, startled.

"Why do I care about what?" Thane had stopped paying attention when he'd started eating.

"Who your father is? What does it matter?" Twitch asked. "It doesn't change who you are or what you do."

"Yeah, I guess," Thane agreed. He hadn't really thought about why he wanted to know, so he said the first thing he thought up. "I just want to know why he left me with the Whitakers."

"Oh," Twitch blinked. "So it isn't him you want, it's information he has?" Thane shrugged, but the answer seemed to satisfy Twitch. "I guess if it's for the pursuit of information I might be able to look into it. But I'll have to see if I can find a back door. If I go at it straight on they'll catch us. But what's the angle? Where can we attack this from? Hey, good idea," he said to his left, and then turned to Thane. "What does your birth certificate say?"

"My what?" Thane was caught off guard. "I've never seen it. Why?"

"You've never seen your birth certificate?" Twitch was aghast. "How do you know it's legit?"

"Why wouldn't it be? Why does it matter?" Thane was getting annoyed. Talking to Twitch always felt like he was missing part of the conversation.

"Because we know that if it says Robert Whitaker is your father than it's a fake and we can start looking for who faked it and when, moron," Twitch answered. "That will give us clues we can start with. I can scan the paper and analyze it to find out where it was made and when. Then I can figure out by who, because whoever it was will definitely know your mom, and she'll know who your dad is."

"My mom?" Thane felt like a moron for not making that connection. Was Gwen his real mother? If not, that would explain her indifference and apathy. If so, then she was at least part blue dragon and would know who his father was. He couldn't believe that hadn't occurred to him yet. Then again, it was such a mundane answer and the last few days had been anything but ordinary.

"Fine, I'm in, I'll help," Twitch said, interrupting Thane's reverie. "Stop pestering me. It'll be a good side project while I monitor-" he cut off and glanced left. "Right. Anyway, it'll only be a side project, so I can't promise results anytime soon. But nothing has happened the last two days, so I should have some down time. Of course I'll keep paying attention, I don't get distracted that easily. Yes, we should go. I'll let you know what I find out." Since Twitch was looking at Thane during the last statement, Thane assumed it was directed at him.

"Thanks," Thane told the older boy, and smiled at him. Twitch started, then smiled back. Then frowned and looked left, muttering as he walked away.

"I don't care if he has a nice smile, we have work to do. And you think I get distracted..." Twitch moved too far away for Thane to hear the rest of the conversation he was having with himself.

Thane slid over to where Twitch's half empty tray sat on the table. There was still some buffalo wings and dipping sauce as well as chips, and it would be a shame to waste food. Besides, the trolls got annoyed if you dumped food into the trash, and Thane didn't want to annoy anyone else today. He picked up a chicken wing and dipped it in the creamy white sauce.

"You run well, human cub," Paka said. Thane glanced to where she sat at the other table, unsure if she was talking to him or not. She was. The panther sat down again on the chair Thane had just vacated, turning it sideways so she faced him. "You made your first kill today," she said formally, "we must beat the drum and scream our defiance to death. It is the way."

"What?" Thane asked, mouth full of spicy chicken. He swallowed. "I didn't kill anyone. Did I kill someone?" He thought everyone got out of the building before it collapsed-- had someone not made it? He felt sick.

"Whenever a cub's first spear passes through an elk instead of a deer, he dances for one day more. If the cub kills a moose, the drums beat two extra days. You have taken down an entire building as a first kill. By right the feasting should last a month, as it is the largest kill any cub has ever claimed." She was smiling at him, or the closest approximation her feline muzzle could make. She put a forepaw on his shoulder. "If this could be known, you would be recognized in song and story as the cub who killed a building with one shot. We must celebrate!"

"Are you serious?" Thane had exhaled and his shoulders slumped in relief when he realized she was talking about building fifteen and not a member of Sanctum. "I blew up a building and you want to throw a party about it?"

"You do not realize the import of what happened here this day," Paka's smiled disappeared, and her too-human eyes stared at him. "This day you have made your first kill. Whether or not you took a soul beyond the stars is irrelevant-- something that once stood by its own power is now laying in the dust. By your hand. Among my people, this day you would no longer be a child to be led around by the hand or plucked by the ear. This day you have grown into your own self." She cocked her head to one side and looked at him. "Is this not something worth rejoicing?"

The way she described it gave Thane a glimpse of something he hadn't even considered. He was so busy feeling guilty about knocking down the building and nearly killing General Gage it hadn't occurred to him how much power he'd held in his hands. The power frightened him, and the memory of the monster was still fresh in his mind, but the general had said it couldn't control him unless he let it. And he wasn't going to let it. He still didn't know how to talk to Charlie about not wanting to touch the lightning Song again. But the monster inside terrified him so much--

"Get out," Paka said, tapping him on the forehead with one padded finger. It jolted him out of his reverie.

"What? Out of where?" He asked.

"Out of your own head, cub. You think too much, getting in your own way." She grinned at him, that feral panther face inches from his own. "Get out of your head and come play with me."

"Okay," he stretched out the word, unsure what she meant.

"Good! We go!" Paka grabbed his arm and stood, hauling him out of his chair and toward the door.

The panther woman held Thane's arm until they were outside. The sun had set while he'd been at dinner, and the stars shone brilliant in the dark sky. "Run with me!" Usiku Paka called, and sprinted off into the night.

"Where?" Thane yelled, pumping his legs and taking off after her.

"Perhaps beyond the stars!" She laughed, a wild sound in the night, and students walking back to their dorms turned to look. Some jumped and others cringed as the black cat streaked past them, Thane pushing himself to catch up. She was still running on two legs and Thane was sure he could pass her if he knew where she wanted to go.

"Are you afraid I'll beat you there if I know where we're going?" he called. She turned back and hissed at him.

"I do not fear you, cub! We go to the plain beyond the hill to beat our drums," Paka answered, and Thane smiled. He put on a burst of speed, forcing his legs to go faster, and drew up next to her furry figure.

"Going on all fours is cheating," he panted.

Across the length of Sanctum they ran, breathing heavily and flying past everyone else. The speed was exhilarating. Thane had never run this fast, not trying to catch the bus or escape from his past or even the first time he raced Paka. Buildings and faces blurred and adrenaline filled his veins. He felt free.

The hill loomed ahead and Paka was behind him. Thane laughed out loud and began to revel in his victory when a streak of black fur shot past at waist level. Before he could cry foul, Paka stood on the top of the hill with her arms raised and roared.

"You cheated!" Thane accused, reaching the top of the hill.

Paka grinned at him. "It is easier for me to run on four legs, as it is easier for you to run on two. It would demean your victory for you to beat me at something you are good at where I have a hardship."

Something about that didn't feel right to Thane, but he couldn't think of a good argument. Instead, he lay down on the grass and stared into the night sky and tried to catch his breath. The stars in the far distance shone like pinpricks in the sky and he watched them, trying to see if he could recognize any constellations.

"What's that?" he asked, pointing to a dark blot above. To his shock, it moved, and brought his attention to at least three more blots that hid the stars behind them.

Paka looked up. "They are a work crew. The dome is cracking with the weight of two dragons within it, and they have to repair it before it forms a breach." She flopped onto the grass next to him, somehow making even that movement look fluid and boneless. "Alpha Team departed for a large perimeter scan to get Gideon away before the cover breaks completely."

"The dome?" Thane watched the dark blotches as they moved, and saw a multicolored shimmer in the air beneath them.

"Yes. It protects and hides us. The Guardian Council claims it even powers us because they hold the net together with thousands and thousands of small panels to catch the sun." She snorted. "I do not believe it."

"Why not?" Thane was surprised at her skepticism. "Solar panels have been around a long time."

"Truly?" surprise flitted across her furry face. "Miraculous. There is no magic in Shae that could capture sunlight." She cocked her head and was still for a moment, before a smile creased her face. "Ah. The drums are coming." Paka sat up and placed a paw on Thane's shoulder. "And you must hear what he who brings them has to say. Do you swear on your life and Song?"

"Why would I--" Thane began, and then Jaeger flew into sight above the hill. The imp carried a set of small drums in his hands, but his tail hung limp and his wing beats were slow. "No. I'm gone."

Thane rose to leave. "Aye understand if hyu don't like me," Jaeger's voice was so mournful that Thane halted. Ready to run, he watched the monkey-sized imp land on the hill. The yellow eyes looked at him with an expression of such sadness it was almost comical on the old man face, and his wings drooped behind him. "But please, Aye haf to say Aye am sorry."

This statement and demeanor was so incongruous with Jaeger's previous behavior that it kept Thane from leaving. He didn't say anything though, just waited. Paka elbowed Jaeger in the shoulder. "Tell the cub the whole apology, Helshvar," she said.

Jaeger's wings fell even lower. "Aye thought hyu were a present," the swirling eyes lowered, staring at the ground in front of Thane. "Aye measured hyu many times, and hyu were perfekt average. It is impossible for a human to be perfektly average in every measurement, so Aye assumed that hyu weren't human." The imp sniffed and wiped his bulbous nose with a bony red elbow. "Brennan said hyu were a human child, but Aye thought he was deceived. The general too Aye thought was wrong. But Twitch showed me hyu's test results and Paka showed me hyu's x-rays, and hyu are a human child, not a robot or a construct like aye thought." He wiped his nose with his elbow again. "Aye owe hyu a debt, Thane human child, and Aye will repay it."

The imp looked so pitiful sitting on the drums with his shoulders and wings slumped down as far as they could go. Thane thought about being driven around in a towel and the welts on his back and being forced to take part in the training exercise where he thought everyone died. And he was perfectly average? That stung a little, but Thane knew how valuable being nothing special could be. It helped him disappear.

"You know I'm a real person now, right?" Thane asked. Jaeger nodded mournfully. "And you won't do it again?"

Jaeger's eyes widened. "Hyu's is the only perfekt head..." he trailed off, shaking away that train of thought. "No, Aye will not use hyu again unless hyu ask. Aye swear."

"Good enough," Thane said. He turned to Paka. "Was that what you wanted?"

"Not all," she grinned, and swiped the drums out from under Jaeger. The imp did a back flip in the air and opened his wings to catch himself before hitting the ground. "We still must beat the drums and scream our defiance beyond the stars to celebrate your kill." She began beating out a complex pattern on the drum. Thane stood there, looking at her.

"What do I do?" he asked.

"Tell the story," she said. When his face remained confused, she added, "of your first kill."

"Oh. No, thanks, I don't--" he began, but she cut him off with a hiss.

"This is not an option, human cub. We honor our people by upholding their traditions. Tell the story."

Jaeger began flapping around in excitement. "Aye love a good story!" he crowed, all signs of his previous regret gone. "Hyu must tell it!"

Paka stared at him, beating the drum and waiting. Thane wanted to disappear. Standing in front of a crowd, even a crowd of two, was daunting. "Close your eyes," Paka prompted. "Listen to the drum." He did so with relief, being much more comfortable pretending to hide and focusing on the rhythm. The pattern of drum beats seemed to match both his heartbeat and his breathing, and a deep continuous thrumming noise joined in. "Find the thread of your story and grasp it," the panther woman instructed. Thane thought back.

"I was completing my Taijiquan kata," he began, listening to the music and the beating of his heart. In his mind, he saw himself going through each pose and felt his feet move in the grass on the hill. "Charlie was leading me to the lightning Song." He remembered listening to Charlie's voice with his eyes closed. "I heard the music." Inside the echoes of his memory came the Song again, the low pounding and rumble of thunder and the high descant of electricity. "I poured it into a ball that I held in my hands," he continued, his hands unconsciously going into the same placement as before.

"But the Song felt unfinished," he said, then hesitated, remembering the sound of his heartbeat and blood and how he'd put them into the Song and how the Song had taken control. His eyes flew open, suddenly afraid that he was going to use his affinity again.

Instead, he saw Paka sitting cross-legged in the darkness on the hill, beating the drums with both forepaws and her tail to create the intricate rhythm. Jaeger sat on the hill above her. But they both were eclipsed by the translucent figure hovering in the air before him. It was an image, as though projected on a screen but fully three dimensional, of himself in the training room with Charlie. The blue dragon was standing by a wall and he, Thane, was in the center of the room with his eyes closed and the ball of lightning growing larger in his hands. The continuous thrumming of Paka's purr surrounded him and wrapped him in comfort and safety while the memory froze before him.

"Finish the story," Jaeger whispered.

Thane swallowed. "The Song felt unfinished, so I reached into my heartbeat and used its rhythm and the flowing of my blood to anchor the Song." He watched in amazement as the chest on his image self glowed for a moment. "But it was too much." The glowing grew brighter, and the ball was as large as his miniature self. "It was pulling me away." The tiny Charlie's mouth started moving as he shouted at Thane, and General Gage entered. He surveyed the room and walked quickly to Thane, placing his hands on Thane's shoulder and whispering in the boy's ear.

The Thane-image's eyes flew open. "I lost control and let go," and the lightning ball that was twice as tall as any of the people in the recreated room flew through the wall in a flash of light. The image faded.

Paka stopped purring to speak, but the sound of the drums went on. "By your hand, Thane dragon son, the building has fallen. Yours is the largest kill in the history of our people. Take your place among the hunters and scream your defiance to that death beyond the stars."

"Do what?" Thane asked.

"Scream," Jaeger whispered.

"Argh," Thane said.

Jaeger rolled his eyes and Paka sighed. "No, human cub, this scream must come from your center. The path to being a warrior is long and difficult, and if you have not come with many scars that was not the path you walked. The pain of every scar you held is for this scream." She rose, still beating the drum with her tail but raising her free arms to the sky.

The panther woman screamed. It was a roar of defiance and pain and somehow made Thane want to laugh and cry and punch something all at the same time. It lasted several seconds before her lungs ran out of air, and Paka slowly lowered her chin to look at him.

He quailed. Screaming like that would draw the attention of everyone in the facility. Pulling out that kind of emotion would make it hard to put away. He had so many scars that screaming out all their pain would take more seconds than he had left in Sanctum, and he wasn't sure he wanted to expend his energy that way--

Paka thwacked him on the forehead. "Get out," she instructed. "Get out and scream."

"Argh," Thane shouted, a little louder than before.

"That was the defiance of a cub who stepped on his own tail." Paka taunted.

"Argh!" Thane yelled in her face.

"You have no pain," she stated. "You have suffered nothing to be free. You are a cub, fresh born and still mewling for mother--"

Thane screamed. It started somewhere in his toes and burned its way up through him, lashing and whipping to drive pain and anger before it. He stood on the side of the hill with his head thrown back and his hands in fists at his sides and screamed a primal scream. Just once, he let all his pain and anger and fear and loss and loneliness show through and didn't try to pull it back. Instead he poured it all into the sound coming out of his throat and threw it at the burning, uncaring stars.

Paka's voice joined with his, and then a high pitched keening that could only have come from Jaeger. It felt amazing. Like he was purging his body of the fear and anger he'd pushed down for so many years. When his breath ran out he refilled his lungs and screamed again, joining the sound of his defiance to those of the panther and the imp. They roared until his throat was too sore to continue, and the only sound he could make was a wheeze and a whisper.

"That is how you scream, cub," Paka said.

"Don't call me cub," Thane rasped.

The panther woman smiled. She leaned forward until her head was over his right shoulder and pressed her cheek against his. Her whiskers were stiff and wiry but the fur was softer than anything he'd ever felt. "Thane," she whispered in his ear, standing on tiptoe. "You have earned your name this day."

She embraced him then, and to his own surprise, Thane hugged her back. "We are family!" Jaeger cried, and wrapped around them both with leathery arms and wings. Paka laughed, but Thane was still uncomfortable with Jaeger being this close and pulled away. The three of them sat back down on the hill, looking up again at the night sky.

"Do you really not have a name?" Thane suddenly asked. Paka didn't reply for so long that he thought she must not have heard his whisper.

"Slaves have no names," she said finally. It wasn't self pitying or angry, it was simply a fact.

He didn't know what to say. He wanted to offer comfort, but was unfamiliar with how that was done. "Don't they pay you?" he stammered. Jaeger crowed with triumph. He'd caught a large glowing insect between two fingers.

She laughed. "They do. I have a stipend and a salary, but I do not know how to use it or what to use it for." Paka grinned at him. "I am the richest slave in all the worlds. But you, Thane," the 'th' sound of his name was emphasized in her feline mouth, "you are not a slave. You have earned a name and have found your power. Why then do you still seem as one in chains?"

Thane was caught off guard by the question enough to answer honestly. "I don't want to be this."

She cocked her head at him while Jaeger studied the bug. "To be what?"

"A--" he almost said 'freak,' but looking at her, changed it to, "someone so different."

"Different from what?"

"From everyone else. I don't want to be a dragon," the word was hard for him to say. "I just want to be me again."

"You never stopped being you," Paka observed. "This dragon blood in you is not something that has just happened. There is nothing different about you than there was three dark moons ago. Why does knowing make it harder?"

He blinked at her. "But I feel so different," he reached for the right words, trying to explain. "I feel... trapped by knowing. Like now I have to be someone else who isn't me."

"You were trapped," Paka stated. "You were a child and led by the hand. But you have found your Song, Thane dragon son. This cannot be the first time you found your deep self, or the result would not have been so dramatic." She looked at him, and Jaeger flew behind her head with fireflies between each of his fingers. The imp was giggling. "Where was your deep self, Thane?"

"Bioluminescence," Jaeger was beside himself with glee, catching fireflies with his toes now that his hands were full. "Aye can build with this."

Thane thought back to being in the desert. The viper faced him, a deadly animal, but only an animal. He'd felt something primal and powerful move within him then and saved himself from the snake.

"I captured a viper that was about to bite me," he confessed to Paka. "We stared at each other, and I knew I was going to die. Then I felt something inside me that was strong, and I caught the snake. I think," he hesitated, never having said this out loud before, "I think it was afraid of me."

"The viper would've seen the dragon. That's why it waited to attack," Paka confirmed. "So why cannot you do this again?"

"People are harder," Thane said. "I can't... I don't want to disappoint anyone."

The panther woman made a sound between a growl and a hiss. "Do not live because someone else wants you to. That makes you a slave, too. The viper would bite, and kill. The person can only talk." She rose on two legs and stretched. The set of drums behind her rose into the air, shining.

"Bioluminescence!" Jaeger yelled. "Aye haf made music glow!"

Paka's human eyes glittered in the light of the drums. The greenish glow lit her fur from one side, and again Thane could see delicate patterns woven through the black. The panther woman saw him looking.

"I wear my name on the outside so I do not forget what I have not yet earned," she said, with the air of someone who is telling a deep secret. "I must re-dye my fur every cycle until I have avenged my parents and my people. You wear your name on the inside, hidden deep where only you can see it." She enunciated each word carefully through her fangs, the green light shining off them strangely. "Stop apologizing for living. You destroyed a building under your own power. You faced down the viper. You sang the Song of lightning and made it stronger with your heart's blood. You survived the training of the Omega Team, and you can outrun a standing panther. Thane, dragon son, you have power in your own life." She bent down until her face was level with his, all her teeth bared in a snarl. "You decide."

Abruptly she sprang away, running at full speed on all fours with her tail flying behind. She was beyond his sight in moments.

He went back through her last statement in his mind. He had done all those things, and more. He had heard the lightning Song when he and his-- and Bert--

had been struck. He'd zapped Jeran, and shocked the nurse, destroyed the power and blew out light bulbs in building fifteen, and heard the music every time. Perhaps he really was the son of a dragon.

Thane thought back to the viper. Paka had said it didn't strike because it recognized the dragon. But the dragon was dangerous and every time he heard the lightning Song someone got hurt. The panther woman's final words echoed in his head. "You decide."

He realized he didn't need to decide, because he already had. He wasn't sure when exactly, but somewhere in the last day he had decided to never use his affinity again. He'd thought about asking General Gage's permission or equivocated on how to talk Charlie into it, but that was over. It wasn't for them to make that call. "You decide."

"I'm not going to be a monster," Thane said grimly. "And if anyone tries to make me, I'll scream at them until they go away."

He squared his shoulders instead of slumping them and lifted his chin instead of lowering it. Thane walked directly and purposefully back towards the building where he and Twitch shared a room. Behind him, the imp Jaeger spun cartwheels in the air catching fireflies until every tiny point of light that drifted over the hillside winked out.

CHAPTER 24

"So Grandpa, I was wondering," Thane began the next morning after breakfast. Charlie had found him in the mess hall and to Thane's surprise allowed him to finish all the breakfast that Twitch had brought over. They were doing the Taijiquan kata together in the large gym of building eleven.

"What's that, tadpole?" the man's arms flowed through the positions in sync with Thane's, moving from Kick with Left Heel to Snake Creeps Down.

"How do I stop blowing things up?" Golden Rooster Stands on One Leg pulled his attention away and he wobbled before finding his balance again.

"Control," Charlie said, balanced and moving to Fair Lady. "Ye learn control so ye use exactly as much power as ye need tae get the job done."

"But what about when I have too much," Thane pressed, "like when Ms. Rasmussen stuck me with the cattle prod?"

"Then ye ground yerself," Charlie said.

"What does that mean?"

"It means ye let the Song dissipate." Charlie and Thane both faced forward and bowed, completing the kata. "Ye dinnae want tae pull more energy than ye need, because letting it go without using it is a mite harder than gathering it in the first place."

"I can't just dump it somewhere?" Thane asked.

Charlie harrumphed. "Dump it? Tisnae trash. Use it or put it back, but dinnae toss it away."

"Oh." Thane was disappointed. He was not going to use his affinity power again, but that didn't mean he would never again hold a charge. Ms. Rasmussen had proved that. He needed something to use, a trick or shortcut that would allow him to discharge safely. "How do I ground myself, then?"

339

"Ye've already been learning it," Charlie smiled at him and thumbed his nose. "Ye have tae be calm inside so all the energy raging about disnae bother ye. Then let it fill ye, and then let it all float away." He moved his hands in an upward motion while opening his fingers.

"All I have to do is let it go?" Thane asked. It seemed too simple.

"Aye. The trick is tae let it all go at once without pointing it anywhere." Charlie clapped his hands and rubbed them together. "Let's give it a whirl. Talk is weak. It's the doing that'll put scales on yer chest."

"Charge me up then, gramps," Thane said, spreading his arms wide.

"Charge yerself up there, tadpole. I'm not yer battery," Charlie retorted.

"But we already know I can get it," Thane argued, "I want to learn how to let it go when I'm charged because someone else did it."

"There isnae going tae be that many people walking around with cattle prods, lad," Charlie said.

"There only has to be one."

"Fine," Charlie threw his hands in the air. "Kids are getting more thrawn every generation," he grumbled under his breath as he neared Thane. He reached out one finger and touched the boy right in the middle of the chest. "Ready?" Thane nodded. "Ye fit?" Charlie asked.

"Yes, do it already," Thane said.

The dragon man grinned and warm energy flowed into Thane. "We'll start small," Charlie said, pulling his finger away after only a few moments. The warmth Thane felt filled only his ribcage, not his whole body, and the lightning Song was faint in his mind.

"Now what?" Thane asked.

"Imagine it drifting tae the edges of yer skin," Charlie instructed. "Once it's there, push it through and let it off."

Thane tried. He imagined that his chest was filled with tiny blue specks, and imagined them floating outward until they pressed against his skin. Then he tried to force all the blue specks through and out, like a water balloon bursting.

Nothing happened. He still felt the warmth of the energy in his chest, waiting. Thane took a deep breath and tried again, carefully creating a picture in his mind of exactly what he wanted to happen. Mentally he watched as the blue dots floated around and slowly separated until they formed a perfectly even line along the underside of his skin. This time he waited for the warmth inside to move before he tried to push the particles out.

But again, the warmth in his chest hadn't moved. The lightning Song didn't vary in tempo or volume, but stayed playing its melody and counterpoint deep somewhere near his heart. "It isn't working," he complained.

The dragon inside the man's body sighed. "Just because ye knocked down a building the first time ye tried tae hold the lightning disnae mean ye'll be good at everything." Charlie looked Thane in the eye. "Breathe. Let the energy drift apart inside ye until it's right next tae yer skin. Ye give it a shove and let it go out intae the air. That's it."

The warmth of the power tingled inside him and he breathed in and out through his nose, slowly. "Drift apart," he murmured, waiting for the heat to spread and cool. The gentle sound of the lightning sound echoed softly in his otherwise empty mind. He found himself humming along with it, altering the pattern of the notes and bringing in more bass-

"Stop, that isnae it," Charlie's voice was sharp and loud, cutting through to Thane's consciousness. Thane realized that more than his chest was warm now. His entire torso from his neck to his legs sparked and flowed with electrical energy.

"Ye were drawing more in, tadpole," Charlie stated. "Yer supposed tae be letting it out."

"I thought I was," Thane said, focusing on the power coursing inside. It was only about half as much as he'd had when he electrocuted Mr. Hoffman, but it was more than Charlie had given him. "I guess no more playing with the Song."

"It isnae for ye tae play with. The Song isnae a toy. It's a name, and everything has a name and that name is the Song and yer calling it in when ye should be sending it back," Charlie said irritably.

"Sorry," Thane said, stung. Charlie immediately recanted.

"Nay lad, I'm sorry. I had a rough night," Charlie rubbed his bald head with one hand.

"What happened?" Thane asked, concerned for his only grandfather.

"Naught much," Charlie gave a weak grin. "That's the problem. I tried tae contact a friend of mine, but I couldnae get a hold of her. It's strange, and I must be a bit more fashed about it than I thought, that's all." He ruffled Thane's hair. "Let's get back tae work. Breathe in."

The Song in Thane's mind was louder now, the intricacy of the melody more apparent. Thane tried to ignore it, focusing instead on the heat and reverberation of energy in his body. "Flow out," he said, clearing his mind and breathing through his nose. Again, the Song seemed to fill his otherwise empty mind. Each separate note was a vibration, and each vibration was an individual piece of the lightning. The electricity in his chest hummed in tune with the Song in his mind, and Thane found he didn't want to let it go. The music was beautiful, and he reached out to it again.

"Hey kid," a familiar voice jarred the melody and pulled Thane's attention from it. He opened his eyes and saw Brennan leaning against the doorway. "How're things?"

"Brennan," Thane grinned, genuinely happy to see the red-haired man. "Where have you been?" The lightning Song tried to flow back into the forefront of his mind, but Thane pushed it aside.

His not-so-imaginary friend smiled. "I've been out on assignment. Since I am full human, I get sent out on recon a lot."

"And because you get lucky a lot," Thane let go of the Song in his mind and strode across the room.

"I told you, kid, luck has nothing to do with it. It's all about honing your instincts. I said I'd give you lessons," Brennan smiled at him, and Thane noticed something off in his smile. There was too much tension in his jaw and around his eyes, and the way he leaned against the doorframe looked more like it was holding him up than he was relaxing against it.

"Are you okay?" Thane asked.

Brennan shrugged, a slow movement of one shoulder. "Good enough."

"Ye seem like something ate ye and plopped ye out the other side," observed Charlie, "and then ye crawled home after."

Brennan chuckled, then winced as if the motion hurt. "You're not wrong. I always said you were an astute worm; too bad I'm one of the few that'll listen to you."

Charlie tipped an imaginary hat to Brennan. "I like it that way. A bad reputation is easier tae keep, and less tae be responsible for." Brennan shifted his weight and winced again. "Och. Ye fit like?" Charlie's tone was light but his face was serious.

"I'm on my way to building one," Brennan admitted. "Someone managed to take a guardian bone from the Rift Circle."

"Shredding holes," Charlie swore. "Who could pull that out?"

"That was my question. I was snooping around to find out, but I came up on the wrong side of some paid thugs."

"Ye got molicated by mercs?" Charlie seemed to think this was pretty funny.

Brennan didn't. "Just thugs. All fists, no style." He pushed against the doorframe so that he was upright, but the effort left his skin pallid. "Somehow their guns jammed and they had to satisfy themselves with beating me half to death instead of shooting me all the way there."

"So why stop here?" Charlie asked. Thane was curious too.

"I heard my boy here blew up a building. Didn't believe it. But when I passed the crater on my way to the infirmary I thought I should stop and say congratulations." Brennan's smile, though weak, was genuine. "Good work, kid. Looks like you're something special after all."

Thane tried to look nonchalant and fought the burning that rose in his cheeks. "Yeah, I guess," he said. Both men laughed, Charlie with a hearty chuckle and Brennan with a flinch and a gasp.

"That's good enough," Charlie said. "Come on, tadpole. We're going tae carry this lightweight tae the medics." Brennan looked like he might protest, but swayed on his feet instead. Charlie slid under one of Brennan's arms and signaled for Thane to take the other.

"Lucky ye ran intae us," Charlie quipped. "I dinnae think ye'd have made it otherwise."

Brennan's lips twitched upwards in an attempt to smile. He leaned heavily on Thane, and the three made their slow way towards the large hospital building on the far end of the base. "By the by, tadpole," Charlie said, sounding as cheerful as if they were on their way to a picnic, "ye did it, in case ye didnae notice."

"Did what?" asked Thane, not struggling under the slight man's weight but certainly noticing it.

"How d'ye feel?" Charlie answered his question with a question.

That was a pet peeve of Thane's. "I'm fine. What did I do?"

Charlie looked at Brennan. "And ye?"

"I'm going to sleep for two days and then eat everything in the mess," Brennan answered. "But as long as we're playing nice, how are you, baldy?"

"Canty, thanks for asking." Charlie's smile was smug. He began whistling while they trudged across the compound.

"What did I--" Thane began to ask again, then cut off. Charlie's whistling reminded him of the lightning Song. The Song that he was no longer trying to ignore. The Song that wasn't there anymore.

He stopped abruptly, jarring Charlie and Brennan and making the injured man suck in hard through his teeth. "Sorry," Thane apologized, chagrined. He started moving again, but instead of paying attention to the world around him he turned his focus inward.

The lightning was gone. No electricity hummed through his ribcage, no warmth flooded his torso from the inside, no power tingled underneath his skin. "I did it," he said with wonder. Then, still carefully walking, he turned to Charlie. "How did I do it?"

"I dinnae ken," Charlie's answer was cheerful. "We were both so concerned about our bleeding kin here that I didnae notice until a moment ago. Whatever it was, it worked." He resumed whistling a jaunty tune.

"Did I miss something?" Brennan asked, turning to look at Thane.

"Charlie was teaching me to discharge excess power," Thane explained. "I had a lot a few minutes ago, but now it's gone."

Brennan was silent for a moment. "Lucky for me it was gone before you touched me," he observed.

"Yeah," Thane turned that over in his mind. "Yeah, it was."

Once their very injured friend had been turned over to the medics, Thane and Charlie returned to their lesson. "So what did ye do tae release the power, tadpole?"

"I don't know," Thane admitted.

"Well, let's try it again then," Charlie placed his finger on Thane's chest. "Breathe in," he instructed, and Thane obediently inhaled. As he did, he felt the flush and tingle of electricity spreading from the point where the dragon man touched him. It flowed until it was about the size of a basketball within his ribcage, and the lightning Song's music sounded seductively inside. "So what did ye do?"

"I tried to push it away, but it didn't work," Thane was thinking out loud. "The harder I pushed against it, the louder the music was."

"Ye can hear the music?" Charlie was truly startled.

Thane looked at him. "Yeah. Don't you? You said it was part of the Song."

"Well yeah, it is, but--" the centuries old dragon was flustered. He held his hands out in front of him, gesturing helplessly. "Ye dinnae hear the Song, it just is. Ye can feel it, but it isnae music the way ye humans ken." He rubbed his bald head with both hands, then looked at Thane again. "Ye really hear music right now?"

"Yeah," Thane said. The song of lightning rumbled and trilled through his thoughts, making it hard to focus. "I hear it every time I touch the lightning."

"What," Charlie paused, his eyes wide. "What does it sound like?"

"Like thunder, and rain. The high parts crackle and the low bits rumble," Thane groped for the right words. The music in Thane's mind grew louder as he brought all his attention to it, trying to find language that would capture the complicated melodies and countermelodies, the descants and subtle syncopation in the rustling vibrations.

"Some of it buzzes, like a phone on vibrate, and other parts crack and sizzle like frying food," he said. "Those are the high parts that run across the top." The song grew louder in his mind. "Thunder plays the bass, but the rhythm isn't constant. It gets faster and slower. In the middle there's two parts that hum the melody, but they always move opposite each other, one goes up when the other goes down and then they switch."

The lightning song was filling his consciousness now, and when he turned his attention away from the music he realized his whole body was filled with energy. Blue sparks crackled across his fingers. The hair on his arms and legs stood on end. It wasn't uncomfortable at all, and since he was just holding a charge and not trying to funnel it anywhere, the monster within woke, but did not try to rise.

Charlie stood in front of him, the man's face wet. Thane was taken aback. Charlie was crying? Thane looked away, unsure what he should do. "Are you all right?" he finally said, his voice sounding distant as the music filled him.

The dragon blinked tears out of his eyes. "I've never really thought about what it would sound like," he confessed. "I never thought much about it at all. But ye can hear it, so loud yer shouting tae be heard." Charlie shook his head. "Ye are something special, tadpole."

"So how do I d-discharge it?" Thane said loudly, stopping himself from saying 'dump' again.

The lightning song filled his mind so completely that it was getting hard to think. Charlie's mouth moved but Thane couldn't hear any of the words that came out. "What?" he shouted. The dragon repeated himself, but still not at any volume that could penetrate the Song. Thane was sure that if the sound had been on the outside his ears would have started bleeding.

Charlie was looking around the room in frustration. His neck flushed sapphire and elongated, and Thane realized he was trying to shift into his dragon form but that this room wasn't quite big enough to hold the full grown beast. Charlie knew that too, so he only half changed, becoming a strange looking dragon/man hybrid and only tripling in size.

But at that size, his chest was larger and more resonant and his voice was three times as loud. "Form the ball," the dragon instructed, "and throw it at me."

Thane shook his head vehemently. No.

Dragon Charlie growled. "It won't hurt me, tadpole. But if you keep all that inside ye yer human bits are going tae short out."

They would? Too bad. Thane held the electricity inside him by force now, as it wanted to burst out in a ball or a bolt and destroy. The lightning song sang to him, so beautiful and powerful it made him want to cry. It wanted to be freed, to dance through the sky with light so fast the sound could not keep up. But Thane was tired of doing what everyone else wanted. He was not going to use his affinity any more or be pushed into using it.

The pseudo-dragon rammed him in the chest and Thane felt the air whoosh out of his lungs with the same speed the electricity drained from him and into the dragon's snout. Thane flopped forward onto the dragon's muzzle. "Why didnae ye shoot me when I said tae?" Charlie asked. He stared at Thane with one unblinking azure eye as Thane struggled back to his feet.

"I didn't want to hurt anyone," Thane said.

"It disnae do anything tae me. But ye ken that. So what's the real reason, tadpole?" As he spoke, his body withdrew into itself and he shrank down until his bulk formed into Charlie the man. His echoing voice dwindled along with his size. The now dragon in human form stared at Thane with that same steady gaze, still waiting for the answer.

"I could've missed and hit the wall. It could've shot out the window and hit someone walking by. Maybe blown a hole in the floor or the ceiling," Thane started to explain, but Charlie cut in again.

"I was phasing. My full dragony self cannae even fit intae the room, and ye think I'd let ye miss? Nay tadpole. Answer true." It wasn't a question any longer.

Thane drew in a breath. Making a decision was a lot easier than saying it out loud, especially when he knew Charlie would be upset. He almost made another excuse, but the expression on the dragon man's face made him think better of it. But not feel better about it. "I'm not going to use my affinity anymore," he said, eyes down and away. He kept his hands open at his sides and braced himself. His grandfather did not respond, and so Thane explained more. "I can't seem to help calling the lightning, but I'm not letting it go ever again.

Three people almost died. Because of me." Still no response, but Thane didn't dare look up. He was afraid to see that look on Charlie's face; that disappointment, anger, and resentment he'd seen so often on his dad's-- Bert's-- face. He tensed, preparing himself to take the hit, and more willing to feel the physical pain then see how badly he'd Charlie let down.

He saw the movement start out of his peripheral vision. The dragon man's arm swung rapidly towards Thane's left side. He closed his eyes. Pain didn't last, and if he didn't see it happen, it wouldn't haunt his dreams later.

Thane felt the touch of Charlie's arm on his arm as the dragon man's hand flew past and grabbed him behind the back. He was jerked forward and felt his face slam into the hard muscles of the man's chest. Nose stinging, he felt another arm go around him. This was a hug. He directly defied the dragon's orders and instead of being beaten was getting hugged. Thane blinked rapidly, his eyes suddenly stinging more than his nose, and for a different reason. "Ye knotted doolie," his new grandfather said. "Yer not going tae hurt someone every time ye use yer power. It's a gift, tadpole, not the curse ye seem tae think. And," Charlie pulled him back, leaving his hands on Thane's shoulders and bending slightly to look him in the eye, "yer a dragon, boy. Ye dinnae have tae do things ye dinnae want. That's for lesser folk."

"So you're not going to try to make me use it?" Thane asked. He cleared his throat to pretend that it was something other than being choked up giving his voice a slight tremble.

"Knots and threads, boy, I'm supposed tae teach ye control. I dinnae think I can do that without making ye use it. But I'll make ye a bargain," Charlie raised a hand to forestall Thane's protest. "We dinnae have time in two days tae teach ye the level of control ye'll need. So we'll work on figuring a way for ye tae discharge it without killing anyone in the process. Then after all this sanctimonious Sanctum muckle is past, I'll come and teach ye my own self. Shiny?"

Thane blinked. It was stalling, but it would teach him what he wanted. And more, Charlie wanted to see him after this week at Sanctum was over. His new grandfather was going to make an effort to spend time with him again, and that was worth any amount of grief about using his affinity. "Sure," Thane said with a smile. "Sounds like a plan."

CHAPTER 25

By dinner Thane had stopped smiling. He and Charlie had spent the entire day working on ways to safely get rid of the electricity that flowed through Thane, but nothing had worked. He stabbed his fork at gooey macaroni and cheese. They needed to try a different tactic soon because Thane only had two days left before they sent him back. Back home to the man who wasn't his father and the woman who may or may not be his mother and the chemistry teacher who was almost certainly insane and wanted to use him as a weapon.

"Bad day, eh kid?" Brennan said.

"Brennan!" Thane said. He hadn't expected to see the lanky red haired man out of the infirmary until tomorrow. "How are you feeling?"

"Starving." Brennan put his tray down next to Thane's. It was loaded with two of everything the mess hall was offering for dinner that night. Pot roast and carrots dominated one plate, while another held nothing but mounds of mashed potatoes swimming in thick brown gravy. Rolls were stacked in the intersections between plates. Brennan's pockets bulged, and he pulled out three soda cans and put one in front of Thane.

"Thanks. I didn't notice they had root beer," Thane said and picked up the cold can, remembering his first conversation with the enigmatic Mr. Tayler. "Healing darts?"

"Yeah," Brennan plunged a warm roll into the mashed potatoes and gravy and scooped out a fist sized portion. He took a large bite and chewed, and Thane followed suit. He hadn't ever thought to dip the roll into the gravy. It was delicious.

They ate without speaking for several minutes and it wasn't until the potatoes and gravy were nearly gone that Brennan started the conversation again. "Thanks for the lift earlier. I did want to check on you, it wasn't just for the lift."

Thane swallowed a mouthful so large he felt his throat stretching. "Sure. It's not like you've never dragged me anywhere."

"That was nothing," Brennan said, but gave Thane a wary look to remind him that they weren't supposed to talk about The Leaf and Dagger.

"How do you do that?" Thane asked.

"Do what?"

"You look around all this insanity and don't even blink. You tell me that you're totally human but you work in a team that's the earth's last line of defense. You seem so normal but you interact with things like Jaeger and the troglodytarum and don't even notice things that would make normal people run screaming. How?"

Brennan shrugged. "I'm from Chicago." He went back to eating.

Thane stared at him. "Really? That's it?"

"It's a long story kid, and I've still got two debriefings after dinner," Brennan stabbed through the pot roast with his fork. "Maybe some other time."

"Sure," Thane said, going back to his own food.

Three or four bites later Brennan spoke again. "Did you have a bad day? You looked ready to punch a wall when I saw you."

Thane snorted. "I'd probably blow it up and kill someone." He meant to say it as a joke, but it didn't come out right.

"Ah," Brennan Tayler took another bite and chewed slowly before swallowing. "Training isn't going the way you want?"

"I can't figure out what I'm supposed to be doing!" Thane's frustration was only tempered by not wanting to draw the attention of the people at other tables. He went on in an undertone. "I know what I want to do but I can't make it work and the way Charlie is explaining it to me doesn't make sense. When I try it his way, it gets worse. And I know I can do it because it worked once but I wasn't paying attention so I can't make it work again." Thane ground his teeth together. "I have to figure it out. I can't go back like this."

"What are you trying to do?" Brennan asked.

"I'm trying to get rid of a charge without blasting something or electrocuting anybody," Thane said.

"And you can't just--" Brennan made a half pushing, half throwing motion with his hand.

"No. Making an energy ball is the last thing I want to do." Thane sighed. "I don't think Charlie even understands what I want."

"What's that?"

"I want to get rid of a charge without anybody noticing," Thane explained. "Like in chemistry when Ms. Rasmussen used the cattle prod on me. If I could've gotten rid of it on my own then nothing would've happened to Mr. Hoffman."

"That seems pretty straightforward," Brennan said. "What do you think Charlie isn't getting?"

"The 'without anybody noticing' part," Thane stuck his fork into the small bit of remaining roast. "He's all about 'dragons are the best' and 'everyone bows to dragons'. I don't think he understands the idea of subtlety." He tore the meat off the utensil with his teeth and chewed.

"He said that?" Brennan chuckled. "What do you think?"

"I think I don't want to be my chemistry teacher's personal science experiment anymore," Thane said. He titled his head back and drank the last of the root beer Brennan had given him.

"That seems fair," the other man paused, thinking. "You said you did it once. What was going on?"

"It was when you came in," Thane said. "You were talking about the bone of the guardian. What is that, anyway?"

"Classified." Brennan shrugged. "Go on."

"I was supposed to be pushing the charge to the edge of my skin and then releasing it out all over. But the lightning Song was too loud in my head and I couldn't make it work."

"The lightning Song?"

"Yeah, I hear music in my head, apparently that's weird." Thane took another bite and spoke with his mouth full. "Charlie was really surprised. He said he's never heard the music."

Brennan looked at him thoughtfully. "That might be important later on. Make sure you tell Twitch so he can add it to your file." Thane swallowed and nodded. "Then what?"

"Then you needed help so I came over and Charlie and I walked you to the hospital building. It was gone before we were halfway there."

"I remember," Brennan said. "It was gone before you touched me." He tapped his three and a half fingers against the table top.

"That's right," Thane agreed. "So it was after you showed up but before we left."

"What were you doing?"

"Talking to you. I had to keep shoving the music out of the way so I could hear you." Thane put the last bite of his last roll through the gravy on the plate and popped it in his mouth. "You were talking kind of quiet."

Brennan cocked his head. "So you had to push the music out to hear me?"

"Yeah." Thane swallowed.

"Did it come back?"

"A few times, but it kept getting quieter." Thane tilted his head back to finish the last of his root beer. Then the conversation they were having sunk in and he gasped. At that moment Brennan grabbed the soda, so the brown liquid stayed in the can instead of going into Thane's lungs. "It's the music!" Thane said.

"It's the music," Brennan agreed. "Your instincts were good to push it away so you could come and help me."

"I have to find Charlie. I have to go try this out," Thane said, getting to his feet and picking up his tray. "Do you know where his room is?"

"No, but Twitch would," Brennan said. He also got up and picked up his tray. "He's in the computer lab. I'll walk you there."

They found Twitch in building two at the same computer terminal he'd been at when he was supposed to be giving Thane the tour. In addition to the huge monitor over his console, the tech specialist had turned two other monitors to face him. Twitch was muttering to himself and glancing back and forth between the three screens.

Each showed a different section of the world with several colored dots. Twitch rose in his seat and drew a circle around a blue dot on the pacific rim. A yellow line appeared after his finger-- they were touch screens. "Chasing ghosts, these are all red herrings," Twitch muttered loudly. "Yes, I know we have to follow them all but I know they're all fake," he shouted at just below the left monitor. "Maybe Brennan will have found something. Yes, I know his report has already been submitted but you know that he always leaves the most interesting parts out."

"Usually on purpose," Brennan said. Twitch jerked back and nearly knocked his chair over before swiveling around.

"Why didn't you tell me they were behind me?" Twitch asked no one. Then his eyes focused on Brennan. "You look awful. Have you been to the hospital yet?"

Brennan laughed. "Yes, but not the shower. Clearly that's next. I'm dropping off Thane." Brennan jerked his thumb toward where Thane stood next to and slightly behind him.

"Oh. Okay." Twitch looked at Thane. "Good, we need to talk anyway."

"Have fun boys," Brennan said and walked out.

"I need--" Thane began, but Twitch shushed him.

"Not yet, wait." Twitch spun back around in his chair and pushed a series of buttons. On the right monitor an image of the hallway outside popped up, showing Brennan walking toward the exit. Both boys watched as Brennan opened the door and exited, and then the door shut behind him.

"I'm looking--"

"Not yet!" Twitch's fingers pressed keys and images flashed through on all three monitors, showing room after room empty. Finally the camera showed himself and Twitch. Thane turned around to look for it. When he looked back, that screen was dark.

Twitch turned around slowly in his chair to face Thane. "Your birth certificate is a fake," he announced. He reached back and touched the keyboard. A picture of a document appeared on the enormous right monitor. The document was faded and blueish in color and had an official looking seal in one corner. The name printed on it was Thane Reed Whitaker, with his birthday and his parents' names filled out. Except that when he looked closer, on the line for 'Father' was written "unknown."

"Unknown?" Thane said out loud. Gwen Elizabeth Marchant was listed as the mother. He thought his mother's middle name was Elizabeth, but he'd never heard Marchant before. "Can they do that?"

"Sure. They can write anything they want. But that's not how I know it's a fake," Twitch said. "The doctor's name. Dr. Sylvia R. Thornton is an actual doctor, but on the date and time this has you listed as being born she was speaking at a medical conference in Europe. And she's an urologist. There's no way she delivered you, even though the signatures match perfectly." Twitch pulled up another image, this one a picture of a severe looking old woman. Underneath it was her birth date and place, city of practice, and a copy of her signature. The computer tech used his finger to drag the image of her doctor's scrawl and superimposed it over the birth certificate. It did match.

"So what does it mean?" Thane asked.

"It means that whoever made this was in a hurry. Otherwise they would've done a more thorough job. Which is good for us, it means that the trail will be easier to follow." Twitch was quiet for a moment, eyes unfocused and looking just to Thane's right. "That's true," he mused. He looked back at Thane. "If I'd been in a hurry and trying to hide you, I would've changed the birth date."

"What?" Thane said. "The whole thing?"

"Not the year, or maybe even the month," Twitch mused, "those things are too easy to disprove. But definitely the day. I'll cross check infant deaths in your birth month and look for inconsistencies."

"Infant deaths?"

"Most likely you actually had a real birth certificate but then they said you died and made you a new one." Twitch did that same pause and distant look, and then turned back. "Especially if they were in a hurry. I'll keep looking."

"Thanks." Twitch shrugged and turned back to his computer console. The images of the birth certificate and the severe old woman disappeared. Pictures taken from cameras flashed through, starting with the one watching Thane and Twitch. The maps reappeared on the three monitors. A list of eight items flashed in the top left corner of the center screen. Six had red lines through them. "What's the bone of the guardian?" Thane asked.

Twitch's whole body twitched. "What? You're not supposed to be looking at that," he said, spinning back to look at Thane.

"You put it up there. What's going on?"

"Nothing. Everything. It's classified." The fingers of Twitch's left hand tapped rapidly on his thigh. "Why are you still here?"

"I'm looking for Charlie. Brennan said you could find him?"

"Oh. Hang on," going back to his computer, Twitch ran a quick program. It popped up a simple screen with three columns labeled "Name," "Rank" and "Location." The columns rolled up the screen so quickly that Thane couldn't read any of the data. In less than a minute a response flashed onto the screen. "Not located."

"Charlie isn't on base," Twitch said.

"What? Where is he?" Thane asked. If Charlie wasn't here, how could he test his new theory?

"I don't know. And I don't feel like executing an unauthorized global search for one of the seven if he doesn't want to be found." One of the blue dots in Asia began to flash yellow, then went orange almost immediately. An alarm sounded from the computer. "Shreds!" Twitch swore. "You've got to get out of here."

"What's--"

"Get out!" Twitch ordered. He began typing and speaking into a microphone. "We have a code orange in sector four, red is imminent." Another light, this one in Africa, went from blue to green. An alarm sounded. "Code green in sector two, recommend dispatch of Delta Team now." Sweat rolled down the back of Twitch's neck. He glanced over his shoulder and saw Thane still standing there. "If you are still there when anyone else comes into this room, we will both wake up in ionized cells." Three blue lights in Europe and one in Canada all changed simultaneously to black.

Thane ran. The threat of the ionized cell was enough to keep his legs pumping out of the building and into the darkness. He hoped no one saw what building he'd come from.

Outside building two and all over the Sanctum base people came pouring out of buildings. Alarms were blaring, broken only by intermittent announcements for this team or that team to report to building three for immediate deployment. Thane used all his skill at navigating crowds to avoid being trampled. The computerized announcement voice cut through the sirens again. "Omega Team--" and every person in the compound slowed or stopped completely to listen. "--report to training building seventeen." Thane watched as the crowd of Shae and Shae-blooded lost a little tension, and resumed their running. Whatever was going on, Omega Team was not being deployed. Yet.

Thane pressed against the side of building seven, waiting until the massive rush had slowed. Tonight was not the night to test his theory. If something went wrong there wouldn't be anyone around who could handle it. Going to bed seemed like the best option, although he was sure he wouldn't sleep.

The world hadn't ended in the morning when Twitch's alarm went off. The whooshing sound of air compressing woke Thane, and he opened gritty eyes. The dart flew through the air and hit Twitch. Twitch groaned and rolled over. Just knowing he was in his bunk made Thane feel better, because Twitch being here meant Omega Team wasn't deployed.

He watched as for several moments his roommate was still solidly asleep. Then without any middle ground Twitch's torso shot up and his blanket flew off and he jumped out of bed with his legs moving. In one jerky motion he pulled the dart out of his arm and put it back in the clock, then spun and walked out of their room.

Thane chuckled. In ten minutes Twitch would return from the bathroom and get dressed, then go to the computer lab before breakfast. He sat up and stretched, taking his time getting out of bed. If Charlie wasn't back, he was going to find Brennan and see if they could figure out a way to test the theory without the blue dragon around to pull the charge. It was Saturday, and he had to go home tomorrow morning.

Thane rummaged around in his backpack for a shirt he hadn't worn yet. He wasn't afraid of their bright colors or bold pictures here-- with creatures like Paka, Gideon, and Jaeger around, one kid in a t-shirt wasn't even noteworthy. He pulled out the red Grand Funk t-shirt and yanked it over his head.

"Thane," he heard General Gage's voice through the fabric. "Can we talk, son?"

He hurried and pulled his head through the collar while turning to face the door. "Yes, sir," he answered, trying to comb his hair with one hand. General Gage entered the small dorm and shut the door. He crossed to Twitch's unmade bunk and straightened it before sitting. Thane stood, facing the older man.

"Sit down," Gage said. Thane did, waiting. "I know you have a lot left to learn, but we have to send you back today."

"What? Why?" Thane was startled. He hadn't had a chance to test this theory about the music yet. How could they send him back? He wasn't ready. He thought of Jeran and Ben and Ms. Rasmussen, and compared them to Paka and Brennan and Charlie. He wasn't ready to leave in more ways than one.

"I'm sure you were wondering about the sirens last night," Gage said. "There was a multi-pronged attack from the Shaerealm. Everything has been contained," some of the tension in Thane's body eased, tension he hadn't noticed until it left, "but there are still several weak spots in the Weave. Enough that we've had to deploy nearly all the teams of the SMG. Upsilon Team can weave each spot back together and make them strong again, but only one at a time. That means we're understaffed here and so there's no one to train you today and if we wait until tomorrow, there won't be anyone who can take you home."

"But Charlie isn't in the Shaerealm Guard. He isn't even part of Sanctum. Can't he still train me? Where is he?" Thane asked.

General Gage grunted. "One of the spots threatened some of Charlie's interests. He got wind of it before we did, so he managed to hold that spot on his own. We've requested that he continue to do so until Upsilon can get to him." Gage gave Thane a reassuring smile. "Don't worry, son, we're not abandoning you. In a year when you're old enough you'll come to Sanctum to stay as a student. In the meantime I'll keep sending Brennan to check on you. And you know how to find me."

"Remi," Thane said. He felt that flush of warmth. He would get to see her again, get to tell her everything that had happened here. He wondered if she would be impressed that he blew up a building or if she would be mad at him for being so reckless.

"Remi," General Gage agreed. " Tell her everything about Sanctum, but not me. I know it'll be hard," Remi's father leaned forward, "but it will allow her to continue trusting me, so that I may keep her safe."

"Yes sir," Thane said. "I will."

"Thank you, son," Gage leaned back and heaved a sigh. "I'm sorry I can only give you a few minutes to pack. Brennan has to be on a transport with the rest of Omega team this afternoon, but he insisted on seeing you on your way home first."

"Omega Team is going?" Thane felt a chill.

"Yes, but only because we need them to cover a weak spot. Every other team is already being used." Gage ran a hand through his thinning hair. "Jaeger is going to get bored. I'll have to move them higher on Upsilon's list." He stood and Thane rose too. "Safe travels, son," Remi's father said, holding out his hand.

"You too, sir," Thane answered, putting his own hand in the general's larger, more calloused one. They shook solemnly, then General Gage left. Thane put his backpack on his cot and started pulling out dirty clothes from underneath it.

"That's what that smell was?" Twitch said, coming back into the room and toweling off his hair. He wore another towel around his waist. "You keep all your dirty laundry under the bed?"

"It was either that or in yours," Thane said, stuffing his clothes into his backpack.

"As long as you're getting the stink out of the room," Twitch said, opening the foot locker at the end of his bed and pulling out his own clothes. "Laundry is in the basement. It's free, so you don't need coins or anything."

"I'm not doing laundry, I'm going home." Thane shoved the last half pair of socks into his pack and zipped it shut, keeping his back to Twitch.

"What? I thought you weren't leaving until tomorrow," Twitch said.

"Change of plans. Everybody's leaving because of the Weave tears, so I've got to go too." He shouldered his pack and turned around.

"Wait," Twitch said, "I've got something for you."

Brennan knocked on the open door. "You ready kid?"

"Not yet," Twitch said, digging through his stuff. "Shreds, it isn't here. I'll meet you at the car," and the older boy ran out of the room wearing pants but no shirt.

"Let's go," Brennan said, jerking one thumb over his shoulder.

Thane and Brennan walked out of the dorm building and into the bright early sunlight. "Will it take long to get home?" Thane asked.

"No. We're cleared for door travel, so we should be back in Payson before lunchtime. The doors closest to Sanctum are on lockdown though, so we have to drive for a while first." Brennan led the way towards building three. "They're letting me drive you this time."

They entered the building from a side door that Thane hadn't noticed before. The room in front of them felt huge, but it was too dark to see anything. Brennan came in after him and flipped on a light. With a buzzing and clicking sound, rows upon rows of fluorescent lights came on. Underneath them were cars in every color, make, and model imaginable. Brennan pulled a set of keys out of his pocket and inspected them.

"Row L, car twenty-five," he read out loud. "Come on, we'd better find it."

They passed rows A-K and turned down row L. Each parking space had a number painted on the floor in front of the car, so they walked down to space number twenty-five.

"Gage must want me to hurry," Brennan observed. "Toss your stuff in and let's go."

THE DARKEST LIE

The car was sleek and black with a spoiler on the back and a red badge on the front in the middle. Thane knew little about automobiles but anyone who had ever even seen a car would know this one was built to be fast. The smooth lines and rounded edges reminded Thane of watching Paka run on all fours. This machine was a panther about to take off, even when it was sitting in a parking lot, and no one could ever hope to keep up.

Even Brennan seemed impressed. "A Veyron. They'll kill me if I scratch it." He shook his head. "Get in."

Thane opened the door reverently. Something about this car made it seem more unreal than any of the creatures of magic and myth he'd been interacting with all week. "It's beautiful."

"It is. Buckle up," Brennan instructed and did so himself. Thane sat in the passenger seat, wedging his backpack on the floor between his feet. Brennan turned the key over, and the engine thrummed and roared.

Thane felt the vibrations in his ribcage. "Whoa," he said.

Brennan had a crazy stupid grin on his face. "Yeah," he agreed.

They slowly pulled forward out of parking space twenty-five and idled their way to the garage door. Brennan had to stop and place his palm on a scanner and enter in a code before the double thick metal door began grinding open. Sunlight spilled onto the car by inches as the heavy portal gradually pulled back.

In front of them Twitch came running across the blacktop, still shirtless. He pulled up short next to them and pounded on Thane's window. "They gave you the Veyron?" He was incredulous. Brennan gave Twitch that same crazy grin and shrugged. "Shredding holes. They'll kill you if you scratch it. Anyway, here," and the tech specialist thrust two objects onto Thane's lap.

One was a stuffed monkey. The other he didn't know. "What is--"

"Shut up, we don't have time. The monkey is for your sister because you talk about her in your sleep sometimes. This," he said, pointing to the grey

363

rectangular object, "is an electrical cell. I designed it myself. It's brilliant, really, because instead of simply putting an anode and a cathode inside--"

"Break it down, Twitch we don't have time," Brennan said. It felt like something that he'd said a hundred times before. Twitch blinked and his left eyelid twitched convulsively.

"It's an empty battery. You get a charge you want to be rid of, put it in here. It'll drain slowly overnight so there's no danger to you or anyone else. All you have to do is grab the top and charge it. Got it?" He pointed to the narrow end where two small prongs stuck out.

"How--" Thane held it wonderingly.

"Charlie told me. I didn't know he was going to pull a Houdini right after. I'll be in touch," and Twitch turned and ran back over the pavement towards the dorms.

"Hey, thanks!" Thane called after him belatedly. He held the electric cell in his hand. It wasn't that big, maybe double the size of a pack of cards. He slid it in the cargo pocket of his pants and buttoned the flap closed to secure it. Then he took the orange monkey and put it in his backpack.

While he was arranging his unexpected presents, Brennan had rolled up his window and driven over the asphalt to a gate, surprisingly similar to the gates of the Kendall Air Force Base. The lumbering half giants guarding the gate were a noticeable difference from the Air Force soldiers, though.

Half again as tall as the trolls he'd seen, these men carried weapons that were easily as long as Thane himself. One of the half giants ran something that looked like a cross between an infopad and a tuning fork across Brennan's head and chest and then read the results.

"They gave you the Veyron?" one of the guards asked. Thane was unnerved. He'd heard the voice whispering in his ear, although the giant's lips had not moved.

Brennan's manic grin was his only answer. "Don't scratch it," the whisper advised, and the gate rose in front of them.

Not only the gate, but the horizon itself seemed to tear in half and separate so that everything beyond them was blackness. Brennan drove forward through the black without hesitation and Thane felt the engine hum with power as the car accelerated and the road climbed upward.

The dirt road became a narrow paved road which they followed for several miles without seeing anyone. Brennan increased the speed again and the intensity of his grin increased with it. Thane marveled at the Veyron. Sanctum must have these specially made. There was no way this was an ordinary production car.

The narrow road merged onto a lonely interstate. Traffic was light this early on a Saturday, so the Veyron made excellent time weaving past what few other vehicles there were. An hour or so later they slowed and exited the freeway. Brennan drove the Veyron through a sleepy looking town and pulled into a barn on the far side. "Last stop, kid," he said, caressing the steering wheel.

"Here?" Thane said, looking at a cow through his window.

"Yep. The door is just outside." Brennan undid his seatbelt and got out. Thane did the same, pulling the backpack and the monkey out with him.

"They gave ye the Veyron?" Charlie said. "If ye scratch it, ye'll get yer head in yer hands and yer lugs tae play with!"

CHAPTER 26

"Charlie!" Thane so glad to see the dragon man it nearly hurt. He'd been worried about leaving Sanctum without getting the chance to talk to his new grandfather again, and here Charlie stood in the barn door smiling at him and looking smug. "I thought you were somewhere protecting a Weave tear?"

"I left a friend in charge for a bit. I needed tae come give my grandson a proper send off." Charlie strode over to where Thane stood and pulled the boy into a rough hug, messing up his hair. It was a short embrace and then Charlie pulled back. "Did Twitch get it finished?"

"Yes," Thane said, fumbling with his pocket and pulling out the electricity cell. "He says I can discharge into it and the charge will drain overnight."

"By the wee man, that lad can do anything. He's quite the techno mage," Charlie said, looking over the grey rectangle. "And ye ken how tae use it?"

Thane nodded. "Twitch explained it."

"Good." Charlie nodded firmly and then put his hand into one of his pockets. "I've a gift for ye too, tadpole. A going away present of sorts."

"Really?" Thane had never gotten so many presents in his life. Charlie brought out a small rectangular box. The dragon man handed it to Thane with a flourish. It wasn't heavy or large, and Thane was at a loss as to what it could be.

"Open it," Brennan was smiling.

Thane lifted the lid off the box and looked inside. It was a cell phone. One of the newest ones, as nice as anything Jeran or the other kids had. The only difference was this cell phone was wrapped in a rubber case.

"There's a thin bit of rubber on the face, too," Charlie explained. "I heard yer last shorted out, and that's a trouble I've had many a day. I had some specialty cases made, guaranteed tae last. Turn it on."

Thane held down the power button until the phone flashed its loading screen. After a moment, an image of a classic bass guitar showed over the lock screen. "I've got coverage here," Thane said, surprised. "Where is here, anyway?"

Brennan and Charlie looked at each other. "Classified," Brennan said. "Sorry, kid."

Thane didn't answer. He was busy playing with his new phone. "My contact list is on here," he said, surprised.

"Twitch," answered Charlie. "I asked him tae set it up for ye. My number's on there too. And I took the liberty of putting some funds in the account, so's if ye find yerself tight they wilnae cut ye off."

Thane scrolled through his contacts until he found "Grandpa Charlie." Seeing it entered like that made something in his chest tighten. "Thanks," he said.

"I'm a tosser when it comes tae answering these things," Charlie said, "but at least it gives ye a way tae contact me."

"Okay kid, time to go. I've got to get back and so does Charlie, no matter how good his friend might be," Brennan said. He pointed out the back door of the barn. "Let's go."

Brennan led Charlie and Thane to a dilapidated tool shed behind the barn. The roof was threatening to fall and the walls didn't seem to be in line with each other, but the doorway was sturdy. "Where should I think about?" Thane asked, looking at Brennan.

"I'll open it," he said. "I'm going in with you for a few minutes."

"Okay," Thane turned to Charlie. "Thanks, Grandpa Charlie."

Charlie smiled. "A tadpole has tae change tae grow up. Ye've got dragon in ye lad, and someday ye'll grow up and turn intae it. My road'll turn yer way soon, lad." Thane nodded, and Brennan opened the door.

On the other side was the lobby of an office building. Brennan and Thane quickly stepped through, and Brennan shut the door behind them. "Come on," the lanky man said, and Thane followed him outside the building and to the street. Brennan hailed a taxi and gave the man Thane's address.

"That's an hour away," the cabbie protested. "I can't make a fare like that."

"It'll be worth your time," Brennan said, and pressed a roll of bills into the man's hand. "Take good care of the kid."

"Yes sir," the cabbie said.

Thane got in the cab and looked back at Brennan. "Have fun?" he said. "Good luck?"

"I'll see you in a few days, Thane," Brennan answered. "This shouldn't take longer than that."

"Don't scratch the car," Thane said, and Brennan barked a laugh.

"Now that is sound advice. Later, kid," and he shut the taxi door.

The ride back to Payson was quiet. Everything was so ordinary that it felt surreal after the last six days. His entire world had been flipped upside down and inside out and he couldn't be the same person he was when he left-- how was it possible that the world he came back to was so unchanged?

He unlocked his cell phone. Now that it had been on for a while it had a chance to sync with the network and notified him he had a voicemail. Surprised, he pushed it and put the phone up to his ear.

"Thane, this is Dr. Bicknell. I have the results of your blood test and they're incredible! You have to come to my office as soon as possible. My office is room four thirty-eight on the fourth floor of Mountain View Hospital. Call me as soon as you get this message!" the date on the phone said that he'd left the message two days ago. Thane wondered what he'd found and what it might mean. He glanced up at the cabbie, considering, but decided it would be best to call Dr. Bicknell back in private. Instead he sent Remi a brief text message. "Back in town. Lots to talk about. Sanctum is unreal."

Within seconds his phone buzzed with her reply. "Call me!"

He typed out his reply, ignoring the glances from the cabbie in the rear view mirror. "Can't. Not alone. I'll call later."

She replied instantly. "You'd better. School was boring without you. CR was gone all week. Had a sub."

She was? Thane pondered that. Where could Ms. Rasmussen have gone? Her being out of the way was nice; she couldn't try to make him electrocute people if she wasn't around. But she had been his backup plan. Charlie said she knew his father, was even actively looking for Thane because of his father. If he couldn't find his father any other way he was going to confront her about it.

The taxi turned onto his street. The tall oaks were stripped of all but a few clinging brown leaves and the bare branches hung over the rooftops. Lanie was playing in the front yard, rolling snowballs. The yellow cab caught her eye and she stared as it drew closer. Thane couldn't blame her. He didn't know if there had ever been a taxi in Payson before. He sent one more text. "Sub is better than crazy. I'll call soon."

When he climbed out of the car and shut the door it felt like he was closing away Sanctum and the Shae and dragons and magic and everything that had made his life special for a few days. What was he supposed to do now? Just go back to school like nothing had changed? The cab started to drive away with his hand still on the closed door and he jerked it away.

"Thanie!" a little voice behind him shouted. Thane turned around barely in time to catch the waist high rocket that hurtled at him. "You're home! What did you bring me? Did you meet the president?" Lanie was full of questions as he spun her around and hugged her. Her small arms encircled his neck and she alternated burying her face in his shoulder and kissing his cheek.

She pulled away as far as she could without letting go of his neck. "You look different," she said. Lanie studied his face. "You look sad. Are you sad? Were they mean to you?"

"How can I be sad when I'm getting hugs from a monkey?" Thane teased. He was happy to see her, and it was gratifying how happy she was to see him. Lanie could be annoying and a pest, but she loved him, and that was worth everything. He hugged her again. "Can you see my backpack?" he asked. He felt her nod against his cheek. "Reach in and see what's on top."

Thane lifted her higher so that she could reach his backpack. The orange stuffed monkey was right on top. She pulled it out and squealed. "Is it for me? Is it because you call me monkey? Now I have a monkey friend?" He nodded and smiled at her, and she squealed again and hugged it close. Then her face fell a little. "But Thanie," she said, "I wanted a friend who wasn't stinky."

He laughed. "Sorry monkey, I need to wash my clothes. He'll smell better after he's been out of my backpack for a while. Why don't you go put him in your room?"

"Okay," she smiled and wiggled to be put down. Thane bent and set her feet on the ground and his little sister scampered up the steps and into the house. "Thanie's home!" she screamed as she entered the door. "Dad, Harper, Mom, Thanie's home!"

Thane breathed in and out through his nose, trying to stay calm. How should he do this? Shoulders down, eyes away? Or would they think that meant he hadn't gotten any guidance or that the counseling had failed? Shoulders squared and chin up was too weird. He couldn't imagine walking up to his dad-- Bert-- his dad, like that. Thane shook his head to clear it. If things were going to be normal, he had to think of Bert as his dad. Otherwise how would he explain knowing? But if he didn't bring it up, how could he ask his mom about it?

"Thane." While he'd been standing in the front yard, Bert Whitaker had come to the door. "You're home early." The man Thane had thought was his father stood in the doorframe and looked at him. The expression on his face wasn't anger or fear, it was curiosity. And then sadness.

"You still don't recognize me," Thane said. It wasn't a question, and Bert knew it.

"I'm sorry. I've been looking for pictures of you all week, trying to remember anything, but we don't have very many. Do you not like having your picture taken?"

That wasn't why, but he looked pitiful enough that Thane decided to help him. "No, not really." It was true anyway.

"Come in, you must be tired. You can tell us all about it over lunch. It's a little early to eat, but I'm sure you're hungry after traveling so much already today." Bert tried to smile at him, but it was a small uncomfortable smile.

"What time is it?" Thane asked.

Bert checked his watch. "Nearly ten. Maybe we'll have brunch instead. Either way, come on in." He turned and went inside. Thane adjusted his backpack and followed.

The inside of the house wasn't the same. The furniture in the front room had all been rearranged and a tan overstuffed recliner sat in one corner. Perhaps not brand new, but it hadn't been there before. The curtains were all open and the blinds were up, bringing in sunlight. The kitchen was cleaner and even brighter, the old dark brown curtains having been replaced with thin light green ones. The table was moved so it wasn't blocking the door or the hallway any more. There were dishes in the sink but it looked like Bert had been in the middle of washing them when Thane arrived. He'd been doing that when Thane left, too.

"What do you think?" Bert asked, watching Thane as he walked through the house.

"It's... different," Thane said.

"When I got home from the hospital everything here was so dark and depressing. Gwen has been pestering me for years to get new curtains, but I never saw the point. When I got back, that was the first thing we changed. Here, I'll take your bag," and he reached for Thane's backpack.

"That's okay," Thane said, flinching reflexively and moving away. "I got it."

Bert put his hand down. "Isn't it just dirty clothes?"

With the electric cell in his pocket, it was. "I can take care of it."

"Suit yourself," Bert shrugged. "Do you want some food? I can whip up some eggs and toast."

"No, that's okay," Thane said. "I'm kinda tired. Is it okay if I go take a nap?"

"Sure," Bert said. His shoulders slumped a little and he looked away. "Of course. Go ahead."

Thane didn't wait. He opened the door to the basement and trudged down the stairs. The skeletal walls of the basement were comforting as he made his way through them to his room in the back corner. He thought he'd call Remi from his mattress and maybe take a nap.

Then he stopped. His room was just ahead, but it too had been changed. The mattress on the floor was gone, and in its place was a bed. A real bed. With a frame to hold it off the ground and blankets on top and a pillow. Behind him he heard the basement door open and footsteps coming down.

"I came downstairs because I thought being in your room might trigger some memories," Bert said. He stopped some distance from Thane, in what would have been a different room in a finished house. "I wasn't going to touch any of your stuff, but I don't think I must have ever been down here before. I don't think I would have let you stay like that so long if I had."

Thane didn't respond. He didn't know how. "I hope you aren't upset that I changed your room around. But leaving it like that just didn't seem right. A lot of things here didn't seem right." Thane heard the man who wasn't his father take a deep breath and let it out slowly. "You and I... we didn't get along, did we."

"No," Thane said.

Bert chuckled uncomfortably. "Lanie mentioned that I... yelled at you. A lot. Was it because I didn't like you, or you didn't like me?"

Thane was a little impressed at the fairness of the question, so he tempered his answer. "Both." Bert didn't reply to that, and so Thane added, "It always seemed... hard, for you, to be around me."

"Why?" Bert tried to hide the pain in his voice, but his attempt to be strong made the pain more apparent to Thane. He was used to being in places where things would hide. Maybe it was easier to recognize because Thane still had his back to the other man. "I always wanted a son. I never had a brother, so a son seemed like the best thing in the world. How did I let things get like this?"

"Maybe because I'm not really your son," the words slipped out through Thane's mouth before his mind could think better of them. He bit his tongue, angry with himself and wishing he could pull them back before Bert heard them.

"What?" Too late. Thane heard Bert come closer, enter the room area where he stood looking at his new bed. "What do you mean, you're not my son? Who else would you be?"

"I don't know," Thane was much better at hiding the pain, having had years more experience.

"Then what do you mean? That you wish you weren't my son?" Bert's voice caught, but he went on. "I would understand that, at least."

"No," Thane moved slowly around to face the man who had never been his father. "I saw my birth certificate this week. You weren't on it."

"What do you mean, I wasn't on it?"

"Gwen Elizabeth Marchant was listed as my mother, but the father was 'unknown'," Thane swallowed. Still unknown. Bert stood thunderstruck, the expression on his face so startled it was almost funny. Almost. "Maybe that's why it was so hard for you to be around me. I was never your son, and you always wanted one."

"That shouldn't have made a difference," Bert disagreed. "But why didn't Gwen tell me?"

Thane shrugged. He thought that his mom didn't say anything because it was easier for her to not get involved. She didn't like dealing with other people's emotions. But Bert was having a hard enough time that Thane didn't want to make it worse.

"I need to go talk to your mom," Bert said. Thane nodded. The man with thinning hair and a weak chin who was not his father turned to leave, and then looked back. "I couldn't do much more than the bed right away, but we'll see about fixing these walls and getting you a real closet. Okay?"

Thane nodded again, swallowing past a lump in his throat. He wanted to ask why but couldn't get the word to come out. Maybe it showed on his face, because Bert added, "Even if I'm not your father, at some point I agreed to take care of you. It's about time I make good on that." He raised his hand as if to pat Thane on the shoulder, but pulled it away without making contact. Thane had flinched.

Bert went back upstairs and Thane pushed his way through the framed wall into his room. Apparently his world had changed. He looked at the bed distrustfully. It was a twin, smaller than his old queen mattress but larger than the cots he'd had in the dorms. The comforter on top was a solid blue and the pillowcase was not quite white. He pulled back the comforter. Sheets. His bed had sheets.

Thane was trying to decide whether to lie down and try out the bed or go throw his clothes in the wash when he heard his mother's voice. "Thane! Get up here!" Clothes then. It was probably better, since he didn't have any clean ones left. He cut through the walls and went back up the uncovered wooden stairs to the kitchen.

Bert and his mother were seated at the kitchen table. Gwen's eyes were narrowed and she breathed rapidly through her nose, but she also bit her bottom lip. Bert was stiff backed and leaned away from Gwen with crossed arms. She spoke first. "Thane--"

"Just a second," he interrupted. Her eyes widened as he walked past them and to the closet behind the kitchen where the washer and dryer were kept. He kept his face turned away while turning his backpack upside down and shaking it to get all the clothes out and into the empty washer. They only filled it about halfway, but he poured in the detergent and started the machine anyway. This gave him time to calm himself and he brought up the memory of screaming on the hill with Paka, and the panther woman's intense eyes as she said, "You decide."

Thane turned back to the table and walked into the kitchen. He reminded himself that Gwen was the one who'd lied, that she should be the one afraid. His sweaty palms and constricted chest didn't believe him. Why should sitting down with these people be so unnerving, even after going through an Omega Team training? Thane rubbed his hands on his legs to dry the sweat, and sat down.

"Are you ready now?" Gwen asked. Thane shrugged. Ready enough. "Who told you that your father isn't your father?"

"I saw my birth certificate," Thane said.

"Why? Who showed it to you?" she demanded.

Thane thought quickly, trying to come up with a truth that he could say. "In the program I went to, part of it was discovering who you were and being okay with that. One of the team members showed me the certificate."

"But why?" Gwen's lower lip trembled.

"Why didn't you tell me that I wasn't his father?" Bert said. He made gestures with his arms still folded across his chest. "I've been driving myself crazy all week about not being able to remember him, asking what kind of person I must be to have forgotten my own son. It's still inexcusable," he glanced at Thane, and then back to Gwen, "but you should have told me. That big of a truth might have jogged something in my memory."

"Did it?" she asked, her voice sounding strained and strange. "Has knowing helped you remember anything?"

"No. But you still should have told me."

"Why?" she demanded, suddenly more angry. Her voice rose both in volume and pitch. "It was perfect! He didn't know you weren't his father, and now you couldn't remember. It might have made everything easier..." she trailed off and took a deep, shuddering breath. "It's been so much easier this past week, without..." she made a vague gesture in the air towards the young man and the middle aged one. "I thought we could stay like that."

Bert's face reddened. Thane looked down and away, tensing. "Lying doesn't make things better, Gwen," the man who wasn't his father said. "We're supposed to be in this together. So Thane isn't my son. So what. We raised him, and he's part of our family, however he got here." Thane glanced up, thrown off balance. Bert was reaching a hand out to Gwen, who stared at it as though it might bite her.

This seemed as good an opportunity as he was likely to get. "Mom," he said, and both adults turned to him. "Who is my father?"

Bert's hand dropped untouched. Gwen shrank in on herself and shook her head. Thane went on. "The birth certificate said 'unknown,' but you'd have to know, wouldn't you?"

Gwen pulled her knees up and rested her heels on the front of her chair's seat, wrapping her arms around her legs and putting her head down. She shuddered. Thane stared at her, and Bert stood up so rapidly his chair clattered over backwards. "You were-- were you-- was it forced on you?" Bert stuttered.

"I don't know," Gwen mumbled into her knees. She was making quiet gasping sounds and her shoulders were shaking up and down a little. It took the two men a moment to realize she was crying. Bert threw his arms around his wife and knelt next to her, leaning his head against hers. Thane was frozen in his chair.

"What happened, sweet girl?" Bert said, running his short fingers through her long blonde hair. "I promise, the truth will only help you heal. Help us all heal," he added with a glance toward Thane.

"I don't know," Gwen said, her voice raspy with weeping. "I woke up in a hospital. They said I'd almost died. They told me a woman brought me to the emergency room and told them I was hemorrhaging inside from childbirth. They said the baby, my baby, was fine. They asked me what my name was." She sniffed, and her shoulders shook harder. For a few heartbeats, the sound of her sobs were the only noise in the room. Bert and Thane were transfixed, the husband still stroking her hair and the son unable to do anything.

"I couldn't tell them. I didn't know." Saying that out loud seemed to be a turning point for Gwen, because her sniffling quieted and her sobs grew further apart. "I still don't." She looked at Bert. "I don't remember anything about who I was before waking up in that hospital. They said my memory might come back, but that there were no guarantees. They helped me get on my feet, pick a name, and even made you a birth certificate."

Gwen picked up a napkin and wiped her eyes. "I got a waitressing job in the next town. And I met you there, Bert. And while we were dating, it was fine. You were kind and you and Thane got along really well. Then we got married and you changed. You could hardly bear to be in the same room with us. Everything got harder, and if I tried to protect Thane you were... it was better if I was awful to him. That seemed to take some of the burden off you. You were so angry I never dared tell you the truth about me after that. I thought you would hate him even more if you knew."

All through this, Bert kept his arms around his wife. He wiped her tears with his hands and stroked her hair. "I'm so sorry," he said. "I'm so sorry." He put his finger under her chin and tilted her face up towards him, then kissed her on the forehead. "We're supposed to be a team, remember?" he said gently. "We'll get through this together. Thane," the man on his knees looked over at the boy, "it seems your mom and I have a lot to talk about. Would you mind if we did that alone?"

"Sure," Thane said, rising to his feet. "I'll go for a walk or something."

"You don't have to leave," Bert argued. "You can go downstairs and we'll go in our room."

"No, it's okay," Thane said, backing away. "I want some air anyway."

CHAPTER 27

It was cold outside. From his front lawn he looked up in Mrs. Knotts' big living room window and saw Lanie and Harper playing there. They were excited, bouncing up and down and running around the room while Mrs. Knotts stood silently laughing in the background. Thane ducked and started walking before his kind elderly neighbor saw him. He didn't want to try and answer her questions right now, like "how are you." Even that was too complicated.

Instead he started in the direction of the Kendall Air Force Base. The late October air was cold, but it was almost afternoon so being in a t-shirt was tolerable. He pulled his new rubber encased phone from his pocket and sent Remi another message. "Free now. You?"

He'd walked almost a full block before she responded. "Calder is bringing me to your house. Be there in 10."

Thane panicked. "No, I'm not home, I'm on my way to you. Don't come here."

Her text was brief. "My dad's not home." Right, that meant he couldn't come in. What should he do? He had to think of a better option.

"Meet me at the park on the way to the school." It was only a mile or so away, and she would have to know where it was. Talking outside was not ideal, but talking in the car where Calder could overhear was worse and having Remi meet his parents was not an option.

"K. Be there soon."

Thane broke into a jog. She would beat him there, but not by much. It felt good to run, and he quickened his pace. He hadn't stretched his legs like this since he raced Paka to the hill. Unconsciously his stride lengthened until the houses were a blur and his legs pumped as quickly as they could. Fortunately

379

there was little traffic on any road in Payson on a sleepy Saturday afternoon in the fall and he encountered almost no cars in his headlong race to the park.

As he pounded up the hill he could see the tall old trees bunched together ahead of him, their bare branches clawing at the sky. Drawing nearer revealed the outdoor stage and the field in the back where all the kids played soccer through the summers. In the furthest back right corner was the playground. There were vacant metal monkey bars, empty slides, and one person sitting in the centermost swing.

Remi. Thane hadn't thought about her much in the week he was away because honestly he hadn't had time to think about much of anything beyond surviving, but seeing her sitting there, gently swaying, brought a rush of heat. He'd missed her, he was so glad to see her, and so grateful to have someone to talk to that he doubled his pace.

She saw him sprinting into the park and jumped to her feet. "The car's over there!" she shouted, pointing. "Calder is waiting in it, he can get us away!"

Thane slowed to a halt several yards before her. "Away from what?"

Her forehead furrowed. "From whatever you're running from." Thane stood there. "You aren't being chased?" He shook his head. "Then why were you running like your life depended on it?"

Thane shrugged. "I like running."

She burst out laughing. "Of course." Thane smiled. He liked making her laugh. She walked back to the swings and sat down again. "You have a lot to tell me, I hear."

"Yeah." Thane walked over to the swings and sat in the one next to her. The seat was black plastic held up by metal chains, which squeaked irregularly as the swings moved back and forth. Thane spent a few minutes drawing shapes in the snow with his feet and trying to think, trying to pull all the different things that had happened to him in Sanctum into some cohesive whole, some story he could relate. Should he start at the beginning with being drugged? Or maybe go through it by person, starting with Brennan and being careful to skip General Gage. Maybe he should tell her about Ms. Rasmussen first, explain all about her motivations and that she knew Thane's real father.

"My dad isn't my dad," he blurted. He was staring at his feet, so he didn't see Remi's reaction. "My biological father isn't Robert Whitaker. I'm not Thane Whitaker."

There was a heartbeat of silence, then she asked, "Who is your father?"

"I don't know." Thane began drawing circles in the dirty snow with his shoes again.

"Can you ask your mom?"

"She doesn't know." Thane looked at Remi. "She doesn't remember anything before I was born."

"Wow." Remi was quiet.

"Yeah." Thane looked back down again. "I just found out this morning."

"I'm sorry," Remi said. He felt her hand on his wrist, her skin feeling impossibly warm and soft compared to the hard, cold chain he held. The warmth spread a little, and Thane realized there was a question he hadn't thought to ask her.

"Where's your mom, Remi?" She dropped her hand and looked down. Thane was immediately sorry he'd asked. "You don't have to tell me, it isn't any of my business."

"She went on a mission and didn't come back," Remi said. It a simple statement, but it told Thane so much about who Remi was and why it she was so upset when people left. "I was six. She was military, like my dad. That's how they met. We were really happy together. Then she went on some secret assignment and never came back." Remi was the one staring at her feet now, and Thane wanted to make her feel better. He reached out to touch her, but didn't know whether to pat her shoulder or hold her arm or what, so he lowered it again.

"I blew up a building," he burst out. She lifted her chin and glanced at him. "You what?"

"I blew up a building. Charlie was training me to use my affinity and it got out of control. When I let go, it blew a hole in the side of the building and the whole thing fell down." He was babbling, he knew, but he was trying to distract her and make her feel better.

"How did you get out? Let go of what? Who's Charlie?" she asked.

"They threw me out the hole with a guy named Travis who had wings," he said. She raised one eyebrow at him, but her mouth still quivered a bit. "An imp named Jaeger rode me like a horse and shot grenades off my head," he added hopefully.

Remi giggled. "A what named what?"

"An imp named Jaeger. He's about the size of a monkey but looks like a little old man with bat wings and a tail and he's red. He thought my head was perfect." She was giggling more now.

"You can't be serious."

"That wasn't even the weirdest thing. Well," Thane paused, reconsidering, "no, that probably was. But every day had something insane. They shot me a lot, too."

Remi shook her head. "You'd better start from the beginning."

"The first thing they did was drug me."

"What?"

"Yeah. Brennan came to pick me up on Saturday morning and he'd drugged my food so I'd fall asleep. He told me the story about why there are holes in the Weave between the Shaerealm and here." He thought back through the story, trying to remember the beginning.

"The Shaerealm. I wonder what that looks like," Remi mused.

Thane shuddered. "I don't want to know."

They sat in the park for hours, staying on the swings until that wasn't comfortable anymore. Then they switched to the fort at the top of the slide, sitting cross-legged on the cold metal inside the circle of wooden slats that had protected it from the snow. Thane told her about meeting Jaeger and Paka, Twitch's tour, and gave her an extended description of being in the mess hall for the first time.

"Imagine our high school cafeteria but three times as big," he began. "Now fill it with every monster from every story you've ever heard or seen. Add a couple of football teams worth of people and give them wings or horns or scales or fangs. That's maybe half."

"Whoa," her response was appropriately awed. He went on to describe the members of Omega Team, skimming over the fight and skipping the part about General Omega coming in. He only briefly described the testing, being tranquilized, and being imprisoned afterwards, glossing over most of the details and emphasizing Charlie. "At first I thought he was obnoxious, but he turned out to be... really great."

"He's where part of your blue dragon comes from?" Remi asked.

"Yeah. He's in my phone as Grandpa Charlie."

"Can I see?" she giggled when he handed her his phone. "Your case is huge."

"Charlie gave it to me. The rubber will keep the phone from shorting out if I get charged. But Twitch made me this," he pulled the electric cell out of his cargo pocket and showed it to her.

"Twitch is the tech guy? The one who always talks to himself?"

Thane nodded. "He's brilliant, though. And he built an alarm clock that shoots him with caffeine every morning."

"No way," Remi tilted her head back laughing. "What else?"

He told her about the training exercise, skipping everything related to the locker room. Remi stared at him with wide eyes as he described running through the weeds outside the warehouse with Jaeger on his head. When Paka rose up and stabbed Twitch, she gasped and tears filled her eyes.

"Twitch is dead?" she asked.

"What? No, no, it was all fake," Thane rushed to explain. "No, they were training, no one got hurt for real. Not permanently, anyway," he amended. "If someone hurts you with a weapon it goes away when the training is done. If they punch you or use their hands, that stays because the people aren't fake. Twitch is fine. Everyone is fine."

"Oh," she sniffed, and wiped her eyes on the bright purple sleeve of her jacket. She laughed at little and added, "Haven't we talked about leading with that?"

"Yeah, right," Thane flushed. "So after, they took Paka and Jaeger and I to the infirmary. There was this doctor--"

"You got hurt?" She looked at him, her eyebrows furrowed and her mouth turned down.

"They said I tore my ACL and my MCL, but they fixed it by injecting me with nanites."

She blinked at him. "Did they take them out again?"

Thane paused. "No."

"So they're still in there?"

He shrugged. "I guess so, unless they dissolve or something."

He told her about Dr. Thunk and talking to Brennan. "So if they tried to close the tears in the Weave and separate Shae and Earth, everyone with any Shae blood would die. They said that's a third of the population of the planet."

"I wonder if I have any Shae blood," Remi said.

"You don't," Thane answered without thinking. Remi looked at him with a raised eyebrow.

"How do you know?"

"Um," Thane tried to think. He knew because all Sanctum personnel and their families had their histories on record. "I asked."

"About me?" she seemed skeptical. "Why would they have records about me?"

"Because your dad's in the military, so he's already in government records and they have access to those," Thane tried to be as honest as possible so he could keep his promise to Remi without breaking the one he made to her father.

"Huh," she said. "What else?"

The tension in Thane's shoulder's and back eased. "Charlie tried to teach me how to control my affinity, but it didn't really work. That's when I blew up the building. Paka said I'd made the biggest first kill ever. I learned a Taijiquan form to keep myself calm and make it so I can hear the lightning Song." This turned into a conversation about the Song and how Shae magic was based on being able to manipulate the vibrations of the world around them.

"I wish I had an affinity," Remi said, stretching out her legs. Thane's were cold and cramped from sitting cross-legged so long on the metal.

"They're kind of a pain," Thane said. "Besides, Brennan is just human and so is Twitch, and General... the general who leads Omega Team is human too." He swallowed, hoping she wouldn't ask about it and chagrined at how close he'd been to saying Remi's father's name.

"How did they get in to Sanctum?" Remi asked.

"Twitch's dad already knew about it, and General Omega was recruited. Brennan I have no idea, he wouldn't ever tell me," Thane said.

"So it's like any other job. It's all about who you know," she sighed. "What are you going to do now?"

"I'm going to figure out who my father is," Thane said, squaring his shoulders.

"How?"

"I don't know," he slumped a little. "Twitch is helping, but I don't know how far he'll get. I can always ask Ms. Rasmussen if she ever comes back."

"Why would she know?" Remi was startled.

Thane realized he hadn't gotten to that part of his narrative. "Charlie knows her, and he says she's got some dragon in her, too. Red, so she has fire resistance. He says she's been looking for me because my father told her to."

"Come again?" Remi said.

Thane repeated the story that Charlie had told him about Ms. Rasmussen, her aspirations to be a part of Sanctum, her money, and her connection to his father. "Charlie can't tell me because there's some kind of rule that dragons can't talk about each other. It's supposed to keep them from going to war or something."

Remi shuddered. "Sounds like a good rule to me."

"Maybe." Thane shrugged. "But it does explain Ms. Rasmussen's interest and why she kept burning me. She was testing for my affinity."

"The sub didn't know when she was coming back," Remi said. "She might be gone for good."

"I doubt it," said Thane. "Charlie thought she wanted something else from me."

"So what's our next move?" Remi asked.

"I find my father," Thane said. "I need to know who he is, and not just for me." Remi looked at him with a raised eyebrow. "For my mom, too. He'll know who she is, what her name was, where she's from. If I can find that out maybe she'll remember. And maybe that will bring her some peace and let her get close to Lanie and Harper so they'll grow up having a mother."

Remi's jaw clenched and she turned her head away so Thane couldn't see her face. He cursed himself for being so insensitive and forgetting that she'd lost her mom when she was Lanie's age. He tried to think of something to say to make it better, but before he came up with anything she turned back to him. Her face was calm. "If nothing else, at least she won't feel so alone anymore."

"Yeah," Thane said. It was stupid, but it was the only thing he could make his mouth say.

"And hopefully, neither will you," Remi said.

Thane didn't respond. It was true, he knew it and she knew it, so it didn't need to be acknowledged. He rose to his feet and stretched the stiffness out of his legs. "I have an idea. Do you think Calder will drive us to the hospital?"

Remi blinked. "Probably. Why?"

"Because Dr. Bicknell wants to see me, and because there's a nurse who hides her horns." Thane smiled.

CHAPTER 28

They rode the elevator up to the fourth floor and walked around until they found an office with the number 438 painted on the door and "Steven J. Bicknell, M.D., PhD." printed on a temporary door plate. The door was cracked open. Thane and Remi looked at each other, then Thane shrugged.

"Dr. Bicknell?" he called. There was no answer. "Dr. Bicknell, it's Thane Whitaker. I got your--"

"Thane?" there was a clattering noise, footsteps, and the door flew open. Dr. Bicknell nearly knocked Remi over getting to Thane. "There you are! You got my message? Come in, come in, it's astounding!"

He turned and went back into his office as rapidly as he'd come out. Thane waved Remi in and then followed and shut the door. Dr. Bicknell's chair had fallen over, and the thirty-something doctor bent to pick it up so he could sit at his computer. "We did a full workup of your blood, Thane, and the results were amazing," he began. "Here, I'll pull up the file. We ran a basic metabolic panel and all that came back within normal ranges. But I ordered a polymerase chain reaction, and that came back unlike anything the scientific world has ever seen! Why is this taking so long?" he tapped an impatient finger on the mouse.

"You did a what test?" Thane asked. Remi stayed quiet in the corner, and Thane was impressed. He didn't think Dr. Bicknell had even noticed her.

"A polymerase chain reaction." The doctor glanced at Thane, who looked back at the man blankly. "A DNA test. We mapped your DNA."

"Oh," that could be a problem. Thane wasn't sure what Sanctum protocol was with non-Sanctum doctors performing tests and mapping DNA, but he was sure that it wasn't something they encouraged. He avoided glancing at Remi so he wouldn't draw the doctor's notice to her.

"Your DNA was breathtaking. I wish I had a blood sample from you before the lightning struck! Why is this taking so long? You had a remarkably low GC-content, which usually means the DNA is less stable, but that wasn't the amazing part. DNA has two base pairs. Yours had three. Three!" Dr. Bicknell ran a hand over his face. "I thought it was a glitch so I re-ran the test myself. Twice more. And the same results came back. Why is this taking so long to load?"

"It says you aren't connected to the network," Thane pointed to an error message at the bottom of the screen.

Dr. Bicknell made a noise somewhere between a sigh and a groan. He clicked through menu windows and tried to reconnect to the network without success. "Fine," the doctor growled, and pressed the power button down and held it firmly until the computer went dark. "Anyway, Thane, this is unprecedented. You have to let me study you." He pressed the button again, while staring at Thane with a flushed face and wide eyes while the computer rebooted.

"I'd need to talk to my parents," Thane stalled.

"Your parents! I need to study them too. Are your grandparents alive? Do you have siblings? I'm not a geneticist, but we'll get one on the research team. This could change everything, all our understanding of evolution and human life and our place in the universe." The computer beeped, and he logged in to the Mountain View Hospital network. This time when he accessed Thane's file it opened. "Look!" Dr Bicknell said, making a grand sweeping gesture with his hand.

Obediently Thane looked at the computer. He saw his name and birth date, and the rest of the monitor was covered with terms, abbreviations, and results he didn't understand. Except the findings at the bottom. Those all said "normal."

"Is this the first part? The metabolic one?" Thane asked.

"No, that's a different file. This is the PCR. See?" Dr. Bicknell pointed to the findings area, and then read what his finger was indicating. "Wait, that isn't right." He closed the file and double checked the file path. When he opened it again, it still said everything was normal.

Dr. Bicknell stared at the computer screen. "This isn't possible," he said. "I saw this yesterday. I uploaded confirmation tests last night. Did they not get linked?" He rapidly searched through the computer file records for uploads. "Here they are. I'll open them in the original location." He waited. "No. This can't be right." He rose. "I'll be right back, Thane. Wait here. I have to go down to the lab and check the samples." The doctor left his office looking slightly dazed.

"Poor guy," Remi said. "You said he's a specialist?"

"He studies lightning injuries," Thane said. He was still looking at the computer files Dr. Bicknell had left open on the desktop. Something about them had caught his attention, and he was trying to figure out what. "Shredding holes," Thane said, grinning, the unfamiliar curse feeling awkward in his mouth.

"What?" asked Remi.

"Look," Thane answered, pointing at the screen.

What he'd seen subconsciously when he'd glanced at the medical records result was clear now. The file looked perfectly legitimate when read from beginning to end, but if Thane stood a little away and looked at them like a picture he saw the words "Twitch was here," spelled diagonally from the bottom right to the top left. Twitch really was a genius. Thane was glad the tech specialist was on his side.

"That's amazing," Remi said. "How did he know to change the records?"

"Who knows," Thane answered. "But we need to get out of here before Dr. Bicknell comes back. We still have to find Delilah and get her to tell us about Shae and the seven dragons."

"Just five," Remi corrected. "We already know Charlie and Gideon."

"Right. Let's go," Thane said.

They left the fourth floor and went back to the nurses' station where the security guard was sitting in his chair. There wasn't a nurse behind the desk so Thane approached the security guard instead.

"Hey, it's the lightning kid," the guard said. "How are you doing?" Thane saw his name badge read "T. Shanafelt."

"Fine," Thane answered. "Have you seen Nurse Delilah?"

"That chatterbox? She just went down to the cafeteria to grab some lunch. She should be back in an hour or so, if you want to wait," T. Shanafelt added.

"No, thanks," Thane said, and he and Remi got back in the elevator.

"What's the plan?" Remi asked him once they were alone.

Thane considered. "I make her nervous, so it's up to you to get her alone. Then I'll come in and ask her what she knows about the dragons."

"That's it? That's the plan?" Remi asked.

Thane nodded. "Why, is it a bad plan?"

"No, no," Remi said, then added, "it's boring, that's all."

Thane blinked, stung. "What would you do?"

"I'd tell her I was from Sanctum," Remi said, eyes shining, "a special messenger from the Guardian Council to gather information on the dragons. But it was a secret mission, so she couldn't tell anyone I'd been here. Then I'd tell her that if she didn't tell me what I wanted to know, she'd be thrown in a cell and interrogated, and if she still didn't talk, we'd throw her against the ionized bars." She grinned at him. "I bet she'd tell us everything then."

"Or run away screaming, which would be bad," Thane said, "or contact Sanctum to verify your story, which would be worse. Besides, I don't like lying." Remi gave him a skeptical look. "I don't."

"I'll remember that," she said, and the elevator doors slid open on the ground floor.

Thane and Remi stepped out into the hospital lobby. "The cafeteria is this way," he said, leading her down the hall. They came to the open double doors of the cafeteria and stopped, peeking in. "There," Thane said, "sitting alone, blue scrubs, about halfway back on the left."

"Brown hair?" Remi asked. Thane nodded. "Got it." Remi straightened up and casually entered the cafeteria. She looked around a little bit and then approached Nurse Delilah where she sat eating her lunch. Remi smiled at her and said something, and the nurse responded. They were too far away for Thane to hear anything they said, but he saw the middle-aged nurse go pale and nod. She stood and followed Remi towards the door. As they drew close, Thane could hear the faint Song coming from her.

Thane stayed out of sight until they were in the hallway and then walked up on Nurse Delilah's other side. He put his arm under hers and said, "Keep walking." She glanced at his face and went even paler, her horns suddenly visible in her mousy brown hair and her Song went quiet. Remi wasn't tall enough to see the top of the woman's head, but she followed Thane's example and took the woman by the other arm and propelled her forward.

There was a room ahead labeled "Probe Cleaning," with an open door. As they drew near Thane peeked in and made sure it was empty before entering with Nurse Delilah and Remi. Remi shut the door and locked it. The room was rectangular and small, with a counter and a sink along one long wall. The short wall furthest away from the door had two metal vats. There was one chair, and Thane led Nurse Delilah to it.

"Sit," he said. She sat. Her horns were clearly visible now, even though the only light in the room came from a single bulb over the sink.

"What do you want?" she asked, her high pitched voice steadier than Thane expected. She lifted her chin and met his gaze. "Make it fast, my lunch break will be over soon and I don't want to get in trouble for being late."

Thane was put off balance by her nonchalance and didn't answer, so Remi spoke up. "We're looking for information and--- you do have horns!" She had drawn closer to the woman and since she was standing while the nurse was sitting, she could finally see the top of the nurse's head. "What are they made of? Can anyone see them? How do you hide them at work?"

"This is why you brought me here? To show me off to your songless girlfriend?" Delilah said, curling her lip. "I'm leaving."

"No," Thane said, throwing out an arm to bar her from standing. "We need some information. What do you know about dragons?"

"Knotted threads," she cursed. "Is that what you are? No, no, I am not getting involved in that. Lightning strike means blue, and blue means trouble. I am not touching that, not getting anywhere near that thank you, I'm going now." She rose, pushing past Thane's arm and talking a step towards the door.

"Not so fast, horn head," Remi planted her feet in front of Delilah, barring the way to the door and enjoying her self-appointed roll as bad cop a little too much, Thane thought. "We're not done with you yet."

"And how exactly are you going to keep me here, songless?" Delilah asked. Thane couldn't see the nurse's expression, but Remi's cheeks flushed and she took an involuntary step back.

"Hey," he said, squeezing around the nurse in the narrow room and getting between her and Remi. He turned to face Delilah.

Her eyes had changed from normal human eyes to the vertical yellow-slitted eyes of an imp. Remi was understandably terrified. Thane, however, had been through an Omega Team training with Jaeger riding on his head. This pudgy woman held no fear for him.

She must have sensed that as he stared back at her unflinching. Her eyes returned to their previous human appearance and she sat back down, crossing her legs and leaning back. "Look, kid, I don't know anything about the dragons.

No one does. That's the point. They can't be found, and they're willing to let the world bleed to keep it that way. You're out of luck, dragon boy."

Thane had the electric cell in his pocket. If he hadn't felt its comforting weight next to his leg, he never would have considered this. "If you know I'm a blue," he said, "then you know what I can do."

"Ha," she scoffed. "Hundreds of people have your little affinity. Most can barely generate enough to spark." She crossed her arms and stuck out her tongue at him. "Do your worst, lightning breath."

"My worst took down a building," Thane said, "and I have more than a little affinity." In his mind he invited the lightning Song. Almost immediately he heard the basso of the thunder and the crackling hum of electricity, and focused the gathering tingle of energy on his right hand. In the weird dim light of the room his fist began to glow with an irregular blue light. He raised it so Delilah could see it clearly. Behind him, Remi gasped. He spared a glance at her over his shoulder and saw that she'd backed away from him, covering her mouth with both hands and staring.

"You can't use that here," Delilah shrieked. "There are millions of dollars of equipment, some of which are keeping people alive."

"Tell me about the dragons," Thane said, but he was only half paying attention to her. The rest of his focus was split between keeping the lightning Song quiet and controlled, and wondering if Remi would ever see him the same way again. Delilah hadn't responded yet and Thane was straining to keep control. He leaned closer in to the nurse's face. "Tell me anything you know about the dragons. Please."

"I don't know anything," Delilah hissed into his face. "But I know someone who might. Ask the Beer Fairy."

"Are you kidding?" Thane asked, louder than he meant to. "Not a chance."

"Then you'll never find them. The Beer Fairy was the only one who ever really knew the dragons, before he was such a pathetic waste. If anyone stands a chance of finding them, it's him." She closed her eyes and pulled away as much as she could sitting down. "That's all I've got."

"By your Oath and Song?" Thane asked, remembering what Brennan had said to Raven.

"Yes," she said.

"Say it."

"By my Oath and Song, that's all I can tell you," she said.

Thane stood up straight and grabbed the electric cell in his pocket. He imagined the lightning song in his head flowing down into the grey metal, and the blue white light on his fist faded and went out. "Thank you, nurse," he said. "I'm sorry this was so unpleasant for you."

"The only reason I'm not going to report you to Sanctum is that the dragons would hear about it and we'd both be dead," she snapped, rising to her feet. Without saying anything else to either of them, she stomped to the door and unlocked it, then left.

Thane waited, still facing the chair. He didn't dare turn around, didn't want to see the look on Remi's face that screamed he was a freak. He wasn't even sure if Remi was there anymore or if she'd fled with Delilah. Who would blame her? Hearing about all the craziness from Thane was one thing, but seeing it first hand was dramatically different. Thane knew that from experience. But if she'd run away, at least she'd be safer. And it would be easier keeping General Gage's association with Sanctum secret if she never spoke to him again.

"That was incredible," Remi spoke behind him. She was still there. Thane slowly turned around to face her. "How can you do that? How can you keep from doing that all the time?" her mouth broke into a wide grin as she reached out and grabbed his fist. "Does it hurt? Where does the electricity come from? I wish I could do that." She flipped his hand over, making him open his fingers and looking at his palm. "My phone battery would never die," her eyebrows lifted and she smiled ecstatically.

This was too much. He pulled his hand away and shoved it in his pocket. "It isn't that great," Thane said.

"Yes it is," she argued. "You're just so used to things that are supposed to be good being bad that when you get something that really is good you assume the worst. Thane," she made sure he was looking at her before she continued, "You could get an electric bass and an amplifier and never have to plug them in."

That image did make him smile. "I don't know if it works like that--"

"Then make it work like that! Figure it out. But later," she said. "First we need to find the Beer Fairy."

" I promised Brennan I wouldn't go looking for Raven's bar again," Thane said.

Remi smiled. "I know. But you told me it was in the back of that old bookstore on Main Street. Right?"

"Yeah," he stretched out the word.

"And it would be dangerous for me to go there alone, right?"

"Yes, it would," Thane said.

"So if I went there and was going to be in danger, what would you do?" Remi asked him with her best charming smile.

Thane put his face in his palm. "I would go in after you."

"You would go in after me," Remi repeated. "I think I need some new books to read until my dad gets back."

CHAPTER 29

The Leaf and Dagger bookstore was exactly as Thane remembered it, down to the bored twenty-something hipster at the cash register. "Can I help you," he said tonelessly, clearly wanting the answer to be no.

"Just passing through, thanks," Thane said.

"Whatever," the cashier waved him on and then ignored them completely.

The wooden door to the back was in the same place, and Thane pulled it open. Beyond was an room that was larger on the inside than the entire bookstore was on the outside. Thane wasn't sick, dazed, or distracted this time so he was able to take a long look around the room that in his memory was so indistinct and chaotic. There were dark oak wood floors and lighter maple wood tables and chairs and one mahogany bar that ran the entire length of the front. It was getting late on a Saturday afternoon and there were patrons in the bar now, two sitting on stools at the bar and at least three tables had people sitting at them.

But the most striking aspect of the room was the doors. Both the wall opposite where Thane and Remi had entered and the wall opposite the bar were lined with doors of various sizes and shapes. Some were only as high as Thane's waist. Some of them were so large four people could walk through and carry someone on their shoulders. But they each had one foot of space between their frame and the frame of the next door, so the overall visual suggested a pattern underneath the chaos.

The bar-tending Sang Evarish Raven was serving drinks when Thane and Remi entered. She looked up, her nostrils flaring, and bared her fangs at him in an approximation of a smile. "Well, if it isn't the dragon boy," she purred. She put her emptied tray under her arm and swayed over to him. "Where's your keeper? Did Rip finally finish eating him?"

"Who's this, Thane?" Remi asked, linking her arm with his and staring down her nose at the silver haired Shae woman. "You didn't mention this place had a waitress."

Raven hissed. "Careful, pet. Sometimes I bite." She turned her attention back to Thane, smoldering again with barely restrained heat. "Rumor has it that you blew up an entire building. That's my kind of party." She fluttered her eyelashes at him and leaned forward. "Invite me next time," she murmured near his ear.

"How did you hear about that?" Thane asked, trying to fight the heat rising in his cheeks.

"Oh, you can pay a mercenary enough to die for you but you can never pay him enough not to gossip," she laughed. "And such stories they bring me over their ales. Alcohol was never very good at keeping secrets."

"Oi! Raven!" A burly, hairy man at a far table called. She straightened and looked over her shoulder to where the half beast beckoned.

"Duty calls," she sighed. "We'll finish this later, dragon boy."

She sauntered off and Remi muttered. "Stupid elf."

"Don't say that," Thane whispered back. "Calling her an elf is a huge insult."

"Really?" Remi's lips curled upward in a smile.

"Yes, like mortal combat," Thane said. "And I don't think either of us would come out of that well."

"Oh," she said. "I'll figure something else out. Now let's find the Beer Fairy."

Thane considered asking why she needed to figure something else out, but decided against it. Remi was right about finding the Beer Fairy. Thane looked around the room, but he saw no sign of the hairy sprite. "Maybe we could ask someone?"

"Okay. Which one?" Remi responded. Thane looked at the other patrons. Ghastly, beastly shapes met his gaze with fangs and claws that glinted in the low hanging lights. None of them looked particularly approachable, and Remi must have thought so too because she added, "How do they get around like this? How do people not notice?"

The door from the bookstore creaked open again, and a man and a woman entered together. Thane started, surprised. They were the athletic couple he had seen walking into the mountain biking store the day he'd been poisoned. The man held the door for the woman and then closed it behind them. Once it was securely closed, Thane heard the barest echo of music, a cheerful, breezy phrase, and saw something like colored mist fly off the couple.

As the mist departed, the man and the woman disappeared too. In their place stood two creatures Thane immediately thought of as werewolves, one a deep russet brown and the other grey and white. They continued into the room and sat at another table near the bar. Thane heard the grey and white wolf comment as they passed, "It's so nice to shake that off once in a while. Holding the Song steady all day is starting to give me a headache," and the russet wolf whimpered in sympathy.

"Oh," Remi said. "I guess... that's how."

Noise in the back corner caught Thane's attention. Raven noticed her new customers and attempted to extricate herself from the group of beastly men, but they were protesting. She stood and started to walk away when one of the men grabbed her around the waist and sat her down on his lap. Her elbow shot back and caught him under the ribs and then pivoted so the back of her fist smashed into his nose. The half beast roared and released her, grabbing at his face while she sprang to her feet.

Raven spun gracefully on the ball of one foot while the other snapped out and caught him at the collar bone. Thane heard the snap of bones an instant before the crash of the table as the beast man landed on it then went through it. There was a spray of splinters and tankards and foamy amber liquid. In the quiet that followed, Raven pointed her finger at one of the doors and the half beast's pack mates lifted him under the shoulders and dragged him out.

Thane turned back to glance at Remi. From the shocked expression on her face, Thane thought he didn't need to worry about Remi using the "elf" insult anymore. Raven moved through his field of vision, going to the bar and ringing a small bell before approaching the two wolf people to take their orders.

Thane could tell the bell had magic because he heard both the tiny tinkle of its sound and the subconscious echo of its Song. One of the small doors opened. Out of it came the slight figure of an old woman barely as high as his knees with wrinkled hands, fingers bent with age, and wispy white hair done up in a high bun. "Can't you go one day without breaking something?" her querulous voice carried across the room.

"Mrs. Cottle," Thane said, and started moving across the room towards her. Remi followed.

"You know her?" she whispered.

"Kind of," Thane responded, "be really polite." As he neared the tiny aged woman, he stopped and cleared his throat.

"What is it?" the old woman snapped, and then looked up. "Oh, young Mr. Whitaker, it's you," and the wrinkles lining her weathered face doubled as she smiled.

"Mrs. Cottle, it's great to see you again," Thane answered with a bow.

This delighted the tiny lady. "Still so polite," she murmured.

"This is my friend Remi," Thane said. "Remi, this is Mrs. Cottle."

"Pleased to meet you, ma'am," Remi said, and made an awkward bobbing motion that Thane realized was supposed to be a curtsey.

"Hmm," Mrs. Cottle said, looking at Remi. "Don't teach those as much as they used to."

Remi smiled her most charming smile. "Unfortunately no, and it isn't something I'd be good at anyway."

Mrs. Cottle studied Remi for a long moment, and then winked at her. "You've got spunk, I like that," she said.

"Can we help you clean up?" Thane offered.

Mrs. Cottle waved her broom at him. "No dear, this is my responsibility for a while longer. But it would be a great help if you would get my bucket, I left it just past the door," and she pointed with her broom handle.

Thane immediately walked to the small opening, carefully stepping over the remnants of the table and spilled tankards. He had to bend down to see through the door. Beyond it was a dark tunnel, lit only by pale yellow lights every few yards. Nothing moved inside that he could see, but there was a bucket the size of a dinner glass on the packed dirt floor. He picked it up and returned to where Mrs. Cottle and Remi were chatting and giggling.

"What's funny?" he asked, placing the bucket on the floor near the tiny woman.

"Never mind dearie," Mrs. Cottle said, daubing at her eyes with a lace handkerchief. "Talk like this isn't for boy's ears. Now off with you, I've got work to do."

"Mrs. Cottle, before we go I was wondering if you could help us," Thane said. He was uncertain how she would react to the request but couldn't think of any alternative.

"I'll do my best, child. What's troubling you?" she asked.

Thane opened his mouth, but paused. What would she think of him after this? "We need the Beer Fairy. Do you know where he is or how we could find him?" Remi said, sparing him.

"Oh," the old woman's eyes narrowed as she looked at them. "Two young people looking for the likes of him? I don't know if I can support that. He's the kind that trouble follows, if you see my meaning." She glanced very pointedly at Remi, then Thane. "I didn't think you were that sort, Mr. Whitaker."

"No, that, um, no," Thane said, struggling for words. "We need to find him because someone told us that he could help us find... someone."

"So it's a quest, then," Mrs. Cottle brightened considerably at that, and patted some of her hair back into her bun. "That's entirely different, and he is the sort who knows things. But you, young miss," she said, leaning close to Remi, who bent down to listen. "Remember this. If a man is being inappropriate, be he shadow, shade, or fae, sock him in the jewels. They learn that lesson once." She nodded emphatically.

"I will, thank you Mrs. Cottle," Remi said with a shaking voice. Thane glanced at her, concerned, then realized she was trying not to laugh.

"Well then," the knee high woman straightened her apron and held her broom like a scepter, "go through that door," and she pointed to one of the smallest ones with the end of her broom handle, "and think about finding the Beer Fairy. It should drop you on the isle of Crete in the Aegean Sea. He hides there, you know," she lowered her voice to a confidential whisper, "when he doesn't want to be found. That's one of the reasons the door is so small, hard to get through. He wants to forget and be forgotten."

She straightened again and turned around, beginning to sweep up the table splinters. Several were almost as long as she was. "Thank you, Mrs. Cottle," Remi said. The old woman harrumphed and shooed them with her broom.

"Off with you. I've got work enough to do without worrying over you youngsters," she said. Her tone of brisk tenderness reminded Thane again of his Grandma Whitaker, and impulsively he knelt down and took one of her hands and kissed it. He had a strong memory of doing that to Grandma Whitaker when he'd been too small to reach anything else, and she'd always loved it.

"Thank you," he said, and two bright spots of pink appeared on her withered cheeks.

"Goodness me, boy. You'll give an old woman a heart attack," she said. Thane was seized with embarrassment and got up quickly, red flushing his face down to his neck. He hurried across the room to the door she'd indicated, Remi following.

He got a sideways look from his best friend. "She reminds me of my grandma," he said, feeling defensive.

"I thought it was sweet," Remi replied.

"This is the door, right?" Thane was desperate to change the subject.

Remi looked. "I think so."

"I'll open it, since I know what the Beer Fairy looks like," Thane said, reaching down for the handle. The top of the door frame only hit his waist and was narrow enough that he wasn't sure his shoulders would fit through. He gripped the ivory doorknob and tried to think about the Beer Fairy, and not how stupid he'd looked kissing that old woman's hand.

He turned the knob and pushed the door open. It moved less than an inch and banged into the wall behind it. "Is that how it's supposed to work?" Remi asked.

Thane didn't bother to answer. He shut the door again and took his hand off the knob. Knowing he was out of sorts and knowing he needed to focus, Thane let his arms drop to his sides and started breathing slowly in and out through his nose. In his mind, he began the Taijiquan form. As his thoughts flowed through each stance of the form, he created a mental picture of the Beer Fairy. Not only what he looked like, but with everything Brennan had said about the once great Shae having fallen and Mrs. Cottle's comment about wanting to be forgotten. Thane knew that feeling was and infused his image of the Beer Fairy with it. When it held steady in his mind, he reached out and turned the door handle.

Remi drew in a slow breath behind him and said, "Whoa." Thane opened his eyes and saw a green field that ran up a hillside. The hill was only the smallest beginning of the mountain behind it. The sky was brilliantly blue and the air felt warm and balmy, a welcome change from the early winter of Payson.

Getting on all fours, Thane put his head through the doorway. His shoulders didn't fit straight on, so he turned them at an angle and pushed through. He sprawled forward, landing on soft grass.

Remi was both shorter and narrower than he was, so she was able to crawl through without difficulty. "Now what?" she asked.

Thane reached down and closed the door behind them. It was nestled between two large rocks and snug against the hill in a small valley. Once closed it was almost invisible as the wood of the door was the exact color and shading of the boulders on either side. "We need to mark this," Thane said. He looked around. "Give me your jacket?"

"Sure. I don't need it here," Remi said and took it off. Thane tucked it snugly under the bottom corner of the door and tugged on it to make sure it was secure. The bright purple stood out boldly. Then he stood and they both marveled.

"It's beautiful here," Remi said. Thane nodded.

"Let's climb that hill," he suggested, pointing. "We'll be able to see more from there and decide where to go next." Remi agreed and it didn't take them long to get to the top. They looked out from their little hidden valley and onto the island below and all around them.

It turned out that they were less than halfway up a mountain in what seemed to be the center of the island. Out of the protection of the hills a breeze blew washing their faces in the scent of wet grass, wild flowers, and the ocean. They couldn't see any signs of civilization, just the uncultivated island and the blue sea beyond.

"I could stay here forever," Remi breathed. Thane knew what she meant. The entire island felt like a place outside of time, where it never mattered what day of the week it was or how old you were. Thane opened himself to the peace and the solitude and heard a flicker of Song. It surprised him, and he lost it. He tried again, and that same flicker came back. This time he focused on it and turned to face it. When he lifted his eyelids, he was facing back down into the valley.

"Come on, I think he's this way," Thane said.

"How can you tell?"

Thane paused. "I can hear music," he answered, "coming from over there somewhere."

Remi appraised him. "All right," she said. "Lead on."

They walked back through the valley, Thane checking again to make sure her jacket was secure and he could find the door again. On the other side they emerged between two hills and saw below a long stretch of excavated ruins to their left, and a path leading up the mountain to their right. Thane closed his eyes and listened again, following the Song with his body. When he opened them, he was facing the ruins.

They hiked down the hill towards the crumbling white columns. It was a much further walk than it had looked from their valley, and they were both hot and sweaty by the time they reached the edge of the tumbling columns.

To Thane's surprise, groups of tourists were walking around in the ruins, commenting on this or that and peering into their guidebooks. He used his skill of going through crowds without being noticed to read over a few shoulders and then returned to Remi.

"This is the island of Crete, near Greece," he said, "and this is the ruins of the palace of Knossos."

"Does that mean anything to you?" Remi asked.

"No," Thane admitted. "But we know where we are."

"But not where the Beer Fairy is," Remi added. Thane closed his eyes again and listened with that part of his mind where his Song was. The music he heard was louder, and he noticed how dissonant it was. Part of it was melancholy and lilting, but that was almost completely obscured by a brash and raucous overtone.

"Don't let me run into anything," Thane whispered, and began walking towards the music with his eyes closed. Remi rested her hand on his arm. She followed him, warning him about uneven ground or if there was a pillar. He moved forward, both pulled and repulsed by the music he was trying to find.

"There's a wall," Remi said. Thane expected her to lead him around it, but she stopped. He opened his eyes.

"Oh," he said. It was a wall, and the side of a cliff that stretched out in both directions. The tourists were all deeper in the center of the ruins, so there wasn't anyone else in sight.

"What now?" Remi asked.

Thane closed his eyes. The music was coming from right in front of him. He lay is forehead against the cool crumbling stone and placed his palms flat against it on either side. "I don't know," he said, pushing against it with his hands to lift his forehead. "I thought--"

The stone under his hands slid forward. He lost his balance and stumbled, pushing the stone even more. It went six inches further into the cliff face and then stopped. Thane tried pushing on it again, but it didn't move.

"Hang on," Remi said, standing back and studying the large stone slab. She came and stood next to Thane, forcing her fingers to dig in the dirt and wrap around the edge furthest from Thane and tugged on it. Nothing. "Try the other side," she instructed.

Thane obediently wrapped his fingers around the other edge and tried to push it towards Remi. The stone slid into a prepared pocket in the mountainside, revealing a passageway beyond. They looked at each other and went inside, sliding the door mostly shut behind them so none of the tourists would follow.

The passage wasn't long, and there was a room filled with orange torch light just ahead. "I think he's in there," Thane's whisper made weird echoes against the stone walls. "I'll check first." Remi nodded, and Thane stilled himself as he had for nearly every day he could remember. He made his thoughts and motions silent so they wouldn't draw attention, quieted his heartbeat and did his best not only to be invisible, but to not exist. Then he crept forward, pressed against the wall until he could see into the room beyond.

The only thing in the room was a large statue of a man with vines and leaves in his hair, holding a large bunch of grapes. Surrounded by empty flasks, bottles and leather wineskins, the Beer Fairy was urinating on the statue with his back towards Thane.

"Burn you," the Beer Fairy slurred at the sculpture. "Burn your thread to cinders." He finished his business and dropped his loincloth, then grabbed a bottle and collapsed onto the square base of the statue.

Thane crept back to Remi. "He's in there, but I don't know if you should come with me," he said. "He looks pretty drunk."

Remi snorted. "I didn't follow you halfway around the world so I could hide in the dark. Besides, I'm around soldiers all the time. I can handle it." Thane was pretty sure that soldiers didn't act like that around the general's daughter.

"Okay, but you can always come back and wait for me here," Thane said. She rolled her eyes at him, but nodded and let him lead down the hall. The two of them stopped outside the torchlight room so that the circle of orange light didn't quite touch them.

"Who's there?" the Beer Fairy slurred. He pushed himself up with his hairy arms and peered into the darkness with red eyes. Remi snickered. "I can hear you," the hairy pixie stated. "It's rude to lurk, you know."

"You look like you enjoy a little rudeness," Remi said, striding into the room. Thane sighed and followed close behind her.

"Who're you?" The Beer Fairy blinked watery eyes. "Do I know you? You look familiar."

"We met--" Thane began.

The Beer Fairy cut him off. "Not you, her. Have we met before, sweetheart?"

Remi laughed. "I think I would remember meeting something like you."

"Something like me, yeah," the Beer Fairy twitched his gossamer wings and sparkles danced in the torchlight as he leaned back and scratched his belly with dirty, uneven fingernails. "I'm something, all right."

Remi opened her mouth to respond, but Thane jumped in. "We need your help. We're looking for my father, and someone said you could help us."

"Your father? It isn't me." The Beer Fairy belched and then hiccupped, his teeth filthy and his breath bad enough Thane could smell it from the doorway. "I stopped doing that kind of thing before you were born."

"No, my father's a dragon, and I--"

"A dragon? No way. I don't mess with the seven, and they leave me alone now. They haven't wanted me around in centuries," he scratched his armpit. Then he blinked and looked at Thane more closely. "I do remember you. You're Brennan's kid, right? But Brennan's not a dragon. Go home, kid. You're more confused than I am," and he hiccupped again, lolling backwards against the statue's legs.

"Brennan isn't my father, and I don't need to know all the dragons, just the blue ones." Thane said.

"The blues? No shredding way, kiddo. The reds you know are out to get you, and the golds will punish then forgive, but the blues are off the charts. Nope." He emptied the bottle in his hand and reached for another, hand unsteady. "Go pester someone else, Brennan's boy."

The music in Thane's head was almost too loud for him to hear the Beer Fairy. The discordant overtone was brash and irritating, and subconsciously Thane started tweaking it. The sad melody underneath was in a weak minor key, and Thane wove the constant of the stone underneath his feet into the bass line to strengthen it. Then he picked the flickering torchlight to add a subtle descant and push away some of the discord, bringing the two clashing melodies closer together.

"What are you doing?" the Beer Fairy demanded.

Remi and Thane looked at each other. "Waiting for you to die of liver failure," Remi said.

The Beer Fairy threw his head back and howled, but in laughter or grief, Thane couldn't tell. "That's the greatest joke of all," the oily sprite said, "I can't get drunk. Here I am, the shredding Beer Fairy, and I can't get hammered. Dionysus, the god of wine, and I can't even get a knotted buzz!" and he threw the bottle in his hand at the statue.

It hit the marble man in the face and shattered, glass tinkling and falling like green rain back onto the pixie who threw it. "I hate you," the Beer Fairy sneered at the statue.

"Who is it?" Remi asked.

"Who is it?" The Beer Fairy spun to face her, his face contorted. "Why, it's me! Can't you see the resemblance? This shredding room is my first temple," he swept his arms out to indicate the square room. "The Minoans worshipped me and I taught them to celebrate. Later they introduced me to the Greeks and gave me a name. Dionysus. God of wine and freedom. Protector of all those who do not fit into conventional society and symbol of everything that is chaotic, dangerous and unexpected."

Tears began falling from his watery eyes and splashing on his flaccid cheeks. "I led men and women to find the wild beauty they held inside. I helped Shaelings find their Song. I spent three centuries helping to create poetry, music, and theater, and protecting and nurturing every soul who didn't belong. And then they left me." He sniffed, rubbing his nose along his hair covered arm. "I became a joke, a caricature of everything I used to be. So I laughed along." He looked down at himself, at the soiled loincloth and the rolls of fat and hair. "I tried to give them something even funnier to laugh at."

Thane was suddenly reminded of Iselle and the story she told him about her father's vineyard. "When every way to forget our loss is taken, how do we move on?" he repeated. The Beer Fairy pointed at him with yet another bottle.

"That's the million dollar question, kid. If you can answer that, I'll tell you who your dad is."

"You know?" Thane asked, heartbeat quickening.

"Of course. You play with the Song just like your dad does." The Beer Fairy took a large swig from his brown bottle.

"If you don't get drunk, why do you drink?" Remi asked.

"Because it's stupid, and so am I. What else have I got left?" the onetime god asked.

Thane was thinking furiously. "You have to find something greater than your loss," he said. "Something that you think is worth fighting for."

"Ha," the Beer Fairy sneered. "What is going to be greater than what I lost? I inspired centuries of artists, was a protector of millions of Shaelings. Now," he punched his rolls of belly fat, "I've been wearing this shape so long I can't even take it off anymore. You know what's worse than being a joke? Remembering all you've lost, but forgetting who you are." He belched, the sound punctuating the discordance in the Song.

Thane ignored the words, and listened to the Song the Beer Fairy was wrapped in. Every drink, every belch, every disparaging remark he made increased the volume of the cacophony and muted the lullaby a little more. It nagged at him, and his mind itched to fix it. Opening himself to the Song, Thane analyzed it the way Ms. Sorenson had taught him in AP Music. Find the themes. The key, the time signature, the tempo and chord progressions all needed to be identified and catalogued. It was easy to assume that these were two very different pieces of music playing at the same time, like listening to songs with your headphones while something else played on the radio.

But that wasn't true. Breaking them down into their most basic parts, Thane recognized they were the same song, but one was broken and haphazard while the other was fading away with nothing to support it. Thane took the pieces of the broken song and wove them back together. He organized phrases that were out of order, fixed broken flats and sharps, and stitched back together the complicated counter melody that ran under and held up the lullaby.

When he'd finished, he was bathed in sweat and breathing heavily. His eyelids felt glued shut, and he released the counter melody back into the Song of Dionysus. It swelled, then vanished. Thane heard the torches blaze and the air around him grew hotter, and Remi gasped.

"What did you do?" Remi whispered to him.

Thane squinted at her with one eye. "His Song was bugging me. I fixed it. Why?"

"He's gone," she said.

Gingerly Thane opened both eyes and looked around the room. She was right; the Beer Fairy was nowhere to be seen. Empty bottles still littered the floor and shards of green glass lay around the base of the statue, but the fat little man with glittering wings was gone.

"Now what?" Remi asked. Thane shrugged. He had no idea what happened.

"I guess we leave," Thane said. "Maybe Twitch can figure out where Ms. Rasmussen went--"

The air around them trembled and the floor vibrated. Thane and Remi both fell to the floor, she catching herself with her hands before her face hit and he landing solidly on his backside and bouncing once. Thane felt pressure building and instinctively threw himself on top of Remi.

"Cover your face," he shouted, and wrapped his arms around his head. He closed his eyes once she did the same.

Behind them cracks were followed by clattering sounds, and then a hollow boom. Thane felt pieces of stone hitting his arms and back, and was grateful Remi was protected from the worst of it. When the stone stopped falling, he opened his eyes and looked down.

Her eyes were open, looking at something behind and above him. "Found him," she said, pointing.

Thane turned to see a young man with shining white skin stepping down off the square stone pedestal. He wore a deep purple toga, and Thane and Remi scrambled to their feet as he drew near.

"You're Dionysus." Remi said.

It was more an observation than a question, but the once god answered anyway. "Yes." He turned to Thane. "How did you do that? I've been trapped so long I didn't think it was possible to get out. How did you navigate the maze?"

"Maze?" Thane asked. "I didn't see a maze. You were playing a song over and over, but it was broken. I fixed it."

Dionysus laughed. It didn't have any of the bitterness and self loathing of the Beer Fairy's laugh, but it still held deep echoes of grief. "Different ways of explaining the same thing. You go through the maze, you took apart the walls and rebuilt my house, you fixed the music."

"I guess," Thane shrugged. "I'm glad you're better now."

"He isn't better," Remi said. The white Shae and the teenage boy both looked at her. "He isn't," she defended. "You don't wake up and suddenly you're better. You wake up and you find you're ready to get better. That's what you helped him to do."

"She is wise for one so young," Dionysus said. Thane silently agreed. "I don't know how you did it, Shaeling, but you returned me to myself. I am grateful. Now I hope to find more artists to inspire, to create theater and music and art again."

"Why don't you do it yourself?" Remi asked.

The Shae gazed at her. "Do what myself?" he asked.

"Create," she said, and made a vague gesture in the air. "You said you spent centuries inspiring other people and then they left you. Why don't you do it yourself? Then no one can take it away." Dionysus was silent, staring into the far distance as if he hadn't heard.

"And if it's good it will inspire other musicians, artists, and writers anyway," Thane added.

Dionysus, the newly freed Shae and former god, stared at them both. "Your father is Ruan de Argos," he said to Thane.

CHAPTER 30

"Ruin what?" said Thane.

"Ruan de Argos, once known as King Minos of this island." Dionysus said. "He is one of the ancient dragons, second of the seven to cross from the Shaerealm. He has been both god and king, and is not satisfied with either. And now you should run," he added, starting to escort them back through the passage.

"Run? Why?" Remi asked.

"Because I named him as a dragon, he'll send some minions to find out why and to whom," the white skinned Shae hustled them faster. They reached the sliding pocket door and stopped.

"I will lead them off in another direction, you go back however you came," he said, and put a hand on Thane's shoulder. "This is all I can do to thank you. Now get out of here."

"Won't you be in danger?" Remi asked.

"No." His answering grin had quite a bit of the Beer Fairy swagger in it. "I'll give them a merry chase and send them back exhausted and wiser. Move it, children," he advised, then vanished.

Beyond the stone, Thane heard inhuman shrieks coming from a long way away. "Yeah, time to go," he agreed, and he and Remi wrapped their fingers around the edge of the stone and pulled.

Twitch stood on the other side, one arm raised as if to knock. "Twitch!" Thane exclaimed.

"Thane?" Twitch asked.

"Twitch!" Remi threw her arms around him.

"Girl?" Twitch's eyebrows furrowed and his left eye began to tick.

"What are you doing here?" Thane asked.

"My sources say the Beer Fairy is here and that he might know something about who your dad is," Twitch looked down the passageway behind them. "What are you doing here?"

"Same thing, my dad's name is Ruan de Argos, and--"

"Shredding knotted holes," Twitch swore. "We've got to get out of here." He turned and started running.

"Wait, you know him?" Thane asked, running after him and glancing back to make sure Remi was following.

"Know of him," Twitch corrected. "Don't say his name again. We need an escape route. I have a vehicle, but it won't get us off the island. How did you get here?"

"There's a door up in those hills," Thane said, pointing. "We marked it so we can find it quickly once we get up there."

"Great, brilliant. Shreds," he said. The shrieking sound was louder now, and coming from the sky. Twitch glanced up and behind them. "Viper birds."

Thane looked back, and then felt sick and wished he hadn't. Grey smears in the blue sky above flapped enormous feathery wings. They broke into two groups and some wheeled off, chasing something Thane couldn't see. The rest drew nearer and screamed at them with near-human female faces.

"Don't be fooled," Twitch called out. "They aren't smart. They're just trained pets, like homing pigeons. Or hunting falcons."

"So if we cover their heads they go to sleep?" asked Remi between pants.

"More like they'll kill us and bring our bodies back to their master," Twitch said.

"Oh," Remi said, and ran faster. "Where are we going?"

"To the edge of the ruins, I have-- there!" Twitch shouted, pointing.

Ahead of them on the side of the trail was something that looked like a dune buggy with two seats up front and a luggage rack in the back. It was triangle shaped with three wheels, two in the rear and one in front. "Get in," Twitch instructed.

Twitch jumped in the driver's seat and Thane climbed on the back before Remi could object. She got in the passenger seat and glared at Thane. "I would be fine there, you know," she said.

"This isn't the time," he answered, and Twitch put the key in the ignition and turned it over.

The engine revved, then sputtered and died. "Shreds," Twitch cursed, and turned the key again with the same result.

"You're the tech wizard, right?" Remi asked.

"Yes," Twitch said. He turned over the key and listened to the engine fail again.

"So with all the magic and technology of two worlds at your disposal you decide to build this thing with a lawn mower engine?" Remi asked.

"Give me a break, I was only ten when I built this," Twitch said.

"You built this when you were ten?" Thane asked.

"It really does have a lawn mower engine?!" Remi screeched.

The shrieks of the viper birds were close enough that Thane could feel the air movement from their wings when the engine roared to life. "Grab something," Twitch shouted as they sped up the trail.

"Your shocks are terrible," Remi said while trying to keep from bouncing out.

"Do you always complain this much?" Twitch asked her, and then added, "She isn't being polite either," to his left shoulder.

"Who are you talking to?" Remi demanded.

"Duck," Thane shouted, and the first viper bird swooped down to attack. Its grey scaly claws grasped the air Thane's head had passed through the moment before, and it screeched its displeasure before wheeling around again.

"Where are we going?" Twitch shouted over the noise of the engine.

"How many are there?" Remi yelled.

"Up the path to a small break between two little hills, and three, maybe four, they're moving a lot," Thane answered. "Twitch, do you have any weapons?"

The tech specialist glanced around at the metal frame of his vehicle. "Take the wheel," he shouted to Remi, then started unscrewing the clamp that held the safety bar next to him.

"Argh!" Remi shouted and grabbed the wheel. They swerved and bounced back and forth across the path. The viper birds swooped down several more times, trying to grab soft human flesh in their claws. But the erratic path of the vehicle made their dives useless, and twice Remi almost ran into one of the attacking birds.

"I've got it," she cried.

"Here," said Twitch, handing Thane the yard long piece of steel. He took back the wheel from Remi and doubled their speed. The viper birds fell back, giving Thane time to adjust to his new weapon.

"Grab my pants," he shouted to Remi as he turned to face backwards on the rack.

She understood and gripped the waist of his jeans with both hands, giving him leverage and keeping him on the vehicle. A viper bird chose that moment to attack. Claws stretched and human mouth screaming, it shot down at Thane like an arrow from the sky. He waited. She was close enough that he could see individual feathers on her wings. He waited. She was close enough that he could count the fangs in her mouth. He waited until he could have almost beeped her on the nose with his finger, and then swung the steel rod as hard as he could.

It connected with the viper bird's head with a bone crunching impact. Her shriek was cut short and she fell to the ground behind Twitch's three wheeler. "That's one!" shouted Thane, and readied himself again.

The other viper birds were more cautious now, hovering back in the sky. There had definitely been four of them because three still wheeled about overhead, shrieking and screeching. Thane held his club with two hands and waited.

"There?" Twitch yelled.

Thane twisted around so he could see the path ahead. The split in the hills was coming up. "That's it," he said, and turned back just in time to get a face full of feathers and feel claws pierce his shoulder.

He screamed in pain and tried to beat it with his steel pipe, but he was too close and couldn't get any momentum.

"Hey, ugly!" Remi yelled. The viper bird turned its face to her and Remi punched it, her fist driving upwards from the base of its human shaped nose.

The claws in Thane's shoulder slackened and the viper bird fell backwards off the ATV and into the dirt behind it. "Thanks," Thane said, gripping the wound.

"Self defense classes," Remi smiled at him. "My dad insisted."

"Good idea," Thane agreed, but kept his eyes on the remaining two birds. His right shoulder felt weak and he bled from four puncture wounds, two in the front and two in the back. Worst of all, his Grand Funk t-shirt was ruined.

"Grip tight!" Twitch yelled, and Thane held on with his left hand as the three wheeler turned sharply to the right and in between the hills. It pulled up onto two wheels but the space wasn't wide enough for it to fall over, and it righted itself on the other side. The screeching of the remaining two viper birds grew louder, and Thane hoped hiding between the hills would buy them some time. He was starting to feel dizzy.

"There's the marker," Thane said, pointing to Remi's bright purple jacket laying on the green grass. Twitch gunned the engine and they raced across the valley floor. As they drew near, he slammed on the breaks and jerked the wheel.

The three wheeler spun to the side and skidded into the nearest boulder, the safety bars bending with the impact.

"Is the door large enough to drive through?" the older boy asked.

Thane shook his head. "Barely big enough to crawl through," he answered.

Twitch was about to say something else when the viper birds crested the hills and saw them again. "I need to tweak the design anyway. Let's go!"

Remi pulled her jacket out from under the door so she could open it. There was nothing but grass and dirt on the other side. "It isn't working," she yelled.

"Move!" Twitch said. "Thane, where do you need to get back to?"

"The Leaf and Dagger, I'll do it, here," Thane said, tossing Twitch the metal bar and secretly relieved to be rid of it. He was getting dizzier and his shoulder ached.

In that moment of transition, a viper bird attacked. It dove at Remi, screaming. Twitch's arm shot out and he grabbed the metal bar in the air, swinging it around like a baseball bat and smashing it against the back of the bald human head with a loud crunch.

The deadly bird dropped and lay immobile on the grass in front of the door. Remi sprang back, her mouth covered by her hands. Thane grabbed the doorknob and twisted, filling his mind with every detail of the Leaf and Dagger back room and focusing on the image of Mrs. Cottle mopping the floor. He infused her with all the life and personality he could. He jerked the door open and saw dark oak floor boards on the other side.

But only a little. The body of the viper bird, about the size of a full grown labrador retriever, blocked the door from opening wide enough to get through. "Help me get this thing out of the way," Thane said to Remi.

She took a step towards it and stopped. Her hands were shaking. "I can't," she said. "I can't make myself touch it."

"I can't move it by myself," Thane growled. "You punched one in the face. This should be easier."

She glared at him. "Fine," she said, and squeezed her eyes shut. Remi reached down and grasped the dead viper bird, shuddering.

"Push," Thane said, and they heaved together. It rolled a little out of the way, but not very much.

"Guys," Twitch said.

"Push," Thane grunted, and they shoved together moving the body another few inches.

"Guys," Twitch pressed.

"What?" Thane and Remi asked together.

"That last one left."

"That's a good thing, right?" Remi said, peeking at him through one slitted eyelid.

"No. That's bad." Twitch pointed to a large black cloud moving rapidly through the sky. "It went to get the rest of the flock."

Distant shrieks and screeches filled the air like high pitched thunder. Twitch threw down the metal bar and ran to help Thane and Remi move the body away from the door. "Push!" Thane shouted, and the three of them managed to move it far enough that they could open the door.

"You first," Thane said to Remi.

"Why? You're hurt, you go first," she argued.

Thane growled and grabbed her with his left hand. "You're already braver than I am," he said, pulling her wrist to the door. He let it go and pushed her head down. "If you get hurt your dad will kill us both," and he pushed her through with his foot on her back.

"Now you," said Twitch, picking up the bar again. Thane was about to argue, but didn't want Twitch to force him through the door like he'd just done to Remi so he got down on all fours and started crawling. He grunted with pain as the punctures on his right shoulder rubbed against the wooden doorframe.

"Come on," Remi said, and grabbed him under the armpits. With her pulling and him pushing with his feet, he popped through. Twitch didn't bother crawling. The moment the doorway was empty he dove in sideways with a viper bird's claws around his ankle.

"Shoo, you filthy bird!" Mrs. Cottle whacked it on the head with her broomstick and beat it mercilessly until it fled back through the door. She reached in with her gnarled fingers and grabbed the knob, shutting one grey wing in the door with a snap.

Thane, Remi, and Twitch lay on the floor in a heap, panting, bruised, and bleeding. Thane saw Raven coming near, and tried to scoot away. "Don't drink my blood," he said, trying and failing to keep his voice steady.

She wrinkled her nose at him. "Wouldn't dream of it, pet. I wanted to see who you brought back with you." Twitch groaned and rolled over, and Raven's lip curled back, exposing a few of her fangs. "Another Shaerealm mercenary. Really dragon boy, you need to keep better company." She sniffed derisively and walked away.

The three teenagers detangled themselves and sat, panting. "You okay?" Twitch asked Thane. "I don't have any darts with me."

His shoulder was burning, but he said, "I'll be fine."

He watched Remi sit with her back to him. She didn't turn around to check on him or ask if he was okay, and that worried him. Maybe he'd hurt her when he pushed her through the door? The thought horrified him. Sure, hurting her a little to keep her safe was the better alternative, but that didn't make it okay. He realized he hadn't asked if she was all right. Maybe that's why she was upset. Maybe it was both.

"Remi, are you okay?" Thane asked.

She didn't turn to look at him and didn't answer him for so long that he almost repeated himself. "I don't need to be rescued," she finally said.

"What?"

"I could've helped Twitch. I got rid of the one attacking you. I'm the smallest, I should've been last because I can get through the door the fastest. I don't need you protecting me or trying to save me." She turned to face him. He was afraid she'd be crying, but her face was cold and calm. "I don't need another father, Thane. I need you to trust me."

"I do trust you," Thane protested. "You've had more combat training than I have. You know how to throw a punch. But that isn't the point." He fumbled, trying to figure out how to phrase the feelings rattling around in his body. "I can't leave you behind. I can't go through the door until you do. It isn't that you aren't capable, it's that I'm not. I am not capable of leaving you in danger. If you hadn't gone through I couldn't have gone through, and we all would've died."

"I'd have gone through," Twitch volunteered. "I'd have left you both."

Remi giggled. Thane smiled too. "We did it," he said. "I know who my father is."

Twitch's stomach growled. "At least I can buy you guys lunch first," Twitch said. "You want to eat? Sanctum is paying."

"Yes," Thane and Remi said together, then smiled at each other. Thane broke off his gaze first, looking down at his feet and then standing up. "Raven makes the best onion rings," he whispered to Remi, "but don't tell her so. Don't say anything good about her cooking."

"Why?"

"She's shadow. I guess if you say anything about them is good they get cranky."

"Really." Her eyes lit up with a mischievous gleam. Thane immediately wished he could take the words back, but the damage had been done. "Hey, your shoulder!"

Thane looked down at the four holes in his shirt. The skin underneath them was smooth and unbroken. "What-- how did that happen?"

"What?" Twitch asked.

"My shoulder. It's better."

Twitch came to look. He pulled a pair of small binoculars out of a pocket and adjusted the settings, then peered through them at Thane's shoulder. "Nanites. When did you get nanites?"

"Last Tuesday, after the training."

"What?" Twitch seemed truly shocked. "That can't be right. They only have enough power for twenty-four hours, then your system flushes them out. How--" the tech specialist stood still, his head cocked to Thane's right. "Right. You generate electricity. You must be keeping them charged. I could do something with that..."

They sat around a wooden table and ate the food Twitch had ordered for them after establishing with Raven that there was nothing harmful in any of it. Remi asked more questions about the Oath and Song, and Twitch was more than happy to talk about anything that was general knowledge among the Shae.

"What?" Twitch said to no one, and then, "yeah, I guess I don't know." Turning back to Remi, he said, "We've been in such a hurry we haven't been formally introduced. I'm Twitch O'Malley, Omega Team, Shaerealm Mercenary Guard." He held out his hand.

"Remi Gage, Sophomore, Payson High School," Remi responded.

Twitch nearly choked on his onion ring. Thane thwacked him hard on the back a few times and the tech specialist stuttered, "You mean you're--" he cut off when Thane pounded him on the back again. "Hey, I'm fine now, thanks," Twitch said.

"Just making sure," Thane said, looking at Twitch with wide eyes and shaking his head back and forth behind Remi.

Twitch caught on. "Oh. Yeah. Thanks."

"I mean I'm what?" Remi asked.

Twitch looked at Thane, then off to his left. "Fifteen. You mean you're fifteen, like this guy?" Twitch jerked his thumb at Thane.

"Yep," Remi answered, sipping her soda. "Tell me more about what you do in Sanctum."

Thane was relieved when they all went home for the night. Keeping his promises was going to be twice as hard if Remi and Twitch were in the same room.

CHAPTER 31

Sunday passed as a quiet, peaceful day spent at home with his family, which in itself was a miracle. Sundays had never been quiet. Thane didn't wake until late morning, stiff from his adventure of the day before and with the name Ruan de Argos on his mind. He wanted to ask his mom about it and see if it jogged any memories, but seeing how frail and unbalanced she was, he thought better of it. The reaction people had to his name, the viper bird minions, and sending Cressida Rasmussen to find him all argued against his father being a hero and Thane wasn't ready to put his mother through more pain.

The alarm on his phone jangled to life too early the next morning. Thane groaned and rolled over, strongly reconsidering his stance of the night before. But Remi would be expecting him, and he had AP Music today. AP Music was turning out to be more useful than he'd ever dreamed, and he desperately needed to learn more. He pushed off his blankets. The basement was frigid but he resisted getting back in bed in favor of a hot shower. He'd finally put away his clothes last night so they were not very wrinkled this morning and ready to go.

He grabbed his platypus keytar shirt and cargo pants and got dressed. He hesitated over the hoodies. Did he really want one? But it was November and his teeth were already chattering, so he pulled on the dark green one.

When he arrived at school he stopped just within the doors and surveyed the hallway. Nothing looked like it was going to try to shoot, claw, blow up, or ride him, so he strode down the middle of the hallway towards his locker. Some people glanced at him as he walked by, and Johanna from Chemistry gave a timid, "Hi Thane," at which he nodded to her.

Remi was two lockers down when he arrived. He smiled when he saw her, and watched her open the locker without trouble. "They fixed it while you were gone," she said.

He opened his locker and found a bass guitarist magazine and an article from the school newspaper about Jeran missing a game winning catch at Homecoming. He glanced up at Remi. "I thought you might like those. School was slow last week without you," she said.

"Thanks," Thane said, unsure how he felt. On the one hand, these were both fantastic gifts. On the other, Remi was still getting into his locker even though she had her own now. His locker was the only personal space he had at school. But the thing that was bothering him was that he didn't care that Remi put stuff in his locker, and not caring about that was not like him. What was going on?

"See you at lunch," she said, and walked away to her first period.

At lunch he sat at his usual table but his tray was laden with food. Bert had left lunch money on the table, and plenty of it. "Hungry?" Remi observed as she sat down next to him.

"No more than usual," he said, and plowed into his food.

"She's back. I saw her in the hall," Remi said before taking a bite of her sandwich.

Thane paused, mouth full of food. "Ms. Rasmussen?" he mumbled.

"I think you said Ms. Rasmussen, and yes. She's here." Remi took another bite and chewed thoughtfully before adding, "I wonder if she heard you're back too."

"We'll find out next period," Thane said, and Remi nodded her agreement.

When the bell rang for third period to start, every student in Ms. Rasmussen's chemistry class was silent and in place. Books were out and pencils sharpened. No one knew what version of Cressida Rasmussen they would be getting and so they prepared for the worst, each student bracing themselves for a hurricane and hoping for a breeze. When she came in, her eyes lingered for a moment longer on Thane before sweeping across the class.

"Open your books to chapter nine," she said. "I understand that's where you left off and you have homework to turn in. Pass it to the center and then forward, please." Her voice was calm and even, not manic, not angry, not like her at all. The entire period passed without incident, and when one of her former favorites inadvertently called her "Cressa," she merely said, "Ms. Rasmussen, please," and allowed her to ask the question anyway.

The only deviance from complete normalcy came at the end of class. "Read chapter ten before Wednesday. Thane, please stay after class to get your homework," she announced from behind her desk. Everyone else gathered their books and left except for Thane and Remi. "Remi, you can go," Ms. Rasmussen said in that same too-calm voice.

"I'd like to wait for Thane, please," Remi said, wanting to be defiant but not wanting to be the one who brought the crazy back out.

"Fine, wait in the hall," Ms. Rasmussen said without looking up from the papers she was grading.

Remi glanced at Thane, and he nodded. She went into the hall and shut the door.

Ms. Rasmussen didn't stand up. She barely even looked up. "I hear you've been busy since we last talked," she said.

Thane nodded. She wasn't looking so he added, "Yes ma'am," out loud.

"Oh don't call me ma'am," she looked at him with a frown and one raised eyebrow. "I'm assuming with you being blue that they pulled in Charlie to help train you?"

Thane had no idea if that was supposed to be a secret or not. She seemed confident anyway, so he said, "Yes."

"Ah. So you probably heard all kinds of psychotic things about me," she scribbled a number on the paper in front of her and flipped to the next one.

He was already being honest, so he committed. "Yes."

"You should know they're all true," she continued grading while she spoke. "I am incredibly rich, dramatically arrogant, and selfish." She glanced at Thane this time and saw his affirming nod. "Good. Then we're on the same page." She scrawled another score in red across the top of a paper and flipped it over, then steepled her fingers and looked up at Thane. "I will get what I want. You can help me voluntarily or be forced into it. I have no issue lying, stealing, or injuring innocents. Like your friend Remi, for example. If I were to threaten her instead of you, I want you to know that I would follow through."

"Leave Remi out of this," Thane growled, his hands balled into fists involuntarily. "She's songless. Pure human. She has no stake in this and messing with her would only make problems for you."

"Really," the red haired woman's eyes sparked and her mouth tweaked up in a small smile. "That is interesting."

"I mean it," Thane glared, stepping forward.

"So do I, boy," she said, and the door opened.

"Thane, we're going to be late and the next class is out here waiting," Remi said.

"Chapters seven and eight with the quizzes at the end," Ms. Rasmussen said, as if finishing a conversation topic. "Don't be late to last period."

Thane stalked out of the room glowering. "What did she say?" Remi asked. "Was it anything about--"

"Yes," Thane cut her off. He glanced around and lowered his voice. "She said she doesn't have any problem harming innocents to get her way if I don't do what she wants."

"What does she want you to do?" Remi asked, her eyes wide.

"She didn't say," Thane was upset and off balance. That was not the conversation he had expected at all, and her calm delivery made him all the more sure she meant every word. He stopped walking so quickly that Remi took two steps past him and had to turn around to look at him again.

"What?" she asked.

He took a deep breath. "She threatened you."

She blanched, her face going pale. "Me? Why?"

"Because you're my friend," Thane admitted. "Because you matter to me and she knows it."

"You're not my bodyguard, Thane Whitaker," Remi said, narrowing her eyes at him.

"I know, but--"

"I don't need you to protect me, I can take care of myself," she insisted.

"You can," Thane agreed, trying to placate her. "That's why I told you. Because I trust you to be ready."

She opened her mouth to say something else, then closed it again. "Oh," she said, her expression clearing. "Thanks."

The second bell rang, making them both tardy to fourth period. "I've got to get to AP Music," Thane said.

"Yes, apprentice, go learn your magic," Remi teased, but that was more true than she knew. Thane hurried and snuck in the back of AP Music while Ms. Sorenson was still taking roll. Sometimes it was useful having a last name at the end of the alphabet.

"Remi Gage, please report to the front office," the PA system crackled to life and repeated the message. "Remi Gage, to the front office please." Thane felt a chill, but suppressed it. Ms. Rasmussen had barely made the threat and hadn't even demanded anything from him yet. Besides, she had a class to teach right now. Thane allowed himself to get lost in the theory of music and was surprised when the bell rang.

He waited to get his make up homework from last week before leaving, then went to get the rest of his books. Remi wasn't at her locker. Had something happened at the front office? His stomach clenched and he shoved his stuff into his backpack and then hurried to where the secretaries were chatting with each other quietly.

"Is Remi Gage still here?" he asked. He tried not to sound abrupt.

"Remi Gage?" Mrs. Wolford blinked at him through her enormous glasses. "No, she was here about an hour ago and talked to Mr. Hoffman about how she was liking school here. He likes to check up on everyone now and then, dear man," she adjusted the binder in front of her.

"She was with Mr. Hoffman?" Thane slumped in relief. "Okay, thanks." Remi must have gone home while he talked with Ms. Sorenson.

He went out to the buses, but wasn't really surprised that his bus had left already. It was a little warmer this afternoon than it had been and his dark green hoodie was thick, so he didn't mind walking. Thane had a lot of homework to catch up on but not as much as he'd feared.

His mom was sitting at the kitchen table when he entered. "Hi mom," he said. "Sorry I missed the bus again."

"That's fine," his mom said, staring out the window. Her face was lacking in expression, and her eyes looked glazed. Her fingers absently traced patterns in the wood grains of the tabletop.

Thane was still thinking about his AP music class and looking at his mother when he had a thought. He closed his eyes and opened himself to the Song, pushing that part of his consciousness towards the woman at the table. Faintly, so faintly it was difficult to hear, she had music. She wasn't songless. But the melody was so faded some of the notes were impossible to decipher, and he couldn't make sense out of the key or phrase pattern.

He tried to draw it out, to make it louder or get closer to it, but it was so delicate he was afraid it would shatter. For a moment, he had it. For the length of two heartbeats he heard his mother's Song. Then it was gone again.

"What..." she trailed off, putting a hand to her forehead. "I must be getting tired. I thought..." she sighed.

Thane felt a little guilty. "Maybe you should go lie down," he said.

"All right. Watch your sisters?"

"Sure. I have homework, so I'll do it here."

Hours later after his dad was home and they'd had dinner Thane emptied his backpack onto his bed downstairs. He was looking for his history notes when his phone tumbled out of a side pocket. It bounced on the cement floor and he hurried to pick it up. Thanks to the thick rubber casing it didn't seem to have any damage, but he turned it on to make sure.

Six missed calls, four voicemails and seven text messages, all from the same two numbers. The blood drained from his face. Nothing about that was comforting. Caller ID hadn't identified either number, so Thane listened to the voicemails first. Three were from Senior Airman Calder, the first two annoyed because he assumed that Thane and Remi were ignoring him or playing a joke on him and telling them to get out to the parking lot now, and a third to say it wasn't funny anymore and he was calling Remi's father. The fourth was from General Gage asking if Thane knew where Remi was and to please call him back at the earliest convenience.

The text messages were more of the same, except for the last one. It was from Gage. It was short, and terrifying. "GPS turned off on Remi's phone and Twitch can't find her. Tell me you know something."

Thane called General Gage back but it immediately went to voicemail. How could he not have call waiting? Thane left a voicemail saying that Cressida Rasmussen had threatened Remi, but taking her now didn't make sense. He hung up and then called right back. Straight to voicemail again. He didn't leave a message this time.

This was bad. Even thinking those words felt like the biggest understatement in the universe. If Remi was gone, Cressida Rasmussen had her.

What Thane didn't know was why, or more importantly, where. He needed a way to track her down. Twitch would know what to do. He went to the contacts list on his phone but Twitch wasn't there. He pressed "Grandpa Charlie" instead. The phone rang, and then went to a generic voicemail message.

"Charlie, it's Thane. Cressida Rasmussen kidnapped my friend. Call me back as soon as you get this," and hung up.

He paced the room some more, and then dove on his backpack. This time he emptied it out completely and went through all the little papers until he found a business card with "Brennan Tayler, Luck Specialist-SMG" embossed on it with a number. He dialed Brennan, and it went straight to voicemail again. "Brennan, my crazy chemistry teacher kidnapped my best friend. Call me back."

Why wasn't anybody answering? Thane smacked his forehead with his palm. Of course. Every team Sanctum had was spread all over the world guarding tears in the Weave. Brennan was in Siberia and who knows where Charlie might be.

"I need Twitch," Thane growled, and then had a thought. He ran upstairs to the computer and opened three browsers. He went to a different search engine in each one and searched for Twitch, Sanctum, Guardian Council, Shae, and any other words he thought might pop up alerts for Twitch.

"Thanie," Lanie called from the girls' bedroom.

"Not now monkey," Thane snapped. He kept running searches, desperately hoping for something to pop.

"Thanie," Lanie sounded more insistent.

"Not now," Thane's face was in his hands and his answer was muffled.

"Thanie," she managed to make his name six syllables long. "My monkey is asking for you."

"I don't have time to play pretend, Lanie," Thane was exhausted and frustrated and afraid.

"Monkey says Twitch says you're a moron and get in here," Lanie said, then added, "It isn't nice to call names, Monkey."

Thane froze, then sprang to his feet and ran down the hall. "Your monkey said what?"

"Her monkey wants to know why you're being a jerk with your web searches and setting off alerts when you know we're busy," Twitch's voice was unmistakable coming out of the mouth of the monkey.

"Twitch!" Thane snatched up the monkey and spoke loudly into it. "Remi's been kidnapped. I need your help to find her, and I need to get in touch with General Gage."

"Back up, you're causing all kinds of feedback. Now what?"

Thane repeated himself slowly. "I need your help. Get General Gage."

"I can't, he's on lockdown. Radio silence. Probably trying to rescue Remi and thinking whoever's got her has access to our communication lines."

"Is that possible?" Thane blinked. "Is this line secure?"

"Please," scoffed Twitch.

"Fine, then you have to help me. Remi was taken by Cressida Rasmussen. Can you run a license plate?"

"And cross check it with every police database and traffic camera in your area," Twitch said. "What is it?"

"P-Y-R-O-4-I-C," Thane spelled slowly.

"Pyrophoric? As in ready to burst into flames?"

"Sure," Thane wasn't interested in what Ms. Rasmussen's license plate meant, just where she was.

"Okay, hang on." The silence felt like it lasted hours. "Got it. Red BMW?"

"Yes," Thane nearly screamed the word.

"Don't yell at my monkey, he's helping," Lanie scolded.

"I've got a traffic cam matching that license plate going south on I-90. Hang on, let me see if I can find the VIN." Another incredibly long silence.

Thane felt like his head was going to burst. "Got it. Excellent, this year, make, and model comes with a standard GPS system. So," Thane could hear the clicking of the keys as Twitch typed, moving so fast and consistently it sounded like fully automatic gunfire far away. "Yes, yes, just social engineer that, will you call? Hmm, yes, I'm listening. Perfect. You've gotta have faith. Thane, I have her car's GPS coordinates."

"Where?" Thane was breathless. He pulled out his phone from his pocket and pulled up maps, typing in as Twitch spoke. The phone searched and brought up a location six miles south of Payson in the foothills a few miles off the interstate.

"Twitch, I'll get you a new lawn mower," Thane promised. "I'm going after her. Come as soon as you can. Tell General Gage and bring help." He handed Lanie back her monkey and kissed her forehead. "Thanks, monkey. I love you."

"I love you love you love you," she giggled.

Thane started to leave the room, then turned back. Harper was in her bed facing the wall and pretending he didn't exist. "I'm sorry Harper," he said. "I love you too."

Thane ran to the kitchen. Bert was in there cleaning up the last of the dinner dishes. "Thane, are you all right?" the man asked, looking at him.

"I need a ride and I need you to not ask any questions," Thane said. "Please."

"I can't do that," Bert argued. "I need to know where you're going and when you'll be back. I'm your--"

"You are not my father," Thane said, and the panic gripping his heart released anger he thought he'd screamed away. "You have never been my father. When I was little and I cried, do you know what you did? You smacked me and told me to shut up. I used to be scared of the dark but I never cried about it, because I was more scared of you."

Bert Whitaker flinched and put down the pan he was washing. "Thane, are you sure you're not exaggerating--"

"You don't remember. I do. I remember when you came home if I'd left any toys out you'd hit me across the face with them and then throw them away. You pushed me down the stairs when I was seven. If mom tried to stop you, you'd hit her too. So I told her to stop, told her that I could take it. I never understood why she let me. Now I know it's because she had nowhere else to go." Thane looked down and away, his fists shaking and his jaw clenched so tightly he was starting to see spots. He started breathing slowly, in and out through his nose. He couldn't afford to lose it right now. Remi's life might depend on him.

"That can't be true," Bert said, sounding like all the air had been knocked from his lungs. "I can't be like that."

"Do you want to see the scars?" Thane was breathing in his calming rhythm, moving through the kata in his mind. Bert backed away as if Thane had come at him with a knife.

"No, please," Bert said. The man who wasn't his father leaned heavily against the counter, his hands shaking.

"You owe me," Thane said. "And I'm calling it in. I need a ride right now, and no questions asked. And when I ask you to leave, you'll leave and won't look back."

"I can't leave you..." Bert protested.

"Get your keys and get in the car, Bert," Thane said. The man flinched at the use of his nickname, and his chin hung down and rested on his collar bone as though his neck had given up. He complied.

Thane climbed in the passenger seat and buckled his seatbelt. "Go south on I-90 and turn off in two exits," he instructed.

Bert Whitaker turned on the car and drove out of Payson and onto the interstate. He drove south in silence, his chin drooping and shoulders slumped forward. Thane counted every second that it took to catch up to where Remi was being held. He would save her. No matter how much she protested or fought him, he was going to save her shredding life.

They took the second exit. "Turn left, go one mile, and pull into the parking lot on the right," Thane said. Wordlessly Bert Whitaker followed his directions and pulled into the empty parking lot. Empty save for one red BMW, with a missing taillight.

The parking lot was for a trail head into the hills south of Payson. There were several different hiking and biking routes that people could take, all branching off this one starting point. Thane unbuckled and opened the car door.

"Would it mean anything if I said I was sorry?" Bert Whitaker said. Thane paused. "Would it matter if I was horrified, sickened by... everything?"

"No," Thane said, and the man who was not his father seemed to deflate. "But it means something that you did this for me tonight." Bert glanced up at him, and some of the air came back. Thane shut the door.

He walked to the trail head, not caring whether Bert actually drove away. He needed to figure out which way Ms. Rasmussen had taken Remi. He followed the trail to the first fork, and the right path had dirt churned up around it as though there had been a struggle there. Thane followed the right fork. The next time the trail split there were four options. Thane eliminated the two biking trails and studied the remaining two choices. There wasn't any difference in the hard packed earth, but his eye caught something glinting gold in the moonlight. It was on the far side of the left trail, and he went to pick it up.

A glass vial of sand. Thane wrapped his hand around it and raced down the left trail. At this point, at least, Remi had been alive and conscious and able to move around enough to drop this. He hoped he would find her at least this well.

The next fork in the trail held nothing. All three choices were equally likely, and Remi hadn't left him any clues he could find. Thane hunted for as long as he dared, but didn't discover anything to help him decide which path to take.

Heart pounding, palms sweaty, Thane closed his eyes and breathed in and out through his nose. He tried to quiet his mind and open it to the Song but it kept slipping away, chased out by thoughts of Remi in danger and Ms. Rasmussen's threats. Thane couldn't find the Song.

Growling in frustration, Thane tried to listen to his instincts. They were screaming at him to go save his friend and to keep moving. He chose the trail in the center. The trail went downward alongside a hill while the path to the right went up. The left path disappeared into the forest almost immediately and he couldn't see it anymore, but he could watch the right path for quite a while as it went up the hill and his went down below it.

Thane caught his breath and held still. He heard something. Somewhere nearby there was a rattling, humming sound that stayed level in volume. There was a cave on the hill above him where the other trail had gone, and the sound grew slightly louder as Thane turned his face in that direction. "Shredding holes," he swore. He'd gone the wrong way.

Instead of taking the time to backtrack Thane started climbing the hill. It was steep and covered in loose dirt and plants with shallow roots that pulled out in his fingers while he tried to get a hand hold. He forgot the plants and dug his fingers into the soil and dragged himself upwards. The gritty soil and tiny rocks pricked the soft skin under his fingernails but he used the pain and discomfort to propel himself upwards.

The trail he hadn't taken ended in full view of the mouth of the cave. Thane was currently climbing up the side of the cave entrance so who or whatever was inside couldn't see him. His instincts had been right after all. He crawled to a point that was higher than a person would be and to the right of the middle. He knew from experience and instinct that few people ever look up, and he would be less likely to be noticed off to one side or the other. Taking a deep, slow breath, he stilled himself, and then leaned over the edge and peered inside.

Remi was gagged and unconscious, but breathing. She lay on the stone floor, her head and shoulders visible from behind a stone outcropping. Light and that loud steady humming noise came from beyond her. Thane crept down the side of the cave and pressed into the stone, trying to get close enough to see where Ms. Rasmussen was without being seen. The sound of whatever machine she was running got louder with every step, until Thane was crouched down behind the rock corner and only an arm's length from Remi.

Pressing his head against the floor, Thane inched forward until he could see around the protruding stone. Remi's hands and feet were bound with thick white rope. Another rope was wrapped around her bonds and tethered to a stake driven into the rock floor. Cressida Rasmussen stood several feet away, still wearing ridiculous heels that clicked against the rock floor when she walked.

She'd set up an old green card table, and on it were three Bunsen burners and beakers with different colored boiling liquids as well as various bowls and containers. On the floor underneath the table was an enormous glass jar. Whatever was inside glowed with a greenish yellow light and moved sporadically, as though it was the biggest firefly he'd ever seen.

The noise was an electrical generator against the far wall. It powered three hanging lanterns in the room as well as being connected to a large black box on the floor. An amplifier, Thane realized. What was going on?

Whatever it was, he needed to get Remi out of there. His teacher was engrossed in her chemicals, recording temperatures and measuring components and comparing them against a scroll she held. Thane crawled forward by inches until his fingers touched the rope that tethered Remi to the floor. If he could untie that, he could carry her out of here, and undo the rest later.

As he slid forward on his belly, thin filaments like spider webs brushed along his hands and in his hair. He resisted the urge to brush them off, worried that unnecessary motion might draw the woman's attention. His fingers tightened around the knot that tied Remi to the cave. Silently and steadily he tugged, loosening the knot. As he did, he felt more spider webs clinging to his hair. The moment the rope was undone he released it, and a covering of hair thin filaments fell on him and engulfed him.

"Hello, dear boy," Ms. Rasmussen said without turning around. "I'm so glad you could make it."

CHAPTER 32

Thane tried to struggle, but the thin wires only tangled themselves around him more fully. "Do you like my net?" Ms. Rasmussen said, speaking loudly over the sound of the generator. "I designed it for you. Now we can really get to work." She turned to face him, smiling down at his prone form, and reached out to grab Remi by the rope that bound the girl's ankles and dragged his unconscious friend roughly across the uneven floor over to the table, far out of Thane's reach.

He'd stopped fighting against the net as the more he twisted the more it constricted. "What are you doing, Ms. Rasmussen?" he demanded.

"We're not in school, call me Cressa," she said, turning around and holding a long, thin object that made Thane's stomach drop and his chest tighten. "And I'm not going to discuss my evil plan with you." She sauntered over, the click of her heels getting louder until all he could see was one of her bright red shoes. "We have too much to do."

She jabbed him in the side with the cattle prod hard enough that the two metal prongs tore through his hoodie and pierced his skin. It didn't hurt that much, and Thane didn't give her the satisfaction of seeing him flinch. He heard the click as she pressed the button. Waves of tingling warmth flowed into him, and the lightning Song filled his mind as the electricity enveloped his body. It was so beautiful and its power so comforting that he embraced it. For a moment. Then he slid his hand into his pocket and held the top of the electric cell battery.

"There now," she said. Thane waited until she removed the prod and walked away. "We can turn this horrid thing off," and she flipped the switch on the generator. It sputtered into silence. The lanterns went dark and the only light came from the three flames on the table. Thane heard the click of another button. The net around him grew warm, and suddenly the electrical charge he held was slowly being leached out of him.

The lanterns came back on. The amplifier hummed and popped. Cressa clapped her hands and laughed. "It's perfect."

"No," Thane said, and dumped the power into the electric cell. He silenced the music so quickly that the cell grew hot in his hand, and the cave plunged back into medieval semi darkness.

"What was that?" Cressa asked. Thane could see her mouth curling up on one side as the flickering firelight played across her face. "Neat trick. Can you do it again?" and again she pierced his side with the cattle prod. Thane tried to push the charge into the battery cell as it entered his body, but the cell was full and overheating. The net tightened around him as the wires and filaments pulled the concentrated electricity from him and returned power to the room. The amplifier popped again and the lanterns resumed their steady electric glow.

"So you did learn a few things from those Sanctum idiots," she mused. "Surprising. But ultimately pointless, like everything they do." And he watched as her shiny red heels clicked back to the table.

He took a deep breath in, then out through his nose. Thane gathered calm around him like a shield, and started to quiet the lightning Song that rushed through him. The lanterns started to dim and the hum of the amplifier weakened.

"Tut tut," Cressa scolded without glancing down at him. "Remember what I said about doing what I want or people would get hurt?" She reached down without breaking her concentration on the scroll and slapped Remi across the face.

"No!" Thane shouted, his calmness shattered. The volume of the lightning Song in his mind exploded as he watched the red handprint slowly appear on Remi's slack face. He wasn't going to let this happen. Grabbing the Song he added more, not just the rumble of thunder but the pounding of distant storm waves as percussion. He fed the shrieking wind to the song, the pounding of rain and the crackling and zapping sound of cut wires. Cell phones buzzing and the thrumming of machines and the sound of every piece of technology he could think of he wove into the music until the Song was almost too powerful for him to hold.

Thane released it all at once into the wire net. The thin metal filaments glowed white and there was a loud buzz. The lanterns glowed brighter, and then the buzzing stopped and the artificial light returned to normal.

"Surge protector," Cressa said. She didn't bother turning around.

"Why?" Thane asked, his voice cracking with disbelief. "What does this have to do with my father?"

"Your father," she measured out white powder in a tiny vial, "is selfish and conceited, which I can admire, and short-sighted, which I cannot." She added it to one of the beakers and the boiling liquid inside flashed. "You know I actually began to enjoy teaching?" her tone was conversational and slightly distracted as she compared notes in a little book to the scroll on the table. "Molding young minds, being admired and flattered by all those young men, and parceling out knowledge. And I was good at it."

She slid a brown leather box out of a satchel under the table and undid the clasp. Thane couldn't see what was inside until she lifted it out. It looked like a knife made entirely from smooth grey stone. She pulled out another, smaller box from the satchel which proved to be a sharpening kit, and she slid the edge of the knife against the whetstone rhythmically. "Every year I taught Chemistry the overall scores went up. I was nominated for a teaching award. And then you came along."

Thane lay captured on the floor, paying attention to her story and trying to find a way out. The lightning Song singing through his mind quieted as he focused on escape, and the lanterns dimmed.

"Boys have such a hard time paying attention," Cressa said. She turned sideways and kicked Remi's prone body in the torso. The girl rolled slightly and groaned, and Cressa kicked her again more forcefully.

"Stop," Thane half demanded, half pled.

"Once for the first time, twice for the second, and you don't want to see what happens the third time you lose focus," Cressa warned with a smile and a wagging finger. "You stupid brat. I couldn't believe that you were the son of a dragon. You, with your mediocre brain and painfully ordinary face. You have everything I've ever wanted," her green eyes glinted, "but you threw it away. I couldn't bring that back to him and say this colossal disappointment was his son. But then you held the charge," she sighed, eyes going distant and mouth softly smiling, "and electrocuted that self-righteous watchdog Hoffman, and I realized how valuable you really are."

Cressa produced two thick black rubber gloves from the bag and put them on. She pulled the large glass jar out from under the table and started unscrewing the top slowly, one turn at a time. The firefly inside darted about more furiously, a yellow green blur. "Do you know who's special, Thane?" Cressa asked, watching the jar intently. Thane didn't answer. Cressa lifted the lid with one hand and the other shot inside the jar, capturing the glowing light in her fingers.

"People who are different," she answered her own question. Now that the light was still Thane could see it more clearly. It wasn't a bug. It was roughly shaped like a person, with two arms and two legs and a round head on top. The features weren't human at all-- its face and head looked more like a budding flower than anything else. "Those who are special," continued Cressa, bringing her gloved hand and its tiny prisoner into the bowl, "aren't afraid to make sacrifices."

He hadn't been watching her other hand. She'd kept him distracted by showing him the flower fairy so Thane had not seen her pick up the stone knife again. Cressa Rasmussen plunged the stone knife into the bowl. The hand that had been holding the tiny body relaxed as the glowing green and yellow light in the bowl faded. "Pure blood of the Shae, to bind their Weave," she said, lifting the small broken body and dropping it back into the jar. She looked at Remi, "And the pure blood of Earth, to bind theirs."

"No!" Thane redoubled his struggles. The wire pressed more tightly into his flesh until he felt it cutting through his skin. Still he fought.

"Don't worry," Cressa said. "You get a part, too. I need you to generate enough electricity to power the sonic wave emitter." She smiled and gently ran her fingers across the top of the black amplifier. "It's a very complicated thing, part science and part magic. You see, I'm going to open a tear in the Weave. And no one is available to stop me." She giggled. "Right now Sanctum's precious mercenary teams are spread across the world guarding tears. They think it's a full frontal assault by a powerful enemy in the Shaerealm. How else would so many points in so many countries be hit all at once? It has to be a coordinated attack, a declaration of war. Idiots." She pulled off one rubber glove and measured a careful amount of boiling liquid, then poured it into the bowl of pixie blood. "As if you can't just pay people in different places to all do the same thing at the same time."

Thane had an idea. It terrified him. If his heart could have pounded harder, it would have. "Here I'm nothing," Cressa delivered her self pity in an even tone. "One of billions of humans with only a little Shae blood. But there?" She glanced at Thane and winked. "Almost all human, and only a little Shae. I will have all the power." She nudged the satchel again with her foot, looking at it fondly. The nudge exposed the barrel of a gun, and Thane realized it was lumpy and enormous because it must contain weapons the Shae didn't have and couldn't make. He wouldn't be surprised if it also had all her chemistry equipment as well, another kind of technology that the Shae would have no knowledge of or defense against.

He had to die. That was the only option. If he wasn't there to be her battery he was certain she couldn't power the amplifier. That seemed to be a key part of her plan. The lightning Song flowed through his mind, bringing a sweetness to his affinity that he'd never noticed before. Thane closed his eyes and took hold of the Song. He filled his mind with it, and then poured his heartbeat into it as an anchoring percussion. Then he focused on the rushing of his blood through his veins and wrapped that into the lightning Song, where it became a flowing harmony. It ran through the different movements of the music and tied them to each other and to Thane more firmly.

Then the wires sucked it out. Since the electrical current was continual instead of being fed into one ball, as Thane grew weaker so did the charge. The lanterns began to dim and Cressa looked at him, annoyed.

"What are you-- oh," she smirked. "Really? The hero sacrifices himself to save the girl? Teenagers are so dramatic." She brought a different bowl down off the table and set it on the floor next to Remi. Then she bent the girl's knee and slid the bowl in the space underneath. "You should know, Thane, that if you die, she dies." Cressa stabbed the stone knife down into Remi's leg just above her knee.

In his mind, Thane screamed. His mouth was too weak to form the sound. He was dying, Remi would die, and Cressa Rasmussen would escape to the Shaerealm and reign with horror and blood.

And the beast inside him stirred. He felt the nightmarish leviathan clawing its way up, demanding to be freed just as the Song badgered him to release it. Thane was drowning again. He was sinking down and away as two forces tried to wrest him under, one dragging from below, one pushing from above.

He was lost. The monster pulled itself out of the pit where he had banished it and drew itself eye level with Thane. In his mind he saw the swirling azure eyes of a dragon starting back into his own, and he remembered the viper. Underneath the lightning Song, quiet and drifting, he heard Paka's words. "You decide." Following close on them was his conversation with General Gage. "Even the smallest bit of human blood gives us the ability to choose. Are you a monster?"

"No," Thane said. The word wasn't loud. It didn't need to be. No one else needed to hear it. He stared into the glowing eyes of the dragon and waited. The sapphire beast roared in his face, spewing chaos and confusion at him. Thane allowed it to flow around him, not breaking eye contact with the monster. The blue dragon replayed Thane's nightmare in full detail, emphasizing every gruesome death and betrayal as Thane destroyed the world in the thrall of the dragon and under Ms. Rasmussen's whip.

"No," Thane said again. The dragon blinked. "You are my blood and my birthright. I'm done fighting it or pretending like it doesn't matter. Because it does. And I'm never going to let anyone else control me again. Not even you."

The dragon bowed his head and then looked up. Thane had the strange sensation of both looking at the dragon and looking back at himself through the dragon's eyes. Then the two images merged, and the lightning Song changed.

It grew deeper and more structured, as though the act of accepting his draconic heritage made him understand the Song more fully. Greater intricacies of melody and counterpoint wove together. He seemed to hear words floating through the Song, words that it plucked from his memory and played back to him.

"Even the strongest of Shae magic couldn't keep you locked in such an unattractive frame."

"Phasic resonance blue-dragon, shifter level four."

"A tadpole has tae change tae grow up. Ye've got a dragon in ye lad, and someday ye'll grow up and turn intae it."

The lightning dragon's Song sang in his bones. He reached for it and felt a familiar sensation, but strange. It was similar to being stuck with a healing dart, where his bones and muscles knit fixing themselves, but different because instead of coming together he felt like he was being pulled apart. Skeleton shifting and bones growing larger, his hands swelling, Thane was wrapped in the Song and allowed it to reshape him.

Since the power kept flowing from him into the net Cressa didn't notice anything was happening. She was busy adding chemicals and boiling liquid to the bowl that held Remi's blood, measuring out each new component carefully. Thane watched her, able to see the numbers on each beaker as his eyes changed and grew stronger. Every crystal of the white power she added stood out in sharp relief. The spreading pool of blood seeping from Remi's leg was startling in how bright and distinct the color, and he smelled iron while his nose stretched. Thane knew his first task was to stop that life from flowing out.

Cressa set both bowls on the table and placed the stone knife between them. Then she turned and walked towards the large black amplifier. With her long fingers she flipped a switch on the side. It began humming two distinct frequencies that grew louder as the machine warmed. "Now, pet, we'll see who is too weak in power," she said, and reached towards the stone knife.

Thane's body was still stretching and shaping, but he couldn't wait. With a growl that was more like thunder than any sound a living creature should make, he tore with claws and fangs at the net surrounding him. The wires snapped and the glow on them began to fade, and he threw it at Ms. Rasmussen. She screamed as the hot filaments draped across her, touching the bare skin on her face and arms. Thane rolled from his back onto his feet, crouching near Remi as the lights from the lanterns faded.

He needed to stop the bleeding. In the flickering of the flames her blood looked black and thick, and there was too much of it soaking her pant leg and the floor. Thane ripped off what was left of his shirt and wrapped the fabric tightly around her knee. He reached for the rope that held her ankles together with the intent of cutting it loose and using it to secure his shirt, but before his black talons reached it he heard a click.

Instinct screamed and he threw himself backwards and sideways without thinking. He heard a gun fire, and felt hot pain blossom in his calf. "I have an entire bag of weapons, dragon boy," Cressa purred into the semi darkness. "And I don't care who I hit."

He'd landed near the stone outcropping and hid himself partially behind it. The dim orange light showed his shirt laying lose and useless under Remi's leg while her blood continued to saturate it. Then he noticed a shimmer in the air behind the table, a roughly circular section of space that shone like a weak flashlight on water.

Cressa gasped. The sound showed Thane's enhanced senses exactly where she was hiding, ducked down behind the black amplifier she'd called a sonic wave generator. "It worked," she said, and sprung towards the table.

Thane leapt out from behind the rocks and crashed into her, knocking the gun from her hands. They landed on the floor in a heap with Thane on top. "Get off," she spat and raked at his face with her long red fingernails. His skin must have changed as well, because it didn't hurt. Thane grabbed her wrist and slammed it against the stone floor.

She kicked him in the groin, hard. Thane suddenly felt nauseous and breathless. His grip slackened and she twisted out from under him, rolling away. Getting back to her feet, she stumbled to the table and threw one of the beakers of boiling liquid at the shining distortion in the air.

The glass hit the light and shattered. The steaming liquid inside drizzled down the light and the acrid smell burnt Thane's enhanced nostrils. The shimmer dissolved slowly and revealed a piece of colorful tapestry, a physical Weave made of color and light and sound. It was beautiful. It was perfect. It was the soul of the universe laid bare.

Cressa grabbed the stone knife to destroy it. Thane struggled to stand as she dipped the tip of the weapon into the bowl with Remi's blood and chemical mixture and slashed at the Weave hanging in the air. There was a sound beyond sound, a cry of dissonance and discordance that Thane felt more than heard, and perhaps half of the threads in the Weave dangled helplessly like broken fingers.

She turned back to the table to dip the stone knife in the other bowl and finish the hole. Before she could get there, Thane kicked. The table leg nearest him folded under and the table with all its contents crashed downwards. The beakers shattered and the boiling chemicals inside splashed onto the burner flames and ignited. Flames spread through the room as the liquid flowed out. Cressa hissed and jumped away, and Thane sprang at Remi, stamping out the fire that had splashed onto her pant leg. He gently scooped her up and carried her from the burning cave to the clearing beyond.

He laid her down in the dirt. His shirt was soaked with blood and it clung to the cloth of her pants, useless. Thane tore off the other leg of her pants at the knee and wrapped it around her wound. He sliced through the rope with his claws and wrapped it around the makeshift bandage, but his claws were too long and unfamiliar for him to tie it off. It was like trying to tie a knot with pencils taped to each finger.

Thane screamed in frustration. "Don't die, don't you dare die," he hissed at the unconscious face of his best friend as he held the bandage in place. "Help!" he yelled, knowing it was dark and they were far away from anyone who could hear him.

Anyone but Cressida Rasmussen. She walked out of the cave carrying the stone knife and a large black handgun, aimed at Thane's face. "Nice stall," she said, "but you still lose."

Thane crouched protectively over Remi and stared up at the barrel of the gun. He also saw movement in the woods out of the corner of his eye. Two tiny darts flew out of the trees and hit her arm the moment she pulled the trigger. The gunshot echoed loudly and pain burned in Thane's shoulder, and Twitch came barreling out of the trees carrying a tranq rifle, Charlie right behind him.

Cressa's eyes rolled back into her head and she fell where she stood, knife and gun clattering to the ground on either side of her. Twitch ran to the prone woman and stabbed her with a needle, pushing down the plunger on a syringe.

"Thane, is that you? The GPS signal from your cell cut out about ten minutes ago or we would've found you sooner," Twitch said. "She must have a signal dampening field set up--"

"Remi's hurt!"" Thane cut in. "She's bleeding out, help her!"

Charlie rushed to where Remi lay and Thane pushed himself back. "There, Cressa cut her there with a stone knife and she's been bleeding and it won't stop and I can't tie a knot..." he was babbling, but couldn't stop.

Twitch came over, pulling things out of a bag he carried over one shoulder. "Press this against the wound, we have to stop the bleeding," he said, handing Thane a large piece of gauze. Thane did so while Charlie examined Remi, listening to her chest and laying his fingers against her neck to check her pulse.

"It's weak and going," the dragon said. "We may be too late tae save yer friend, lad."

"No," Thane shook his head, which felt strange and off balance. "No, she won't die. Remi doesn't need anybody to save her. She'll be fine."

Twitch cut through the pant leg above the wound to get a better look. He pushed Thane's hands and the gauze away, pulling a needle and thread from the bag. He wiped the cut and the skin around it with something that made Thane's eyes sting and then rapidly started sewing the torn skin back together.

Remi's skin was pale and sallow, her cheeks looking sunken. Her breathing was so shallow that even with his dragon enhanced senses, Thane couldn't see her chest rising and falling anymore. Her body shuddered a little, just once. Then she relaxed into the dirt.

Charlie pulled his fingers from her neck. "She's moved on, Thane." The ancient dragon wrapped his arms around the boy. Thane struggled against him, trying to reach Remi and ignoring both the fiery pain in his shoulder and the much worse agony tearing through his chest, but his grandfather held him still.

"Shredding holes," Twitch swore. He sounded surprised. Both Thane and Charlie looked to see what had caught the tech specialist so off guard.

Remi's body was glowing. It was faint, only a reddish orange light that in daylight wouldn't be noticed. Here at night she shone like firelight.

Thane felt Charlie's grip around him tighten until it hurt. "No," the dragon said, the word edged with so much torment that Thane felt it stab his heart. "No, this isnae right."

The light receded from her arms and legs and began to pool over her abdomen. As it gathered together it grew brighter until it hurt Thane's eyes. But as he would rather go blind than look away, he saw the light coalesce into a form rising out of Remi's chest.

It was a bird. Similar in shape to a swan, it had a long neck and large wings. The outline of the bird was red, lightening into orange, yellow, and then white as if the fire was fueled by the bird's heart. Half of the body of fire was still inside Remi, but the bird was spreading long wings of flame and preparing to fly.

"No," Charlie repeated, releasing Thane and pushing him aside. He crawled to the bird on his knees. Thane and Twitch watched in silence. Thane didn't understand what was happening. Remi was his best friend, the only person he felt he could talk to about anything, the crazy girl who made him laugh and left stuff she knew he'd like in his locker. The girl who punched a viper bird in the face. What did any of that have to do with this glowing fire bird coming out of her?

"Yer going tae die now?" Charlie accused, still on his knees. He was directly in front of the creature, his arms spread wide as if to catch it if it tried to fly away. "Ye cannae leave now, not the moment I find ye again."

Like a lightning bolt in his mind, Thane understood. Charlie's phoenix love. The soul of the bird that would be continually reincarnated unless she died without being loved enough. If that happened her soul would fly beyond the stars and never return.

And that was Remi? "I'll not lose ye forever," Charlie's voice was choked. "Please, Cleo, Aellai, Lucja, Maresol, Giselle, Katyusha..." with each name the bird's head drew away from him as if being slapped. As Charlie continued the list the phoenix turned her head away from him and up to the stars. She spread her wings fully.

It made Thane angry. "Remi," Thane called. She looked back. "Her name is Remi. That's who she is now. That's who you have to call back. Remi."

"Remi," Charlie said. He spoke the name as if it were a prayer, or a battle cry. The phoenix pulled her gaze back from the stars and her wings lowered slightly. "Remi. Come back. I promise ye a life full of joy. Do ye know me at all?"

Slow, tentative, the spirit bird nodded. "Then ye ken that I will never break a promise tae ye. Please. Hold the darkness away." The last word caught in his throat and the bird of flame leaned towards his face. From his vantage point Thane could see a tear sliding down Charlie's rough cheek. This had caught the phoenix's attention, and she nuzzled the tear with her beak. Charlie's entire body shivered at the contact.

Then the phoenix extended her wings above her head to their full length and shrieked. It was both the roar of a raging fire and the scream of a woman in pain. Then the phoenix soul melted, tongues of fire and flame flowing across Remi and being absorbed by her. The light dimmed, then disappeared, the night twice as dark with its absence.

In the silence left by the phoenix's departure, Remi's first rattling breath was disproportionally loud. Charlie knelt next to the body of the girl and sobbed. Thane wrapped his arms around his grandfather. Charlie accepted the gesture, and hugged Thane back.

"Shredding holes," Twitch said and rolled his eyes at Thane.

CHAPTER 33

The small clearing in front of the cave was crowded. Remi was awake and resting on a stretcher in a large open tent that the Sanctum team had brought, with Dr. Thunk inspecting the wound on her leg. The lumbering ogre-man turned and bopped Twitch on the head. "Sloppy," he said, pointing to the stitches.

"Field medicine!" Twitch protested, rubbing his scalp. "I was in a hurry."

"Bad excuse." Thunk shook his head and held the wound pinched shut while he removed the stitches to apply better ones.

Charlie hadn't left Remi's side. "Ye fit, love?" he asked again.

"Stop calling me that," Remi said, trying to scoot away. "I told you, I don't know you."

Charlie gave her his most charming smile. "Ye will. I promise."

"Dad?" Remi called.

General Gage excused himself from his conversation with Brennan and Turcato, who were going to be responsible for getting Cressida Rasmussen's still unconscious form back to Sanctum and incarcerated. "Yes, princess?" he said, the steadiness in his voice a stark contrast to the tightness around his eyes.

"Can you make him go away?" she asked, pointing at Charlie.

"Certainly," Remi's father said. "I've only been waiting for you to ask."

Charlie held up both hands placatingly. "Aye now, I hear ye both. Let me say my farewells tae my grandson, and I'll be out." He grinned and bowed.

Remi rolled her eyes. "Whatever."

Thane watched this from where he sat on the ground, wrapped in a blanket. Charlie had managed to talk him through most of the transformation back so his face had returned to normal. The blue dragon sauntered over to him and mussed his hair. "Thanks, I enjoyed the party. Next time I'll arrive afore the fun begins."

"Yeah, your timing sucks, old man," Thane said. They smiled at each other.

"How's the shoulder, lad?" Charlie asked, looking at the blanket Thane held.

"Seems fine now. Twitch thinks it was the nanites again," Thane answered, and Charlie looked pleased.

"Our roads will cross again soon, tadpole. Til then," and Charlie walked off into the woods, whistling.

Thane watched him go until he couldn't see the dragon shifter anymore, and then stood and walked over to Remi, being careful to stay out of the long reach of Dr. Thunk. "How are you feeling?"

"Better," she said, and smiled at him.

"What happened?"

"I was walking back from the front office and I saw her go into the faculty parking lot," Remi said. "She was acting weird and I knew she was supposed to be teaching a class, so I followed her. That psychopath was waiting for me and threw me in the trunk of her car. She drove off and I kicked the tail light out and stuck my arm out and waved, like you taught me," she said, looking at her father. He smiled at her, but there was a look in the man's eyes that made Thane cold and he held his blanket tighter. She turned to Thane. "Did you get my clues?"

He nodded. "I don't think I would've found you without them."

She grinned. Kari Loren called General Gage over, and he excused himself with a long look at Remi.

"Where's Paka and Jaeger?" Remi asked. "I really wanted to meet them."

Thane shrugged. "Maybe they're still watching the tear." His blanket started to slip and he glanced down, alarmed, and pulled it back around him sharply.

Naturally, Remi noticed. "Are you all right?" she asked.

"Yeah," Thane said. "I need to go talk to your dad. Are you okay here?"

"Sure," she said, and gave Dr. Thunk her best smile. "I'm in great hands."

Thunk blushed. Thane almost stayed just to watch that longer, but he needed to find General Gage.

He walked through the crowd of Shaerealm Mercenary Guards and Sanctum professionals. Remi hadn't asked her father why he was here with them yet, and Thane assumed the general was going to avoid that conversation for as long as he could.

He saw Kari Loren, her tall graceful form bending over an infopad. "Excuse me," he said. She looked up at him. "Do you know where General Gage is?"

She sighed, managing to convey in that one soft sound eons of annoyance with human stupidity. Thane waited for her answer anyway. "I believe the general has gone into the cave to check the inventory of items," she said, and returned to her infopad.

"Thanks," Thane said, but she didn't acknowledge him again. Thane walked back through the cave entrance, avoiding contact with anyone else. He assumed Gage would be in there alone and this would be a good time to ask the question burning in his mind, but he heard voices ahead and stopped.

"Do you understand what you are to do?" General Gage spoke.

"Aye do," Jaeger answered. Thane peeked around the outcropping of stone in surprise. Jaeger was here?

General Gage was standing near the back, studying the broken Weave where it hung in the air. Jaeger was crouched on the floor inspecting the burnt remains of Cressa's science equipment.

The general spoke again. "Once your objective is achieved, return and report directly to me in person. Do not make contact with the target under any circumstances. Do you understand?"

"Aye, sir," Jaeger said, picking up a large shard of broken pottery. There was still something inside, and the imp stuck his finger in the liquid and tasted it. "This is the one hyu want," he said, handing it to Gage.

Cressa's weapons were laid out in neat rows along the floor. General Gage paced along them until he came to the stone knife, laying apart in the leather box. The general reached down and picked up the knife by the hilt. "We have to seal this tear immediately. You will be responsible for your own returning."

"Aye haf a way," the imp said.

"Good." General Gage returned to where Jaeger crouched. Thane's mind spun, disbelieving, as General Gage dipped the tip of the knife into the thick green liquid the bowl fragment held and then slashed at the broken Weave. There was a rushing of air and a single note of Song, so powerful and huge Thane nearly blacked out from the weight of it. He stumbled back behind the outcropping and huddled into his blanket.

The note ended, cut off as sharply as it had begun. Thane crawled out of the cave on hands and knees, shaking his head to clear it. Outside, no one had any idea what had happened. Some equipment had gone haywire, and monitors and infopads beeped erratically. Several of the mercenary guards who had visible amounts of Shae heritage had fallen to their knees or on their backs. Remi was stroking Dr. Thunk's bald held as he knelt next to her, looking dazed.

General Gage emerged from the cave with the leather box in hand, clasp closed. "We need to return the bone of the guardian immediately," he ordered. "Having it too near the tear is making the Weave unstable." Several people jumped to their feet and within moments a helicopter had departed, the team inside carrying the leather box.

Thane had crawled to the edge of the hill and sat with his back to everyone else, holding onto his dirty blanket. He should have felt better. Maybe not happy, but at least relieved. Ms. Rasmussen was gone, on her way to some classified prison where Thane knew Remi's father would make sure she never came back from. But the only feelings Thane could muster were exhaustion and dread.

The sun was rising and bathing the woods with soft yellow light when General Gage came and sat next to him. "You all right, son?" General Gage asked. He watched the sun rise from the edge of the hill. "You've had a long night."

Thane shrugged. It felt like a lot more than just one night. It felt like his whole life had been one unending fight to survive. He pulled his blanket closer.

"I don't think I can go home," Thane said.

"Why not?" General Gage placed a hand on Thane's shoulder. "If it's a problem with your father--"

"Bert isn't the problem." Thane clutched his blanket tightly, and then let it fall. His body had returned to his previous human self. Except for his hands. They were the right size, but where there should have been warm skin there was instead blue scales. Fingers that should have ended in pale pink fingernails ended in black curved talons.

"You should change those back now," General Gage said.

"I can't." Thane paused, then looked out at the sunrise again. "I can't hear the music anymore."

"Oh," General Gage cleared his throat. "Burnout isn't uncommon. The Song should come back after you've had a few months of rest."

"Months?" Thane clenched and unclenched his curved claws. "How did this happen?"

"We're not sure." Gage sighed. "Somehow Cressida Rasmussen got access to a scroll of the ancients and learned how to make a tear in the Weave. That information is supposed to be heavily guarded." Remi's father rubbed his face with his hand. "I always thought she would be safe, that I was off battling the monsters to keep them away from her..." He took a shaky breath, then looked forward into the sunrise again. "Fortunately, I left her with someone responsible." He held out his right hand to Thane. "Thank you."

Thane looked at General Gage's outstretched hand, and then down at his own draconic ones. He lifted the right one and turned it over, glancing at Remi's father. The general's face was impassive as he moved his hand forward towards Thane's and gripped inside the curved claws. The general shook it with firm strength.

"Can we ever fix the Weave completely?" Thane asked, "Couldn't we find a way that wouldn't hurt anyone?"

"It would be the best long term solution, if we could guarantee both worlds would be stable after. But the cost of that would be astronomical." Gage sighs. "There isn't any way to prevent the death of everyone who has Shae heritage. The less the blood, the longer it would take, but in the end billions would die. How could we justify that kind of cost? It would take something truly horrific for the Guardian Council of Sanctum to support such a cause."

"Like what happened here?" Thane asked.

Gage shook his head. "Much worse. But speaking of the Guardian Council," Gage turned to face Thane. "They've made a decision about you. They are willing to bend rules in the face of extreme circumstances, and you've already proven yourself capable of facing a tear level threat. You are to be admitted into the Sanctum school immediately."

Thane swallowed, emotions and thoughts warring. Could he leave his family? They would be better without him, he was certain. But being admitted into Sanctum was a lifelong commitment. Was he sure they were on the right side? Was there a right side, or was there just the best choice based on what was going on? All this ran through his head, but what came out was, "I'm not leaving Remi behind."

General Gage smiled at him, the first sincere expression Thane had seen on the man since his arrival to the cave. "I banked on that, and got them to admit

Remi, too. She'll be safer there, and I am not leaving her without protection again. Hiding all this from her has only caused pain." Gage looked behind Thane, as if there was someone there. Thane glanced back but the trail behind him was empty. The general sighed, then focused on Thane again. "What do you say, son? Ready to carry the burden of the fate of all worlds?"

"They won't look at me like I'm a freak there." Thane said, "I won't even need to wear gloves. I won't be alone."

"Alone is the lie, Thane. We're never alone."

"Then I'm in." He lifted his chin and squinted at the bright light as the sun finally broke over the horizon.

"Welcome to Sanctum. Classes start Monday. Go start learning to save the world."

EPILOGUE

Ruan de Argos stood on the balcony of his seaside villa, gazing out over the storm tossed waves of the Mediterranean Sea. "You are sure of this?" he said, keeping his voice smooth and calm. Marcos was a good servant, and he wasn't ready to show his displeasure quite yet.

"Yes, Mr. Argos. The reports confirmed the incident happened less than eight hours ago. The team Omega responded. The source is sure." Marcos spoke with a quaver in his voice. Ruan smiled at that. Without turning around, he knew Marcos would be standing in the middle of the white and grey marble floor, twisting his hat in his hands. Marcos always did that when he brought news that might displease his employer. This predictability was something Ruan found endearing about the little Moroccan man, although at this moment it was... annoying.

There was nothing he liked less than being annoyed. "Did the source say why?"

Marcos gulped. "No, no sir. Only that she was taken by Sanctum and that two children were injured."

"Two children." It was both a statement and a question.

"Yes sir. A boy and a girl about fifteen years old."

Ruan's eyes flashed and the Song of lightning and dragons played in his mind unbidden. "Fifteen?"

"Y-yes, sir."

"Dear Marco, that is the most interesting thing you have said all morning." Lightning crashed in Ruan's eyes and thunder echoed in his mind, but he spoke calmly and resisted the impulse to fry the toad where he stood. That would damage the marble, and Ruan was fond of his marble palace. "We need more information. Run along, dear Marco, and find out where all this took place. It looks like we might be taking a vacation sooner than I expected."

"Yes sir." Marco fled the room, his bare feet slapping against the marble as he made for the closest door. Ruan heard it slam as his servant left.

"You lied to me," he said, his hands clasped behind his back and his face still turned out over the ocean.

The Woman stepped out from behind one of the many marble columns, her bare feet making no noise at all against the stone. He could hear the clink of the chains around her wrists as she moved, the chains that he had committed the last decade and a half and nearly all his vast resources into acquiring. Holding her was no paltry trick. Ruan kept his back to her, unwilling to look into those piercing green eyes as she spoke. "I have never lied. I cannot."

"You were supposed to be unable to interfere, either," he growled. The seduction of the Song in his mind swayed him and he almost gave in. Almost.

"The balance was threatening to tip, changing the face of this world. That would change its Song, and the tension of the Weave would grow until it shattered. I am obligated to interfere." The music of her ageless voice soothed him, and that made him angry.

That flash of anger was enough. He gave into the Song in his mind, embracing the music and sending bolts of lightning to destroy The Woman. They crashed into her, their sound and power making the entire building shake and the servants flee. Ruan could hear their screams as they ran from the building and he fed their terror into his Song.

As quickly as his fury came, it vanished. The Woman stood, calm and untouched, although the floor around and under her was rubble and the column closest to her had fallen.

"Feel better?" she asked.

"A little, yes," he smiled at her. "And knowing where you are, that you are powerless, this helps too."

"The child has grown up and may choose for himself now, and he may not choose you," she answered.

"I am his father," Ruan did not need to shout. The words carried their own weight. "He will not have known any father but me. When you stole my child and tried to make me believe he was dead, I cursed you. But that gave me an idea." His smile became angelic and he raised his hands upwards to the mural of a storm painted on the ceiling. "I gathered the best mages and men of chemistry and biology. The strongest combination in this world, that of our Song and their science, I used to place a curse on any man who would think himself a father to my son." He glowered down upon The Woman and raged inwardly at the pity in her green eyes. "He would never have peace in his own home. He would not be able to look upon my son without anger and fear. And he would never be able to walk away."

"You condemned your own child to a life of abuse," The Woman's accusation carried the pain of billions of children whose spark of life had passed through her.

It brushed past Ruan without touching him. "Of course not. My son would never allow himself to be abused. He would drive them away from his cradle. Why would he not?" the question hung in the air, a challenge that The Woman did not accept. "And even if he endured it, Amelie would never let it stand. If she was strong and clever enough to escape me, even with help," he flung the accusation back at her, "why would she remain with some songless male who beat her child? No. My son will have grown up without a father but always wanting one. And then there will be me, a father, a friend, a mentor who understands his power and his pain," Ruan's pale blue eyes glittered with greed.

"Why do you want the child?" The Woman asked. "I had understood that you abhorred all half-breeds and mixtures."

"Yes, that's true." Ruan shuddered. "Rutting around with those songless humans is filthy. But my son is more dragon than any songless blood can weaken. But as part human, the rules of Shae don't apply to him. Neither do the rules of the Alpha."

"Oh," The Woman said. "You don't want a son. You want a tool, a weapon that the dragons don't control because of his human heritage and with power that few can match because he is so much a dragon."

"I want my son to be proud to be that weapon," Ruan corrected. "One of the hunters I sent to look for him was captured by Sanctum this morning. Omega Team itself, which draws my interest. There were children involved, and if rumors are to be believed, a guardian bone knife." He had the satisfaction of seeing The Woman's eyes widen. "Yes, it peaked my interest too. So I'm off to get her and find out what she knows."

A cell phone in his pocket buzzed. He pulled it out and read the message on the screen. "Ugh. America. So little culture, so much arrogance. Ah well, off to rescue Cressa." He bowed to her mockingly. "I'm afraid I must bid you good evening, Sylphie."

ABOUT THE AUTHOR

Angela Day has loved fantasy ever since she was too young to read. Her father read the Chronicles of Narnia out loud to her when she was four years old, and she's had her nose in a book ever since. The only thing she wants to do more than reading is writing. Mrs. Day currently lives in Texas with the best husband in the world and two wonderful, brilliant sons of whom she is very proud. Visit her website at www.awriterbyday.com

Made in the USA
Las Vegas, NV
25 September 2023

78120327R00260